PRAISE F

"A gripping mother-daughter story set in the highly competitive dance world, *What's Yours Is Mine* had me hooked from the first page. Jennifer Jabaley is a fresh new voice in women's fiction, and I can't wait to read what she writes next."

—Camille Pagán, bestselling author of *Good for You*

what's
yours
is
mine

OTHER TITLES BY JENNIFER JABALEY

what's yours is mine

A Novel

jennifer jabaley

LAKE UNION
PUBLISHING

Text copyright © 2025 by Jennifer Jabaley
All rights reserved.

Published by Lake Union Publishing, Seattle

www.apub.com

Amazon, the Amazon logo, and Lake Union Publishing are trademarks of Amazon.com, Inc., or its affiliates.

EU product safety contact:
Amazon Media EU S. à r.l.
38, avenue John F. Kennedy, L-1855 Luxembourg
amazonpublishing-gpsr@amazon.com

ISBN-13: 9781662527791 (paperback)
ISBN-13: 9781662527784 (digital)

Cover design by Eileen Carey
Cover images: © bvb1981, © Connect Images / Getty; © bluehand, © FabrikaSimf, © New Africa, © Rocio S / Shutterstock

Printed in the United States of America

For Sam and Izzie

ONE

Valerie Yarnell had been a mother for fifteen years, and this was what she knew about parenting: absolutely nothing.

There had been times when she'd thought she was winning—when Kate was crowned spelling bee champ in the fifth grade, when she used her manners at the grocery checkout, when she snuggled next to her on the couch. Then, the teenage years barreled through their home like a bad storm, transforming her once sweet, loving child into something unrecognizable. All Valerie's efforts to forge a friendly conversation were greeted with darting glances and indecipherable grunts as Kate's fingers flew across her phone, communicating with someone who obviously knew her far better than her own mother.

It's fine, Valerie had repeatedly reassured herself. This was normal teenage behavior. She wasn't worried that Kate had discovered her long-buried secret. She didn't fear that her daughter was on some downward trajectory toward depression or violence. She wasn't scouring news sites, fearful of finding her child in a police report.

At least not yet.

Kate was just distant, maybe a touch secretive. And now, as Valerie glanced at her clock, she could add inconsiderate to the list. She had said twice the previous night that she could not be late to work; she had an important meeting with her new boss. Kate had promised to be on time, while averting her eyes and creeping back toward her room like a feral cat.

"Kate!" she called now. Her voice echoed in the vacuum silence.

This was all Valerie's fault. She'd completely failed at raising her daughter. Well, to be fair, she'd kept her alive and fed, which as a single parent was a major accomplishment. But somehow, she hadn't instilled basic kindness and consideration in her offspring, even as she'd tried so vigilantly to model good behavior. She thought of all those times she'd held her tongue when a car cut her off in the horrendous Atlanta traffic. Or how many times she'd held in her frustration about the insane dance moms who Kate adored.

She should never have enrolled her daughter in that damn studio. Its collection of orbiting mothers promoted the idea that the girls' entire existence revolved around dance. That's why her daughter was so self-absorbed; she worshipped those other moms. Especially her best friend Colette's mother.

Elise Carrington. She of the country club elite, with her understated elegance and obvious judgments. The queen bee of the dance moms, always clad in expensive athletic wear, like she was ready for an impromptu yoga class or, more likely, as a constant reminder that she'd once been a professional ballerina.

Lately, a crippling fear had gripped Valerie that Kate, fueled by teenage drama, would emancipate herself and go live with that woman. She recognized the irrationality of it, but Kate had grown so moody, so mysterious. Did she really even know her daughter anymore?

Valerie took a sip of her coffee and looked around her condo. She'd splurged on cheap imitations of the home decor found inside Elise's mansion, desperate to create a place her daughter would want to stay. But between the carefully arranged picture frames and the artfully tossed blankets, she could still sense it. The emptiness of the space. The void in her life. She glanced at her watch. If they left immediately, she could drop Kate off at school and be only ten minutes late. We need to leave now, Valerie texted. The phone announced the message had been delivered and then read, yet her daughter still failed to appear.

Last night, Valerie had suggested she take the bus. Just this once. Kate's mouth had hinged open in complete horror. *Nobody rides the bus to school.* Kate's declaration had cut through the air like a knife. It was hard to compete with those kinds of mothers, the kind who didn't have to work and could drive their kids to school, no matter how long it took to fix their hair in the morning. Kate spoke of her friends' mothers with such blatant admiration, Valerie felt coated in thick shame, like she was doing something wrong. Motherhood was a never-ending simmering pot of guilt. She'd acquiesced and said she'd drive her to school. She'd never be like the dance moms, ever-present and doting, but Kate would have to see that she was trying.

Five endless minutes passed before she charged down the hallway. She imagined opening the door, tapping her watch, saying, "My meeting?" It would be comforting to see Kate's eyes widen in realization of her mistake and maybe, if the universe were gracious, her daughter would apologize and race out the door.

As Valerie approached the bedroom, Kate's voice fluttered into the air. On her cell, most likely FaceTiming a friend so they could critique each other's outfits. She clenched her hand into a fist, raised to knock.

"Please." Kate's voice, heavy on the sarcasm. "Mom's never there. She doesn't give a crap."

Valerie sucked in a breath. A knee to the gut. She blinked back tears, slinked away before she was caught. She sat back down in the kitchen chair and waited, wondering how long it would be until her child left her. Just like everyone else.

A few minutes later, Kate emerged, backpack slung across her shoulder, hair pulled high into a topknot. "Ready?" As if it were just a typical morning. She flashed a casual smile, wide and false.

Stabbing Valerie's heart.

❧

All day at the hospital, Kate's words swarmed in Valerie's head. As she instructed her laboring patients to take quick, short breaths, her inner voice chanted: *She. Doesn't. Give. A. Crap.*

Her best friend, Jazmin, eyed her with suspicion as they left new parents with their babies washed and swaddled. "What's wrong? I thought you'd be flying high after getting that raise."

"Yeah. That was a surprise." Valerie raced through the staff lounge toward her locker. "Nothing's wrong; I just need to hit the road."

"Oh." Jazmin brightened. "Big date?"

As if. "Absolutely. That hot husband decided to dump his wife and newborn and take me out for tacos and margaritas."

Jazmin chuckled. "The butt on that one, right? But seriously, where are you off to?"

"Dance."

"I thought Kate's class ended at seven? We've got time. Let's grab a quick bite."

Sure, she'd much rather hang out with Jazmin than sit in the stuffy dance studio. But that was the problem. If she were a good mother, if *she gave a crap*, she'd want to go. Even if she didn't understand it—the jazz, tap, ballet, contemporary all smeared together into one big blur. But apparently, each genre was unique. And Elise, expert on all things dance, quietly mocked her ignorance with each not-so-subtle glance at her friends and a barely perceptible eye roll. Valerie massaged the tension creeping up her neck. "I want to watch Kate practice."

"Oh my God, why?" Jazmin grimaced. "Oh no. They've gotten to you. The hysterical studio moms. They've invited you to wear a bedazzled *Dance Moms* T-shirt and sit on the bench with them, bouncing with every move their kid makes." She did a theatrical impression, swaying and gasping as she pretend-watched a performance. "Look at her feet! So quick and light and elegant! She's going to be a *star!*"

Valerie laughed. "Actually, I'm going to silently gloat while snapping pictures for later braggy posts on social media: *OMG! Kate finally nailed her routine! #challengingmoves #lovemygirl #dancemom.*"

Jazmin winced. "Gross."

"I know. But for once, I don't want to be the only one who shows up right at the end."

"Why?" Jazmin pulled on her puffer coat, more suited for Alaska than Atlanta.

A stir of vulnerability swirled in Valerie's stomach. Just thinking about what Kate said made her queasy.

"What?" Jazmin looked genuinely concerned, so Valerie told her everything.

Jazmin leaned against the heavy door to the parking deck. "Val." Her voice took on the compassion she reserved for her patients, and that made Valerie want to cry. "It's not true. You're a great mother. Everyone knows how much you love Kate."

She tried to smile appreciatively, but instead, her lips did a weird twitch. "I'm just not the kind of mother who gives a crap enough to watch her lessons."

"Yeah, because you have more pressing things to do—like a job— that pays for all those classes, by the way."

"Well, if I had a better job, like Colette's father, Kate wouldn't have to clean the studio to offset the tuition." Just another division. Kate never complained, but Valerie could feel the slump of her daughter's shoulders as they pulled up to the empty building on Saturday mornings.

Jazmin pushed open the steel door, and a gust of wind swirled up and smacked them in the face. "So, what happened? Did you tell her you overheard what she said?"

"I pretended like I didn't. I don't know how to act around her anymore." They stopped in front of Valerie's ten-year-old silver Corolla. "The other day, I had to resort to changing the Netflix password just so she'd come out of her bedroom. She spends so much time cooped up in there, who knows what she's doing."

"If I learned anything after ten years in pediatrics, it's that teenagers are hard," Jazmin said. "They're irrational and impulsive. Their brains aren't fully developed. They make stupid decisions."

Valerie paused. She knew Jazmin was referring to Kate's harsh words, but suddenly, Valerie wondered: Was her daughter irrational and impulsive about other things? Surely Kate wasn't doing anything disturbing, nothing *dangerous*. Not like her father. A pit of panic descended.

"Don't worry. Kate's fine," Jazmin said. But the idea was already out there, like a foreboding.

Valerie said goodbye, climbed into her car, and accelerated onto the highway. Immediately, she slammed to a heart-pounding standstill, stuck in the middle of a traffic jam, trapped, unable to get to Kate, like in a bad dream.

She recalled how she'd been plagued with nightmares when Kate was an infant. She'd bolt upright in bed, convinced she'd left the baby in the hot car, still strapped in the car seat. Or she'd awaken thinking she'd lost her grip on the stroller, that Kate had careened down a steep embankment. Once, horrifically, she'd dreamed a man was at the door with a gun, so she'd thrown the baby on a roasting pan and slid her into the oven. That last nightmare had sent her running through the doors of Suzanne Crowell, PhD, clinical psychologist, who'd reassured her that she was simply overtired, overworked, and overly concerned as most new mothers are, single parents especially. "Not to worry!" the counselor had said.

"I'm not a terrible mother?" Valerie's voice had been strangled with tears.

"Oh no," Dr. Crowell had reassured her. "Quite the opposite. It shows what a good mother you are. How hard you're trying to protect her."

But somehow, all that must have changed, because her daughter thought her mother didn't give a crap about her.

Valerie finally skidded into the parking lot of Volkov Studio, realizing with a sigh that class had been in session for more than an hour. She jogged toward the studio entrance wearing only her cream-colored scrubs. Hunching her shoulders against the sharp wind, she encountered yet another roadblock. Smack up against the glass door blocking the entrance were two teens, their arms wrapped around each other. The girl's head was tilted back, eyes half closed, glazed with desire. Their kissing, so noisy and sloppy, made Valerie recoil, but then an unexpected yearning bubbled up inside her. She could almost feel her toes curl with a rush of longing. She realized she was staring, so she cleared her throat, but the make-out session proved impenetrable.

Until an enormous gloved hand reached over Valerie's head and landed on the glass door above the teen girl's head. He banged three times, as if knocking to enter. "Excuse us." The deep voice sounded familiar. At last, the girl's eyelids blinked open; the boy removed his mouth, displaying a smear of berry lip gloss across his chin. They both stared for a moment, as if not knowing where they were, then straightened their clothes and shuffled away.

Valerie craned her neck. Andrew Carrington was so close, she could feel the exhale of his breath on her cheek and smell the faint whiff of his aftershave, which brought to mind pine trees and leather. "Oh, hey," she said, suddenly embarrassed, fully embodying the role Kate had cast her in: apathetic mother, showing up at the end of class. Once again. Nothing like Andrew's wife—the perfect, petite Elise. Valerie's face flushed with shame. "I hate that I'm so late. I . . . I got caught up at work."

Standing there, in the February cold outside the dance studio, Andrew looked at her with a hint of a grin. There wasn't an ounce of judgment on his face. Instead, he shrugged. "Probably more fun there, anyway."

His words stirred the same sense of unexpected pleasure as finding an old wad of money stuffed into a jacket pocket. He might have only meant it to dismiss her tardiness, but in that moment, she took it as she needed it—as affirmation.

He pushed the door open and gestured for her to enter. With her towering five foot, ten inches in flats, she had to stoop like a long-necked giraffe to pass under his outstretched arm. But still, she smiled up at him, thankful for his kindness. She knew it was wrong to be looking at a married man with even a hint of attraction, but being that he was married to Elise, the woman her daughter adored, it also felt right in a small, vindictive way.

TWO

Elise Carrington entered Volkov Studio at exactly 3:40 p.m., five minutes before class started. She sat on the long wooden bench and flung her designer bag on the space next to her, saving seats for Ling Li and Susie. She was always the first to arrive, and even if she were running late, everyone knew that the center seat on the bench belonged to her. Just as center stage belonged to her daughter, Colette.

The studio had a wall of glass providing viewing opportunity from the parent lobby, but Elise preferred to be on the bench, sharing the same thick, sweaty air and melodic music as the dancers. Roza Volkov, owner of the studio, had insisted parents were not allowed inside the practice rooms, but a small smile and a sizable donation changed that policy. Some days Elise would find herself counting the notes of music, which carried her away, back to her ballet company days in New York. Her toes would lift on pointe as she imagined doing a series of pirouettes, ready to flutter across the stage. Her face would flush as she felt the long-ago spotlight beam; for small moments, she'd be back in her youth, living her dreams. Before they'd been stolen away.

Now, at least her daughter would have the opportunity to fulfill that destiny.

When the door burst open, the calm of the studio was replaced with teenage laughter and gossip. A swarm of girls passed by, their overstuffed dance bags slung over their shoulders, their hands twisting hair into sloppy buns. The smell of hair spray, body lotion, and vanilla-flavored lip gloss floated through the air.

Parents showed up, filling the bench or hovering against the wall. The girls emerged from the locker room, like a long train of pink satin, finding their spots across the wooden floor, stretching their legs and reaching their arms. Elise riffled through her bag but couldn't find her phone. Damn it! She'd left it charging at home, and now she couldn't video today's lesson. Ling Li and Susie walked in. Susie's face was red, and while it was unseasonably chilly outside, Elise didn't think it was from the cold. "Something wrong, Suse?"

Her friend sighed and gave a tug at the neck of her sweatshirt, pastel blue with a retro *Flashdance* neckline, dropping off one shoulder— something meant to be worn by a teenager with soft silky shoulders, not a middle-aged woman with sunspots and crepey skin. Elise had noticed Susie's recent propensity to copy the fashion choices of her daughter. Last week she'd shown up at the studio in an actual leotard tucked into ripped jeans. Embarrassing.

Susie licked her lips. "If I ask you guys something, do you promise to be honest?" They nodded. "Do you think Avery might have . . ." Susie looked over her shoulder, leaned in, and whispered, "Unusually long arms? Like, out of proportion for her body?"

The three women gazed across the room to Susie's daughter, whose leg was propped up on the barre, stretching. How had Elise not noticed? She tried not to cringe. Whenever she watched Avery dance, she recognized her clumsiness, like her limbs were made of tin cans on string. But she'd failed to identify the true problem: The girl's arms were never-ending. No selfie stick required for her. They fell into an uncomfortable silence.

Finally, Ling Li spoke. "Well, it's not like her knuckles are dragging on the ground."

"Oh my God, like a gorilla?" Susie fanned her face with her hand, and her voice ticked up. "Avery asked me this morning if her arms were crazy long, and I just stood there because it's not like I'd ever really looked. But after she left, I pulled up pictures . . ."

Ling Li shrugged. "Better than short arms. No one wants a dancer who looks like a T. rex."

Susie's breathing became shallow. "Do you think it could hurt her chances at professional dance? To be a little . . . disproportionate?"

Elise winced. Not because knuckles almost dragging on the floor would curtail Avery's career, but because if she were honest, Avery didn't stand a chance at professional dance. Period.

No one ever said the words out loud: *soloist. Company. Performing artist.* These dreams were just as much the parents' as the children's. More so, if truth be told. Why else would the mothers agree to leave the more reasonably priced local studios and travel across town to log upward of two, three hours a day inside the damp studio? Why would they spend thousands of dollars on lessons, costumes, and performances, if not for the possibility? And when a child's dream was crushed, so were the parents'. Maybe it was easier for a parent to ignore their child's weaknesses. Some girls' movements had become sloppy; others didn't have proper extension. And then there were certain undefinable qualities, like effortlessness, luminescence, and polish. Elise had known that Avery had fallen in the ranks even without recognizing her gorilla limbs. But then, she had experience as a professional dancer and that critical eye for aptitude.

Susie sat beside her, panting slightly, waiting for reassurance, so Elise gave her a version of the truth. "I never even noticed."

They watched Avery spinning around, her arms extending out farther and farther like a two-tentacled octopus. The music stopped—a welcome halt to their new fixation. The girls dropped to their flat feet; their chests heaved in and out with little breaths. Miss Roza pulled Colette to the front of the room. As the music began again, Elise's daughter floated through the air, then dropped delicately to the wooden floor like a puppet on a wire. How could the other mothers watch the fluidity of her child's torso, the extension of her neck, and not realize that she embodied that magical mixture of precision and pure elegance? Did they not realize their girls, who watched in obvious awe, were amateurs compared to her Colette?

Elise leaned in and squinted. While the execution of Colette's moves was flawless, today something seemed off. She seemed distracted. How many times had Elise told her that the face must always be engaged? And for this to happen on the day she didn't have her phone to record the lesson was a real disappointment. How would she show her exactly where the problem was?

No one else seemed to notice. Ling Li tilted her head and said, "Damn, that girl can dance." Elise beamed.

But then suddenly, Miss Roza walked through the cluster of girls and pointed to Kate, gesturing her to the front of the room. Next to Colette. That was new.

Miss Roza whispered to the girls, who began basic kicks, moving in unison, stepping front, side, and back, then amping up into a high-energy jazz routine. Elise's eyes were glued on Colette, the way she held her hands in just the right way. Her body alignment was pristine.

Ling Li sighed. "They're flawless."

They. *They* are flawless? Not *she*? Not *Colette*? Elise wrenched her gaze over to Kate. Her daughter's best friend. Her son Trey's girlfriend. The little lost puppy who'd latched on to her household for the last decade, sitting at her kitchen table and sleeping in their guest room more than at her own home. She idolized Elise like a loyal groupie, and Elise thrived on adoration. She should be proud right now, she knew. Her pseudo-daughter was brilliant on the dance floor. Instead, she found it difficult to breathe. An anxious feeling stirred, like she'd been blindsided. Like she'd slipped on last year's jeans and couldn't zip them up. Sure, she'd noticed the small, almost imperceptible creep of change that had exposed itself recently. In a way, it had reminded Elise of her biggest rival in New York—a bit of a late bloomer on the stage, an unexpected surge of competency. But Kate had never looked this good. Dangerously close to as good as Colette.

She leaned in and analyzed her with her trained eye. Kate's performance was impeccable. Elise sat up straighter, a ripple of concern moving down her spine. *It's like she crept onstage and stole my dreams!* That was what Elise had screamed so many years ago when her life had crashed and burned. But Kate wasn't creeping. Wasn't stealing anything. Not from Colette. No way. Still, she knew how it could happen, how someone could blast from the sidelines. A twist of panic stabbed at her eye, and her lid twitched.

Susie placed a hand on Elise's arm. "Hey, are you okay?"

"Oh, I know," Ling Li said. "You've heard."

"Heard what?" Elise's voice was tight. Had Miss Roza said something about Kate? Called out her improvement? Complimented her on her form?

Ling Li scooted closer and jutted her chin toward another mother sitting at the end of the bench. "Dena told me she was in line behind Kate at CVS. Kate filled a prescription for *birth control pills.*"

Susie inhaled sharply. "Do you think Kate and Trey are having *sex*?"

The accusations swirled around her, but Elise couldn't think about her son's sex life. She was too busy obsessing over Kate's seamless routine and Colette's distracted demeanor. Why wasn't Colette focusing? Did she not realize all that was at stake? That Kate had unfolded her tucked-away talent and presented it now like a peacock—proud and confident? Elise's world tilted off its axis. She gripped the edge of the bench.

"Well, sex or no sex," Susie continued, clearly clueless of Elise's panic, "maybe Kate's infatuation with Trey means she'll be distracted, and it'll, you know, clear the limelight just for Colette."

Clear the limelight? Just for Colette? Elise's heart turned to a brick and dropped into her gut. She inhaled sharply, needing air, the studio hot and heavy with sweat. The low ceilings seemed to dip. Ling Li's and Susie's shoulders squeezed her from either side. Everyone had noticed. Kate's slow rise. Her creep toward center stage.

All those times Kate had said, "Elise, you're amazing. Elise, you still dance like a prima. Elise, I want to be just like you." She'd been thrilled that someone had actually seen her. Not like her preoccupied husband.

Not like her oblivious children. But no. Kate hadn't been just observing Elise and complimenting her. She'd been secretly studying.

An awkward silence ensued. Ling Li and Susie followed Elise's gaze to Kate. Her moves were dreamy, at once chugging and hopping with excitement, then suddenly softer and luscious and luminous.

A prickle of fear cascaded over Elise's skin.

Susie shifted uncomfortably beside her; Ling Li gestured with her finger across the dance floor through the glass window at Kate's mother. "The moppet has arrived," she said, trying to break the tension. "Just in time for class to end."

A loud thud reverberated across the room. They turned back toward the girls. Avery crash-landed, her legs angling awkwardly on the ground.

"Oh my God." Susie's hand flew to her mouth. "Not the ankle again."

The girls froze on the dance floor, clearly not knowing whether to proceed. In slow motion, Kate turned her head, searching until she found Elise. Their eyes met. Kate looked so eager and desperate for some sort of recognition, Elise felt the base of her throat clench. It was obvious Kate wanted to know that Elise had seen her hit those jumps, land flawlessly, execute the routine perfectly. She wanted Elise to love her. To approve of her.

Elise's eyelid spasmed again. Why, suddenly, were those requests difficult?

She was not a terrible person. She was not. She nodded at Kate and flashed a reassuring smile.

Kate beamed, then turned back to her instructor.

She thought of all those nights Colette and Kate had practiced in their basement, Elise correcting and guiding, never really comprehending that Kate was there, not just as Colette's friend, not just as an adoring groupie, but as an ambitious student, benefiting from all of Elise's expertise.

What had she done?

All this time, had she coached, coddled, and unintentionally created her daughter's biggest competition?

THREE

Valerie and Andrew walked inside the dance studio parent lounge, filled with gray couches and a glass-topped coffee table, vending machines pressed against the wall. "Thanks for rescuing me," she said. "I thought I might be stuck watching live-action soft porn."

"Yeah." He laughed. "I remember those days. All that . . . desire."

Valerie bristled. A long time ago, that insatiable craving had left her pregnant, scared, then alone.

"Ah, young love." He turned and looked at her. "What? Why the frown? Don't tell me you've never felt that way?" he asked, half joking.

"Well, I guess." A surge of embarrassment crawled up her neck. "But I wound up with a baby at eighteen, a bag full of diapers, and puke on my shirt. So, my view of young love might be slightly less idyllic."

"Oh," he said softly, shaking his head. "That's not how it's supposed to be."

Something inside her stirred. She and Andrew had known each other for ten years, had seen each other a million times, but they'd never talked like this. Their conversations were typically a quick hello as she picked up or dropped off Kate, a reference to an upcoming performance or a pulled hamstring. Nothing personal.

"Well then, lucky you. You still have that to look forward to. A real romance." His face paled, and he shifted on his feet. "I mean, assuming you aren't with anyone now. I don't think you're involved?" he stammered.

She shook her head. "No. Not involved." They were silent for a beat, just the sound of their breathing, inhaling and exhaling in unison. "So," she finally said, breaking the awkward silence, "did you come to watch Colette?" Elise Carrington never missed a practice. Andrew, on the other hand . . . Well, she couldn't remember ever seeing him at the studio.

He pulled out an oversize iPhone from his coat pocket. "Elise forgot her phone. I knew she was probably freaking out. She videos all of Colette's lessons."

Valerie looked through the glass viewing panel at Elise sitting on the bench, and something tugged in her stomach. If Valerie forgot her phone, it stayed put. Lucky Elise. "She videos every class?" Her voice came out more judgmental than she would have liked.

He let out a small laugh. "Welcome to the land of the crazies." He twirled a finger by the side of his face. Valerie paused, wondering if she'd heard right. "I want to know how you've done it," he continued with a playful tone. "Avoided the helicopter-, tiger-, dance-mom thing? You know, sitting on the bench analyzing every move? And even if you're not recording lessons, surely you watch hundreds of YouTube videos on how to shellac hair into the flawless bun. Right?"

Valerie tried to understand. Was he joking? Poking fun at the fanatic dance moms? Did he roll his eyes at their notebooks tracking water consumption? Did he laugh at the way they spoke with such confidence of their children's future stardom?

"Come on," he said. "I'm sure you own a toolbox full of sequins, glitter, and fabric paint to dye leotards the perfect matching flesh tone."

Her lips lifted into a smile. "No toolbox."

"You're lying!" He threw his palms out. "Your daughter is so good. You must be behind the scenes orchestrating her success."

She stood there both stunned and speechless, yet also strangely excited that someone else saw the absurdity of the dance moms. But this was Andrew Carrington. His wife was the queen bee, his daughter the star. Could it really be that he, of all people, agreed with her about this

16

dancing thing? That it had taken over their daughters' lives, and even his wife's, a bit too much? Did Andrew Carrington *not give a crap* either?

His face turned serious suddenly, as if he'd read her mind. "Don't get me wrong. I applaud Elise's commitment. It's just become a little . . . intense." He took off his gloves, stuffed them in his pockets, slid out of his heavy coat, and tossed it over his arm. He wore dress pants and a light blue button-down shirt, sleeves rolled to his elbows. His forearms were ropy with long muscles, the arms of an athlete.

"Well." Valerie's eyes lingered on them for a second too long. All that sloppy kissing outside must have triggered too many hormones. She forced her eyes back to his face. "I know my daughter wishes I was as enthusiastic as Elise is."

He waved a hand through the air, as if to dismiss her concerns. "Kate has a good head on her shoulders. You've raised her to understand the world doesn't revolve around the studio. She studies. Talks about college. I wish that would rub off on Colette."

A pulse of pride swelled inside her. Andrew got it. Dance was not the be-all and end-all. "Still," she said. "It's a battle. It's hard to study for AP classes or fit in SAT prep when you spend two or three hours a day dancing."

"Not to mention the yoga and Pilates."

"And all of the time icing and taping the injuries."

"The dozens of trips to the ER for the sprained ankle, the broken toe." He ticked off the injuries on his fingers.

They smiled like they were the only ones in on a secret; the whole conversation had turned deliciously scandalous. Like they'd crossed a virtual line.

"Well," Andrew said, "it's going to get a lot worse if they get accepted to that regional competition."

"What?" It came out sharp and a touch panicked.

"You know, that Duncan dance thing or whatever it's called?"

Of course she knew what it was. The Duncan Dance Prix, named for Isadora Duncan, the mother of modern dance, was the second-largest dance competition in the world. Kate and Colette had obsessed over it for months, so she couldn't help but know every detail. It featured one of the largest cash prizes of any dance contest: First prize took home $100,000. Second- and third-place winners received $50,000 each. Five additional dancers were awarded scholarships to dance schools worldwide. Not to mention there would be agents and famous choreographers present, ready to offer contracts. The competition required all dancers to qualify for an invitation by submitting a video performance. She and Kate had discussed it for hours—well, *argued* about it would be more accurate. What was the smarter choice? To spend endless hours training for a future career as a professional dancer—a prospect that was not only extremely difficult to ascertain but near impossible to maintain? Or focus on keeping her GPA eligible for the HOPE Scholarship, and working toward a college degree and a more practical future? Kate had acquiesced and agreed not to submit a video audition. So why was Andrew acting like she had?

"I don't think Kate entered that . . ." Her words trailed off as he nodded his head.

"Oh yeah, she did. She and Colette spent hours with Elise in our basement, perfecting their auditions. Elise videoed and entered their submissions." He shoved his hands in his pockets. "I thought you knew?" His voice trailed off with an apologetic hitch.

Valerie's eyes lost focus, the lounge becoming a smeary gray blur, the lines of Andrew's face losing their edges. So that's what Kate was doing at the Carringtons'. Not studying with Trey and hanging out with Colette, but . . . shooting audition videos for the Duncan Dance Prix? With Elise? Who was always around and available to fill Kate's head with nonsense while Valerie was off working to pay the bills. Had Elise informed Kate that her own prima ballerina career had ended almost immediately after it started? That she could afford to hover all day only because she'd married a successful lawyer? Valerie's heart raced, and her face heated up. She reached a hand against the wall to steady herself.

Andrew's crystal-blue eyes registered concern. "Hey, are you okay?"

No, she was not okay. How had she screwed everything up so badly? Not only had her daughter spent all her time at another woman's home, but she'd also followed *her* guidance instead of her own mother's. And what kind of a woman was Elise to go behind another mother's back? Valerie restrained herself from telling Andrew that his wife had completely overstepped her bounds. "I didn't realize that Kate had entered the competition." She closed her eyes, hating the tremor in her voice, how it made her look like she and her daughter didn't communicate. With horror, tears brimmed in Valerie's eyes. She blinked fast and swallowed.

Andrew placed a hand on her arm with a gentle touch. "I'm sure she was going to tell you." He pulled his hand away and pointed to the folded paper sticking out of Valerie's bag. "What's that?" he asked, obviously trying to change the subject. He scanned the Realtor's logo in the corner. "In the market for a new house?"

She tucked it out of sight, embarrassed, thinking of the Carringtons' two-story with the waxy green shrubbery, lap pool in the back, and the outdoor kitchen and fireplace. Her dream home would be the size of their garage. She suddenly felt stupid, thinking Kate might actually stay home more if they had that big patio in the backyard. She'd imagined barbecued chicken and board games. But why would her daughter want to stay anywhere except at the Carringtons', where her best friend and boyfriend lived? Where the woman she wished was her mother ran the show? The woman who *gave a crap* about her dreams and did things undercover to make them happen.

What else did Valerie not know about?

The loud bass from the music in the studio reverberated through the wall; she and Andrew glanced through the glass partition. Past the line of dancing girls, Elise's eyes landed on her husband and Valerie, and only then did it hit her how close she and Andrew were standing.

He stepped back. "I better get this to Elise." A hint of urgency painted his tone. He held the phone out so his wife could see. He looked at Valerie with a note of regret. "Hey. Sorry. I didn't mean to spring the news about the Duncan thing on you."

She suppressed her bizarre mix of sadness and rage. "Oh, no worries."

He gave her a sideways smile. "And, hey, stay strong. Resist it." He swirled his hand in the air, mimicking a helicopter. He gave her a wink and disappeared around the corner.

While his teasing had been a satisfying surprise, it couldn't counteract the trickle of despair she now felt about her daughter's lies. She walked closer toward the glass window and spotted Kate among the swath of sweatshirts and leggings. Her daughter, long and lanky, towered above the rest of the petite, pixie-like pack.

The music rose an octave, and the girls began to dance in unison, the long line of legs jumping and twirling, ponytails of hair swirling through the air like cotton candy. They flowed across the floor, creating an expression of beautiful artistry even Valerie couldn't deny. They rose into the air like a wispy cloud, then landed together against the wooden floor. Another jump, another landing. This time, Kate touched down closer to another girl; their shoulders almost brushed. Quickly, Kate sidestepped, but there was a sudden thud, loud and echoing, and the girl crashed down, her leg splayed at an unnatural angle. The music paused. The air stifled.

Valerie took in a breath, pressed her face on the glass. The crush of dancers blended together as they raced to the fallen girl. It was Kate's friend Avery, her face strained in agony. Kate stood beside her, staring down at her. Why wasn't Kate helping her? All the girls, in fact, just stood there, motionless, their arms still extended, their legs still semi-straight, like they were unwilling to break their own form to help another. Valerie's heart stilled.

What the hell was going on? She looked from the bizarre image on the dance floor, like a video paused, to the moms on the bench, equally immobile. She'd read about the obsessive world of dancers—how the fierce level of competition could stoke rivalry and sabotage. She'd heard about broken glass shoved into shoes, subtle shifts on the floor to make another dancer fall. She'd assumed that was the stuff of melodramatic movies. But what if . . . no. Kate had just missed her landing. In fact, Valerie didn't think their bodies had actually touched. But why was her daughter just standing there?

Valerie banged on the glass. "Kate!" she shouted. "Help her!"

Kate looked up. But oddly, her gaze didn't find Valerie. Instead, she glanced toward Elise on the bench.

Colette's mother, catching Kate's questioning expression, gave her a small, almost imperceptible nod and a tight-lipped smile, a gesture Valerie didn't understand. But Kate clearly did. Because quick as a flash, she spun away from her prostrate friend and jetted her leg up toward the ceiling. Like a flipped switch, the remainder of the girls followed suit, dancing the routine as if nothing had happened.

Miss Roza, the instructor, darted between the dancing bodies and tended to Avery, whimpering.

Valerie turned away, unable to watch. Stricken.

When had her daughter become so self-absorbed that she was unwilling to help a friend?

When had she become a liar?

Screwing her eyes shut, Valerie mentally bulldozed through a mountain of panic.

FOUR

Colette had only thirty minutes of practice left, but to be honest, it was a total struggle not to call it quits. She was off her game. Zero focus.

Miss Roza called out commands, and her body obeyed in some weird hypnosis. But her mind was stuck in fifth-period language arts, replaying Finn McAllister asking, "Hey, Colette, can I screenshot your notes?" After he'd snapped the picture, he touched the inside of her arm and said she should get a tattoo. "Right there."

She kind of freaked that hot senior quarterback and all-around perfection Finn was actually making physical contact with her and laughed like a psycho. "My mom would straight-up flip."

And instead of making her feel like a loser for talking about her mommy, he'd smiled and said, "I get ya." Just about killed her.

Was he into her? Maybe he only needed her notes. But even if he had a legit crush, Mom would dead-end that before it even started. She had Colette so scheduled, she could barely take a shit.

Now Colette glanced across the wooden dance floor to the bench where her mom was sitting. Mom squinted at Colette, her pale blond eyebrows pulling in. Oh yeah; she was totally going to call her out for daydreaming. Colette could predict tonight's conversation. "Your eyes were glazing over. Your face must always be engaged." If Colette ever missed her mark, Mom had an arsenal of criticisms locked, loaded, and ready to fire.

Mom always said every practice was a performance, and every performance must be perfect. And even if a dancer nailed all their jumps and landings with technical precision, she could pinpoint the exact moment a performer disconnected with her audience. So, Colette always focused. But today was rough.

I get ya. God, he was a stone-cold hottie.

None of the other moms would notice if their kid was distracted, but hers was different. Elise had been nineteen when she'd landed at a prestigious company in New York City. There were pictures of her onstage, decked out in glittering costumes or at glamorous parties with brightly colored scarves wrapped around her neck. Newspapers featured her and called her a rising star. But she didn't rise. Colette didn't know why. Whenever she asked, Mom simply said she'd met Dad, fell in love, and that was that. Her life had changed. But Colette always suspected there was more to her story. She'd tried searching online, but social media started after Mom had already left New York. All she could find was a few random articles about her performances.

When Colette was five years old, Mom signed them up for Mommy and Me dance class. Colette instantly loved it—the precise technique of the moves, the speed of the spins, the sparkly costumes, and the glitter dusted on her cheeks. She liked that people said her personality popped onstage. Mostly she loved how happy it made Mom. Like, if Mom couldn't dance, at least Colette could. She didn't realize how big a job that would become: keeping Mom happy.

Together, they'd planned Colette's future. Each night, Mom would show her the proper stretching techniques, teach her when to ice, when to soak in a hot bath, how much Advil was too much for a delicate stomach. They did everything together. People noticed them. One woman had said, "You look like a mother-and-daughter pair of movie stars."

Mom had beamed and corrected, "Dancers, actually."

The woman had smiled. "Even better."

One day Colette caught her mom staring and was about to tell her she was creeping her out, but then Mom said, "Colette, you have that undefinable quality people cannot replicate."

"What?"

"Stage presence." She'd gotten a little teary. "Do you understand?" And when Colette shook her head, she'd continued. "Many girls want to dance professionally, but there are few opportunities. But with your ability, your passion and radiance—you have stage presence. You can make it all the way. To prima ballerina."

Colette had stood there, frozen. Her mother's eyes had narrowed and lasered in. "What? Is that not what you want?" Her voice had practically hit the ceiling.

Looking back, Colette was surprised she'd had the guts to be honest. "I'm not sure what I want."

Drop-dead drama had ensued. Mom sprang off her feet. "What? What?"

Colette had to explain. She wanted to dance. Of course she did. But ballet was so . . . old school. At the word *old*, Mom caved in like she'd been punched. She'd had regular appointments with the Botox people and was 100 percent freaked out about aging. Colette shifted tactics. "Miss Roza said if we want to be employable dancers, we need to not have a narrow focus but be trained in every genre—not only ballet, but tap, jazz, lyrical, contemporary."

Mom's mouth twitched like she was trying not to take it as a criticism of her career choices. Finally, she sat back down. "That's smart advice." She'd taken a long breath. "One of my colleagues had a long career in contemporary dance at Alvin Ailey. So, the goal is still the same: a company. Not Broadway or"—she pulled her lips downward—"working as a backup dancer for Taylor Swift or doing cruise ship performances." She twisted her mouth like she was tasting something awful. "Or dancing for the Dallas Cowboys."

Actually, working as a backup dancer for anyone sounded pretty awesome to Colette, but that discussion would totally have to happen at a different time. She could push Mom only so much. "Yeah, a dance company. Of course."

Mom spent tons of time studying all the dance genres to help Colette progress, to help her get to the top. And here Colette was, blowing practice by obsessing about a senior quarterback who was too stupid to pass language arts. She felt so ungrateful.

She forced his dimples out of her mind and sharpened her concentration. She tuned into the sound of the music, found her reflection in the mirror, and created the illusion of confidence. Over the years, she'd perfected the art of shoving everything inside and letting the world see only a mask of perfection. That's what performers have to do. Mom drilled that into her head.

Now Mom cracked the tiniest smile. Not approval, but at least maybe Colette wouldn't get a lecture.

While Colette was totally fixated on smoothing things over with Mom, some serious drama went down. Suddenly everyone stopped dancing, and Colette realized Avery had fallen. They all stood there for a minute, looking at each other, waiting, she guessed, to see if Avery would pop back up. The girl did fall a lot. She, like, *just* got her boot off from the whole ankle fiasco.

The room buzzed with confusion. Colette looked to Kate; Kate looked to Colette's mom. Emma shrugged, like, *What do we do?* Miss Roza had preached that they were to ignore any interruptions during a performance, but this was practice. And what if Avery were really hurt? Still . . . Mom was super strict about following rules. And Colette had already gotten the stink eye for dancing distracted. Avery looked up at her, like, *Help.* Her insides were torn: friend or Mom?

But before she had to face that no-win choice, there was a swoosh of air, and she realized everyone had started dancing again. She quickly caught her mark and joined them. Avery's mom ran by, wearing some tacky sweatshirt that kept falling down and giving them a scary view of her mom bra.

Together, she and Miss Roza carried Avery away. Colette immediately thought of the spring gala. Routines hadn't been posted yet. It wasn't like Avery would get a solo or anything, but still, Colette wondered how another injury would affect Avery's future.

They were always petrified about how injuries could rob them of their dreams.

Miss Roza dismissed everyone except Colette and Kate. She pointed with her bony finger in the direction of her office. Kate gave Colette a slight eyebrow lift. *Do you think?*

She meant the Duncan Dance Prix. Could they have heard back about their auditions? Colette opened her eyes wide. *Really?*

They walked into Miss Roza's small office and sat on metal chairs facing her desk. On the cement wall hung a framed picture of Judith Jamison's induction into the National Museum of Dance and Hall of Fame. A quote underneath was highlighted: *It's time to write our own story.*

Miss Roza walked in. Tall and wiry, she wore her gray hair pulled into a tight bun. Her eyes were silver, her lips thin, and she spoke in a thick Russian accent that gave all her words an intimidating edge. Colette had read that the last name Volkov meant *wolf* in Russian, a perfect description of the woman who was the owner and artistic director of the studio. The day Colette walked into the Volkov Studio, her whole life had changed. Miss Roza hadn't glorified her abilities or her looks the way other instructors had. Her face had pulled into that now-familiar tight expression as she'd eyed Colette's body, asked her to do simple leg extensions and jumps. Mom had simply said, "We want a pathway to the top." Without any further questions, Miss Roza had pulled out a piece of paper and created a bulleted outline. Workouts. Stretches. Nutrition. Performances. Competitions. A road map to success.

"It's a major commitment," she had told them. "Not just for Colette, but for the family. There will be sacrifices of time, energy, and money."

Mom didn't say she needed to talk to Dad about it. She didn't even look at Colette. She simply nodded and said, "We're in." Sometimes, when Colette was exhausted and sore, or wanting a normal life where she could hang with a guy, she'd think back to that moment and get pissed. Because Mom had done this to her: imposed this life. But it's not like Colette had stopped it either. She loved dance.

And so, it began: the journey along the bullet-point road map. Miss Roza prepared a schedule of classes with a variety of instructors, including herself in the elite Jazz One and Contemporary Dance. When she suggested a summer intensive workshop in a different city, they paid the fees and went. Six months ago, Miss Roza had pulled out the old piece of paper she'd kept all these years. She'd used a bright-red pen to cross through each accomplishment, and then at the bottom, she'd added: *the Duncan Dance Prix.*

"The Duncan?" Colette had asked breathlessly.

"It's the world's second-largest and most respected dance contest," Miss Roza had said.

Her mother's green eyes had spun like she'd downed a can of Red Bull. They had done all the normal competitions, but the Duncan was different. It was a place where you could secure your future, whether through immediate acceptance into a company, or a signed contract with agents, or scholarships to prestigious schools.

The Duncan Dance Prix became the final bullet point, the Holy Grail, the event Colette spent her life preparing for. The video audition for the regional level had to be perfect.

They began to prepare.

And since Kate was always around, she prepared with them, too. Miss Roza had told all the top dancers about the competition, but no one rehearsed the way Kate and Colette did. Every extra moment they had was spent in her basement, music blaring, windows fogging up with heat and energy. When the time came to submit the video auditions for regionals, they had their routines polished and perfected.

Now, Miss Roza sat with a hint of a smile tugging at the corner of her mouth. She reached over and pulled out two sheets of paper, placing one in front of Kate and one in front of Colette.

Dear Ms. Colette Carrington,
It is with absolute pleasure that we offer you the opportunity to participate in the regional semifinal competition at the Ferst Center for the Arts in Atlanta, Georgia, on March 26 through 28.

Colette didn't even finish reading. She and Kate exploded out of their chairs, hugging, crying, laughing.

Then Kate did something unexpected. She pulled away, threw a fist in the air, and said, "I made it!"

But Colette was thinking, *WE made it.*

And to be honest, it *was* a little shocking that Kate had made it. Not to sound full of herself or anything, but come on: Everyone assumed Colette would make it. But Kate? She wasn't a guarantee, you know? She'd never been stopped on the street and asked if she was a movie star. She didn't have a mother who was a former dancer. She didn't have the genetics and the bone structure and the tiny hips. Miss Roza hadn't pulled her aside and formed a seventeen-item bullet-pointed road map to success. Had she? But she had pulled Kate up to demonstrate today.

Colette looked at Kate again—the girl who was like her sister. She should have been proud that she was finally getting recognition for her hard work. But deep down, there was a little whisper of fear. A forewarning.

Of what? Colette didn't know.

FIVE

Standing alone in the parent lounge, Valerie watched as the dancers emerged from the locker room and exited the studio. Through the viewing window, she saw the door in the corner of the practice area open, and Colette raced out, practically airborne, in the direction of her mother, who was still seated on the bench. Colette said something with wild enthusiasm, and Elise's face nearly exploded with joy. She popped up off the bench; they were hugging and taking little hops with their tiny bodies, up and down. The words *Duncan Dance Prix* stirred in Valerie's mind. She thought of Andrew, full of charm and smiles, unknowingly dropping a bomb: *Elise entered both of their submission videos.*

Kate finally emerged from the same door, slower, tamer, her face emotionless. A tiny flicker of hope sparked; maybe she hadn't gotten accepted. It would be the perfect solution. The decision would have been made by the hands of fate, not her. But then Colette pointed toward Kate, and Elise smiled, extended her arms, and took Valerie's child into a tight maternal hug. Kate pressed in, dipping her head down toward Elise's shoulder; the intimacy of the gesture made Valerie's mouth go dry with a cracked mixture of envy and resentfulness. They all disappeared into the locker room, and Valerie stood alone, watching her daughter follow Elise like a puppy.

The silence of the lobby was all at once flooded with high-pitched, jubilant voices. Elise, Miss Roza, Colette, and Kate walked toward her. "What's going on?" Valerie feigned ignorance.

Miss Roza handed Valerie a letter with an unfamiliar twinkle in her eye. "Kate and Colette have been accepted to audition for the Duncan Dance Prix competition this spring. This is a major honor. Many applied, but only these two have been accepted."

The words sailed over Valerie's head like clouds swirling across a stormy sky—untouchable but looming. She felt everyone staring, waiting for an appropriate reaction, but all she heard was Kate's voice from weeks ago: *You're right, Mom. It doesn't make sense to enter that contest. A future in dance isn't practical.*

The room had gone quiet, just the distant hum of the vending machine filling the air. Valerie stood, her insides scooped out, hollow and vulnerable. She tried to smile but didn't think she hit the mark. Cheeks straining, she manufactured an artificially enthusiastic tone. "Wow. That's incredible. Congratulations, you two." She zeroed in on Kate, who fidgeted—scratching her ear, tucking her hair, curling her hands inside her sweatshirt. Valerie narrowed her eyes. *Busted.*

Miss Roza nodded in one brisk motion. "What's incredible will be the amount of work necessary to compete at this next level. We have just a couple of weeks to prepare. Kate and Colette will need to be at the studio before school, after school, on weekends. Now may be a time to consider homeschooling."

Not that conversation again. She'd filled out mountains of paperwork to maintain Kate's scholarship at the elite private school, and she refused to let that go down the drain so Kate could dance all day. Plus, would extra studio time mean an extra expense? "That's not a consideration. At least for us."

After a moment of awkward stillness, Elise sighed. "Us either. My husband." She tsked, laying the blame on that perfect man.

Miss Roza straightened. "The schedule and intensity of the training will be grueling. Stress will be high. It's a good thing Colette and Kate are such great buddies. Friendships are hard to maintain when you're essentially each other's rivals."

Elise's body twitched, and her eyes darkened strangely. An ominous gust of wind blew through the studio, deep and cold.

The car ride home was silent, the air tight. Kate didn't turn on the radio, almost as though she were waiting for an argument. But Valerie restrained. The parenting guide she'd bought years ago, now highlighted and dog-eared, said it was not wise to have a meaningful discussion in the heat of disappointment. She would not scream: *Why did you lie? Why do you take Elise's advice over mine? Why did you run to her first, wrap your arms around her like you haven't done with me in years? Why do you love her more?*

The back of her throat clogged with tears. She sniffed them back before her lips started quivering, then parked at their condo complex. Kate opened the car door and bolted inside, Valerie silently following.

Valerie sat on the couch and took long, deep breaths. She hadn't failed at all the basic motherhood demands that had plagued her nightmares. She'd kept Kate alive. The problem was that no matter how many times she tried, she couldn't bridge the connection. Her daughter simply preferred Elise. She'd have to forget about competing for Mother of the Year and figure out the real issue: why Kate had lied.

Gathering her courage, she knocked on Kate's door. It opened almost instantly, as if her daughter had been waiting for her. Valerie noticed the diary open on the bed, a pen next to it. What awful things Kate must have written about her. Valerie crossed the room and sat on the desk chair. *Do not attack*, the parenting book said. "When did you decide to enter the Duncan?" She managed a nonaccusatory tone.

"A few weeks ago." Kate averted her eyes, taking hold of her ponytail with a sudden interest in her split ends.

"Why didn't you tell me?"

Kate's face crushed with anger. "I knew you would tell me not to do it. You don't want me to dance . . ."

"It's not that I don't want you to dance—"

"You weren't even happy that I made it! Do you get what a huge deal this is? Miss Roza said there were thousands of entries, but I made it! And you don't even care!" She pulled a pillow into her lap like a shield.

"Of course I care. And I'm proud of you. But I'm upset that you lied."

"I didn't lie. I just didn't tell you."

"What else are you not telling me? Why did you just stand there and not help Avery when she was hurt? I thought I raised you to help others, not just worry about yourself. But this morning, you didn't care if I was late for my meeting, and now, apparently, you don't care about your friends."

"I'm sorry! I forgot about your work thing, okay?" A look of condemnation crossed Kate's face. "And you have no idea what you're talking about. It's not like I passed an injured person on the street. The rules are different inside a dance studio."

"What are those rules? It's okay to land a little too close to throw someone off-balance? Someone who was a competitor for the Duncan?" She hadn't meant to verbalize her fear, and from the horrified expression on Kate's face, she knew she'd crossed a line. "I'm sorry."

"You know nothing about dance!" Kate shrieked.

Valerie threw her hands out. "Tell me! You never take the time to teach me."

"Maybe because you're never home."

Valerie recoiled, the words knocking the wind out of her. She rolled her lips in, trying to camouflage the agony her daughter's words had inflicted. "I'm sorry that for the last few years, I've had both work and school. It took a long time to finish my degree, but now I have a better job. I'll be home more. And at that meeting today, I got a raise." She reached into her purse and pulled out the crumpled real estate flyer. "I was going to wait until I got the final approval for the mortgage, but look." She extended the glossy page toward her daughter. "It's perfect. It has a yard. We could plant a garden. We could buy one of those porch swings and have long conversations." Valerie's voice broke. It was pathetic. A mother begging her daughter to love her.

Kate didn't even glance at the brochure. "Yeah, but those long talks would all be the same. Maybe I spend so much time at the Carringtons' because I get encouragement there."

"I encourage you, Kate. Why do you think I've been working so much? So I can continue to afford to send you to Chandler Prep because I know how smart you are. What a future you could have. I don't understand why you'd want to throw all that away to go to some . . . dance school." Her voice escalated in desperation.

Red blotchy circles flushed Kate's cheeks. "See? You only support the things that you think are important! You don't care about my passions!"

Valerie burned with resentment. Elise had filled her daughter with impractical dreams, and now she'd have to undo all that damage. "Look, even if you beat out the thousands of other competitors and become a professional dancer, how long does that last? Realistically, what? Ten years? Maybe fifteen? When you're thirty years old, what are you going to do? How are you going to support yourself? Or are you going to wait for a handsome lawyer to rescue you, wrap you in cashmere, and build you a French country cottage on a grassy green hill?"

Kate's eyes narrowed with a look of disgust. "Why do you hate her so much?"

Valerie clamped her mouth shut and resisted the urge to scream, *Because you love her so much.*

Where was the parenting book that was honest? That said, *Some days, motherhood will feel like swallowing glass.*

Maybe she was going about everything wrong. Maybe she should be more like Elise and say, *Follow your passion, Kate.*

But no. She couldn't even think of the word *passion* without triggering memories of Kate's father, Valerie's first love, and how his *passions* were like a hamster wheel of rotating aspirations. One day he'd declared he was going to open a hardware store. When Valerie had asked how he'd compete with large chains, he'd waved her off, maxed out the credit card, and filled a storage unit with tools. But then, he'd realized, his true calling was actually electrical work. He just needed to be trained. And on and on, leaving Valerie to pay off and clean up after each unfulfilled dream.

They'd been teenagers when Chad had taken Valerie's face in his hands and said, "I want to be with you forever." Valerie had been doubtful; Chad had a history of brief romances. But then, the summer before their senior year, she'd gotten pregnant, and abruptly, his quick-exit strategy halted. Instead of prom, they'd taken a baby to the pediatrician. Instead of a senior trip to the beach, they'd scraped together enough money for rent. After graduation, her mother had convinced her boss at Dollar General to offer Valerie a minimum-wage job stocking shelves.

In ninth grade, Valerie's guidance counselor had pulled her aside and said, "You're smart, and you're ambitious. I'd love to see you break out of here." Valerie had imagined herself behind the wheel of a convertible, yelling *Adios!* as she drove over the mountains. Then she'd wound up pregnant. She'd used the same doctor who'd delivered Valerie when her mother was a teen, and suddenly, she understood the words of her counselor from years before. Not necessarily *break out of here . . .* but *break out of the cycle.*

She'd gone to Chad and offered a different plan. They should go to college. But Chad had a better plan: a coffee shop—here, in their hometown, where he knew everyone. He'd memorize their orders, offer morning smiles. He'd be their barista hero. So, they'd stayed. It turned out opening a café required start-up costs and a lot of hard work. Instead, Chad did landscaping while Valerie stocked shelves at Dollar General.

At first, it was good—cutting grass paid decent money, but Chad felt squashed. He was meant for something bigger. When Valerie insisted they had a baby to feed, that now was not the time for grandiose, impractical dreams, his charming lopsided grin shrank. His face and his mood became dark and sullen. His tone escalated. Why wouldn't she support him? Was she jealous of his big ideas? Why was everyone holding him down? A creep of paranoia descended. People were judging him, laughing at him. When a man at the park pointed out there was a safety strap for Kate on the swing, Chad had flipped. Did that man think he was stupid? Incapable of protecting his daughter? A bystander threatened to call the cops, but the man, thankfully, apologized and left.

The suspicions amplified: Why was Valerie finding yard work for Chad miles away? Was it so she could screw her manager while he was gone? When her boss showed up with a black eye, Valerie had blanched. "It's my fault," she'd explained. "I've destroyed his future, made him work a job he hates to help pay for our baby." Her kind boss had put a hand on her shoulder and said, "You deserve better."

Chad's behavior spiraled. Bar brawls. Disorderly conduct. Assault.

But she knew Chad could be fun-loving and caring; she'd seen it before. Like the time he'd planned a surprise picnic for Valerie when Kate was still an infant. He'd packed a wicker basket with a checkered tablecloth and all her favorite snacks. Or the time he'd rescued an abandoned puppy from the street, nursed him back to health, walked him, fed him, and loved him with complete adoration. He never got mad when the puppy had an accident in the house. He kept his cool when the puppy chewed his favorite shoes. Valerie knew he could be a good guy. There was a time when everyone in school had been hypnotized by his captivating charisma. He'd been voted most fun in their senior superlatives. It was her fault he'd taken such a dark turn.

She'd decided she would work overtime so he could pursue his newest passion—whatever that turned out to be. She'd even prepared a whole speech about how she'd encourage his dreams, but when she'd returned home one night, there were two suitcases lined up next to the door. Chad had emerged from the bathroom with his hair wet from a shower. "Baby," he'd said, cupping Valerie's face in his hands, "I can't live like this."

A kernel of hope had blossomed inside her. Was he going to college? Getting a full-time job?

"There's this place in Costa Rica," he'd said, taking a step back and pulling out a glossy page from a travel magazine. "Life there, it's, like . . . incredible. There's rafting, hiking, and kayaking . . ."

"We can't move to Costa Rica. Kate starts kindergarten in the fall."

He'd stuffed the shiny travel advertisement into his back pocket. "I know." He'd bitten the edge of his lip. "I'm going."

"What?" Valerie had flinched. "What are you talking about?"

"I'm going to go." He'd pointed toward himself as if that explained everything. "I'm going to get some ideas; then I'll come home and start an outdoor adventure company. It'll be awesome. I'll be an *entrepreneur*." He'd said the word like it was a prize.

Valerie's body had gone cold. "You can't just leave. What about Kate?" *What about me?*

"Oh, doll, I'll be back." He'd walked over to the couch, given Kate a high five, and promised to be in touch. He'd grabbed his suitcases, planted a kiss on Valerie's lips, and then he was gone.

So, with nothing else holding her there, she'd packed up her things, loaded Kate into her car seat, and driven a hundred miles to Atlanta, with only a dream of a better life. She'd found an apartment and a job at a day care. Kate had decorated her new room with pictures of her father taped to the walls. Every night, she'd pray for his call.

Finally, after months, Kate had received a long, gushing letter, a handmade beaded bracelet, and a beach-shell necklace. Kate had adorned herself with each item, proudly telling everyone they were from her father. That was enough. Valerie had put dinner on the table every night, furnished a wardrobe, cobbled together money for dance lessons and a private school education, but Kate never spoke of her with such raw admiration.

A couple of years later, Valerie had received a collect call. His deep voice and thick Southern accent made her stomach burn with a bizarre cocktail of desire and resentment. There had been an incident, he'd explained. A guy was eavesdropping on Chad's conversation. He was stealing Chad's ideas and life plans! He hadn't meant to shove him so hard; he didn't realize they were that close to the edge of the dock. It wasn't like he'd *planned* to kill the guy. He needed Valerie to wire him money to cover the lawyer.

She was so mad, she'd hung up. Several more collect calls and increasingly desperate voicemails thundered across the phone lines. But it took her time. Time to squelch her anger, to vault over her lingering abandonment, and decide to help the man she still bizarrely loved. The father of her child. Except she had no way of finding him. So, she waited for him to call again.

But he never did.

She still toted around the jagged pieces of her failure, stuffed into a tiny slot in her soul. She couldn't do that to her daughter.

Now, sitting in Kate's bedroom, their argument about the Duncan still heavy in the air, Valerie realized that if she didn't want to lose Kate the way she'd lost Chad, if she wanted to reel her daughter back from the grip of Elise, something would have to change. "All right," she said, the words coming out soft and a little scared. "If this is what you want, I'll support you. I'll be there for you." It felt so huge. This moment. This bridge she was laying down.

"Don't bother," Kate said in a blasé tone, insulting Valerie's huge concession. "I learned long ago I have to rely on myself to make things happen."

Valerie's heart crushed, hopes of fixing their broken relationship suffocated.

SIX

Elise pulled out of the studio parking lot in a frenzy. Colette yammered on, elated about the Duncan. Yes, it was fantastic—that critical next step in their plan—but Elise couldn't properly celebrate. Not yet. Not when the victory had been overshadowed by the realization that somehow, before her eyes, Kate had blossomed. Enough to earn an audition to the competition. Her palms sweated against the steering wheel.

"Slow down!" Colette shouted, flattening her hand against the glove compartment as the car swerved around a corner.

"Sorry, sorry." Elise jacked up her tone with gusto. "Just so excited!" She could hardly catch her breath. She felt sideswiped. Like someone had stolen something precious right from her hands.

She drove up the driveway and slammed to a stop in the garage, the smell of burned rubber wafting through the air. Colette hurried into the house, fingers flying over her phone, a smile glued to her face. Elise followed, waiting until her daughter was out of sight, then collapsed into a kitchen chair. She was lightheaded, queasy, her mind racing. She had to examine the evidence, see if Kate's talents could actually challenge her own daughter's.

Fumbling in her purse, she pulled out her phone, opened up her photo app, and clicked on the dance album. Two hundred sixty-two videos. Looking at the endless squares of recordings, she scrolled back in time, randomly tapped one, and began to watch. Time dropped away as she viewed one clip after another, observing the slow, creeping evolution. Barely able to blink, her dry eyes burned. Still, she stared in horror and disbelief. She had been blind. Hyperfocused on Colette. Nitpicking every detail of her daughter's performances, thinking her biggest threat was the slight lack of control in landing her jumps. Good God. She scrolled to more recent footage and was now practically catatonic, totally ripped raw from her oblivion. They looked elegant. Flawless. Both of them.

There was room for both Kate and Colette to succeed, she reassured herself. But no.

She recalled those brutal memories of the professional dance world, how there could only be one prima. How every bloodthirsty ballerina would stop at nothing to reign supreme: toe pads that went missing before a performance, needles stuck inside tutus, costumes purposely mistailored and ill-fitting. Nothing was off-limits. Elise knew that firsthand. All the drama and backstabbing from her years in New York bubbled to the surface. Could Kate be capable of such deception?

Stop! Elise fanned herself with her hand. Kate and Colette were like sisters. This was not like all the treachery she'd witnessed in New York. And contemporary dance offered more options for success. Sure, there were the coveted solos and showcase dancers, but it wasn't like her experience, the quest for prima. Was it? She googled and was disheartened to learn that cutthroat actions did indeed infiltrate all genres.

She clicked on a video from a few weeks ago, when Colette and Kate had been perfecting their auditions. Graceful performances. Excellent choreography. Suddenly, her spine jerked straight. *What was that?* She blinked. Refocused. Replayed.

Using her thumb and forefinger, she enlarged the image. Advancing the video in slow motion, she paused, on the precipice of a true anxiety attack. It couldn't be. Surely her eyes deceived her. Surely she was ruminating too much about her own rivalry. She stood up and walked away. She went to the sink, filled a glass with cold water, and drank the whole thing in one long gulp. Her heart pulsed. Back at her phone, she watched it again.

Kate and Colette were side by side, their bodies in a deep plié followed by an energetic leap. While airborne, they tucked both legs and rotated while traveling across the floor. In the recording, Elise's voice called, "Really stab the floor."

On video, Colette adjusted her leg position. Kate glanced at Elise, then back at Colette, leaned off her mark, her foot extended, slanting in the direction of Colette's path. As if to trip her.

Elise's heart seized.

Rewound. Replayed. Reexamined.

Could it be a trick of angles? Lighting? Could it be that Kate had simply missed her mark?

But how, when her sequence otherwise had been pristine? It didn't appear like an accidental misstep. Rather, it appeared intentional.

On video, Elise had stopped them before they'd completed the movement. So how could she know what would have happened next?

It felt like a bird was caught in Elise's rib cage, flapping its wings ceaselessly. She played the video again, this time observing only Kate's face. The sensation accelerated. Fear sank into her gut. Kate's face looked determined. Determined to get the combination right?

Or determined to make Colette fall?

The video was too damn ambiguous.

Why would Kate do that? The question reverberated along with the flapping in Elise's chest. Her voice whispered the answer in her head: *because every bloodthirsty dancer would stop at nothing to command center stage.*

She'd always thought Kate was honest and kind. Desperate for a family and a home. A horrible suspicion crawled into her brain. What if Kate had tricked them all? What if her friendship with Colette and romance with Trey were nothing more than plots to reap the benefit of Elise's expertise? And now that she was ready for the Duncan and prepared for her rise in the dance world, she had to eliminate her competition? Colette's audition would suffer with a turned ankle, a bruised knee.

No. No. No.

Elise put her face in her hands to halt the hamster wheel of thoughts. The video was not clear. It was a trick of lighting. Angles. She was simply reliving her own anguish and deception. Kate was a sweet, nonthreatening girl. Wasn't she?

A heavy hand gripped her shoulder. She screamed.

"Geez. What are you doing?" Andrew hovered.

"Nothing." She turned her phone over, smoothed her hair, and stood up. "How was your day?"

He had a thoughtful look on his face, eyes skyward, lips slightly pursed. "It was interesting." He tossed his keys on the counter and walked past her.

She watched him as he headed toward the bedroom, an inexplicable pinch in her gut. If something noteworthy had happened, why didn't he want to share it with her? Why had he breezed right past her with barely a glance? She was wearing leggings. There was a time when tight workout clothes had been a green light for sex. He couldn't resist groping her butt anytime her attire was hip-hugging spandex. But not today. Not in a while, now that she thought about it. Could that be another thing she'd glossed over—his growing disinterest? Sure, over time their relationship had morphed from passionate lovers to more . . . what? Business partners? Shuffling the kids and paying the bills and organizing schedules. But that happened to all couples after almost two decades of marriage, didn't it?

She thought of seeing him through the window at the dance studio earlier that day talking to Valerie. She hadn't given it any thought. Andrew was a schmoozer—he made everyone feel special, a part of what made him such a good lawyer. But now, she realized it had been a long time since he'd acted like that with her.

It was like someone had placed glasses on her face, and now she could see her world clearly. Not at all the life she'd thought she was living.

Her chest hitched; she couldn't get enough air.

She could fix this. All of it. Colette. Kate. Andrew. She'd start with him.

The way to a man's heart was not through his stomach, like the old adage advised. It was about six inches lower. She took a breath, settled her nerves, and walked up behind him in the bedroom. When he startled, she walked around to face him and pressed a hand to his chest. "I want to thank you for bringing my phone to the studio. It was so nice of you." She tugged the back of his neck until his face came toward her, and she kissed him. If he was surprised by her initiation—something she realized she hadn't done in ages—it was quickly overshadowed by sheer desire. They locked the door and landed hard and swift on their plush, down-filled duvet, and she convinced herself she'd done this because she loved him. Not because she was trying to prove to herself that she hadn't let cracks form in her marriage. The way she'd inadvertently let huge gaps form in her understanding of Kate's ability and possible intentions.

She wrapped her arms around him, moving in for a kiss, but before their lips touched, he turned her around, her face meeting the pillow. It was fast and intense; clearly, her initiative had sparked desire, but it lacked the intimacy and connection she craved.

As he rolled over, spent, she felt like he'd done a quick cardio session rather than made love to her. Had she really let their relationship diminish to this? To the outside world, and maybe, if she were honest, even to herself, she'd viewed them as the golden couple. Was it all a farce? Her pulse rumbled with hysteria.

Andrew's breathing slowed, and an idea sprang to mind. New York City. They should go back to where they'd fallen in love. To the city where they used to hold hands and eat candlelit dinners; where he'd looked at her not only with longing but admiration. They could ride a carriage in Central Park and show the kids where he proposed. He would be reminded of all they used to be. And while they were there, Colette could visit the headquarters of the Duncan Dance Prix and put her name and face in front of influential people. The trip could both reignite her husband's passion and get a leg up for her daughter. A way to help Colette win, even if the competition was fiercer than Elise had realized.

She wouldn't allow Colette to wind up, twenty-five years from now, nestled in midlife with no real accolades of her own, just an old pair of pointe shoes hidden in a wooden box, newspaper clippings announcing all she might have been if she hadn't allowed one person to destroy her dreams. Colette would never stand in front of a man who'd once looked at her like a grand prize but now walked by with barely a glance. This was Colette's chance to always burn bright. An inside look at the Duncan could be the answer.

Elise nestled closer to Andrew, slid a hand around his waist, and pulled them into a perfect spoon position. She leaned close and whispered, "Let's go to New York. Show the kids where we fell in love."

He didn't turn toward her, but she thought she detected a nod. "Okay." He unraveled himself and tugged on his pants while she spoke of things they could do in Manhattan. After she remade the bed, they wandered back into the kitchen. She brought the serving dishes to the table.

Trey and Colette walked in. Andrew pulled a beer from the fridge and popped the top.

"We've decided to take you to New York! And . . ." Elise said, with a fortuitous lift in her voice, "you have a couple of days off from school for Presidents' Day weekend, so it works out perfectly."

Andrew walked toward the table. "Wait, what?"

She looked at him. "Didn't we just agree?"

"I . . . I . . ." He sat down and fumbled with his spoon. "I didn't realize you meant this weekend. It's a holiday. Won't that be outrageously expensive?"

She raked her hand through her hair, trying to hide her alarm. They had to go to New York right away. It was the only way to fix everything she'd somehow botched. She took a tremulous breath.

Andrew looked at his children staring at him, then back at Elise. "I . . . I guess I didn't realize you meant now."

Elise swallowed, feeling on the verge of tears. How had she let this happen? All these little cracks ready to split wide open. "Please?" Her voice was fragile.

"Uh, okay. I guess," he said with an almost panicked look in his eyes.

She would repair. Rebuild. Everything would be okay.

Still, she felt a steel belt tightening around her chest. Breathless.

SEVEN

The whole plane ride, Dad and Mom acted crazy tense, Colette thought. Mom kept shushing him. But anyone who knows Dad knows the man doesn't whisper. He tried big, splashy court cases for years, so he's not about keeping a low profile. He yelled about expensive last-minute flights and a pricey hotel. It was weird. Those two fighting about money. Kate always felt bad because dance classes cost a fat wad of cash, and it was hard for her mom. But it had *never* been a thing for them. At least, not that Colette knew of. Guilt creeped up her spine and tingled her scalp. But she wasn't the one who dreamed up this trip. Everyone knew Mom was doing this for Colette's "future."

Colette had seen the famous New York City skyline on TV and in movies. But the actual thing? It was insane. The plane dove through clouds; then all at once, there it was. Buildings everywhere. The sky was pink and orange. Lights flickered from windows, like bulbs on a Christmas tree. Even Mom and Dad stopped fighting to look.

They landed, got their bags, and grabbed an Uber. The hotel was right near the entrance to Central Park South. They stepped out of the car as snow started falling. They all looked up because it was, like, just too on point. Like a freaking Hallmark movie. Snow. Horses and carriages decked out with red velvet and fake flowers. Colette pulled out her phone and took a selfie because could it get any more Insta-worthy? *#NYCinwinter #snowincentralpark #familygetaway.*

Dad put his hand on Mom's shoulder. "This is nice." His apology for being an asshat. Mom smiled. Colette's neck loosened, and her scalp stopped tingling. Everything was going to be cool.

Mom was on a high after Dad's mood change. She talked up the guy at check-in; she was all, *It's so good to be back in the city, and I used to be a professional ballerina, and this is where we fell in love.* Next thing they knew, the front desk dude upgraded them to a suite.

In the room, Mom waved a stack of index cards with stuff to say to the people at the Duncan headquarters: *I live to dance, and I dance to live! This opportunity will catapult me toward future stardom!* "That's not how normal people talk, Mom."

Her face got all smooshed up, and she looked like she was in pain. Suddenly, Colette thought about Dad on the plane. She didn't want to be another person getting onto Mom. "I mean, it's close. But maybe I can tone it down a little."

Mom nodded and reminded Colette to sit up straight and smile. Like it was an interview. But it wasn't an interview. Was it? Actually, Colette didn't have a clue what they were doing, so she asked.

"We're going to get a leg up on the competition. Remember," Mom said with a strange sound to her voice, "there's no telling how far you can go. How high you can soar." She paused, glanced across the room, then back at Colette. "As long as you don't let anyone get in the way." Her face was dangerously close and she waited, but what was Colette supposed to say? Her emotions pushed and pulled, like a door swinging in the breeze. She wanted to do everything in her power to make Mom proud. But she was starting to feel smothered by the effort. She got that weird feeling all across her scalp again. Like she wanted to yank out her hair, one strand at a time, just to make Mom stop talking. Thankfully, she finally went to bed.

The next morning, the Duncan headquarters was a quick cab ride away. Mom told a security guard they had an appointment with Tamara Suches, and he directed them down a maze of hallways. When they entered her office, Tamara said, "I loved chatting with you the other day. I must admit, I did a little snooping." She looked down at a paper and read. "*What her body does in response to the rapturous music is a work of beauty.* That's just one of the lovely reviews I dug up."

Mom flushed.

Tamara paused, maybe waiting for an explanation for why Mom's dance years ended so abruptly. But just like with Colette, she offered no answers. Tamara cleared her throat. "Well, I'm so impressed by Colette's desire for an inside look—such ambition."

"Oh, thank you," Colette said, feeling like an impostor. "I want to be prepared. It's a chance of a lifetime." She delivered the dictated flash card speech, with a surge of resentment toward her mother for forcing lies, the pretense that this had been her idea.

"So," Mom said, sitting up straight, "I guess what we're wondering is, everyone competing at regionals is technically superior. How can one stand out, especially if some dancers are from the same studio and have worked with similar choreography and artistic direction?"

Mom had always insisted Colette was the best. So why was she suddenly scared of the competition? Why was she wringing her hands like she was on the verge of a panic attack? What had changed? A chill spread across Colette's skin.

Tamara nodded, then turned toward her computer and typed; the screen loaded a page of results. "What most people don't know is that before our competition, we research the dancers, peruse their social media for drama. More importantly, we note competitors who have a positive online presence, or even better, a platform. We send scouts to preview highlighted competitors at local events. By the time regionals starts, our judges already have an idea of who the top contenders will be."

Mom's face got all serious. She pulled out her phone, opened up the Notes app. "When you say platform . . . ?"

"Colette's search results are very typical for a fifteen-year-old girl," Tamara said, pointing at the screen. "But look at this." She typed *Skyler Schetner* into the search box and opened an Instagram page. The avatar

51

was a teen girl, soaring through the air, arms and legs extended in a perfect barrel roll.

"When Skyler was thirteen, she began posting a series of five-minute instructional videos aimed at young dancers who couldn't afford studio lessons. She taught combos and jumps but also provided inspiration. By the time she auditioned for us last year, she was sixteen and had forty thousand Instagram followers, a robust TikTok page, and a sponsorship from Danskin. And that, my friends, is a platform."

Mom's mouth fell open.

"When someone like Skyler shows up at a competition, beyond the cash prizes, it becomes a bidding war between companies, agents, and choreographers about which avenue she'll choose."

Mom took notes frantically. *Instagram. TikTok. YouTube. Platform. Sponsorship.* She shook out her wrist. "But how . . ." She sounded desperate. "How can we build that kind of following in such a short amount of time?"

Tamara took her tortoiseshell glasses off and twirled them between her fingers. "In all honesty, it will be a challenge. The trick is to find something new." Tamara smiled at Colette. "But look at you. You're absolutely gorgeous. I'm sure you look incredible on video. People will want to watch you if you have intriguing content, if you formulate a certain aesthetic. You may not be able to score a huge number of subscribers before the competition, but if you find a unique approach, show that you're building toward something with potential . . ." She let the end of the sentence dangle.

Mom stood up. "Thank you so much," she said. "You've been unbelievably helpful."

"Happy to do it." Tamara pointed her eyeglass frames, still in her hand, in Colette's direction. "I expect great things from you, Miss Colette Carrington."

"That's a name you won't forget," Mom said. "We'll do whatever it takes."

Whatever it takes. A weight landed on Colette's shoulders. Then, a revelation barreled through her like a sledgehammer. Why they had come. Mom thought Colette was good, but she was worried. Mom had lived this life. From the outside, it seemed like she'd had all the makings of a star—the looks, the talent, the opportunity. But something had derailed her. She wanted to protect Colette from similar roadblocks. In an instant, she forgave Mom for all her annoying control and decided she would dedicate herself to achieving the destiny Mom had lost.

They talked the whole way back to the hotel. Colette searched for Skyler Schetner on her phone; she had many copycats. They had to find a new angle. But what?

The cab pulled to the curb across the street from the hotel. They got out, and Mom pointed at a patch of ice. "Careful," she said. "The last thing we need is an injury."

Colette walked around the spot, thinking how one wrong move could spell disaster. She stopped right in the middle of the sidewalk, jamming up people in the crosswalk. "Injury prevention," she said.

"What?" Mom looked over her shoulder.

People pushed past, cursing under their breath. "What about a video series on injury prevention? Like how if Avery had done the strength exercises Miss Roza suggested, maybe she wouldn't have twisted her ankle?"

Mom was quiet for a moment, then sat down at a metal café table outside a restaurant. Colette sat across from her. "A focus on preventing injuries common to dancers?" Mom pulled out her phone and started tapping. Colette searched, too. There were random articles or videos. But not a series. Not a channel dedicated to it. Not a platform with an appealing aesthetic.

Mom looked up, a sparkle in her eyes. "Colette . . ." She didn't finish. But Colette knew. It was perfect. Mom was crazy happy. Her smile was like a thousand-watt lightbulb. She tucked the chair against the table, and together they walked. The city seemed brighter, dipped and coated in fairy-tale charm. Windows twinkled like stars; streetlights glowed like gems. Pedestrians' breath puffed out in frosty cotton-candy clouds. Everything was magical; Colette's future filled with success.

At their hotel entrance, the suited doorman smiled, tipped his hat. "Welcome back, beautiful ladies."

Mom winked. "It's a beautiful night." It was weird, but Colette felt responsible for Mom's great mood. Like in that moment, she was exactly the daughter Mom had always dreamed of. Colette wanted to feel like this forever.

They crossed the lobby and got on the elevator, beaming. When the mirrored doors slid closed, the lighting darkened, and Mom's reflection suddenly morphed, dimming her joy. Shadows cut angles into the sides of her cheeks. Her smile faded into an expression of sternness, like a fairy godmother ripping off her mask. "Do not talk about any of this to anyone: what Mrs. Suches told us, having an online presence, sending scouts to local performances, and especially about our plan for your channel."

"Okay . . ." Colette sounded as confused as she felt. "But I want to tell Kate—"

"No!" Mom snapped. "Do not mention any of this to Kate!"

The slice of her voice ripped through Colette's gut. "But . . . but she's my best friend. We tell each other everything."

"Listen to me." Mom leaned closer, her perfume clogging the air. "Everything has changed. You and Kate are competing for the same thing. You have now become *rivals*."

The word echoed in the cramped space. Colette winced.

"Do you think she's worried about your success?" Mom hissed. "No. She's thinking about her own future. You can still be friends, but it will never be uncomplicated."

A shiver blew through Colette. Like a punch, she recalled getting their letters of acceptance. Kate's celebratory jump. *I made it!* Not *We made it!* A prickle of anxiety crept into Colette's head again. She ran her hands through her hair with an urge to pull. Mom stared at her. Colette forced her hands down. All this time, she'd thought of Kate as her best friend. But . . . did Kate think about their relationship differently? Colette's heart raced. While she was willing to share the spotlight, could Kate be wishing for a solo act?

The elevator doors opened. Light flooded in, blinding Colette.

She refocused, shoved aside Mom's scariness.

Because there, in front of Colette, was someone else she needed to target.

EIGHT

Valerie walked in from work to find Kate sitting at the kitchen table. "Can you drive me to Colette's?" her daughter asked by way of greeting. "I haven't heard a thing about the Duncan headquarters, and I'm dying to know how it went."

Why couldn't they have a normal conversation like all those mothers and daughters on TV, bonding for hours over fancy lattes? Instead, Valerie was a chauffeur. She sighed. "Fine."

The drive to the Carringtons' wasn't far mileage-wise, but in that short distance, the aesthetics of the neighborhood changed drastically. It wasn't that Valerie lived in a bad part of town, but once they drove out of the condo complex, past shops, restaurants, and a large sprawling park with basketball and tennis courts, the streets became quieter with a mix of hundred-year-old cottages and bungalows, roomy midcentury ranch homes, and a smattering of newer developments. The Carringtons lived in a historic section of town filled with a mixture of original architecture and some new construction, leading to an interesting and eclectic mix of homes. The streets, wide and tree-lined, bordered a very prestigious country club.

Their house was tall with sloping hipped roof lines and long rectangular windows in a natural stone facade. The windows of the first floor had arching wood shutters, aligned in perfect symmetry, looking almost like rounded eyebrows on a surprised face. As Valerie pulled up, she saw another car idling in the driveway. The door opened, and Avery popped out, still a little wobbly on her ankle.

"Oh," Kate said. "I didn't realize she was going to be here."

Valerie wanted to ask why Kate sounded disappointed. But Kate had been so aloof all weekend, and she was afraid her daughter would say she was being intrusive, or reading into things. So, Valerie held her tongue, hating all these conversations left unsaid.

Kate opened the car door and left without a thank-you, let alone a goodbye, and that was too much for Valerie to ignore. She rolled down the passenger-side window and called out, "Bye!" with an irritated snap. "Love you, too!"

Without warning, Andrew's face appeared by the open window. Valerie gasped, both surprised and embarrassed that he'd witnessed her little outburst. She slammed her hand into to her chest. "Oh, you startled me."

"I have a defibrillator in the garage if you need it." He smiled. "Next to the bedazzled toolbox." That wink. Again. Oh . . .

Valerie blushed. There was an undercurrent beneath their conversation. Confirming they had a secret joke. It made her feel electric, special, and a touch nervous. "I think I'm okay. No electrodes necessary."

His gaze moved to where her hand still pressed against her chest, and she found herself thinking about her plain white bra beneath her shirt. It was old and ordinary, with sagging straps. Her face heated. Why was she thinking about lingerie? She quickly removed her hand, worried he could somehow sense where her mind had traveled. "What are you doing out here?" She steered the conversation away from her.

He held up a chainsaw, then gestured with his other hand toward a behemoth, sprawling oak tree that grew from the center of their yard and draped a huge umbrella of thick, gnarly limbs in all directions.

"Oh no!" Valerie said. "Please don't say you're chopping down that tree."

"Nah," Andrew said. "Just trimming some branches." He looked like a college kid in his old faded jeans and dark navy hoodie. He was wearing a UGA ball cap that covered the sprinkle of salt-and-pepper hair that tinged his temples. "Elise wanted to replace it with a Bradford pear. But I won that battle. I reminded her of the tire swing that hung right there." He pointed to a sprawling limb. "All the summer nights Trey, Colette, and Kate would pile on and swing for hours."

"It was so much easier then." Valerie felt a tug at the base of her throat. "When a simple tire swing made them happy." To her embarrassment, the words hitched.

Andrew leaned in through the window. "They're just teenagers." His voice brimmed with kindness. "I know they're like aliens now, but they'll come back to us. Eventually."

She studied his face, the soft creases folding in the corners of his eyes and the slight tilt of his head. His look of compassion stoking such a strong pulse of intimacy scared her. She leaned back against her seat, allowing some space between them, and shifted the tone back to a more comfortable, playful banter. "Such confidence. Or is it delusion?"

He chuckled. "I've never been accused of being totally sane."

Laughing, she shook her head. "Join the club. Well, good luck with the tree. See ya." She started to drive away, but after only a few yards, she caught sight of him in her rearview mirror, waving frantically. For a flash, she imagined that he didn't want to end their interaction either.

"Stop!" He ran to her window. "You've got a flat. Don't worry. I'll help."

She turned off the engine. "I know how to change a tire." She unbuckled her seat belt and got out.

His eyes stayed on her for a beat longer than necessary. "I'm sure you can. You handle everything on your own. But it's okay sometimes to let someone help you."

A lump appeared in her throat again. She swallowed hard. "Okay. Thanks."

He pointed toward the curb, and she sat. He pulled a jack and a spare tire from her trunk, then bent down, loosening the lug nuts. "Junior year of college, me and three of my fraternity brothers were going to the beach for spring break. The guys were pounding Miller High Life, thinking they were high class because they had bottles, not cans. I was driving because I was the responsible one."

"Naturally," Valerie said with a smirk.

He chuckled, placing the jack under the car and raising the tire off the ground. "But I failed to realize that throwing glass bottles out the window could have an unfortunate side effect."

"Like a flat tire?"

"Like two flat tires."

"Yikes."

He laughed. "Of course, I had a spare . . . but not two."

"So, you called a tow truck?"

"Four broke college students? Hell no. We improvised. I searched through all our crap and found a skateboard, which had . . ." He raised an eyebrow.

"Wheels?" She laughed.

"We duct-taped the skateboard underneath one flat tire and drove the car to the nearest tire shop."

"Wasn't the car off-balance?"

He shrugged. "They were already bombed. Everything looked tilted." He grounded her car, tightened everything up, and put the flat tire in her trunk. "Make sure you get yourself a new spare ASAP."

"Will do. Maybe I'll also throw in a skateboard. Just for good measure."

"Now you're talking." He grinned.

She reached out and touched his arm. "Thank you." She meant for all of it—not just the physical labor, but the conversation, the laughter, the reassurance about Kate. He held her gaze, and for a fraction of a second, she felt something: that tingle when you suspect someone enjoys spending time with you as much as you enjoy them. Something a hair past friendship.

And just for a flash, Valerie thought perhaps Elise could deliver on every whim of her children and even Kate, but maybe she wasn't able to satisfy her own husband. And wouldn't it be just a smidge satisfying to retaliate?

But no. Valerie shook it off. She wasn't mean-spirited.

She climbed in her car, waved, and pulled away, driving home in silence. When she walked inside the condo, it was quiet and lonely. She was used to Kate being gone, but after her sparkling conversation with Andrew, the emptiness left her feeling isolated, in a vacuum of silence. When was the last time Kate had shared a story like that with her? Lately, she'd been all secrets and lies. Her deception about the audition still stung. What else was she hiding?

She walked toward Kate's room. Standing in the threshold, she looked at the space her daughter had claimed for herself. The soft palette of gray and pale yellow. The clear glass pencil holder that contained a rainbow of colored gel pens. The biology book pushed to the corner of her desk. On the far wall stood a small white corner bookcase filled with rows of neatly aligned journals, several of them stacked spine to spine like tall soldiers in a row. From a very young age, Kate had been an avid diary keeper. But what, precisely, did she write about?

Valerie's heart ignited. She looked toward that neat row of spines with a burst of longing so strong, her mouth began to water. Kate's thoughts, fears, anger, joy, all of it—lost to Valerie's ears for the last several years—could spill out before her like a gift.

But she respected Kate's privacy.

Could her entries explain how Elise had drawn Kate into her orbit? Did she write about how Valerie had failed as a mother? Then she thought of the day Avery had fallen and twisted her ankle, how Kate had landed unnaturally close. Had it just been an accident? Were there any words to explain it?

Her need to understand her daughter suddenly outweighed her moral code. It wasn't even really a decision. She took one step. Then another. Then she was down on her knees, fingers grabbing at a random notebook nestled in the middle of the stack. Valerie's fingers felt thick, desperate, as she flipped the pages open, landing exactly in the middle. Her eyes raced over the beautiful cursive writing. She waited, heart throbbing, to see the criticism, the parading commentary on her mothering. Or to see the love and admiration for Elise. Or her intense desire to succeed in dance.

She held her breath. Scanned. Flipped a page. And another. And another.

But she was nowhere to be found. And neither was Elise. Neither were any typical ramblings about Trey or any boys, crushes, or first kisses.

Everything, absolutely everything, was about Colette.

NINE

Satisfaction poured through Elise as she looked at the drawings and plans to renovate the basement. Currently, it was a teen hangout—with pool and Ping-Pong tables, a sixty-inch smart TV, and a six-piece dual-power reclining leather sectional. There was a small area in the back where Colette practiced, but it was basic: a laminate floor and a small, full-length mirror. In New York, Elise had realized they needed a space to film Colette's videos, and in order to create a reputable channel, an authentic setting was essential. She wasted no time, phoning from the hotel and sending photos to every remodeling business within a twenty-mile radius until she found a team willing to begin immediately. Time was of the essence!

The plush carpet would be ripped up to reveal a sleek light-stained hardwood floor. The TV would be replaced with a complete wall of floor-to-ceiling mirrors, and a wooden ballet barre would hang at waist height. The contractors suggested pushing the gaming tables into the far corner to allow for the creation of a home Pilates studio, complete with a Cadillac reformer and a stability chair. They would build a new mini kitchen with a stainless-steel refrigerator and stocked cabinets with trail mix, apples, and water.

Footsteps pounded on the stairs. One by one, Colette, Kate, and Avery descended into view. Elise struggled with a strange urge to hold up her hands and stop them, to keep this project only for whom it was intended: her daughter.

Elise stood awkwardly at the base of the stairs, blocking their entry. "Oh, hey, girls. What are you doing?" Even to herself, she sounded phony.

Colette's eyebrows pulled into pale blond slashes. "Um, we're, like, *stranded* on the stairs, Mom. How about a little space?"

Elise reluctantly sidestepped, sending telepathic commentary to her daughter with the pulse and jab of her jaw: *This is for your SECRET YouTube series!*

Colette, oblivious, walked her friends down the stairs and showed them the AI-generated images of the proposed remodeled basement that were printed and taped to the wall. Avery gasped as she balanced delicately on her recently healed ankle. "This . . . is . . . amazing!"

Avery's tone was pure awe, but Kate remained silent as her gaze roamed over the drawings with an expression that was unfamiliar to Elise. Her eyes sank, looking hurt or abandoned.

A battle tugged inside Elise. She'd rescued the girl from her lonely latchkey life, giving her not only a home but a mother figure who doted, inspired, and provided in a way her own mother could not. Elise recalled the first time she'd met Kate at a Mommy and Me dance class when the girls were five. Kate's mother, Valerie, had looked like a wide-eyed doe, perpetually flustered. Elise had wondered how she'd landed in Atlanta with a baby but no other family, no friends, and no husband. She was barely old enough to drink. Valerie had explained she was estranged from her mother, and Kate's father had died in an accident years ago. She was all alone.

Elise had taken Valerie under her wing, relishing the role of adviser and friend. She'd helped her fill out financial aid forms to enroll Kate in the private school her children attended. Once the girls started kindergarten, Elise had envisioned morning power walks, followed by coffee shop conversations, Valerie becoming the little sister Elise had never had. Instead, the minute the heavy school doors banged shut behind their kids, Valerie had enrolled in community college in addition to her full-time job at a day care.

Elise recognized that Valerie had no experience with dance, and watching her essentially ignore Kate's passion tugged at too many memories. She wouldn't let Valerie do to Kate what her own mother had done to her: disregard her dreams. Elise had tried to school Valerie, to let her know how critical it was to be at a more expensive studio, how important it was to be present at the lessons. But each time Elise had attempted to advise, Valerie had stood wordless, like Elise's guidance was drivel, her world shallow. Like she had no time for the friendship Elise was attempting.

So, when Kate gravitated to Elise's home, to her advice, to her maternal love, maybe it was the universe's small ripple of retaliation.

Now, when Kate looked at the proposed basement transformation and mumbled, "When did this happen?" it triggered guilt. Because, for the last decade, Elise had kept nothing from the girl—her home, her love, and her teaching. This new act of secrecy plucked a wire of doubt. Because what if Elise was wrong? What if that little two-second clip on that video was misleading? What if Kate had never harbored ill intentions against her daughter?

"We *just* came up with the idea for the remodel," Colette gushed. She threw a casual arm around Kate's waist and leaned in conspiratorially. "I'm pushing for a massage table right over there."

Elise looked at them—Colette and Kate, pressed against each other. Inseparable. They were like yin and yang, the petite pale blonde with crystal-blue eyes juxtaposed with the lanky giant with long hair that fanned out like a lion's mane. She looked at her daughter, eased up against her friend, so trusting. Just like Elise had trusted Gina in New York. They had been friends until Gina had threatened Elise's success. What else was Elise to do? Her whole future had been at stake. Elise understood that sometimes drastic actions were necessary. But she couldn't allow that to happen to her daughter! Kate wasn't as ambitious as Elise had been. And yet . . . Elise couldn't stop thinking about that video. What if Kate were more driven than Elise had ever realized? What if she *had* tried to trip Colette?

Footsteps thudded down the stairs. "Emma's here." Andrew peeked his head into the room.

The girls raced upstairs, leaving Elise and Andrew alone in the basement. Things still felt a little off between them for no real reason. Elise's big plans for romance in New York had been hijacked by the excitement of Colette's video series. Now, Andrew let out a long sigh that felt weighted with disappointment.

"What?" Elise asked, hearing the tinge of irritation in her own voice.

He looked around, his mouth pulled tight, and shook his head. "Did I hear something about a massage table?"

"Uh-huh." Elise saw his expression, his jaw twitching. "What?"

"Don't you think it's a bit much? Most people are worried about things like a flat tire and paying the rent, not spending a fortune on something as frivolous as a massage table. And what's Trey supposed to do? Sit on a hard floor and stare in the mirror . . ."

Elise was frustrated. Why was he talking about flat tires and acting like she'd done this on the sly? "We discussed this. The importance of the right setting for Colette's videos. And besides," she said, pointing, "I'm not getting rid of his stuff."

"How kind. You'll put the TV and couch in the corner." He took an exasperated breath. "I'm sure he won't feel pushed aside."

"What are you saying? Do you think I favor Colette?" Her insides swirled. "Maybe it's because I understand Colette's dreams. They were my dreams, too. I guess I want to give her everything I didn't have. If Trey asked for something, I'd give it to him. How is this different? If you didn't want me to renovate, you should have said so." She was fed up with trusting people, only to worry she might have been duped. Was this really about the basement? Or was it something else? "What's really wrong?" she demanded.

"You just seem . . ." He looked up at the ceiling as if carefully choosing his words. "A little hyper-obsessed lately. About dance."

"I'm not *obsessed*." She put her hands on her hips, thrust up her chin. "It's a critical time. I'm trying to help."

He let out an exasperated sigh. "Your commitment to Colette's success . . ." He let the words drop off.

"What?" Her tone ticked up. "It's *what*?" Blood rushed up her neck and heated her face. She leaned forward, waiting.

"Well . . ." He held her gaze. "It's suffocating."

Her breath caught; her lungs squeezed as if she'd taken a blow to the back. She felt blindsided. Her emotions barreled past anger and slid down into despair. Once, she'd been the brightest light in the room. Now, she took away all of his air. She was silent, dumbstruck. But he went on, the floodgates now open.

"You're spending too much time, too much money, too much brainpower on dance!" His voice escalated. "You've completely ignored your own son!"

Her shock turned to anger. "The kids have friends upstairs!" she whispered harshly. "Please don't embarrass them with your cruel criticism of me!"

"Always worried about how things look." He shook his head and headed up the stairs.

Elise was furious. He was bailing midargument; nothing was resolved. She wanted to follow him, to demand they finish talking, but her eyes were misty, and she could feel the flush of her cheeks. The kids would know she was two seconds away from losing it. So, she stayed in the basement until her breathing returned to normal, and the haze of tears cleared. She climbed to the top of the stairwell and heard Colette's voice echoing from the living room. She walked in that direction, her daughter's voice like a calming salve.

Colette stood in front of the stone fireplace, beams of light from the setting sun filtering in through the window, like a spotlight illuminating her radiant skin. Elise could almost imagine the word *STAR* flashing around her like a brilliant neon sign. How did Andrew not understand that everything she did was for this—so their daughter could shine? Colette wore an emerald green sweater dress and her bright-red signature lipstick—a color most fifteen-year-olds wouldn't be brave enough to wear. Seated around her in a semicircle were her three besties. Trey and his friends were off to the side, talking among themselves.

"Guys," Colette said, her voice theatrical, her arms outstretched, "this trip has changed . . . my . . . life!"

Elise clenched. Had she not made herself clear? Kate was sitting in there like a sponge. Their intel on the Duncan was top secret!

Kate leaned forward, a flame of curiosity ignited in her eyes. "The competition headquarters?"

"Yeah," Avery agreed. "You ghosted us. We know nothing. Was it awesome?"

"Yes, but I'll tell you about that later. First, I need to tell you about . . ." Colette paused, pulled her shoulders back. "Marcus."

Marcus? Elise inched as close to the wall as she could without letting herself be seen.

"Marcus. Six feet tall. Brown eyes. A legit surfer. From Florida. He was staying in the same hotel, and at first, when we kept seeing each other, I thought . . . random. But then he smiled. And it was, like, *Whoa.* He accidentally on purpose brushed against my arm. I accidentally on purpose brushed into him in the elevator. And it was obvious—*fate.*"

"I thought you only friend-zoned guys. No hooking up until you're accepted into a company?" Kate asked.

Exactly! Elise thought. This was not the time to start thinking about romance.

"I know," Colette said. "But something about Marcus was . . . different. On Saturday, I got off the elevator, and there he was. At the lobby Starbucks. I didn't say a word, but he turned and said, *Meet me here at midnight.* I pulled off a total *Mission: Impossible.* After everyone was asleep, I put on my ripped black jeans, black chunky sweater, gloves, and a hat. I shot out of there like a panther and met him. We sat on a bench at the entrance to Central Park and talked for six straight hours."

A swell of nausea roiled through Elise. She'd noticed the dark circles under Colette's eyes, mistakenly assuming she hadn't slept because she was excited about the YouTube channel. But no. She had been sneaking out with some boy she'd just met. How incredibly stupid!

"He totally gets me. Because he's as serious about surfing as I am about dance. It's not like he spends his summers working at Chipotle. He's in competitions, too. He has a life plan." She inhaled wistfully. "He kisses like it's his superpower."

Elise held in a gasp. Colette allowed that boy to kiss her? How long had her daughter been making bad decisions? Acting reckless?

Colette sat down on the edge of the beige couch. "It was like a major Netflix binge: six hours of pure awesomeness, and then . . ."

A shadow loomed over Elise's shoulder. "Seriously?" Andrew's breath was hot on her cheek. Her hand flew to her mouth, startled. "You're eavesdropping?" His eyes narrowed to slits.

"I just . . ." Her heart thudded. She pointed toward their daughter. "She's talking about some boy she met in New York. She doesn't have time for a boyfriend! The Duncan's in a couple of months!"

"She's fifteen," he said through gritted teeth. "She has a little crush. It's not a monumental roadblock."

"But it could be!" Elise's voice was desperate. He didn't understand! "This is exactly the kind of thing that could derail her future! Is that what you want? Years of training to be sidelined for a couple of Snapchats with a surfer? And while she's spending time with her *crush*, someone else"—she pointed toward the living room—"could be refining their technique and soaring past our girl!"

Her breathing quickened. Her neck felt clammy. "Stop looking at me like that; I'm not obsessed! I'm just trying to help our daughter," she hissed, clenching her hands.

Her husband blew out a long, disgusted breath, turned, and walked away. Like she repelled him.

The silence that lingered in his wake was as loud as a ticking bomb.

TEN

It was freaking cold on Colette's morning run. Sweat froze into ice crystals in her hair. She stopped for a quick selfie and posted to her socials. Then she busted her final mile.

At their driveway, she hit "Stop" on her watch. *Damn.* Her time was good. She walked in through the side door, buds in, music still playing. The kitchen smelled like a Starbucks, which meant Mom was up. Colette rounded the corner into the kitchen, and there Mom was. Scowling. Lips moving. Colette paused her playlist.

"How many times do I have to tell you that running this early when it's still a little dark, with your music blaring, is dangerous? Someone could come up behind you, and you'd never hear them until it was too late."

Like their neighborhood would be featured next on *Crime Watch*. Whatever. There was no point in arguing. "Sorry. I'll just play music from my phone next time."

"Maybe don't play music at all. It could be a distraction. You could trip and get injured. That would derail everything! Just run in silence. Mentally review your practice from the day before."

Suffocating much?

Trey came into the kitchen, black circles under his eyes, hair still matted from sleep. How long had he and Kate stayed on the front porch talking after Colette went to bed?

"So, Mom," Colette said, "I met this guy in New York, Marcus. He was staying at our hotel. He and his parents are coming to Atlanta for some work thing in two weeks. Can I have him over that Friday night?"

"No." It came out loud and clipped.

"What? Why not?"

Mom reached across the counter and touched Colette's hand with the tips of her icy fingers. "Honey," she said. "Your whole future rests on these next few weeks. That's what we need to focus on. Not some boy you hardly know."

Colette scrambled. "I *do* know him! He's a competitive surfer, so he understands commitment to a sport. A relationship could be a good thing. Look at Kate—she's dating Trey." She pointed at him. "And it hasn't been a downfall. If anything, she's gotten better!"

Something weird happened to Mom's face. The muscles around her lips tightened, pulling her mouth into a hard line.

Trey threw up his hands. "I'm a downfall? Very nice."

"That's not what I mean," Colette said. "It's just not fair that you can date and run with earbuds. Just not me."

"Don't drag me into this," Trey said.

Mom didn't even look at him. "I don't want your hearing muffled while you run. It's a safety issue. It's much more likely that you'd be a victim, not your six-foot-tall brother."

"A victim? Come on. It's not exactly high crime on these streets." Colette pointed toward the window.

"Crimes can happen anywhere. You need to be careful. A girl like you could easily be a target." There was a look in her piercing eyes that said, *I am the boss.*

It sent a bullet of anger through Colette's core. "Well, I guess I'll just bubble wrap myself and stay protected from everything." Resentment flooded her voice.

Dad walked in. "What's going on?"

"I can't go for a run. I can't have a boyfriend. I can't do anything!"

He looked at Mom.

"She wants to see that boy she met in New York. I told her—"

"Let her be a teenager," he interrupted. Mom's eyes bulged, like she was going to unleash on him. But he turned away from her and looked at Colette and Trey. "Don't you guys have school?"

"The kids have a four-day weekend for Presidents' Day," Mom answered. "I told you that, but I guess you weren't listening." Ice cracked her voice.

Trey and Colette looked at each other. Something strange was brewing.

Dad picked up his wallet and keys and left without another word.

Mom's lips pursed. She cleared her throat. "Fine. Text me his number. I'll call his parents and invite him over."

Whoa. Twist. "Um, okay. Thanks."

Mom exhaled loudly but said nothing as she walked out of the room.

Colette quickly texted Marcus before Mom changed her mind. Then, scrolling through her phone, Colette realized Kate still hadn't responded to her messages. "Have you talked to Kate?" she asked Trey. "I've Snapped her, like, five times, and she's totally ghosting me."

He used his napkin to wipe his mouth, obviously stalling.

"Hello?" Colette said, annoyed.

"She thinks you're purposely not telling her about the Duncan. Even though she asked last night, all you talked about was that guy."

Crap. That's exactly what she'd been doing. But what was she supposed to do? Mom had forbidden her to say anything.

Trey pointed toward the basement door. "Do you think it was easy for Kate to see Mom's whole freaking HGTV renovation plans to give you a private studio when she feels bad asking her mother just for lessons?"

"She can use the basement anytime!"

He shook his head. "Kate said Mom was weird last night. Like, maybe she wasn't invited to use the new studio."

"Really? Why didn't she just ask me about it?" It'd never been awkward with Kate before, but suddenly, she worried: Was Mom right? Had the Duncan changed things? *You have now become rivals.*

Trey fiddled with his phone. "I don't know. She said ever since New York, you're being secretive. It's bothering her." His tone became irritated. "And Mom told me not to say anything to Kate about some videos or something. I don't know what she's talking about, but it's BS. I'm not keeping any secrets." He got up and left.

Ugh! How could he unleash a verbal grenade and just disappear? She did feel guilty about Kate; she wasn't entirely wrong about Mom. Colette needed to tell Kate something about New York, but not about her platform. She ran her hands through her hair and massaged her aching scalp.

She texted: Hey, sorry I've been checked out. Too much Marcus on the brain. Come over? I'll give deets on Duncan. Bring your bathing suit.

Three little dots flashed, but then they disappeared with no reply. Colette's heart raced. Five full minutes went by. Torture. Finally: OK. Be there in a few.

Kate's mom dropped her off thirty minutes later. She stood in the doorway for a second, just looking at Colette. Then, in a flash, she was back to normal, digging into her bag for her bathing suit. "Girl, it's cold out," she said.

Colette laughed. "I turned up the pool heater. Come on."

They got changed, threw on fluffy chenille robes, stuffed their feet into fur-lined boots, and darted outside to the pool. They jumped into the warm water and floated, looking up at the cobalt-blue sky through the bare limbs of the birch trees lining the patio.

"So, why are we swimming in the middle of February?" Kate asked.

Colette had unearthed an interesting fact while in New York that was fair game to share. She could give Kate insight but not exactly about the Duncan. "You know how Mom is petrified I'm going to veer off her precious plan and wind up dancing on a cruise ship?"

"God forbid." Kate clenched her jaw and mocked devastation.

They had agreed that going the route of commercial dance by way of the entertainment industry wasn't a bad gig. There seemed to be more options and better pay than in contemporary companies. But, according to Mom, a company was "legit." "In an effort to push her agenda, Mom took me to a contemporary studio in the city. I have to admit, it was pretty incredible."

Kate looked at her feet, and her cheek hollowed like she was biting the inside of her mouth. Colette realized while Kate wanted info, she didn't want a flowery five-minute reel of their perfect trip. Because Kate felt left out. Colette edited her story. "Anyway, I found out that at the company school, they practice lifts in the water."

"Why the water?"

She shrugged. "I don't know. You pay more attention in science than I do. Something about buoyancy? Becoming weightless?"

"Like I could ever be weightless! I'm not a stick figure like you." Kate laughed. "Hey, Trey said I'm going to meet the infamous Marcus soon."

Colette broke into a huge smile. "I don't know about *infamous* . . ."

"Look at you!" Kate pointed at Colette's face. "I've never seen you crush so hard."

"I know. Mom said he's nothing but trouble." She swirled her hand through the water. "She's probably right. I bet he's a total player."

"Nah! I bet he's totally crushing on you, too."

In the distance, Colette heard the bounce and spring of a neighbor jumping on his trampoline: up and down. Like her emotions. Was Marcus really into her? Was Kate acting different? Colette decided to trust things were normal between them. "He did this thing where he put his hand on my arm and just rested it there. Then he kind of slid it around my back and squeezed, like, *I'm into you.* Not *I just want to hook up*, you know? Is that stupid?"

"No," Kate said. "That's sweet."

"No, I'm an idiot. He was probably trying to feel my boob, right?" Colette laughed and pulled her foot toward her thigh and massaged the arch. "He was cool. Oh, well, whatever. I'll probably never see him again."

"You will." Kate looked away for a second. "You always get everything you want. You'll see him next weekend. And he'll be perfect. You'll win at regionals, and then nationals. You'll get tons of money and a spot in a company." There was a weird twinge in her voice that Colette didn't understand. And Kate's mouth twitched like she was trying to smile but couldn't.

"We'll *both* win," Colette said. "It'll be the happiest day of our lives."

Kate leaned against the hard edge of the pool. "What if you win, but I don't?" Her voice was low, a whisper, with a hint of a challenge.

A prickle crawled up Colette's spine. "You wouldn't . . ." She hesitated. "You wouldn't be *mad* if I got accepted to a company and you didn't, would you?"

Kate gave a false smile and clutched her hand to her chest dramatically. "I'd kill myself out of jealousy." She paused, staring. "Or maybe I'd kill you and take your spot."

"What?" Colette's voice cracked high and stunned.

Kate splashed me. "Chill. I'm kidding!"

Colette's heartbeat was firing like gunshots. Because, for a hot second, she thought Kate had gone straight-up psycho. But then Kate laughed some more, and Colette relaxed. "Come on," Colette said, ready to ditch the bizzarro world they'd crash-landed in. "Let's do a reach." She gestured for Kate to walk closer.

"This is totally unnecessary. You'll be the one doing lifts. Like you always do."

Like you always do. Colette blew it off. "Come on. Tighten your core."

Colette held on to Kate's hips from behind, counted, and on three, Colette dead pressed Kate up and out of the water. Kate lifted one leg out and spread her arms wide, looking like a soaring eagle. It triggered a strange, unfamiliar emotion in Colette—Kate above her, powerful and majestic.

"This is awesome!" Kate cried.

"Stop talking! It's making you wobble." Colette took two quick steps backward, trying to balance. "Don't break!"

But Kate dove into the water. She waded over to the wall and climbed on. She ran her hand over her eyes, flicking droplets aside. "That was totally awesome. I know it's no big thing for you because you get to do it all the time. But it was cool for me."

Colette looked at her. Was it her fault Kate was five inches taller and fifty pounds heavier? Colette was the obvious choice for a lift. And a few minutes ago: *You always get everything you want.* When had Kate started keeping track?

"Stop staring at me," Kate said, squeezing the water off the ends of her hair.

But she couldn't. Mom's voice trickled through Colette's ears: *Your friendship will change. You have now become rivals. It will never be uncomplicated.* "C'mon. Let's do it again."

"No, you don't have to. That was enough."

"I want to." Colette moved toward her. What happened next was unclear. Colette extended her arms. Kate's leg flew out. Water splashed. A hard kick landed in Colette's gut. Pain shot through her. She caved in, falling back into the water. Her mouth, nose, and ears filled up. She gagged. Thrashed. Tried to get air. Her heart raced with panic.

A tug pulled her wrist. A yank. Hard. Then she was up and out of the water. Cold air slapped her face. She coughed. Spit. "What happened?" She gasped. Water dripped into her eyes, burning.

Kate's mouth dropped open. "I'm so sorry. I pushed off to swim toward the ladder. I didn't realize you were right there." Her lips trembled. She threw her long, gangly arms around Colette.

But for the first time, Kate's hug felt like a choke.

Because if Kate was just turning for the ladder, why was the kick so hard? So . . . fierce?

But what other explanation could there be?

They got out, shivering, goose bumps sprouting across their arms and legs. They grabbed towels and went inside. They took turns in the bathroom, stripping their bathing suits off and wrapping back up in their soft robes. Kate sat at the kitchen table, but Colette couldn't sort out her feelings. She busied herself making hot chocolate.

Trey came home from the gym. Kate recounted the story of how she almost accidentally drowned her best friend. "You do, like, a thousand pliés a day." Trey laughed. "How could you not realize how freaking strong your legs are? You're like Quad-zilla."

At that, Trey and Kate laughed and laughed.

ELEVEN

While sitting in the staff lounge drinking coffee, Valerie handed Kate's notebook to Jazmin, opened to the passage she'd marked with a pink sticky note. "Read this," she said.

> *Today Colette wore her hair in a messy top bun, pale pink nail polish, diamond stud earrings, three bracelets on her left wrist, and a new lipstick shade—a cherry red. I spent two hours looking up videos on how to fix a messy top bun so I can look like her.*

And another:

> *Today she wore the red lipstick again. She hasn't said anything, but I think I get it. It's going to be her "signature look." I want a signature look, but nothing works on me.*

Yet another:

> *Colette is so flexible. I can't even get my splits in second position! When I got frustrated, she said to me, "You don't have to be perfect to be a great dancer!" And that was really nice. But also, easy for her to say because she IS perfect.*

Jazmin put the notebook down. "Well," she said with a touch of hesitancy in her voice, "I'm not sure what to think." Her smile struggled to be nonjudgmental.

"It's a little weird, right?" Valerie squirmed. "This bizarre mix of friendship and admiration? In the five notebooks I looked through, there's only a few entries about Trey—and he's her first real boyfriend! And even her other friends are nowhere in these pages." She paused, swallowed. "You don't think she's . . . obsessed with her, do you?" A stab of disloyalty pierced her words.

Jazmin's face twisted like she was contemplating. "I think friendships are complex. She loves her, but maybe she's also a little captivated by her. A little . . . envious."

Two paper cups filled with coffee rested between them. A small TV hung in the corner, the channel set to a game show, but the volume was turned down to a distant mumble. Outside in the hallway, there was a shuffling of rubber-soled shoes and the squeaks of carts as they passed, but overall, the labor and delivery wing was unusually quiet.

Valerie absentmindedly flipped through the pages of the journal. Jazmin wasn't alarmed. *See, nothing to worry about.* She tried to subdue the memories that had cycled through her mind all day: Chad talking incessantly about a guy he'd met at a local bar; how he'd hiked the entire Appalachian Trail with his GoPro, documenting on TikTok, and ultimately gotten a book deal. They'd become best friends! He was going to help Chad do his own documentary. A few weeks later, a restraining order had been filed. *What an arrogant prick!* Chad had screamed. *He's just worried I'll get a bigger deal than he did.*

Valerie had googled *obsession* and *stalking* and uncovered that the behaviors were linked to mental health disorders that could be genetic. But Jazmin wasn't bothered by the entries. Of course, she didn't know about Chad's mood swings. His erratic behavior. His delusions. But Kate wasn't like that. She was just a normal teenager. And friendships could be complex. Her daughter was fine. So why were her hands trembling as she held the journal?

She was about to shove the whole discussion away, but instead, she pulled out another notebook with her daughter's most recent entries, then handed it to Jazmin, her insides tight.

I know Colette's life is, like, perfect. But I've never been jealous because she's always been like a sister. What was hers was mine. Then she went to New York. Something changed. She ghosted me. I panicked. What if she learned something at the Duncan and didn't want to share it with me?

When she got home, she said she'd met a guy. Marcus. That's why she was MIA. Okay. I chilled. She invited me over to practice lifts—which was random—and even though it was incredible, I felt like she was just swerving me off the topic of New York. I was pissed. But IDK, maybe I was totally going off the rails. So, I let it go.

Then, a couple of days ago, we were at her house working on our biology projects. When Mom came to get me, Colette said Trey had something for me downstairs. But he was clueless. I didn't think anything about it. She handed me my backpack, and I left. The next day, I went to turn in my project, and it wasn't in my bag. I got a freaking zero! Later Colette texted that I'd left the project in her room. But I know I packed it up. I KNOW I did.

I keep thinking about her sending me to Trey. Her alone with my stuff.

But here's where it gets whacked. This morning, she asked, "Did you get in trouble? For the zero?"

I said Mom was pissed.

And she said, "She, like, didn't make you drop out of the Duncan? Even though you failed?"

What the actual fuck?

I can't stop thinking: Did she hide my project? On purpose? So I'd fail? And hope Mom would be so mad, she'd take me out of the competition?

I have a huge kink in my neck. I feel tricked. And now I think back to her trip to New York, and I know I wasn't imagining it. Something weird is going on.

Jazmin set the diary back on the table. She tipped her head sideways. "I don't get it." She tapped the page. "If Colette is always the star, why would she want Kate out of the competition?"

"I don't understand either," Valerie said, bewildered. "Kate's never mentioned any of this." Valerie shifted in her seat. "It's like there's this whole side of my daughter that I don't know."

Jazmin softened her voice. "All teenagers pull away from their parents."

"Yeah, I know. But she's built this huge wall between us." Valerie's voice cracked, once again thinking about Chad—he had symptoms of a mental illness, Valerie's therapist had explained, possibly borderline personality disorder. But how could she know the difference between that and normal teenage behavior?

The door swung open, and Peter, another labor and delivery nurse, came into the lounge. "Two things," he said, sitting down at their table. "One, we've got an incoming delivery. She and her husband are stuck in traffic, and contractions are coming fast and hard. We'll need all hands on deck in about five minutes. Second . . ." He took a deep inhale, then bit his lower lip. "There's a guy here to see you, Val." His face registered confusion, eyebrows creasing, followed by hesitation. "He says his name is Chad. Chad Jensen." His voice sounded muted and far away, like she was wearing earplugs.

She thought of all those late-night shifts: she, Jazmin, and Peter, sharing their stories. Both Peter and Jazmin had praised Valerie for raising Kate on her own. They hadn't spoken of Chad in ages.

Adrenaline made her heart pound, her fingers go numb, and her eyes prick with tears. She couldn't pinpoint her feelings. They swirled relentlessly through her mind. Confusion. Nausea. Fear.

"Honey?" Jazmin said.

"I . . . I . . ." Peter stumbled. "I thought you said Chad died?"

Oh, shit.

TWELVE

Mom was acting totally off-script lately. Ever since returning from New York, she had random "errands" after dance, so she never invited Kate over. Every night, it was just her and Colette. Which was strange. And lonely. But anytime Colette thought about asking if Kate could come over, a memory of practically drowning in the pool surfaced, Kate's foot still imprinted in Colette's gut. And even though Kate swore it had been an accident, that kick was fierce. Like she had a lot of jacked-up anger or something. Colette didn't know what to think.

It was hard getting back into the swing of school when prepping for the Duncan had added so much to her schedule. Plus, time seemed to slow as she eagerly waited for Marcus's visit. Colette was heading to finish her homework when Mom suddenly appeared at the top of the stairs. She stood there, like a roadblock. "I did some research." Mom looked at her phone and read: "For building a platform, Instagram favors quick Reels and images, while YouTube favors long-form videos." She looked up. "I created a YouTube account. Also, the best times to post content are Thursday and Friday afternoons between noon and three p.m. So, I was thinking, if we film your first video tonight, I can upload it tomorrow during those prime hours while you're at school."

Colette had a brutal test in history that day. She'd run a mile in gym, then had two hours of dance. Her brain was fried. Her legs were jelly. Her feet were numb. And she had at least an hour more of homework.

The last thing she felt like doing was making a video. "I'm exhausted. Can't we do it another day?"

Mom's face got pink and splotchy. "Time is ticking. We have to act strategically if you want to build a platform before the Duncan."

Colette inhaled long and deep. She was just so freaking tired. But Mom's lips pulled taut, like she was in pain, and Colette realized Mom might be reliving her own dance career obstacles—whatever they were. She wanted to offer Colette an easier path. So, of course, Colette gave in. "Okay."

Mom's eyelid did a twitch, and she sighed loudly. "You're acting like it's a chore. Like you don't want to capitalize on the valuable information I worked so hard to get."

Everyone assumes it would be awesome to have a mom who does so much. What they don't realize is that it's not easy being the kid of a so-called perfect parent, because they expect the perfect daughter in return. "Sorry. It was a long day. I'm afraid I look like crap. I need my aesthetic to be on, you know? Like how Ms. Suches said everything has to look good? Not just the content, but me."

Mom got quiet and nodded. "That's what concealer is for. Come on."

What choice did Colette have? She followed Mom into the bathroom and sat at the vanity. Mom used brushes and sponges and dabbed all around Colette's face. But Mom never looked in Colette's eyes. Never saw how tired she really was. And maybe even a little scared. Because going online like this was like showing up to school with a radical new hairstyle and praying people liked it.

Mom misted Colette's face with a setting spray. "Just enough color. Just enough shine." She walked into Colette's room, reached into the closet, and came out waving a red sweater. "I've researched the psychology of colors in marketing; red creates energy and excitement." Her hands shook a little, like she'd been downing energy drinks, which Colette knew for a fact Mom would never do. Her intensity was just on the verge of scary. As invested as she'd always been in Colette's future, she'd never been like this. Jacked-up. Totally consumed. It was a little creepy. Colette grabbed the shirt and changed.

The basement renovation was almost finished. The smell of fresh paint and floor varnish lingered. Her mom had set up an area to film. There was a monster two-tiered light and a little contraption attached to an iPad, which worked like a teleprompter. "You did all this?" Colette asked, instantly feeling like a bitch, getting all irritated. Because, wow. This wasn't going to be like all the stupid TikTok videos half the girls in dance posted, expecting to be *discovered*. Mom was doing it high dollar. Professional. Like the Instagram influencers who have tons of followers and get free merch. Could that . . . Could that happen to Colette? Were there really enough people out there who cared about injury prevention? "Maybe the channel should be about dance wear. Like, top-rated fabrics that don't stink when you sweat."

"What?" Mom's voice jerked up. "What are you talking about?" Her eyes bulged.

"I just . . . I mean . . . What if people think it's lame? Or say I'm not . . . qualified to post this kind of stuff?" Colette spiraled, thinking about how the internet was a cesspool of haters and trolls. "What if someone makes a meme of me with, like, an ACE bandage, and it goes viral, and everywhere I go, people point and say, *There's the bandage girl!*" She backed up against the wall, shaking, raking her fingers through her hair.

"What's wrong with you?" Mom snapped. Something in her tone sent an icy chill up Colette's neck.

How could she explain? The pressure felt so huge. To be beautiful. To create a following. To dance professionally. To achieve Mom's idea of success. What if Colette failed? And humiliated herself trying?

Mom closed her eyes for a moment, then eased her shoulders down. "This is a brilliant idea. We have to keep it a secret because it's so amazing, others will want to steal it. We can't let someone steal your future!" Her eyes were all glassy and unfocused, and they freaked Colette out. Mom blinked and came back. "Your platform is going to build, and it's going to catapult you to a huge win at the Duncan."

Colette swallowed. Nodded. It all sounded so easy. But the tingle in her scalp, the threat of complete burnout, and the crush of Mom's expectations made Colette fear it'd be nothing but excruciating.

THIRTEEN

Elise entered the Pilates studio and grabbed three towels from the stack in the front of the room. She tossed one to Ling Li and another to Susie. The instructor was running late, so the three sat on the reformers and waited. Ling Li gave Elise the eye, nodding ever so slightly toward Susie, who was wearing a crop top with printed leggings, a new pair of transparent eyeglasses, and a gold-plated *Susie* necklace. She looked like she'd ordered her ensemble from her daughter's online wish list. If this kept up, they were going to have to have an intervention.

Maybe Susie's recent bizarre style was a sign she was battling something she hadn't had the courage to talk about. Elise thought about how things in her own life had recently changed. Andrew disregarding her concerns for their daughter's future, Colette ignoring her warnings about friends turned rivals. No one listened to her. Could dynamics at Susie's house be changing, too? Was her flashy wardrobe an attempt to be seen? She looked at her friends. Was it possible they all had unsaid worries buried inside? "Do you guys ever feel . . ." She glanced at the other women in the class, then lowered her voice. "Like everything is changing?"

Ling Li nodded with dramatic exaggeration. "Completely. I can barely get out of bed in the mornings. Eugene said maybe if I didn't drink a bottle of wine every night, it wouldn't be such a challenge. I said maybe if he wasn't such a drag, I wouldn't hit the booze so hard. I asked for Ritalin because I heard it can be a mother's little helper."

She winked. "But Dr. Schwartz said it was unethical. So, I'm back to double espressos."

Susie pulled at the neck of her crop top, then fanned her flushed face. "I think we're all perimenopausal. Metabolism tanks. Energy tanks. Everything tanks."

Elise massaged the nape of her neck and tried not to show disappointment. "That's not exactly what I mean."

"Well, what do you mean?" Ling Li asked.

Elise thought of all the time she'd spent typing up the scripts for Colette's videos, all the research and money for the best teleprompter and microphone, the forethought to pick the perfect outfit to set a tone for the show. Yet her daughter seemed almost annoyed by her efforts. Then, after Andrew accused her of being partial to Colette, she'd ordered a $1,500 basketball hoop for Trey, but instead of applauding her, Andrew flipped out about the money. She'd fixed spaghetti with homemade meat sauce—his favorite—as an apology, but he'd said nothing. All those processed carbs with no payoff. "Do you ever feel invisible? Like no one appreciates you?"

"Oh my God." Ling Li straightened her posture. "You're having a midlife crisis."

Elise deflated. "I'm not having a midlife crisis."

Ling Li raised her pointer finger with authority. "It's totally a thing. My friend quit her job to raise her kids. Now all she does is drive the twins all over town and watch HGTV. Bored out of her mind, she ripped up the carpet, stained her wood floors, and repurposed her kitchen cabinets. When she finished redoing her house, she started redoing herself—face, boobs, butt. The whole package. She got her leg veins lasered, then in a moment of weakness blasted the veins in her hands. But she had a reaction; her hands blew up like baseball mitts." Ling Li leaned toward Elise. "Please don't laser your hands."

"I have no intention of lasering my hands." Why had she even brought this up? Of course, they wouldn't understand.

But then Susie dipped her chin, and her eyes looked watery, like maybe some string of sadness had been plucked from deep inside. "For fifteen years, it's been go, go, go. There was barely any time to shower, to read a book, or watch a movie. Someone was always crying or whining or fighting. But in a weird way . . . it became my world." Her eyes misted. "My purpose. Now, it's like . . ." Her voice caught.

"They don't want your input anymore. Or your efforts are suffocating," Elise finished. She smiled at Susie. Strangely, she thought having someone articulate her same pain would lessen it. Yet the opposite happened. It felt more real. She swallowed back tears. She couldn't lose it in the middle of the Pilates studio.

"Well," Ling Li said, "consider yourself lucky. I swear, if Emma could reattach the umbilical cord, she would. I had to pull her off the tit when she was two. That was the first clue. She'll be forty and still living in our basement. But you"—she pointed from Elise to Susie—"if your kids are pulling away, I say embrace it! Rediscover you!"

But who was Elise if not the supervisor of her children's lives?

"If I could ever get Emma to leave me alone, maybe I could get a little action." Ling Li made an exaggerated wink. "I'm like a drooping daylily. I need some tending to. And Elise, it's immeasurably unfair how Andrew is aging like a freaking movie star. Those Paul Newman eyes! Those salt-and-pepper temples! Who wouldn't want to spend some extra time with that? Not that I'm drooling or anything. Poor old bald Eugene can still water my garden."

"Does he?" Susie blurted. "Still turn the faucet on?" She leaned toward Ling Li, clearly curious.

"What?" Ling Li's face scrunched up. "Like, can he get it up?"

"No. Shush." Susie put a finger to her lips. "I'm just asking if he . . ." She craned her head left, then right. "If you're still as active?"

"Please. I told Eugene I was going to discontinue his gym membership if he kept initiating sex so much. All those endorphins. I think it revs him up. But Emma is always around. So, he waits until she's asleep. And who wants to be groped at midnight? It's like we're constantly buffering . . . waiting for the right time."

"Oh." Susie's voice teetered between surprise and embarrassment. "Patrick's not . . . revved up. I mean, we still . . ." She lowered her voice. "Do it. I just get a feeling, like, in the middle of it, he's mentally balancing the checkbook." She looked over, and Elise felt her cheeks burning. Susie and Ling Li stared, as if waiting for Elise's contribution.

"I don't know." Elise fidgeted with the straps of her tank. She thought of Andrew walking past her, missing the green-light yoga pants. How she had to make the first move. "I mean . . . It's not like when we were first married. When his hands were permanently planted on my butt."

"Well, that's because your butt is perfection," Ling Li said. "If I had your ass, I'd wear leggings every day of my life."

"Well," Elise said, "lately, even when I wear leggings, it's not like he even notices."

"You're not having sex?" Ling Li's mouth dropped.

"Hush!" Susie put her finger back up to her lips again, like a schoolteacher.

Elise dropped her voice. "We're not *not* having sex. It's just . . . different. And less frequent."

"How less frequent?" Ling Li asked.

Elise looked down at her feet. How less frequent had it been exactly? Her neck was clammy. She wanted to go back to talking about feeling invisible. But then again, wasn't this directly related?

"Do you think he's having an affair?" Ling Li had a strange mixture of horror and intrigue on her face.

"What?" Elise gasped. "No, he wouldn't."

"Of course he wouldn't!" Susie said. "Look at her! Who would cheat on that? She looks like a model."

"It happens all the time," Ling Li said. "Good men tempted and led astray."

Elise's lip began to tremble. Her stomach hollowed. Andrew was a charmer, but he wouldn't take it past that. A wink and a smile. Only that. Right? She thought about how not only had he been distant recently, but when he was present, he was snappish. Could it be because he was pulling away from her? Thinking of someone else? Her heart raced. Heat flooded her neck. She needed to leave. She was too dizzy to work out.

Susie put a hand on her arm. "Andrew is not having an affair. Do not spend another minute thinking about it."

"Right," Ling Li said. "I'm sorry. I shouldn't have said that."

Elise was quiet. Never in a million years had she thought it was possible. Was it? Would that explain the changes lately? Her career had been stolen from her. Was her husband next? Where was the Pilates instructor? She needed to stop talking about this. She'd shared enough.

Ling Li tapped Elise on the thigh. "I'll tell you what happened. One day he made a move on you, and without even realizing it, you flinched. And he took that as rejection. Then you wore your leggings to highlight your ass, and he had a rough day at work and didn't notice. And you took that as rejection. And now both of you are feeling rejected, waiting for the other to make the next move."

Elise nodded a little. "Yeah. Maybe."

"Okay," Ling Li said. "We need a plan."

Elise shook her head. She didn't have time for a plan. Colette had regionals coming up. And a YouTube channel they needed to tend to. But maybe that was it. Was Andrew's criticism of her obsession with dance simply a way of saying he felt abandoned?

"Yes, a plan," Susie said. "To lure Andrew back in."

"Lure?" Elise's voice was uncertain. "Come on. This sounds like something our kids would do. A way to attract the hot quarterback . . ."

"Exactly. Just a more adult version. We'll call it . . . a sexy seduction scene," Ling Li said.

"Code Triple S." Susie chuckled.

"And what exactly is this plan?" Elise asked, skeptical but willing to listen.

"Well, you're going to seduce him, of course." Ling Li nodded authoritatively. "You are going to remind him of all the reasons he should never even think of straying."

"Oh!" Susie said. "Can I do that, too? Seduce Patrick?"

"Not in that outfit." Ling Li looked at Susie's clothes and shuddered.

A pink flush crept up Susie's face. She tugged the hem of her crop top.

The glass door opened. The instructor flew in with apologies and excuses. She turned the music up. The women all took their places on their equipment.

"Okay. After class, I'm taking you to get some sexy lingerie. And tonight, you'll remind Andrew of everything he's missing." Ling Li rubbed her hands together. "This is going to be fun."

FOURTEEN

The air was still in the hospital staff lounge. Valerie was paralyzed. "Chad is here?" *In Georgia? In her hospital?* "How?" she whispered, her mind whirling in a windstorm of panic.

Jazmin angled her body toward Valerie and hinged forward. "I don't know. Did he rise from the dead?" There was a whiff of anger in her tone. A volcano of emotions exploded from Valerie.

"I'm so sorry. I'm not a liar. I swear. I just . . . I didn't know what to do." Her diaphragm collapsed, and her breathing got short, shallow. Then she was sobbing.

Peter closed the staff room door and came to her. The fire behind Jazmin's eyes melted, and her face filled with compassion. "Val, tell me. What's going on? Do we need to call the cops?"

Valerie sniffed back tears and let her tone simmer back to normal. "I don't know. I don't think so."

Jazmin's shoulders relaxed, and she sat silently next to Peter. All those years of guiding women through long, intense labors had infused them with patience.

Valerie took a sip of coffee, the liquid now cold and bitter. She started at the beginning. "It was the same old story: Girl falls for the wrong boy. He lived on the wrong side of town, raised by a drunk father. He spent more time working odd jobs to pay the bills than in school. You know the kind?"

They nodded.

"But by high school, he'd transformed into a star running back with magazine good looks—a mane of shaggy blond hair, chiseled abs, a killer smile." Valerie closed her eyes and recalled the small gap between his two front teeth that made him look so innocent, so irresistible. "He had a chip on his shoulder about growing up the way he did, but everyone wanted to massage that away—not just girls, but the coaches, the teachers . . . Half the town credited him for the team's run to the state championship. He could work a crowd—not only from the football field but anywhere. He'd cock his head when he listened so you felt like you were the most important person in the world. And if he really liked you, he gave you a nickname. The whole team proudly wore jerseys with stupid names like *Stubby* or *Tank* or *Slim Jim* because Chad had christened them." Valerie took a long inhale. "He was a womanizer, rotating through girls every month or so, and yet, even with that reputation, not a girl in town was immune to dreaming of the day Chad would brand them with a nickname. When it was my turn, I felt like I had won the lottery. I was convinced I'd be the one he'd stay with. And he did. But only because I wound up pregnant."

Jazmin and Peter leaned back into the couch. Even knowing the bones of the story, they were mesmerized by the details.

"It was flattering at first. How excited he was about having a kid. He promised he was going to do everything differently." She halted, the next chapter like a dark hole she wanted to jump over to avoid admitting she hadn't been strong enough to climb out. "You know how hard early parenthood is. We spend our lives handing out pamphlets to new mothers about postpartum. Well, it was really hard on Chad. The responsibility. The lost opportunities—he thought he'd be playing college football. It was like he'd climbed to the top of the hill and seen the beautiful possibilities on the other side, only to slide back down. He kept trying to find his way back . . . to glory. Football was no longer an option, so he kept creating new desires, new dreams, outlandish ideas that would bring him fame and fortune. When each one crashed and burned, he sank deeper and deeper into depression. Anger." She sighed. "Violence."

"Did he hit you?" A splotchy rage colored Jazmin's face.

"No," Valerie quickly answered. "That was the issue. It was never us—me or Kate. I guess . . ." She slumped, chin to chest, staring at her rubber-soled shoes. "I guess that's why I never left." She looked up and saw puzzlement cross her friend's face. "He left us." Valerie brushed a sweaty strand of hair off her forehead and explained how Chad went to Costa Rica, then called from prison. "After I refused to send money, I never heard from him again. I searched online to see if he'd been convicted, but I couldn't find any information. It's hard to look into criminal records abroad. I didn't know what to believe. Was he rotting in jail? Had he married a local and was living happily?" She gazed across the lounge, the story spilling out of her mouth felt like a novel she was retelling, or a TV show, not her life. Not her own bad choices. "When Kate started asking where he'd gone, and all these pristine dance moms with their expensive cars and catalog-perfect families inquired about our circumstances, it just seemed easier . . ." *To be a victim of a tragic accident. A widow.* "To lie." Emotion strangled her voice.

"Oh, sweetie." Jazmin wrapped her arms around her. "You could have told us."

The back of Valerie's throat hitched in a muddled whimper. She knew it was true. But once a lie is told, a thousand strings need to be pulled to craft the perfect web of deceit. She couldn't risk the rupture. Never did she imagine the unraveling would descend like this. With Chad's return.

Peter put a hand on her shoulder. "What do you think he wants?"

Valerie gave a slight shake of her head. "I have no idea."

Just the thought made the hairs on her arms stand and sent a chill down her spine.

"I'll go with you," Peter said.

Jazmin nodded. "I'll cover the incoming patient."

Valerie's insides buzzed like her veins were filled with swarming bees. She was nervous, afraid, confused. Slowly, she stood and followed her friend down the long hallway into the elevator, which deposited them on the first floor.

It was his voice that hit her like an old song on the radio—instantly transporting her to a different time and place, his thick Southern drawl sinking into her skin with every syllable. He had his back to them, the broad expanse of his shoulders pulling his T-shirt at the seams. Shaggy dark-blond hair peeked out from the back of a ball cap. He was squatting down in front of an injured young boy. The face of the boy's hovering mother lit up. Just then, the boy's mouth creeped into a smile, and Valerie imagined Chad had called him *Chief* or *Captain*. *Macho* or *Boss Man*. Something delightful enough to make the boy's mother flirtatiously laugh so hard, she'd be hoarse in the morning. The sound of it, a woman so eager, so captivated, was like a splash of cold water in the face.

"I . . . I can't do this," Valerie whispered urgently into Peter's ear. "I have to go. Please. I can't. Tell him I've left already. Tell him I'm not here."

Peter nodded. "I'll get rid of him. You go." He gave her a gentle nod. "It'll be okay."

She swallowed hard, turned, and raced away.

FIFTEEN

After class on Friday, Colette was blow-drying her hair, getting ready for the party downstairs when there was a knock at her door. Kate and Avery walked in. Avery sat on the bed. "I know your secret!"

"What?" Kate looked at Avery, then Colette.

Avery flashed her phone, showing the YouTube video. "How come you never told us you were starting a channel?" She read aloud: "Injuries can rob athletes of their dreams." She looked up. "This is ah-mazing! You're, like, going to be Insta-famous! You totally kept it on the down-low." She acted impressed with the covert mission, but Kate squinted at the screen, and her mouth did a strange jerk. While Avery went on about how cool it was, Kate stayed silent. She stood there like a statue in a black miniskirt and boots, her face losing all color. Colette couldn't tell if Kate was shocked, impressed, or pissed. Things had been weird since the pool drama, but her nonexcitement seemed extra odd.

"What?" Colette asked her.

Kate turned. Their eyes met, and for a flash, Kate had this crazy look: eyes narrowed, nose a little flared. But before either of them could say anything, Avery pointed out the window and said that everyone was here. They headed downstairs. Everyone gawked at the gorgeous renovation, now complete.

Trey had moved the Ping-Pong table right onto Colette's practice hardwoods. Mom would combust! "Trey," Colette started, but he flashed a grin and pointed to a smuggled bottle of Malibu rum tucked into his jeans. She shot him a look. *Mom will kill us.* He put a finger to his lips. *Shh!* then splashed huge shots of rum into cups of lemonade.

The guys started playing foosball, and the girls took selfies and posted pictures to their pages. *#fridaynight #hangingwithfriends.* Everyone was getting drunk, looser, and louder, and Colette wanted to laugh, too, but where the hell was Marcus? She checked her phone again.

Emma leaned in and slurred, "GPS can totally screw up around here. He's just lost. Guaranteed."

"Yeah." But Colette looked back at her blank screen and started to freak. She tossed her phone on the coffee table and accidentally spilled lemonade and rum all over her pants. What was wrong with her? She went upstairs to change. And have a small breakdown. As she flew through the kitchen, Mom was over by the counter. She was looking at her reflection in the mirrored toaster and dabbing at her eyes. She was wearing a dress. And heels. Like maybe she and Dad were going out. Not that they'd ever leave an unsupervised party. Still. The dress. It was weird. "Where's Dad?" Colette asked, fanning the smell of booze off her pants.

Mom jumped. "Oh. Sorry. You scared me. He, um, he went out for a bit." She waved her hand dismissively through the air. "Too much noise for him. No worries. Have fun."

No worries? Have fun? What was this bizarre world? The doorbell rang. *Yes!* Colette raced into the foyer, ignoring her wet pants, and flung open the door. The porch light threw a halo around his mop of hair. He bit his lip, looked her up and down. "Damn, girl."

"Marcus!" She went to him, and he did this thing where he tucked a strand of her hair behind her ear and kissed her. Right there. In the hallway. Where her mom could easily see. But he didn't care, so with another quick glance to confirm Mom wasn't watching, Colette didn't stop him.

He pressed his mouth against hers, and the heat of his lips made her body pulse with an unexpected energy. She wanted to tell him this was her first real kiss, and it was perfect—*he* was perfect—but the basement door swung open, sending loud music streaming into the hallway. He looked up, eyebrows raised. "Does the dancer also know how to throw a party?"

She nudged him playfully, taking his hand. "Let's go see." She entwined her fingers with his and quickly darted past the kitchen. But Mom was gone. A lightweight feeling channeled through her. Like she was helium, going airborne through a vast open sky. Never before had freedom laid out in front of her like a big red carpet. A party. A boy. A kiss. She was breaking open a new life and was 100 percent there for it.

On the stairs, she paused, tilting her chin up for another kiss. His lips grazed hers, soft and wet, but his eyes were open, taking in the scene. Plastic cups were everywhere. A new bottle of vodka rested on the coffee table next to the empty rum. Scattered empty Gatorades littered the ground. A rowdy Ping-Pong game was going on, and music blared. Colette shot a glance up the stairs. The party was on the verge of being out of control, but before she could panic, Marcus let go of her hand and said, "Awesome."

He blended right in, teaching the guys how to play Texas Hold'em and impressing the girls with stories of surfing waves. She stared at him, thinking, *Now I get it.* What all the fuss is about. Her heart was on fire, and the replay of that kiss was on auto in her mind. Every time he passed her, his hand reached out and skidded along her back, like he needed to touch her, and she needed to feel him. She mentally planned an escape route for them to be alone, thinking of the double-seated swing on the back patio, when out of the corner of her vision, she saw Marcus lock eyes with Kate. An intensity flashed between them that made Colette's legs go weak. But then just as fast, he jumped on the coffee table—like it was a makeshift surfboard—and started another story. "The waves were brutal. I looked over." He pointed . . . it seemed directly at Kate. "And there it was. A shark. Huge. With a mouth like this." He stretched his hands wide. "And teeth as sharp as nails." He jutted his chin at her. "Show 'em your teeth."

Kate gave a huge double-row-of-teeth grin, and everyone burst out laughing. Colette's stomach fell like a roller coaster on the downturn. Why was he pulling Kate into his story instead of Colette? He squatted down and pretended to surf away. Kate did an impression of a vicious killer shark, chasing after him. Like *they* were a couple. Trey was too hammered to notice his girlfriend flirting, but Colette was right there! Watching whatever the hell was happening.

She wanted to scream, *She's too tall for you. Too plain. Too taken. And I'm supposed to be yours.*

Instead, she plastered on a stage smile and snapped a pic. "You guys are hysterical."

He hopped off the coffee table and poured himself another drink. Her nerves settled. It was the vodka. Making her crazy. She needed some food to soak up the alcohol. She told him she was going to get snacks.

Starting up the stairs, she sensed someone on her heels. She turned and practically banged into Kate. "Oh!" Colette said, startled. She wanted to say, *Why were you flirting with Marcus?* Instead, like a chicken, she said, "I'm hunting some chips. Want to come?"

"I gotta pee."

"Oh, okay." It was a normal thing to say, but Colette could hear the tiniest bit of hesitation in her voice, wondering why their friendship suddenly felt strange. She went to the pantry; Kate headed toward the bathroom. Colette's phone dinged with a notification that her video was getting a ton of comments. Excited, she scrolled through the feedback as she grabbed the chips and exited the pantry. She glanced up and stopped dead in her tracks.

Just a few feet down the hallway were Marcus and Kate, their backs turned. They were standing so close, there was barely a sliver of air between them. Some strange intuition froze Colette.

Alone in the hallway. So close. Colette thought about him locking eyes with Kate. Her ease with playing his sidekick.

Colette took a step back into the pantry and watched through the cracked door, every muscle in her body going rigid and scared.

Marcus leaned closer, his mouth inches from Kate's ear, and whispered something. Kate angled her head to look up at him. Colette's chest thudded, and for a horrible second, she thought . . . But no. Come on. They were just talking. Then his hand moved to Kate's arm, resting against the yellow fabric of her sweater. Colette held her breath. *No. Please, no.*

In horror, there it was—a slow slide of his hand across Kate's back. A squeeze. *I'm into you.*

Standing there, pressed into the pantry door, Colette wanted to flat-out die. Because she had seriously thought she and Marcus had this intense connection. All those hours, sitting on the bench in Central Park, talking. All those late-night text marathons and Snap streaks. Her first kiss. The way his hand kept finding her back. Soulmates, she'd actually thought. But no! It all meant nothing to him.

Humiliation. Her insides burned. She watched Kate standing there, letting his hand rest on her back. Then Colette got mad. Like, crazy mad. Was Kate going to let him make the move Colette confided had meant so much to her? When Kate had a boyfriend of her own? Was she going to . . . steal Colette's? Even just for a minute?

Then, as if it could get any worse, he dropped his head like he was going to actual, in real life, *kiss* Kate! Colette's heart pounded; her palms got sweaty. She was ready to unleash on both of them. She would charge out there and tell them both to get the hell out of her house! He could get his ass back to Florida, and Kate could find a new best friend. And a new boyfriend—not Trey! But before Colette could, a sharp pain sliced in her chest. Her breath caught, jagged and stinging. She doubled over, hands on her knees, heart pounding so hard, she could hear it in her ears. Was she having a heart attack? She couldn't breathe. She was so scared. A ton of bricks landed on her ribs. She was suffocating. Air. She needed air.

A memory surfaced: She was young, choking on a grape. Dizzy. Breathless. Gagging. Mom had grabbed her arms and raised them above her head. Clearing the airway, Mom said. So now, even though there was no food trapped, Colette reached up, begging her body to breathe, her head to stop swimming, her heart to stop throbbing. She counted inside her head: *one, two, three.*

Slowly, her chest expanded, her lungs filled, and cold air entered. Tears streamed down her face in fearful relief. What had just happened? She'd been out of breath before on hard runs, but never like that.

She took another wobbly breath, reassuring herself she was okay, then inched toward the door, desperate to see what was happening. She gazed through the sliver of opened door. They were still there. Kate's head angled up. Had they kissed?

Suddenly Emma appeared. Kate and Marcus flung apart like balls bouncing off each other. Like they'd been caught.

Colette turned away, facing the rows of canned vegetables in the pantry. Her eyes burned with tears. None of it made any sense. She'd been so happy. So convinced he was the one. Confusion and darkness hung over her. What had happened? Why had the two most important people to her stabbed her in the back? Rage raced through her.

She wanted to smash their skulls. Break them into a thousand little pieces.

Just like her heart.

She wanted to charge over to Kate and rip her hair right out of her head.

Instead, Colette jammed her hands onto her own scalp and gripped. Then, in complete rage, she pulled. An intense slice skidded over her scalp. She clamped her mouth to stifle a cry. It hurt. It hurt so bad.

But she instantly felt better.

SIXTEEN

Valerie's hands trembled as she unlocked her car door and got inside. She had been a zombie for the remainder of her shift, barely able to breathe, fearful that when she exited the hospital, he'd be there, waiting. But he wasn't. She walked through the cold, damp parking deck, looking over her shoulder, fumbling with her key fob as she opened the door.

She sped home in a frenzy, grateful that Kate was spending the night at Colette's. She planted herself on the couch and googled, searching for any information she could find. It's not that she hadn't googled before; of course she had. Embarrassingly often. But beyond the rap sheet filled with arrests in Georgia, there was scarce information available. She had stopped looking years ago, figuring he was probably spending the next several decades behind bars in some dingy beach town in Costa Rica.

Now her fingers quivered as she tapped the keys and spelled his name into the search bar. Google delivered the same search results she'd found previously, the familiar rap sheet followed by a lone video from an American couple who'd been vacationing at a resort in Costa Rica and had captured the argument between Chad and a man on a fishing dock. The words were muddled on the audio, but Chad's expression of fury dropped a liquid bomb through Valerie's veins. From the vantage point of the recorder, it seemed obvious that Chad's aggressive shove was the reason the man had fallen overboard.

Just like previously, when Valerie tried to research Chad's fate—Had he been convicted? What was his sentence?—she circled the drain of never-ending links that led nowhere. International law and criminal justice were not an easy map to read.

As she continued to search, she found a new result she'd never seen. It was a Tripadvisor review, with Chad's name highlighted. She clicked. Six months ago, a family from New Jersey had vacationed in Costa Rica and used an adventure company for a volcano zip line and river tubing excursion. Their guide, Chad, was *amazing*, the reviewer posted. There was a picture attached. Valerie enlarged the small square to full screen. The backdrop was a dark, foamy river. The cloudless blue sky played peekaboo between the lush trees. Standing at the water's edge, balancing a hand atop a vibrant red tube, was a ruggedly handsome man with sun-streaked skin and a gap-toothed grin.

She leaned in, her vision pulsing with her heartbeat. She blinked. Focused. Pulled the laptop closer, then held it farther away. Her heart clattered fast, the sporadic beats climbing up her throat. It was him. Chad. Not in prison. Working. Looking happy. Getting rave reviews.

So why was he here? What did he want? Had he been acquitted? Maybe he'd never served time at all. How could she find out? Who could help her navigate the judicial system of a foreign country?

Suddenly, Valerie thought about Andrew wearing a tweed blazer and a navy striped tie, looking like the definition of attorney. It wasn't that long ago when he'd said, "It's okay to let someone help you." He'd been referring to her flat tire, but maybe he could help her with this? Help her understand if Chad had served time? If he had more recent offenses? How could she determine if he was dangerous? Would she need to keep him away from Kate? And if so, how would she go about doing that legally?

She opened the contacts on her phone, pausing at Andrew's name. If she asked for help, she'd have to explain why she'd lied. It would be embarrassing but also . . . intimate. Trusting him. Was it crossing a line? But did Elise ever feel guilty for stealing Kate and treating her as a daughter?

She took a deep breath, exhaled, and texted Andrew: Sorry to bother you. I know you have a house full of teenagers, but whenever you have a chance, can I ask you some legal questions? Thanks.

Her heart raced. She had jumped the gun. Before she could spiral, her phone dinged with a response: Uh-oh. Need bail money? ☺

She exhaled, relieved. Why did this man always make her feel better. Not tonight.

So, what's up?

Well . . . I have some legal questions. But it's complicated.

I'd give you a call, but the volume in here is OOC. These kids . . .

Valerie had to google *OOC*: *out of control*. She smiled. No rush! I appreciate it!

A moment later, the front door opened, and Kate stumbled in. Valerie looked up, surprised. "I thought you were spending the night with Colette?" she asked.

"I changed my mind." Kate's eyes were glassy. Had she just slurred?

"Who drove you home?"

"I took an Uber."

"What? Why didn't you call me? What happened? Why'd you come home?"

"The party . . . something happened." Kate's voice was tender; it almost sounded sincere.

Valerie was very still, thinking maybe Kate was going to finally talk to her. "What? Tell me."

Kate curled her lips in and looked hesitant.

"You can tell me anything," Valerie said softly, begging for this bridge, knowing she might also have to unload a difficult conversation. But not now. Not when Kate seemed to need her.

"Colette's been talking to this guy she met in New York. Tonight, he came to visit."

"Was he nice?"

She nodded. "Yeah. Life of the party." Valerie could smell the alcohol on Kate's breath and was disappointed but also recognized that it might render her daughter less guarded.

Kate was quiet, and Valerie waited patiently for the rest of the story. Kate looked down at her fingernails, like she was debating. Finally, she spoke. "At one point, Marcus and I were alone in the hallway. He leaned really close and said, 'You're superhot.'" The hairs on the back of Valerie's neck prickled. "Then he said, 'Colette never said you were hot.' Then he tried to kiss me."

Tensing, Valerie sat very still. "What happened?"

"I pushed him away," Kate said emphatically.

"Good." Valerie slumped against the couch, relieved.

"Emma showed up, and I bolted to the basement. Later, Trey and I walked into the kitchen and saw Colette, like, full-on freaking on Marcus."

"Oh no. So, she saw?"

"I don't know," Kate said. "We just heard her scream and tell him to leave. I tried to talk to her, but she ran to her room, locked the door, and wouldn't answer her phone. So now what am I supposed to do?"

Valerie's palms were sweating. She thought of all the diary entries, the already fragile relationship between the friends. Something like this could tip the scales, escalate emotions.

"Why don't you just tell her the truth?"

Kate sighed. "It's not that easy. Things have been . . . different between us lately."

"Oh yeah? Like how?" Valerie faked ignorance.

"It's just . . ." Kate hinged toward the laptop. "Wait . . . who is that?"

Valerie tried to quickly slam the laptop shut, but Kate was too fast. She pulled the computer into her lap, her lips moving as she skimmed the Tripadvisor review.

"Let me explain," Valerie insisted.

"Chad? *Chad? Chad Jensen?*" Kate's voice escalated. "What the *hell* is this, Mom? You told me he was *dead*!" She threw the laptop across the room.

"Kate! Please!" She had her hands out, palms up, desperate. "Listen!"

"Listen to what? How my whole life has been *a lie*?" She stormed down the hallway.

"You don't understand," Valerie begged, chasing after her.

Kate slammed her door shut.

Valerie crumpled to the ground in a heap of sobs. How had they gotten here? It wasn't that long ago that she and Kate had fallen to that exact spot on the hallway carpet, except they'd been laughing, hysterical tears streaming down their cheeks.

"It's not that bad," Valerie had said as Kate had convulsed with giggles outside her door.

Valerie had finally succumbed to Jazmin's insistence that she enter the world of dating apps. In preparing for her first date, Valerie had attempted to do her makeup and hair. It had not gone well. Kate had pulled her up off the carpet and ushered her to the vanity in her bedroom. First, she had removed Valerie's disastrous face paint, then methodically applied shadow, liner, and mascara. "If you go with a dramatic eye, you tone down the lips, okay?"

Valerie had smiled at her daughter in the mirror. Kate had sorted through a pile of lipsticks—more than any normal twelve-year-old would have, but on par for a performer—and found a soft nude pink. She'd swiped it across her mother's lips. Next, she'd found her curling wand and wrapped a long strand of Valerie's hair around it.

"But my hair is already curly," Valerie had protested.

Kate had grimaced dramatically. "Not the right kind of curly." And that had sent them into another fit of giggles. When Kate had finished, they'd stared at each other's reflections. "You look really pretty," Kate had said. Then her voice had gone soft. "Your date is going to fall hard, and it'll never be just the two of us again."

Valerie had reached for her phone and tapped out a message. "C'mon," she said, taking her daughter's hand. "I just canceled. It's you and me tonight."

"No, you should go . . ." Kate had tried to protest, but Valerie could see the excitement in her face, the yearning.

They'd wound up at a neighborhood Italian bistro where they'd ordered spaghetti and laughed all night.

If only she could have frozen time when their love was so easy and pure, where her lies remained hidden and inconsequential.

Now, still on the floor outside of Kate's room, her phone dinged with a text from Andrew: Hey. I had to run an errand. I'm in your neck of the woods. Want to meet at Joe's Café and talk about your legal questions?

She grabbed the phone and stared at it like a lifeline. He might be the only one who could help her.

Joe's Café was a small diner tucked into a strip mall a few miles from Valerie's condo. It had cheap food, late hours, and was a favorite of the younger crowd. Valerie had driven past it millions of times but had never entered. Sporadic tables were filled with teens and twentysomethings shoveling in burgers, fries, and gossip. Andrew was seated at a small round table pressed against the window. Two steaming mugs of coffee were already waiting. And just that—not only his willingness to meet her, but to have beverages waiting—made the hornet's nest in her gut settle.

"Thanks for giving me a reason to escape the mayhem of the kids' party." He started with small talk, but Valerie, unable to banter, cut him off.

"I've made a big mistake. I don't know what to do. I need help." His face blanched, and she realized he probably thought she meant she'd broken the law. "I didn't commit a crime," she quickly amended. "I just need to talk to someone with knowledge of the law."

"Okay." He leaned back into his chair, looking relieved.

She wondered, behind her lanky frame and monotone wardrobe, what kind of imagined criminal did he speculate she was. Shoplifter? Gambler? Pill popper? She almost laughed out loud. Then she remembered her situation. "Is there a way you can help me investigate someone's criminal history? Like if they served jail time?"

"Sure," he said casually, taking a sip of coffee.

"What if the crime happened in another country?"

"A US citizen who committed a crime in another country?"

She nodded. "Yes."

He rested his chin in his hand, looking thoughtful. "Well, it depends. Each country is sovereign, and its laws apply to everyone, regardless of nationality. But the US offers services to its citizens to navigate the foreign legal process. I guess I need to know the story."

The story. Those words hung in the air like a dark cloud, a slippery slope, a black hole. Once she started, she could never back out. She paused, debating, then decided to take the step.

He listened quietly, his face not showing shock or judgment. Maybe, she thought, he'd heard it all at his job. But still, she was admitting to lying to his family for the last ten years. It didn't feel good. But he glossed over that detail, instead focusing on the task at hand. "So, we need to find out if this guy is dangerous before we let him back into Kate's life and yours."

Tears sprang to her eyes. Hearing him say *we*. His willingness to join her efforts. The protective look that splashed across his face. But just then, there was a creak as the glass door swung open, and in walked two of Kate's dance friends. They stood for a moment, staring.

A flush of red dotted Andrew's cheeks. Valerie volleyed her gaze, not knowing if exiting now would deem their rendezvous scandalous. Andrew raised his hand, asking for the check, making the decision for them both.

SEVENTEEN

After concocting the Triple S plan with her friends to fix her marriage, Elise had envisioned a whole romantic scene—the kids in the basement with their friends, the music drifting up into the kitchen, she and Andrew slow dancing around the island. She'd imagined whispering about the ivory silk lingerie she'd bought that afternoon. But somewhere between scrolling through YouTube comments and the arrival of floppy-haired Marcus, Andrew had walked out to "get some air." When the kids had all left and her husband still hadn't returned, she'd texted him. He'd simply replied: Wound up doing work stuff. Be home soon.

Andrew had never lied before, so there was no reason to doubt him, but work at 10:00 p.m.? On a Friday? It didn't sit well. After she'd fallen asleep, a jostle of the sheets told her he'd made it home, but by morning, he was gone again, leaving a note: *Went to play golf.* She looked out the window at the frost still covering the lawn. A knot of doubt formed. She shoved aside Ling Li's accusations.

Heading to the kitchen for coffee, she saw Colette slumped on the couch in the living room. She was dressed in loose lavender pajamas, her platinum blond hair spilled across her shoulders. As Elise fixed coffee, her daughter called to her. "Do you think Kate is prettier than me?"

"What?" Elise dropped the mug. It landed with a thud on the floor, cracked, then splintered into shards. She stepped over the mess and went to the living room. Sitting on the coffee table opposite her daughter, she said, "Why would you ask that?" Her voice was rattled and angsty.

"I don't know." Colette's lashes fluttered like the wings of a butterfly. "I mean, haven't you noticed? Like all of a sudden . . ." She looked up at the ceiling. Her lips quivered, and for a horrible moment, Elise thought she was going to cry. "She's got it together. Everywhere. Even onstage, she seems different. Better."

The bitter smell of spilled coffee wafted into the living room. An acidic tinge burned the back of Elise's throat. She recalled the videos on her phone: Kate's incremental leap in aptitude, her slow creep into center stage. Elise's skin tingled with anxiety.

"She's so much curvier than me," Colette continued. "What if people think she looks like a star, but I look like a child?"

Why was she saying this? "Colette, what's going on?"

With trembling lips, she explained. "Last night . . ." She took a long, shaky breath. "I saw Kate and Marcus . . ." She turned away, burying her face in the couch cushions.

"You saw Kate and Marcus . . . what?" Elise inched forward.

Colette craned her head back again. "Flirting. They might have kissed."

Elise's mind tripped over thoughts and emotions. She'd tried to give Kate the benefit of the doubt. Other than the brief clip of possible suspicious behavior, there was no other evidence that she was anything other than genuine. But now . . . had Kate cheated on her son? Was she playing mind games with her daughter? Trying to tweak Colette's insecurity? Could it be that Kate wanted to steal Colette's entire life? The Duncan, the boyfriend, the home . . .

Realization landed hard and swift. Whatever Kate's end goal, this was clear: Elise's instincts had been correct. The girl was not to be trusted. Elise would have to delicately convince her daughter to distance herself from that threat, then convince Trey their romance was fractured. But she'd have to be strategic. And subtle. Or risk driving a wedge between herself and her children. But that was for later. Now, the immediate task: Boost Colette's confidence.

"Did you see them kiss?" she asked.

Colette sighed. "Not exactly."

"Have you asked Kate?"

"No."

Elise laid a gentle hand on Colette's arm. "Then why waste all this energy if you don't know the facts?" She got up and retrieved her laptop. Gesturing for Colette to move over, she sat beside her on the couch and placed the computer between them. She pulled up Colette's first YouTube video and scrolled through the comments: *You are amazing. Love this! You're so beautiful and well spoken! Would love to see a video of you dancing!*

"Now tell me people don't look at you and think you're a star," Elise said.

Slowly, the corners of Colette's mouth pulled into a smile.

"Don't forget this," Elise said. "Find your confidence. Because when you're dancing at the Duncan, judges will notice who is self-assured." She hesitated. "Hey, how about we work on your next video?"

Colette nodded. "Okay."

Elise sighed with relief. Another well-received video would help her daughter's spirits. Another step. Soon her family's ties to Kate would be severed.

Two days later, Elise sat on the bench at the ballet studio. Ling Li and Susie slid in beside her. Little bullets of anticipation shot off their skin.

"Operation Triple S? Was it a success?" Ling Li put a hand up in the air, as if expecting a high five. But Elise didn't move.

"Uh-oh." Susie pulled her mouth tight, grimacing. "What happened?"

Elise slumped. "Friday night, all the kids were at the house. It was loud, and Andrew said he had a headache. He went for a drive."

"He used the headache excuse?" Ling Li put a hand to her heart. "I thought that was earmarked for desperate housewives."

Elise straightened her posture. "He didn't say he had a headache to avoid sex. He said it because a mob of teenagers in the house is ear-shattering. By the time he got back, it was late, and I'd gone to bed."

"What about Saturday?" Susie's tone was delicate, like she'd anticipated trouble.

Elise fiddled with her bag, pretending to be distracted, like this was no big deal. "He played golf and was gone most of the day." Plus, she'd been consumed with her new insight about Kate. But she couldn't tell her friends about that. At least not yet. It was easier to whitewash her concerns about Andrew with the idea that they were both busy.

"So, it just never happened?" Ling Li asked, clearly incredulous.

Susie leaned in. "Do you think he might be avoiding sex because he has erectile dysfunction?"

"He's not avoiding sex!" Elise said defensively. Dena, another dance mom sitting at the far end of the bench, looked over. Elise lowered her voice. "I think it's normal that after many years together, frequency declines."

Ling Li scrunched her nose as if to say, *Excuses* . . .

"He could be embarrassed," Susie said. "You know Trista? From PTO?" Susie had this annoying habit of reminding you where you knew people from. Of course Elise knew Trista! She'd sat next to her at every PTO meeting for the last ten years. "Trista said Noel had to start taking *Cialis*," she whispered. "You want me to see if I can snag one of his pills, and you can drop it in Andrew's coffee and see what happens?"

"No, I don't want to secretly give my husband Cialis. He doesn't have erectile dysfunction. Geez." Elise blew out an exasperated breath.

Ling Li bit her bottom lip. "Well, if he doesn't have ED, there is another possibility." Insinuation was in her voice.

Elise threw her hand out. "Stop, Ling. I know what you're implying, but Andrew would never cheat. He just wouldn't."

Ling Li clicked her tongue. "The penis has a mind of its own. Reasonable men do very unreasonable things."

"Guys, come on. You know Andrew." Elise's voice chopped the gossip in half. "He wouldn't have an affair."

"You're right." But Ling Li's expression contradicted her words. She raised a finger like a revelation had struck. "I know! You should try porn. That'll tell you straight up if he has ED."

Susie's eyes went wide, and she clamped a hand to her mouth.

"Oh my God!" Irritation flooded Elise. "Did you start taking that Ritalin, Ling? Because you're acting crazy." Right? It was crazy. Even though lately he'd been different, she knew him. He wasn't built that way.

On the dance floor, Miss Roza clapped her hands three sharp times. The moms stopped their banter and gazed toward the class. Miss Roza stood broad and erect, her fingers slicing through the air as she spoke. The girls moved to the edge of the wooden floor and sat, pressed up against the mirror. Everyone except for Colette.

Miss Roza often spotlighted Colette's technique, making all the girls take in her perfection. Elise relaxed, grateful the focus was off her sex life and onto something she could be proud of: her daughter.

The music began, and Colette raised her right leg impossibly high, her muscles long, lean, and taut. Slowly, she began to turn on her supporting foot. Typically Colette really shone with artistry, but today her eyes were vacant, her smile forced. She looked shellacked in plastic.

Elise scooted to the edge of the bench, her heart picking up speed. It wasn't bad. Technically, it was spot-on and fluid, but she'd never looked like this: despondent, dejected—the way she'd looked in her lavender pajamas, strewn across the couch. What was going on? This weekend, Elise thought, she'd fixed Colette's minor bout of insecurity, but now, she looked shaken to her core.

Then, it almost appeared as if someone had pushed Colette. No one had. But her limbs jerked robotically, like a toy losing its battery charge.

Elise held her breath. Colette began her turns; then she floundered, missed a mark, then improvised to fill the time to the beat of the music.

"Oh, shit," Ling Li muttered under her breath. "Sorry." She put a hand on Elise's shoulder.

But Elise couldn't feel it. Her skin was on fire. Her whole body ignited with a scorching panic. What the hell was going on? She grabbed a cold water bottle and pressed it to the back of her neck.

Miss Roza clapped and gestured for Colette to stop. Colette put her leg down and returned her arms to her sides. Her mouth was frozen in a little guppy fish *O*, and her chest puffed out and in fiercely as she caught her breath. She stood there, the fabric of her top pulsing with each breath, as if not realizing she was finished and supposed to exit to the sidelines. Beads of sweat dripped down Elise's spine. Miss Roza whispered something, and Colette's mouth pulled closed. Her expression dropped like an avalanche; then she walked to the sidelines in a trance.

All the moms were silent. Elise could hear her own breathing—in and out quickly, like she was running.

Miss Roza's back was turned. Elise didn't know what was said, or how it happened, but suddenly, Kate stood up and glided toward the center of the floor. The music restarted.

All the other moms sat hinged at their waists to see exactly what would happen next.

Kate, tall and elegant, floated her first jump with the weightlessness of a bubble. Elise's stomach plummeted like an elevator suddenly untethered and careening toward a crash. Her daughter, her perfect daughter, had been thrust to the sidelines and outperformed. By Kate.

Kate, who was unreasonably tall. Entirely too chesty. Gangly and gawky and with all those limbs that sometimes made her look like a praying mantis springing across the floor.

But no.

Not now.

Kate whipped through a pirouette, and as she spun, Elise caught a glimpse of her honey-brown eyes. She thought of all the subliminal messages of encouragement and parental love she had pressed the girl's way all these years. She thought of all the times in her mind she'd whispered, *You can do it, Kate! You've got this, Kate!*

A force deep inside Elise, like the repel of magnets, suddenly split her loyalties in two. She was no longer on the fence. She had spent all those years helping Kate, praising her, loving her, because she reminded her of herself. A lonely girl with no parental support. When Elise had told her parents she wanted a career in dance, they'd laughed at her, told her she'd never survive New York City. She knew Valerie didn't understand the desire to dance, and Elise had wanted to be that whisper of encouragement that she'd longed for when she was young. But Elise knew how desperation for success could breed sinister plans. In wild recklessness, she had succumbed to wickedness. And so would Kate. She could feel it in her bones. Elise's heart raced. She had tried to rescue a child in need, but in being helpful, she'd hurt her own flesh and blood. Poor Colette, undermined unintentionally by her own mother.

She had to fix this.

Elise zoomed in on Kate now, finding that mental clarity and homing in on their strong connection. She knew it was awful. She knew it was terrible, unforgivable, but Colette was her daughter. Not Kate.

Before she could stop herself, Elise intensively zoned in and stared toward Kate, stared until she caught her eye, and then with all her might, she thought: *Fall.*

EIGHTEEN

The music ended. Kate stood, holding her perfect pose, shining in the spotlight. Colette's spotlight. Colette's fingers and toes went numb, her skin prickling with goose bumps. She never realized how cold it was on the sidelines.

When Kate dropped her long arms down by her sides, everyone spontaneously started clapping, like she was some superstar. Like she was some brand-new dancer they'd never laid eyes on before who'd strolled in and absolutely wowed her audience. What the hell? Would they still be clapping if they knew that Miss Supposed Best Friend had tried to swoop in and steal Marcus? And went MIA all weekend? Avery forwarded a Snap from Kate with tears on her face, a message that said, *Total meltdown with Mom*. But that was it. Kate never contacted Colette.

Then, right before practice, Kate came to Colette in the locker room and swore up and down that it was him. *Marcus* scammed on *Kate*. Well, Colette found that hard to believe when he drove six hours to see *her*! Then, what did Kate do?

Totally upstaged Colette! In front of everyone! Miss Roza! Her mother!

Mom. Colette couldn't even imagine what Mom was going to say. Blood rushed to Colette's head, and she could hear throbbing in her ears. She couldn't look up. She couldn't get up. She couldn't possibly walk out into the lobby, face Mom, and have to explain why it hadn't been Colette standing there. Perfect.

She flashed back to the pool, Kate's foot coming at Colette hard and fast. And now, again Kate had knocked her down.

Colette raced into the locker room, grabbed her bag without changing, without uttering a word to anyone, and darted out into the lobby, where everything felt like a potential threat. She couldn't make eye contact with Miss Roza. She couldn't talk to any of her friends because, after Friday, Avery had texted that she didn't want to *get trapped in the drama*. Like Avery wasn't always trying to stir the pot. Whatever.

Colette walked fast and silent, straight through the crowd of mothers. Without even looking, she knew Mom wouldn't be there. Sure enough, she was inside their car, behind the wheel, engine already humming. The radio was turned down low. Mom gripped the steering wheel tightly, her knuckles white, and one lone vein pulsated in and out, down the side of her neck. They drove in thick, heavy silence for six and a half minutes. Every switch of the digital clock on the dashboard took an eternity. Was she ever going to talk again? The back of Colette's throat tightened; the tip of her nose grew cold and wet. Her eyes burned and fogged with tears.

"One time!" Colette blurted. "I messed up one time!"

Mom drove in torturous silence for three more minutes until they reached a red light. Then, keeping her hands on the wheel, she turned to face Colette. Mom's mouth was tight, her eyes brimming with tears. "What's going on with you?"

Colette looked away from the pure disappointment on Mom's face. Why did there have to be a reason? Wasn't Colette allowed a bad day? Her head pulsed. Slowly, she pulled her dance bag into her lap. Her hands shook as she pressed the button to lower the window and raised the bag up. A harsh smack of air sliced inside the car, whirling strands of her hair loose from the ponytail.

"Stop!" Mom screamed, reaching over and yanking the duffel from Colette before she could toss it.

The light turned green. They sat, staring at each other, the energy like fire sparking between them.

A car honked.

Mom hit the accelerator and drove, still clutching the straps of the bag in her hand. A whistle of air whined as Colette closed the window.

Mom threw the bag into the back seat. "What? Are you going to quit? After one tough day? Did I really raise you to be that weak?"

Colette's eyes burned.

Mom's hands looked like swords as she sliced them through the air. "Do you want to?" she asked again. "Quit?"

Tears tangled at the back of Colette's throat. Her chest contracted, and she started to sob. She loved dance. She loved the person she was onstage. She loved the acceleration of the jumps, the impact of the landings, the emotions of the stories. But if being a dancer meant constant pressure to always be perfect, then yes, maybe she should quit. "I don't know. Maybe I'm not good enough."

A squeal of tires.

A sharp turn.

And then they were parked in front of Mike's Tire Shop, under a streetlight. "What?" Mom sounded frantic, like someone had told her Colette was missing or dead. Mom looked Colette square in the eye. "She is not better than you." Mom's voice was low and gravelly, on the verge of creepy. "She is not better than you." A little louder. "She's not better than you!" she screamed.

The hairs on the back of Colette's neck stood at attention. She hunched back into the seat. But what if Kate was better? What if Marcus *had* picked her? What if Mom had arranged the meeting at the Duncan headquarters because, deep down, she saw Kate leaving Colette in her dust and figured they needed a strategy. What if . . .

"She's not better than you!" Mom screamed, rattling the car windows.

Colette sat very still, tears streaming down her face.

"She is not better than you," Mom said, quieter this time. Breathy. Almost a whisper. Like she had collapsed a lung.

Colette stopped crying, stunned by all of it. Mom's crazy eyes. Frantic voice. Finger-combed hair.

"Okay," Colette said, desperate. "I won't quit."

Mom took a deep, quivering breath, nodded. "You want it? Regionals? Nationals? A dance company?"

Colette was afraid to speak, afraid to say, *Of course I want it! But how much more do I have to give?*

"Colette?" Mom's voice rose higher.

"Yes," Colette whispered. "I want it all."

"Okay. Okay." Mom spoke rhythmically, as if soothing herself. "I will fix you. I will fix you. I might not be able to fix everything that's wrong, but I can fix this."

"What else is wrong?" Colette's voice was small. What could be worse than destroying all Mom's dreams for the future? Colette thought about the random Snap Emma had sent Friday night: a pic of Dad and Valerie sitting at Joe's Café. *Weird*, she'd written. Colette had been too consumed by Marcus to really think about it, but yes. It was weird. Could it also be a clue? A reason Kate had a meltdown with Valerie? Something that now Mom needed to fix?

Mom ignored Colette's question. "If you give me an extra hour a day of training, continue to commit to the video and platform building, I'll work on your mind. The mental block. We'll figure it out. I promise." She started the engine again.

The lights clicked on, illuminating the empty parking lot. She hit the gas, and her face softened. Like she could now put that disappointment behind her because they had a plan. Colette looked at her bag, crammed in the back seat. Should she leave it as a symbol of her faults, or retrieve it as a symbol of her future commitment? Sometimes it was impossible to please her mother. She decided to change topics.

"I found out about Kate and Marcus," Colette said. "Before practice. Kate said *he* tried to kiss *her*."

Mom slowed the car, stopped at the curb right in front of their house. She didn't pull up the driveway like normal but just let the car idle. She looked at Colette, and her eyes had that crazy swirl to them again. "Kate said *what?*" her voice shrieked.

"She said he tried to kiss her." Colette swallowed hard and tried to control her voice because Mom's face got all twisty, and Colette couldn't figure out why she was so mad.

Mom went silent, then stared intently. "Don't you think it's *interesting* that she told you that right before dance? Not on Friday when it happened. Not on Saturday or Sunday. Not even at school today. But she waited until you were in the studio." Her whole face was engulfed in a wave of rage.

Colette thought about the unanswered texts. The way Kate never showed up at lunch today. Had it all been on purpose? To unnerve Colette right before practice?

"This is what I tried to warn you about," Mom said. "She may say she's your friend, and maybe she once was, but here's the thing about prodigies and super athletes: Sometimes it takes a cutthroat personality to attain that level of achievement. I'm speaking from experience. Sometimes people betray others, not intending to hurt them, but on a rash impulse." She looked away, and Colette was pretty sure they weren't talking about Kate anymore.

A cold chill came over Colette. She thought about the tension between her parents. The strange text. "What are you talking about, Mom? Who betrayed you? Did Dad do something?"

She whipped her head around. "What? Dad? No. Why would you ask that?"

"I . . . I don't know," Colette stammered. "I've heard you guys fighting."

Mom was quiet for a minute, rolling her lips. "Parents fight sometimes. That's normal."

"So, what betrayal are you talking about?"

She took a long inhale. "When I was a ballerina in New York, things got . . . scandalous."

"What happened?"

125

Her eyes were glazed, her jaw slack, lost in a memory. "It's a long story." She hit the accelerator and drove up the driveway and into the garage.

Colette wanted to understand. What had happened in New York to make her not only quit dance but become so distrustful of other dancers? Even Kate? But she had shut down the conversation. They walked inside. On the table in the foyer was a huge box.

"What's this?" Colette asked.

Mom shrugged and got a pair of scissors. They tore it open. Inside were about ten plastic bags with leggings, sweatshirts, tank tops, and sports bras, all in a variety of colors and patterns.

Mom pulled out a note and read, "'Dear Colette. We love your instructional videos about injury prevention for dancers. We'd be honored if you would consider wearing some of our new athletic clothing in your upcoming shows. We look forward to watching your subscriber numbers soar.'" Mom's mouth dropped open, and she pulled Colette into the tightest hug. Then Mom was cheering and congratulating her, acting normal again. Like the whole bizarre car ride had never even happened. "See! It's working! The platform is working!"

And it seemed all thoughts of Colette's crappy performance were now buried beneath the new excitement.

Lying in bed later that night, Colette's heart raced like it had in the pantry. She couldn't breathe. She knew from googling that she'd had a panic attack, and she could tell another one was coming on. Her scalp tingled. She wanted to pull. But the website she clicked on gave suggestions for how to lessen anxiety, and one of them was to talk about what was bothering you. So, she got out of bed and texted Kate: I need to know what happened Friday. For real.

Kate called. Right away. "He scammed on me, Col. I don't know what else you want me to say." It wasn't exactly comforting. But then after a pause, she said, "I'm sorry." And her voice cracked just enough to let Colette believe her. And then Kate was sobbing.

"What?" Colette asked, somehow knowing it wasn't about Marcus.

In between gasps, Kate told the craziest story ever. Her dad—the one everyone thought had died in an accident—was actually alive. For real. Like this was a Netflix series or something. But Colette thought about what Mom had said—people can betray people unintentionally. "Maybe your mom was trying to protect you or something?" Who knew? Maybe her dad was straight-up nuts. Or criminal.

"Well," Kate said with a gritty tone to her voice, "I'm going to find out."

It sent a shiver up Colette's spine.

But then she realized that was why Kate had been unavailable all weekend. That's why she hadn't offered any info on Marcus—not because she was secretly plotting to ambush Colette but because her life had taken a true plot twist. And then, it dawned on Colette that Kate had trusted her with this giant secret. Because they were friends. Not rivals, like Mom kept saying.

And everything seemed back to normal.

It didn't last. After practice the next day, in the locker room, Colette saw a white sheet of paper taped to the wall next to a panel of light switches. With all the focus on the Duncan, she'd forgotten about their own studio performance. They'd been practicing the routines; Miss Roza just needed to divvy out the roles. All the girls raced toward the wall.

As Colette got closer, the words came into focus: *Annual Volkov Studio Spring Gala.*

There were several group pieces—a hip-hop number where everyone, even the younger dancers, participated, another group jazz routine, a trio contemporary number featuring Colette, Kate, and a boy named Xavier. Colette gazed down the list to the most elite performance, The Stair Walker. Everyone was so excited for that one. Miss Roza had used a new choreographer and hired set designers to build an actual rolling wooden staircase for the stage. The solo dancer's costume would be fire-engine red and sport high-heeled sequined shoes as they strutted down the center stairs while the remaining dancers parted like a giant wave. And there in bold type:

STAIRCASE SOLOIST . . . .
. . . . KATE YARNELL

Colette's eyes went blurry. The edges of her vision went black, like she was walking down a long, dark tunnel. She blinked and blinked, but the paper still said the same thing. Kate had the lead. For the first time ever, Colette did not.

Her heart was like a gun firing: *Boom, boom, boom.*

Kate had a broad smile across her face. Colette tried to say, *Congratulations*, but her head was swimming, her scalp was tingling, and her voice shaking. It came out indecipherable and desperate.

Like she was falling right down that rolling staircase.

NINETEEN

The hospital suddenly seemed like a dungeon. Valerie had never noticed how dark the parking garage was, how long and empty the hallways could be. She walked on edge, half expecting Chad to appear around every corner. But he hadn't returned. At least not yet.

After witnessing him in the hospital lobby consoling the hurt little boy, charming the pants off his pretty mother, Valerie wondered if, somehow, through maturity or medication, he'd dialed back to the captivating boy he'd been. Before all the anger and violence. She wished she'd been brave enough to confront him, but fear gripped her, worrying that he was still like a magnet, able to attract people with an invisible force, holding tight until he decided to repel them.

Now, Valerie sat in the staff lounge and told Jazmin how Kate had seen Chad's picture, freaked out, and given her the silent treatment. Valerie admitted she'd reached out to Andrew. He had listened, and it wasn't that he'd excused her terrible decision, but he seemed to understand it, the depths you would go to safeguard your child. He'd promised to help, starting with unearthing any criminal information from the last ten years of Chad's life.

"Andrew sounds like a really great guy," Jazmin said.

"Yeah. I don't understand how he's married to that awful woman." Valerie then told her that Kate had avoided her since finding out about her father. Desperate to see how her daughter was coping with such a bombshell, she'd resorted to snooping again. Now, she retrieved a diary from her bag, opened to the place she had marked with a sticky note, and handed it over. "Nothing about me or Chad," Valerie said. "Just this."

I'm the featured dancer. Oh my God, the staircase solo.

This day was 100% EPIC.

Of course, it was kind of hard to be happy when Colette stood there looking like a ghost—fading from shock.

I've always thought that Colette and I were like sisters—super close but maybe with a hint of competition. I mean, sometimes it sucks to watch her live her perfect life—always the star, always with the best clothes and most expensive vacations—and yeah, sometimes I'm jealous, but still, I'd give her a kidney if she needed it. And I always thought she'd give me one, too.

But today she stared at the roles for a long time. Then she turned toward me and we stood there, still sweating from practice, looking at each other. That's when the craziest thing happened. Her face changed. Like a secret door opened, and I saw, just for a second, resentment. Rage.

And I knew, all this time, I'd been wrong. She wouldn't give me a kidney. She didn't even want me to have a minute on her center stage.

Jazmin took a sip of her latte, then wiped her lips with a napkin and leaned back into the chair, looking exhausted. They had just finished their shift, and it had been a doozy. A full moon always brought babies, and the labor and delivery ward was busting at the seams.

"Is she so obsessed with dance that finding out her father is alive takes a back seat?"

"She might still be in shock, Val. It was a big surprise." Jazmin propped an elbow on the table. "What do you think about the fact that Kate actually got the solo? Does it make you reconsider her aspirations?"

"Should it?" Valerie asked, then squirmed at how inflexible she sounded. "We're talking about a studio performance. That's great to put on a college application, but it doesn't change my mind about her future. I'm proud, of course. And I understand it's a huge deal to her. But how does a lead role take up more space in her mind than her huge argument with me? Or the fact that her father is alive? It doesn't seem . . . healthy." Her phone dinged, interrupting her. She scanned the text. "Oh, it's Andrew. He's asking to meet."

"Hmm." Jazmin's tone was filled with implication.

"He's married!" Valerie said. "To Elise—the ice-blond supermodel wrapped up in a teeny tiny perfect package."

"Still." Jazmin cocked her head.

"Still nothing." Just then, another message came through. If you have time, I want to ask you something about the girls. Oh. She'd assumed he had information on Chad. "He wants to talk about our daughters. I bet it's about the performance roles." She would never admit it, but she felt let down. After their initial flirtation and then heartfelt conversation, she thought there'd been a jolt of electricity between them. And even if they both knew it couldn't go anywhere, still she wanted more of that intimacy. Not talk about dance. She replied that she could meet in twenty minutes. He suggested a Mexican restaurant.

The early-evening temperatures had plummeted with the sun; Valerie shoved her hands inside her coat pockets as she walked from her car to the restaurant. Inside, loud, tinny Spanish music played above the hum of conversation from the crowd. She spotted Andrew in the far corner, sitting under a television turned to a soccer game. He was still wearing his heavy wool coat with a plaid scarf wound around his neck. He looked up from his phone, caught her eye, and waved her over.

131

She hated the way her heart picked up speed at the sight of him. Thank God Jazmin wasn't there to tease her about her burning cheeks. She pulled a chair up and sat across from him. The waiter appeared and offered menus. Valerie shook her head. "I have a roast in the Crock-Pot. I'll just take a Diet Coke. Thanks."

Andrew ordered queso and a beer. Once the waiter was gone, he said, "It looks like Chad did serve some jail time in San José for manslaughter."

"Manslaughter?" Valerie gasped.

"An altercation occurred between Chad and another man on a fishing dock. He pushed the guy, and he fell backward into the water. His head hit a boat anchor, and the impact killed him."

It was the story she'd seen on the video and had heard snippets of all those years ago across the staticky collect call. She'd assumed, since she had sent no money, he couldn't afford a lawyer and wouldn't have a way to get any counsel from the United States. A bizarre wave of guilt swirled inside her. What if it was really just an accident . . . just a simple shove . . .

Andrew reached out a hand and rested it on top of hers, halting her spiraling thoughts. "The good news is there's no evidence that he caused any problems while serving his time. He got released and worked for an outdoor adventure company in Costa Rica. There are no documented additions to his arrest record." Andrew pulled his fingers down so they almost threaded inside of hers. The heat of his palm melted against the top of her hand. Whether he was offering comfort or preparing her for a blow, she wasn't certain. But the gesture incited a longing deep and strong. "It's unclear when he returned to the States or where he's currently living or working. Honestly, his footprint is pretty invisible. And he hasn't tried to contact you again?"

"No."

With his free hand, he reached into a pocket and retrieved a note. "This is the name of a private investigator if you want to pursue that. I've worked with him before, and he's great at accessing information I can't. I . . . I . . ." He fumbled. "I wasn't sure how far to go, what my boundaries are."

She wanted to tell him that she had no boundaries. She wanted all of his help, all of him, but his gold wedding band pressed into her skin, reminding her of what she couldn't have.

The waiter came with their drinks. They pulled their hands apart. A compassionate look crossed his face. "Have you told Kate?"

She explained how Kate had seen Chad's picture online and exploded, shunning every discussion Valerie attempted. "She'll never forgive me."

"She will." He tilted his head in contemplation. "Kate is reasonable. Balanced. Once she gets over the shock, she'll listen and understand. You've done a great job."

Valerie raised an eyebrow. She was a liar. A fraud.

"Kate's a great girl. Sure, she's angry, but once she listens to you, she'll realize it was a decision made out of uncertainty and fear. She'll forgive you." He raised his shoulders in a gentle shrug. "I never realized how much you had on your plate, not only a full-time job but all this worry, and yet you've raised this awesome girl all on your own."

His flattering image of her hung in the air like a mirage, like the perfect mother she strived to be. But instead of graciously accepting his compliment, she stammered, flustered, like a teen giddy from her crush's approval. "Well, I'm not doing it totally on my own. Elise has been a huge help. All the times she's picked Kate up, fed her. You know, she practically lives at your place." She laughed uncomfortably. Why was she pretending Elise was a savior? Sure, the bones of those words were true—Elise had been a resource to lean on. But her help had come with so many strings. She'd used her physical presence to impart her own values and ideas in Kate's mind. But she wouldn't say that out loud. Instead, she sipped her soda and let the false words of praise cover her deep-seated resentment.

A hesitant look crossed Andrew's face. "Well, actually, that's what I wanted to talk to you about. Elise."

Valerie's palms turned damp. He'd texted he wanted to talk about the girls, not his wife. Her mind raced along with her heart. She watched his fingers flexing as he peeled the label off his sweating bottle of beer.

"I'm worried that Elise is putting too much pressure on Colette. She logs practice hours, charts her food, endlessly watches dancers on the computer. Now she's started this YouTube thing with her. I tried to tell her to tamp it down. Stop putting so much emphasis on winning that damn competition. I think she should celebrate the effort, not the outcome, you know?"

"Yes. Absolutely." She looked at his startling blue eyes. They looked so genuinely concerned.

"Has Colette said anything to Kate about her mom being too demanding?"

Valerie shook her head.

"Elise says she's just trying to do everything that her mother never did for her." He threw his hands out, palms up in a surrender. "What do I know? But she's very secretive about her time as a professional ballerina. It makes me wonder what really went on. The dance world is often portrayed as cutthroat. I worry she's promoting that intensity. Lately Colette just seems . . . anxious, fidgety. Last night she was sitting in the kitchen, just staring into space, running her hands through her hair. At three in the morning! She said she couldn't sleep. I tried to probe, but she just smiled and said everything was good. It didn't look real; it looked like her stage smile." He glanced down at his beer.

Valerie thought for a moment. "Do you think maybe she's upset about the spring gala?" She felt strange bringing it up, but it seemed like an obvious explanation.

A blank expression crossed his face. "What do you mean?"

The waiter returned with queso and a huge basket of tortilla chips. Suddenly, Valerie realized she was famished. She spooned the cheese dip onto a small plate, then grabbed a handful of chips. The waiter disappeared and the air was silent and expectant. Andrew didn't know? For a moment, she was relieved. She wasn't the only parent in the dark.

But that meant now she'd have to tell him that Kate had beat out Colette for the solo. It reminded her of not too long ago when he'd told her Kate had applied for the Duncan. They were each other's informers.

"What?" he asked, curiosity in his eyes. "What are you not telling me?"

He looked desperate, so she said it simply and to the point. "Kate got the solo for the featured performance. Not Colette. They just found out."

Andrew closed his eyes and inhaled slowly through his nose. Was he sad for his daughter or worried about his wife's reaction? Valerie shifted in her seat. She had a strange urge to blurt out that the only reason she even knew any of this in the first place was because she was a horrible mother who snooped through her daughter's diaries. Instead, she shoved a chip into her mouth.

Andrew opened his eyes and, seeing her, his whole face changed. His expression slid into a grin, and a small chuckle followed. "Finally. A woman who loves chips as much as I do. I haven't seen Elise eat one in fifteen years."

Valerie swallowed, dusted the salt off her lips. "Well, that's why she's a size zero and I'm not."

He leaned in, just a fraction, but close enough that she could see the stubble on his chin. "Let me give you a little insight. Guys like curves."

Every nerve ending in her body sprang to life. Electricity tingled all the way down to her toes. She didn't say a word, fearful that her tone would reveal something deep inside her heart; a feeling stirred that she would never tell a soul about. But for so many years, Elise Carrington had hijacked her daughter and claimed her for her own. Was it so outrageous if, just for tonight, just for a moment, Valerie wished she could hijack Andrew?

He smiled, clueless that she'd imagined what it would be like to have his hands on her curves, his breath on her neck, his lips on her skin.

She laughed nervously at how dangerous her mind could be.

But it was wrong. Even to think it. She had to change the conversation before she said or, God forbid, did something she regretted. "My mother made me do beauty pageants."

He cocked his head. "What?"

She closed her eyes and cringed at the memories. "I hated it. The spray tans, thick makeup, the four-inch heels." She pointed at her face. "So not me."

He nodded, intrigued. "So why did you do it?"

"Because it made her happy. Not only to earn a cash prize, which we desperately needed, but to see me dolled up, getting attention from men. She said she'd squandered her youth and beauty, and she wanted me to live out her lost opportunity."

"Oh, I'm sorry. That's a lot of pressure." A small grin played on his lips. "But I'd sure love to see you in rhinestones. I'm going to search the internet, find pictures. I bet you were Miss Photogenic," he teased.

"Don't you dare!" They laughed for a minute. "She was so angry when I got pregnant and couldn't do pageants anymore. She could no longer live vicariously."

They were silent for a few moments. Then he leaned forward, bridging the small space between them, and lowered his voice. "You're wondering if your story isn't so different from Colette's? If Colette sees that Elise is happy when she's the star . . ."

Valerie shrugged. "Maybe?"

He nodded slightly, then reached over and rested his hand on top of hers, again threading his fingers. "Why is it so easy to talk to you? Why do you always make so much sense?"

His hand was big. Strong. Warm. Touching hers. And she knew. He wasn't just being helpful, seeking information about Chad. Something was brewing. She looked into his eyes, and he held her gaze. It felt like everything was about to change.

"Andrew?" The voice was high-pitched and almost urgent.

His hand retracted quickly.

They looked up. It was one of the dance moms who always orbited just outside of Elise's circle.

"Dena!" Andrew said it too loudly. "How are you? How's John? Been busy at the hospital?"

Dena nodded. "Yes. Very busy." Her eyes were glued to Valerie. "Picking up dinner for him now."

"I'm giving Valerie the name of a friend. He's going to help her with some . . . business stuff."

Valerie was frozen. They'd been *caught*. Again. But this time, not by teens who were self-absorbed and uninterested in their parents' lives. She felt nauseated; she had to leave. Before she caused Andrew any trouble.

She waved the paper with the private investigator's number in the air dramatically. "Thank you so much, Andrew. For the recommendation." She stood up quickly. "I've got to run." She smiled at Dena, avoiding Andrew's eyes, then grabbed her coat and left.

TWENTY

Elise walked into the Pilates studio and joined Ling Li and Susie by the juice bar. She ordered the Energizer: an apple, carrot, and ginger concoction that always gave her the perfect boost of adrenaline. She paid, turned around, and saw the women staring at her. Sighing, she mentally prepared for yet another inquisition on the state of her sex life, but then Ling Li made a strange grimace and said, "Since I didn't get a 911, you must not know."

"Know what?" Elise asked.

Susie looked uncomfortable, turned away, and tucked her tank top into the waistband of her leggings. Ling Li screwed up her face. "Susie, honey, the tuck is not happening."

The door swung open, and Dena Loudermilk walked in. What was she doing here? She never did Pilates. She was a strict barre devotee.

"Oh my God," Ling Li whispered, jutting her chin toward Dena. "Total gossip hound."

"Gossip?" Elise said, frustrated she was in the dark. "About what?" She'd left the studio thirty minutes before the end of class yesterday to meet with the electrician about adding extra lighting in the basement. What could she have missed? Colette hadn't mentioned anything.

Dena bounded over, arms pumping, breath accelerating, as if desperate to unload whatever juicy tidbit was circulating. "Oh, hey, guys," she said with a note of false surprise in her tone. Like this meetup was a coincidence. "So . . . did you hear?" A smile stretched across her face, exposing just a sliver of her top gums that made her look youthful and innocent, thereby softening the rumors she loved to slingshot around town.

Ling Li straightened her spine and snapped, "Yes, we've heard, Dena. *Obviously.* And it's sensitive. So, we need a little privacy."

"Okay." Dena put her hands out. *Excuse me!* She looked at Elise. "I'm not one to judge, but she's always been a little sketchy to me. Hate that she's going after your family. I'm here for you, hon. If you need anything."

"Thanks?" Elise squirmed. She turned to her friends. "What's going on? Who's going after my family?"

Ling Li and Susie said, "Kate," at the same time Dena said, "Valerie." Everyone's gaze volleyed back and forth. "Wait, what?" Ling Li asked Dena.

Dena beamed. "Okay, so you *don't* know."

"Know *what*?" Elise's voice edged higher.

Dena cleared her throat, bent in conspiratorially. "Last night I bumped into Andrew at Tacos and Tequilas." She paused dramatically. "He was with Valerie."

Susie gasped. Ling Li's eyebrows cinched. Elise froze. *What the hell?*

Dena relished the attention. "They said they were discussing business?" She cocked an eyebrow. *As if.* "Not sure why Valerie would need legal advice . . ." She went to sit down next to them, but Ling Li shooed her away.

"Okay, thanks, Dena. Good to know. See you around," Ling Li said, standing in front of Elise like a shield.

Dena sighed and went across the room to the only open reformer but craned her neck to eavesdrop.

Elise's breath was ragged, like she was already working out. She looked at her friends desperately. She could barely say the word. "Affair?" It squeaked out like a screech. "With Valerie?" Elise thought back to the previous night. He'd had a work dinner and came home smelling of salsa with a strange look of satisfaction in his eyes. When she tried to talk to him, he'd been evasive and headed up to take a shower. At nine o'clock at night? He hadn't gone to the gym. Her stomach had bottomed out. She'd spent the night googling: *signs that your husband is cheating*. She'd checked his underwear drawer for new boxers, his wallet for any receipts from romantic restaurants or flower shops, his laptop for suspicious emails. Nothing.

"Honey, no," Susie said. "Not an affair. They were probably talking about . . ." She looked at Ling Li, hesitated.

Ling Li whispered, "Kate got the staircase solo."

"What?" Elise gasped. Her mouth went dry. Not an affair, but the gala? And how could Kate get the solo? That made even less sense.

"None of us understand the decision," Susie said. "And why did Valerie go run and tell Andrew? She's never been interested in studio business before."

"Maybe she's after him," Ling Li said. "He's handsome, charming . . ."

Elise's heart raced. The instructor shouted, "Everybody on their reformers!"

Elise stood. "I can't do this." She grabbed her bag and juice and raced out the door. Gusty wind smacked her in the face. Gray clouds rolled over the horizon. Storms everywhere.

Ling Li and Susie scurried after her. "Colette deserved it!" Susie said as they got to Elise's car.

"Of course she did," Ling Li called over the roaring wind. "This reeks of foul play. Miss Roza wouldn't do this on her own. Someone's behind this."

They stared at each other, contemplating this theory. But who? Surely not Valerie. She didn't even want Kate to dance. But why was she running to Andrew with the news? A prick of tears burned Elise's eyes. Nothing made sense. "Thanks, guys. I've got to go." She clicked open her car, climbed in, and peeled away. She thought back to her time in New York when her artistic director had taken a sudden shine to Gina, Elise's supposed best friend. Then suddenly, Gina started getting more stage time than Elise! One day, Elise had walked in on Gina and the director having a private meeting. *Just talking about a sore toe*, Gina had explained. But Elise was no fool. They were conspiring to catapult Gina to stardom! Had Kate done something similar? Somehow coerced Miss Roza into letting her be the featured dancer? But how did Valerie fit in? Why had she run to Andrew?

She dialed her husband, but he didn't answer. She texted him, Please call. It's important. Parking in a random lot, she waited. Five long minutes went by. She dialed the office directly and asked Andrew's secretary to please get him immediately.

A moment later, he came on the line, breathless. "What's wrong? Are you okay? Are the kids okay?"

"What were you doing with Valerie last night?"

He was silent for a beat. "I was in an important meeting, Elise."

"I want to know why you were with her when you said you were doing something for work." She couldn't breathe. An image of them laughing in the studio lobby crashed through her mind. Her lungs tightened. She thought of that strange smile on his face. Disappearing into the shower . . . No. It wasn't possible. Valerie was practically a child! And she was plain. Tall and lanky. She probably didn't own a blow-dryer! But still . . . she remembered watching them that day, the way they'd laughed, the way Valerie had seemed rapt by his attention. There was a streak of lightning. Her whole body went rigid, waiting for the crash of thunder.

"It was work," Andrew said. "I was helping her with some legal stuff. Single parenting is challenging."

That was what Dena had said. But why had he been cryptic about it? "Well, why didn't you just say that?"

"Because most of the time, you never hear a word I say unless it has to do with dance."

"And did she tell you?" Elise plowed past his hurtful comment. "About the gala?"

"Yes, actually, she did."

Elise's whole body shook. She was positive Valerie had invented a need for advice to be alone with her husband. Then she'd casually told Andrew about the roles so he'd drop the bombshell on Elise. Passive-aggressive bitch. But Andrew hadn't mentioned it. Fat raindrops splattered on her windshield with a *plink, plink, plink*. "Why didn't you tell me? I was at Pilates, sitting there like a fool because everyone in greater Atlanta knew except for me."

"Aren't you wondering why Colette didn't tell you?"

A trickle of ice streamed through her body. "What are you implying?"

"That maybe she was afraid of how you'd react . . . just like this . . . like she's some *failure* because of a stupid dance recital."

"It's not a recital! This isn't little Debbie's neighborhood dance class! This is an elite preprofessional training program!" Her whole face heated in frustration. She hung up and tossed the phone onto the passenger seat. How, how after all this time, after seventeen years of marriage, could he still not appreciate how important dance was to her and to their daughter? Did he think that not just dance, but her entire life, her passion, her *identity* was stupid?

Her heart throbbed. Her head spun in a million different directions. She didn't know who to focus her anger on. She drove in a tense, pulsating panic. Wipers skidded across the windshield in time with her heartbeat. Once home, she went straight to the computer, coat still on, juice still in her hand, and started searching. "I will fix this," she muttered as her fingers flew across the keyboard.

⌒☺

Six hours later, Trey and Colette returned from school. They chatted casually as they tossed their umbrellas and rounded the corner into the kitchen. They stopped and stared at Elise. She was sitting in front of the computer, papers strewn all over the desk. They looked from her to the mess to each other, an entire conversation with just their eyes.

Elise promised herself that she would remain calm and composed. Andrew's biting words—*Aren't you wondering why Colette didn't tell you?*—still clamped around her heart. She would not put her daughter on the defensive. She would only be her advocate. "I've been trying to figure out how, after ten consecutive years of dancing solos, you were suddenly cast in a subpar position."

Colette flinched. She looked at Trey, then back at Elise and plastered on a smile. "I'm on the first stair, though. I'll still get a spotlight. It might be even more difficult than Kate's routine to nail that stick-out while rotating off the stair." She was trying so hard to sound excited and justified, it broke Elise's heart.

"No!" Elise barked. "The name of the routine is the Stair Walker, for crying out loud. You deserved to strut down those stairs." Thoughts rained down like the shower outside. She would not allow Colette to suffer the demise of a career at the hands of a supposed best friend, the way Elise had all those years ago. How had Kate done it? Convinced Miss Roza? Outside the kitchen window, a bird feeder rocked violently in the wind.

Colette glanced across the kitchen to where Trey hunted for a snack. She leaned in and whispered, "I think it was a pity solo."

Elise froze. "What?"

Colette sat in the chair closest to her mother and covered part of her mouth, shielding her voice from Trey. "I think Miss Roza felt bad because Kate couldn't go to New York. And now I'm getting all this attention from the YouTube channel." Her gaze jumped around skittishly, the edges of her tiny nose flaring.

Elise let out a long breath, tension spooling out of her body. Her brilliant daughter had figured it out. "Of course it was pity." It came out louder than intended.

Trey snapped his head in their direction. "What did you say?"

"Nothing," Elise cooed.

Trey slammed the cupboard shut. "Kate is, like, part of this family. She's my girlfriend. She's Colette's best friend." He pointed at Elise. "I don't know what is up with you, but we see it, me and Kate. How effed up you're acting toward her."

"Trey!" Elise scolded.

He came toward them. "Don't make me pick sides, Mom," he warned. "Because I'll pick her."

Elise laughed. "Is Kate going to pay for your car? Your college?"

"Whatever." He turned and walked away.

Elise turned toward Colette. "Don't worry about him. Deep down, he must know that's the only reasonable explanation. Kate is talented, but she's not you." She imagined a giant chess board, Kate striking another calculated move, dropping hints to her teacher about all she'd missed out on, fishing for sympathy. Kate was not as clever as Elise had been years ago. Elise's moves were calculated and indetectable. It would have worked if Gina hadn't stumbled upon evidence.

"Listen," Elise said now, pointing to the laptop. "This is how you're going to regain the spotlight." She clicked on the keyboard, and an image filled the screen. A photograph of a man with silver hair gelled to perfection, sharply cut cheekbones, and parchment-thin skin wrinkled in the corners of his honey-colored eyes. "This is Ashton Parker. One of the world's most famous choreographers. He became most known for taking young dancers and mentoring them to stardom. He retired and disappeared into obscurity. But I tracked him down. We had a very nice conversation."

Colette's eyes widened. "You spoke to him?"

Elise nodded. "An hour ago. And I just booked a one-way ticket for him to come to Atlanta. It will be his mission to work with you until you become the very best. Until you become flawless. Until you outshine everyone and anyone else in your way."

TWENTY-ONE

Sitting on the edge of her bathtub, Colette pressed a cold washcloth to her eyes. She was losing it. What if it wasn't a pity solo? What if Miss Roza actually thought Kate deserved to be featured? What would Colette do if she weren't number one?

There was a knock at the door. She ignored it. The bathroom door swung open. She jumped. Before she could say anything, Trey burst in. "Do you think that, too?" Trey yelled, pointing a finger at her, his cheeks red. "That Kate didn't deserve it?"

Her lip shook. "No."

"Then why didn't you defend her? I thought the three of us were, you know . . ." He paused, emotion sliding across his face. "Everything." He bit his lip. "And she told you, right? About her dad?"

Colette nodded.

"And after all that, you still couldn't let her have one good thing?"

He stared at Colette, but how could she explain? "You didn't see the way Mom freaked after I had one sloppy practice. Now, to lose the solo?" She ran her hands through her hair. "If she thinks there's a reason, it makes it easier on me." Her voice cracked. "But now she hired a private coach to help me regain perfection. If that's even possible. So, I'm sorry. Maybe I'm a bitch. Maybe I should have stopped Mom from saying that. But can you think how hard it is to be happy for Kate when her success is literally screwing up my life?" She burst into tears.

Trey froze. Slowly, the flush of anger on his face softened. He sat across from Colette on the edge of the toilet. "Do you dance . . . for you? Or is it for Mom?"

All of her life, everyone had always told her that she was going to be a star. Somewhere along the way, she forgot if it ever even was her dream to begin with. But when she was onstage, life was perfect. That was true. She couldn't imagine doing anything else. "I love dance," she said.

He locked eyes with her, like he was searching for holes in her story. "Okay. Then do it for you. Not for her."

She nodded, but the idea was hard to even imagine. Colette, Mom, and dance were all wound up like a big ball of tangled yarn. She swallowed. "Please don't tell Kate."

"I won't," he said. "But next time, defend her. Be a better friend."

She nodded. But Mom had told her the opposite.

After he left, Colette paced, thoughts crashing into her like bumper cars. If she really was as good as everyone always said, why hadn't she gotten the solo? Did Kate have something to do with it? Why had she waited three days to tell Colette about Marcus? Was Mom right? That Kate set Colette up to fail right before the gala roles were cast? Why had Marcus tried to kiss Kate? Marcus. What a douchebag. He'd started this mess—the tension between Colette and Kate. Yes. It was so much easier to be mad at him.

Colette rushed into her room and grabbed her phone. Scanning through her texts and pictures, she screenshot, edited, and crafted the absolute nastiest, most embarrassing post. Then, she dropped it all over social media. *There, Marcus McWilliams. Take that.* She'd show the world that nobody screws with her.

And finally, she could breathe.

❧

The next day at the studio, Avery rushed to Colette's locker. Avery's face was pink, her phone outstretched and waving. "You hammered him," she said. "I didn't think you were someone who believed in paybacks, but damn, girl, when you get mad, you get even." She gave Colette a high five.

Kate wandered into the locker room, bag slung over her shoulder, head cast down at her screen. Remembering her promise to Trey to be a better friend, Colette went to her. Kate was wearing a pumpkin-orange sweater. Random curls had pulled loose from her high messy bun. She had on lip gloss and looked pretty. "Hey," Colette said. "I'm sorry things have been weird. Can we, like, push a button and restore factory settings?" She gave a small laugh. "Congrats on the staircase solo."

Kate let silence linger for a beat, her eyes like daggers. "Well, if that's true," she spit, "maybe you should stop spreading the rumor that it's a gift from Miss Roza given out of *pity*."

Oh, shit. A creepy feeling skidded up Colette's neck and across her scalp. Like a needle scratching. Everyone in the locker room halted and stared. The air turned hot, like everyone had just blown out long breaths of surprise. Sweat beaded at Colette's hairline.

Kate waited for Colette to respond, but she was speechless, sucker punched, and scared. What exactly was happening? "I . . . I never said that," Colette stammered.

"Oh, really?" Kate's voice was low and intense. "You're a lot of things, but I never thought you were a liar."

Acid rose in Colette's throat. She turned and ran past Kate, past Avery, past all the girls pressed against the wall, all the way out onto the studio floor, where her mother was watching from the bench. What was she going to do? Could she fake a fever? Miss Roza and the rest of the girls appeared, so with no options, she plastered on a smile and somehow started to dance in a hypnotized trance. She moved to the music that she couldn't even really hear, feeling the white-hot stares of every girl on the dance floor. She inhaled long and slow, so she wouldn't pass out. Avery whispered, "Are you okay?" But Colette ignored her. She just kept going. What else could she do? Everyone stopped, so Colette stopped. Everyone walked toward the locker room, so she walked toward the locker room. When someone tapped her shoulder, she almost screamed.

It was Miss Roza. Her gestures were animated, hands waving in the air, and she was saying something, but Colette couldn't hear the words. They were drowned out by the whooshing in her head. She nodded, clueless. Miss Rosa signaled to Kate and flagged down Colette's mother. They walked down the hallway. Kate and Colette repelled like opposite magnets, the air thick with hatred.

In the office, Colette wedged herself into the corner. Her mother hovered. "What's wrong?" Mom pressed the back of her hand to Colette's forehead.

Miss Roza cleared her throat. "Just to let you know," she barked in her brusque manner, a wedge of newly cut black bangs swung across her forehead. "I received an email from the director of the Duncan. Two judges will attend our spring gala to assess Kate and Colette prior to the regional event. Very good news. They don't scout everyone. This is very exciting." She extended her beefy, freckled hand and gave two taps on Kate's shoulder, but Colette was out of reach. There was no congratulatory tap from Mom. Her eyes had suddenly gone dark.

Those judges' first impressions would be of Kate dancing the solo and Colette on the sidelines.

∞

As soon as Colette got home, she went to Trey's room. He was at his computer. She tapped his shoulder. He pulled his headphones down onto his neck.

"Kate knows. About the pity comment," she said.

Resentment flooded his face. "Mom's probably told everyone." He reached for his phone, but Colette put a hand on his arm.

"She thinks I said it." Colette prayed he hadn't heard that she actually had been the one to suggest it. "Kate's really pissed. Can you talk to her? Tell her it wasn't me?" He paused, phone still in his hand but not contacting Kate yet. Something in his expression made Colette panic. The way his head tilted, his eyes locked on hers. Like he was torn between her and Kate. Colette's stomach burned because, for the first time ever, she wasn't sure he'd pick her. Kate had been through a major shock, and now Colette was making her life worse. "Forget it. I'll work it out." Colette left before he could say anything.

She'd barely made it down the hallway when Avery messaged. Have you seen Marcus's Insta? There's been some . . . retaliation.

Colette sat on her bed, opened her feed. She stared at her phone as a simmering hysteria boiled. There was a pic of her face with the word *psycho* written across it. And a screenshot she'd sent him of her in a sports bra and panties. *Too bad her abs are bigger than her tits,* he'd captioned. The phone was slippery in her sweating hands. Mom had lectured her about sharing explicit photos—obviously—and she hadn't! Not like what other girls do. But still. Even though she wasn't naked, everyone would know how into him she was. And he picked Kate! Colette was an idiot! Humiliation burned through her. What an asshole.

She would get even.

She scrolled through her pics from the Friday night party. There was a shot of him on the coffee table, bottles of booze all around his feet. He'd been telling his stupid surfing story. His eyes were red and glassy. She captioned: *Is this who you want representing your sport? Winning your competitions? Wearing your brands?* She linked every surfing competition, association, and clothing brand she could find. She hit "Post" and went to bed.

She thought she'd feel better, but all night, her scalp burned.

When she woke, long platinum strands littered the sheets.

TWENTY-TWO

Two days had passed since Valerie sat across from Andrew at the Mexican restaurant, and she'd neither heard from nor seen him. A dull ache cascaded over her like she was a lovesick, rejected teenager. Which was ridiculous. He was married. And yet, she was certain she hadn't imagined the sparks igniting between them. If that dance mom with the brown bob and snooping stare hadn't interrupted them . . . But, really, what had she honestly thought was going to happen?

The number of the private investigator was hidden deep in a pocket of her purse. She'd told herself she'd wait to tell Kate everything until she knew the whole story. She hadn't dialed the number yet. She justified the delay because of the expense, but if she was being honest, deep down, she knew her hesitation was because she wasn't sure she wanted to know all of Chad's history.

Sinking back into her couch with the premade pasta dish she'd picked up at Whole Foods, she flipped channels, looking for a Friday night movie. When her phone dinged and Andrew's name lit up the screen, her heart gave a little jump.

On my way home from work. Trey asked if I could swing by and pick up Kate's phone. She said she left it inside her dance bag.

Valerie replied: Surprised. Usually, it's attached to her fingers.

🙂 right. They're going to the movies and can't watch a movie without a phone. Obviously.

Valerie smiled. No problem. I'm home.

Okay. Be there in a few.

She went to her bathroom and brushed her hair. She swiped a rose-colored gloss across her lips, walked halfway down the hallway, turned around, went back into the bathroom, and wiped it off. *Don't be ridiculous! He's running an errand. Not dropping in to see you. Not checking up to see if you're okay since Kate still hasn't spoken to you.*

After a loud knock at the door, she swung it open. Her smile dropped. Her chest squeezed.

Chad. Standing there, as handsome as the damn devil.

Yes, the picture online should have prepared her. But that was just a photograph. This was him, flesh and bone, energy and heat pulsating off him, the smell of woodsy outdoors permeating the air around them. He was too tall, too muscular, too rugged. Too angularly attractive for real life. He looked Photoshopped and flawless. A breath strangled in her throat.

"Hey, stranger." He locked eyes with her, staring like he could see right through the hard shield Valerie had built around her shattered heart. "Time's been good to you." He reached a hand out and, with barely a flutter, grazed his index finger across her cheek. Just the hint of his touch sent liquid lava cascading down her body, weighing heavy in her limbs. She was cemented in place, at his mercy.

At eighteen, when Valerie had told her mother she'd fallen in love, her mother had bristled, scolded: *That boy is no good, Valerie. Sleek, sexy, oozing with seduction. No Mr. Football Hero and Good-Time Charlie is going to settle down and be a respectable husband. And even if by some supernatural phenomenon he did marry you, that's just delaying disaster. He has too much power over you with his husky drawl and moves like a jungle tiger. No decent-minded woman can make decisions when she melts like damn caramel just looking at a man.*

Valerie had insisted her mother was wrong. But even after his smile had faded and his drawl turned bitter and loud, Valerie still had fallen to the floor, hands out, desperate, and begged him to stay.

Now, years later, stronger and wiser, it killed her that she was rendered speechless, breathless, almost pliable, by just the barest graze of his touch. She delved deep into her years of counseling to gather strength. She stepped back. "What do you want, Chad?"

He threw a playful hand to his heart. "That's the welcome I get?" He dragged his gaze over her body, lingering, smiling. Then before she realized what he was doing, he bridged the space between them and landed a gentle kiss on her lips. Like a snowflake melting on her tongue, it evoked nostalgia, yearning, and suddenly, she was a teenager, pressed against the cold, metal locker in their high school hallway. The hint of cinnamon on his breath. The swell of lust. The promise of love. She flung a hand out, pushing him and her memories aside. "Stop."

He did, grinning widely, like this was a game, like he knew the power he still possessed over her.

Valerie inhaled deeply. She would not succumb to his deception. She forced her mouth to stop quivering.

Still smiling, he gazed beyond her open door, letting out a long, sexy whistle. "Look at this. Nice digs, doll. I heard you've got yourself a fancy job at the hospital. Must pay well." His eyes twinkled with approval.

"Yes." She angled her shoulder to shield the view inside her home. "I've worked hard to provide for our daughter while you've been gone." Valerie's hand seized the doorframe to steady herself. Thousands of white stars danced in her vision. She thought she might pass out. "I had to get a good job, Chad, because you were no help when Kate needed her tonsils out, and I had to put the hospital bills on my credit card. You were gone when she broke her toe, and I had to miss work to bring her to the ER, and I got fired. I had to figure out how to care for our child while you were off *finding yourself* in Costa freaking Rica, never sending me a dime!"

Across the walkway, the door of condo 6A opened, and Mrs. Seneca appeared, a look of disgust on her face. "Could you argue about money somewhere else, please?" The door slammed shut.

His beautiful face turned hard and eerily dark. "I would have been able to help. I could have *been here* if you would have answered my damn call!" His tone, harsh and accusatory, stoked some long-buried trepidation. Her knees weakened. "If you had sent me a little bit of cash, I could have hired a lawyer and proven the whole damn fiasco was an accident!" A vein throbbed down the left side of his neck. "I wouldn't have been stuck behind bars, not able to help out with my daughter!"

Valerie thrust her chin, aiming to appear resolute. "It's always an accident. Or someone else's fault. You're misunderstood. No one gives you a fair shake. I was tired of it!" Her voice echoed across the hard stucco of her threshold.

But he didn't flinch. In fact, his shoulders relaxed, and his entire disposition softened. He tilted his chin in a sweet, consoling manner. "Doll . . ."

"Don't call me that!" she barked.

"You're so angry. So hard." He moved closer. His words were like thick syrup coating her in shame. "If you had just given me a chance, it all would have worked out. You would have understood that I was innocent; I would have been acquitted. I could have come home to you with all my research, and we could have built an empire together. You wouldn't have been all alone. And so angry. But you push people away. You knock people down."

She wanted to protest, but her mouth was dry, her tongue thick. Like her words were trapped in a ball of half-eaten taffy. She wanted to say no—*he* was the problem. But nothing came out. Instead, her head throbbed with the possibility: Maybe she *was* too hard. Maybe she *did* knock people down. That's why Kate avoided her and loved Elise. That's why she and her mother were estranged. That's why she'd yet to find a true love. It was her, her, her. She choked on a sob.

He edged a finger along her jaw, tracing the line from her ear to the base of her throat. "I forgive you, doll. We can start over. You help me; I'll help you."

She almost fell into him, into his strong, muscular chest, but the old words of her therapist echoed over her heartbeat: *He's a classic manipulator. He uses his charm to get what he wants.* She wasn't sure what he wanted now, but she'd bet it wasn't her love. She inched back, her shoulder blade hitting the hard wall. "No," she said. She would not let him crash in on her carefully reconstructed life, her stability, her money—everything she'd worked so incredibly hard for. "No," she repeated, louder this time. "It's over."

His eyes narrowed ever so slightly, and he gave a small closed-lip smile that made a chill drop down her spine. "It's never over, doll. We're forever bound. By Kate."

The truth of those words froze her bones.

Just then, a voice broke through the air. "What's going on? Valerie, are you okay?"

She looked up through tear-streaked lashes. Andrew—walking up the concrete pathway. Chad took a step back. "Who is this?" Andrew asked, a protective edge to his voice.

Chad flashed another smile toward Valerie. "It was great seeing you, doll." He gave a small nod toward Andrew, then walked toward the parking lot. The material of his jacket caught the flickering light from the streetlamp, highlighting his broad shoulders and thick arms.

Andrew stepped toward her. "Was that him?" He brushed away some tears on her face with his thumb. His tone was concerned and caring, which made Valerie submit to a fresh new onslaught of sobs. She turned and walked back inside her house with him on her heels.

Her mind was so overloaded, at first, she didn't understand why Andrew was at her place. Then she remembered: Kate's phone. She retrieved it and pressed it into his hand. She wanted him to take it and leave, so she could collapse and cry, but he held her hand inside his own, not letting her go.

Her throat was raw, her nose still dripping. "Yes. That was Chad." Her lip trembled. "Kate's dead father."

"Did he hurt you? Threaten you? What happened?" Before she could answer, he pulled her into his arms, the soft, expensive fabric of his coat like a cashmere blanket. "You're safe," he whispered.

How could she explain? It wasn't that he'd threatened her, but rather his presence brought out the worst in her—the insecure, desperate girl who still thought she wasn't worthy of a good man. A man who would truly love her. "He acted like . . ." She looked up at the ceiling, searching for words. "Like we would just . . . get back together."

Andrew's eyes fired. "Did you . . ."

"No! I'm sure he just needs a place to stay. Or money . . . I don't know."

He pulled her into a full hug, their bodies pressing against each other. She was hit with a sharp pang of need to erase the lingering pull Chad still possessed. To know she could be attracted to another man. A better man. She had to replace the imprint of Chad's lips meeting hers. It was wrong, on so many levels. But she was overwhelmed, engulfed in emotions, and a deep, raw desire. She reached up and grabbed the back of his neck, pulled his mouth down to meet hers. He didn't resist.

They kissed, hot and desperate and passionate. Her whole body was on fire with chaos, but then, it just felt like lust. As he moved his mouth on hers, she glanced at the couch, and for a moment, she thought: *Just once.* No one would ever know. She could swap the image of Chad with Andrew and lessen the grip of her old longing.

"Val," he said softly as he kissed her. His voice was so tender, so intimate, so genuine, it made her stop.

What was she doing? Andrew was a good man. She couldn't corrupt him. He was married! "No. We can't. It's not right." She stepped back, putting distance between them. She'd made so many mistakes. She couldn't falter any more. "I'm so sorry. I don't know what came over me. I'm terrible." She put her face in her hands, tortured.

He pulled her hands down. "I wanted it, too. I've thought about it a thousand times." His eyes got misty, and she believed him. "Lately . . . you're all I think about."

"But it's not right. You're married." To Elise. *The woman my daughter worships.* "And our kids . . . it's too messy."

"I know," he said, then rolled his lips in, hesitantly. "It's not that I don't love Elise. We have a history. A family. But . . . I don't . . . Things have changed." He exhaled loudly. "When I talk to you, you listen. With her, it's like she's not interested in anything I have to say. All she cares about is Colette's rise to stardom." There was so much hurt in his voice, it made Valerie ache.

"I tried to tell her something a few months ago. It was important, but she didn't hear a word I said. I was incredibly frustrated. So, I just stopped trying. I just feel . . . Empty." He looked at her. "And then that day at the studio when we talked, a little flame sparked inside of me. And for the first time in a long time, I rediscovered what it felt like to have fun. Laugh." He paused, looking at her. "And I know that doesn't make it okay. But I'm not . . . happy . . . except when I'm near you. When you're upset, I want to comfort you. I want to protect you. When I saw that guy, I was wildly jealous."

Every inch of Valerie's skin scorched with desire and longing to be touched and held by someone who saw her. Who liked her. Wanted her. Who was a good man. But there was that old hardened heart that asked, Was he a good man if he was willing to cheat? And didn't she deserve more? "I'm sorry that you're unhappy." She swallowed. "But I can't swoop in and be your distraction."

"That's not what I want!"

"Well then, what?" she asked.

He looked out the window with a defeated expression. Because really, what were the options? "I don't want you to be with that guy." He swallowed.

"I don't want to be with that guy." *I want to be with you.* "I won't be the other woman."

He nodded. "No. You deserve so much more."

What else could she say? What they both wanted seemed unattainable.

TWENTY-THREE

When Colette walked in from school, Elise was waiting. Ashton Parker was due to arrive in fifteen minutes; she didn't have time to waste. She yanked out her phone and shoved it in front of her daughter's nose. "What is this?"

Colette froze, eyes wide, mouth open. She swallowed. "I can explain."

"Yes, please do. Explain how my daughter, who I know was raised not to be vulgar, has a picture online half naked for the world to view."

"I . . . I'm sorry. It wasn't . . . I didn't mean . . ."

"Aside from it being humiliating, it appears you managed to associate yourself with an apparent obsessive teenage psychopath." Elise inhaled a sharp gust of air through her nose. Thank God she was a diligent mother who kept tabs on her children's social media. "I told you nothing good would come of that boy. But no one listens to me." She flung a fist to her chest. "Did you forget that Ms. Suches told us they scout competitors for internet drama? What do you think they'll say when they see . . ." She glanced at her phone. "*Surfin Waves* posted vulgar language across a picture of you? I'll tell you what they'll think: Colette Carrington is aligning herself with a derelict!" She extended her hand out, palm up. "Hand it over."

"What?"

"Your phone. You've lost privileges."

"No! That's . . . Mom, I can't . . ."

"I don't have time to argue with you. A world-renowned dance mentor I pulled strings to hire is on his way. Hand me your phone. I'll return it when I'm certain there's no actual damage from this boy, and I can trust you to adhere to our online objectives."

"Are you kidding me right now?"

"Colette!"

She slammed the phone on the table and charged upstairs. As she changed, Elise scrolled through and found that the boy had been blocked. Additionally, Colette had since deleted and removed tags of her name from his other offending posts. Good thing Elise was so on top of everything, or she might have missed this online war. She still hadn't cracked the code on Snapchat, though. There was no telling what outrage was occurring on that site. She'd have to investigate.

Ashton arrived dressed in a tight black ensemble with a waist-length purple satin vest buttoned up the front. He was flashy and impressive. Elise prayed that he was their beacon of hope, the one who could heave her daughter out of her slump and propel her back to her rightful place in the spotlight.

Colette appeared. Ashton walked two full circles around her, like he was tabulating a mental list of her assets and flaws. He stopped abruptly, clapped his hands, and announced in his distinguished British accent, "Now we shall begin."

They walked to the basement. "A few years ago, I got a call," Ashton said, leaning against the mirrored wall. "There was a competition— not the Duncan. That's relatively new, but a similar event. You get the drift. There was a woman. Average height. Average looks. A plain, shaggy mutt trying to stand out among a stage filled with Westminster purebreds." Noticing Elise's mortified expression, he held up a hand. "Not that I'm calling anyone here a mutt, obviously. Look at that hair! Look at those cheekbones. Colette's gorgeous. That's not the point." Elise relaxed. "So, I get this call from the girl, the mutt, and she says she has exactly two minutes and fourteen seconds onstage. No solo. Not even a minor showcased combo. She was literally a backdrop."

He paused, dramatically lowered his chin. "This was her last chance. She was down to her last fifty dollars. She said, *Ashton, if I can't employ myself, I'm forced back to Claremont, Oklahoma, to take that job at the post office.*" He grimaced and held up three fingers. "We had three weeks to work. It was brutal. There was sweat. Tears. Begging. But when she got onstage for two minutes and fourteen seconds, all she did was walk from the back of the stage to the front; she did one kick." He flung his spindly leg into the air. "Just one kick." Long pause. "After the performance, she booked an agent. Got a job. All from one walk and one kick. That's what I can do for you. You will make the audience forget everyone else; they'll leave raving about the platinum-haired minx who stole the show."

"Yes!" Elise cried, sounding a little breathless.

Colette nodded, but her face blanched, and her hands clenched into fists.

Ashton, seemingly oblivious to any resistance, walked to the mirrored wall. "Let's commence." He snapped, and Colette shuffled toward the barre. "Sixteen swings, and a first, and a fifth. A first and a fifth. A first and a fifth. That's good. Long hands. Short wrists."

The hours vanished. Elise's breath was short, her heart fast, as if she were doing all the work right alongside her daughter.

After two hours, Colette, dripping with sweat, grabbed the barre and moaned. "My calf is cramping." She massaged the muscle. "I think I need to stop."

"Colette," Elise scolded, "you must be tougher than that! If you want to get noticed, the training will be tough. The body will break." *The body will break.* She hadn't meant it to be quite so intense. But her daughter was staring at her with wide, terrified eyes.

"Well, perhaps it's time to call it a night," Ashton said. Elise wanted to yell, *No!* but Colette hobbled away like a wounded animal. Ashton and Elise followed upstairs and ran into Andrew in the kitchen. Ashton gave a bow to Andrew and exited in a whirl of purple satin.

After the door shut, Andrew turned, perplexity splashed across his face. "Who was that?"

163

"His name is Ashton Parker. He's a world-famous choreographer and mentor. He's agreed to help Colette prepare for the Duncan."

Andrew stood there, wordless, obviously put off that she'd made this decision without even discussing it with him. But if he could privately dine and discuss business with Valerie, she could certainly arrange instruction for her daughter without a conversation. Elise's stomach growled. "It's almost eight p.m. Where have you been?"

"Trey asked me to pick up Kate's phone on my way home. She left it."

"At her house?"

"Uh-huh. It was on the way."

It *was* on the way from his office, and after a decade of the girls' friendship, they'd often had to go to each other's homes, but why did it make her skin prickle today? Something didn't feel right. The way her husband averted his eyes, the way he shifted from foot to foot. A sour taste filled her mouth. Ling Li's accusations crossed her mind. *An affair.* She thought again of Valerie's youthful, radiant glow, and a trickle of anxiety coursed through her. "And what? You . . . hung out over there? Chatting?" She could taste the bite in her tone. Accusation.

He jerked. Guilt? Or shock, maybe? "Actually, Kate's father was there."

Irritation plowed through her. The man never listened. "Kate's father is *dead*, Andrew."

He hesitated, fiddled with his shirtsleeve. "No. He's not."

"What are you talking about?" Bewilderment clouded her mind. She was certain that was what Valerie had told her all those years ago. How could she have gotten that wrong? She recalled all the kind sympathy she'd given poor, young, widowed Valerie. But as she zeroed in on her husband's antsy, jittery movement, a thought floated up. He was covering for her. Had she . . . *lied* about her ex?

"Kate's father is alive? And at their apartment? Where's he been all this time?"

His face sharpened at the judgment in her tone. "He's been abroad."

"I don't understand." Elise shook her head. "None of this makes sense."

"It's not our business to understand," he said matter-of-factly. But Kate had practically lived at their house. Of course it was her business! She couldn't wait to tell Ling and Susie. But he went to the table. End of conversation. "Let's eat."

She deflated. She'd have to tease out the details later. She called to Colette, but she said she wasn't hungry. She put the chicken and a large chef's salad on the table and grabbed two plates. She handed Andrew his beer, then sat and opened the napkin in her lap. After he sidestepped her inquisition about Valerie two more times, she shifted topics to Ashton and the decision to hire a mentor.

He took a long sip and placed the bottle down. He sat in silence for a moment, looking like he was fighting some internal battle.

"What?" Elise asked.

"How much does this guy cost? From the look of his outfit, he's not cheap."

Elise balked. "You said you wanted me to back off from training Colette, so that's what I've done. But if I'm not going to do it, someone else has to, and that costs money."

"What about Miss Roza? What are we paying her for?"

"We're at a critical juncture. Colette needs more. And why the sudden interrogation about my spending? You've never been so interested before, but suddenly, it's just another thing for you to criticize." Her voice shook.

He exhaled heavily. "Forget it. Let's talk about something else."

She thought he'd be happy that she was stepping back. Wasn't that what he wanted?

"Isn't there anything else you want to talk about?" He looked at her, unblinking, almost desperate. "Other than gossip about other mothers, the spring gala, and pushing our daughter to the point where she can't even walk?"

Elise flinched, her frustration funneling down to hurt. "I . . . I don't understand why you're acting like you're mad at me? Or . . . bored by me." Insecurity scraped through her. "I'm sorry if my world seems little to you. But I think it's valid to be curious if a woman I've known for a decade has misled me. And while you're out mixing and mingling with the dignified elite at your corporate law office, I'm home doing laundry, cooking meals, chauffeuring. And so, if I talk a lot about dance, that's because it's the highlight of my glamorous day. I've spent the last seventeen years molding our children, cementing our family. I'm sorry if that's not enough for you." Her voice cracked. "It used to be enough."

"You're right. I'm sorry," he blurted. He massaged his temples. His tone sounded so sincere, the back of her throat burned.

She took her napkin and blotted at her eyes. "I know I seem hyperfocused. And maybe I am, but I want our kids to have great lives. I want them to succeed."

"I know you do, but Colette and Trey are smart and kind and generous. Shouldn't that be enough? It seems like the only way you'll be proud is if Colette is a star."

"She has so much talent, Andrew. I want to give her the opportunity to reach her potential. I wouldn't be doing my job if I didn't push her to maximize her gifts."

"What about Trey?"

His words slammed into her. "What?" Her voice was thin, rattled.

"Trey. Your other child. Don't you worry you'll wake up one day and realize you've missed out on his life? Missed his basketball games to . . . what? Hover at a dance lesson?" He waited, but she was sucker punched, couldn't respond. "He's captain of his team."

"Yes! I know that!"

"But you didn't devote your entire existence to making that happen. He did it on his own." Andrew looked at Trey's empty chair, highlighting his absence, subtly asking, *Do you even know where he is?* She didn't, but that wasn't the point. He was trying to muddy her argument.

"It's different, Andrew. Trey loves basketball, but he never expressed a desire to make it to the NBA or even try for a college scholarship. Colette has said she wants a career in dance. When I told my mother I wanted to be a prima ballerina, she laughed at me! Maybe if she had shown support, I would have succeeded."

"Do you regret this life? Are you still so hung up on what you never accomplished that you'll only be happy if Colette does it for you?"

Elise sucked in a breath. "What?"

From across the kitchen table, he stared at her with disappointment, and her heart clenched tighter. He used to look at her with amazement. When they'd first met in New York City, he had told her she lit up the stage, lit up the city, lit up his heart. He'd believed in her the way no one else ever had.

They'd become inseparable, and when he had graduated from law school that year, a job in Atlanta pushed forward a conversation about their future. There was ballet in Atlanta, he'd said with a trace of worry that she would pick her career over their love. He hadn't known what had happened. How the tension between her and Gina had escalated. There had been betrayal. Lies. Elise wasn't proud of her actions, but she'd been forced into a counterattack. She wasn't going to let Gina hijack her job! But Elise's strategy had backfired, leaving her without a contract renewal, and worse—a tarnished reputation known throughout the small world of dance in the city. No one was going to hire her in New York. Andrew was the only good thing in her future. And if she went with him, she could start fresh at a new company where no one knew of the scandal. So, she had agreed to join him.

Six months later, they were married. She had just started pursuing ballet in Atlanta when she found out she was pregnant. It was another unexpected roadblock in her dance career. At first, she was upset, but Andrew was so happy, and he promised together they were going to build a family. A new life. She thought maybe it would be enough.

But now, all these years later, without even realizing it, a crack had formed between them. Slowly, underneath the daily grind, tectonic plates had shifted their foundation. He sat across from her in their designer kitchen, looking like he was disgusted with who his rising star had turned out to be. She was no longer a young beauty, no longer lit up the stage; she had not turned out to be the wife or mother he had anticipated either.

Over her dead body would she let Colette meet this same fate.

TWENTY-FOUR

Colette was not killing it on her morning run. Her calf was still sore, and she was exhausted. Another no-sleep night. She'd stayed awake until Mom had gone to bed, retrieved her forbidden phone. She'd created a new anonymous profile so she could monitor Marcus online. He continued to go ballistic, like he knew even after blocking him, she would see his bullying. She would know he was still angry. The last thing he'd posted? A picture of Colette with a giant red circle and slash through it. Underneath, he'd captioned: *Remember, I know where you live.* Was that, like, a threat? Fear. Like little pinpricks over her skin. Because who was this guy, really? She'd opened her heart to a stranger. When she couldn't hold her eyes open any longer, she'd slipped the phone back into Mom's room.

Colette accelerated hard and fast now, running her last mile in record time, ignoring her throbbing muscle. Panting and sweating, she walked in the side door and saw Mom at the kitchen table, staring at a vase of flowers, a little yellow card crushed inside her hand.

Mom jumped like she didn't even realize anyone was in the room. "Oh!" Her eyes were all red, like she'd been crying. Colette looked from Mom to the flowers.

Mom blinked with a glazed look on her face. "Have I been a good mother?"

"What?" Colette looked at the way Mom's lips shook while she squeezed the card. Something flooded through Colette. Shame. Guilt.

She was such a bitch. Telling Mom she was helicoptering and too up in Colette's business. But the truth was, Mom was always right. She'd warned Colette that Marcus would be a problem. She'd said Colette's relationship with Kate would change. She'd predicted the success of the YouTube channel. Now, trying again to handle all Colette's screwups, Mom had flown in Ashton Parker, and what had Colette done? Acted like a total wimpy bitch because she was sore, pushing Mom to back off. But what if Mom was right, again? Maybe this intensity, this never-ending training, was necessary. Colette had to stop resisting. She had to just do it. She sat down and wiped the sweat from her face. "Mom—"

"Do I . . ." Mom interrupted. "Do I push you too hard? I just . . . I just never had anyone believe in me, and I believe in you. I want you to know that." Her face crumpled.

"Mom," Colette said, her voice cracking. "You're the absolute best mother ever. I'm sorry sometimes I don't listen to you, or I argue . . ."

Mom got up and threw her arms around Colette so tight, she thought she might suffocate.

The little yellow card dropped from Mom's hand and landed on the floor. The message seemed so much scarier the way it was written in all block letters: *COLETTE IS GOING TO CRACK.*

Colette's eyes filled with anxious tears. When they pulled apart, Colette grabbed the card, her hand shaking. She crumpled it into a ball and shoved it in the garbage where no one could see it.

Mom handed Colette her phone back. "I think he's moved on," she whispered, since it appeared like Marcus had stopped posting.

Colette nodded wordlessly.

How had everything gotten so out of control? She needed to fix her life. So, she did the only thing she knew to do: She listened to her mother and focused only on her training.

When Ashton said, "Keep your eyes off the floor," Colette kept her eyes off the floor.

When he said, "Close your ribs," she closed her ribs.

When he said, "Dance beyond your bubble," she danced beyond the bubble she didn't even know she had.

"Stay in the air." She did.

"Don't come down." She fought gravity as best she could.

"Don't sit on your heels." She wasn't sure that was anatomically even possible, but she sure as shit didn't do it.

She danced until he left, pushing her homework until the middle of the night.

She ignored the fatigue that made her feel like she was climbing stairs made of marshmallows.

She ignored the pain that made her feel like she was dancing on floors made of knives.

She ignored the fear when she viewed Marcus's continued threats.

She ignored the sick feeling she got when Trey asked if she and Kate would ever make up.

She ignored the way her heart ached with loneliness for her friends. Even Kate. Especially Kate.

She ignored the way her heart raced at night when she couldn't sleep.

She ignored her GPA as it dipped.

She focused on only one thing: being the best so she could make her mother smile.

She'd never see Mom cry like that again. Not because of her.

TWENTY-FIVE

Valerie sat on the couch, conflicted by a seesaw of emotions. It was true: Chad had no arrests since his release, but she couldn't squelch the fear that his arrival was intentional. What did he want? And Andrew. She sighed. Why was the first truly good man she'd allowed herself to have feelings for married? She grabbed the remote and surfed, landing on the tennis channel, mindlessly watching the little yellow ball bounce back and forth over the net.

The door swung open, and Kate walked in. Ever since finding out her father was alive, she'd ignored Valerie, walking by with a glare of anger. Now, she dropped her bags on the floor, faced her mother with a hand on her hip. "I saw Dad."

Valerie straightened. "What?" Her heart jumped.

"He came to Volkov. He said he did a lot of research to find me because *you* wouldn't cooperate. He stayed and watched me dance because he's interested."

Valerie's lip twitched. "Kate . . ."

"No! Don't *Kate* me." She stood like a statue, cold and unmoving. "He told me everything. How he would have loved to have been here, be involved, if you hadn't abandoned him."

She stood. "That's not how—"

"He was, like, *so impressed* with my talent," Kate interrupted. "And he knew all about the Duncan. He'd looked it up. He kept saying I was good enough. I could win that hundred grand. Or fifty thousand. He would do *whatever* to help me win. It would be like he was helping me get all the money he could have made if you hadn't let him rot in jail."

Understanding landed like a brick. Chad needed money. When he couldn't sweet-talk his way back onto Valerie's payroll, he'd found out about Kate's potential cash prize. She had an overwhelming urge to grab her daughter and drive far away. But her body was trapped, like a bird in a cage. "Kate, listen to me. Please," she begged. She patted the couch next to her. Kate sighed heavily and reluctantly sat. Valerie tried to explain her and Chad's trajectory—how they had been young and Chad was irresponsible. Valerie was left holding down the fort. "I'm sorry I led you to believe there had been an accident. I was only trying to protect you."

"Protect me? From what?" She made a dramatic shrug. "He seems like a pretty great guy to me."

Of course he did. Charming Chad. How to explain? "He has a tendency to lavish love and attention and then . . . well, get a little angry if things don't go his way. I didn't want to subject you to that . . . to always seek approval, to feel responsible if he became sullen. I didn't want you to feel like he left because you weren't enough." Valerie's throat closed with emotion.

Kate's head tilted slightly, and her jaw pulsed, as if contemplating. "So, you're saying Dad took off and never tried to contact me?" Agony plowed through Valerie to have to admit this. But before she could answer, Kate shook her head. "Because that's not how he made it out."

"What do you mean?"

"I don't know. More like you wouldn't let him talk to me. Like you were always mad at him. Angry. So, you hid him from me. He said he sent packages and letters, but you never told me. Then when he needed help, you deserted him and kept me all to yourself."

"That's what he said?" Valerie tried to conceal her outrage, but her tone was sharp. "What a liar! He sent one package. One! Then nothing. Until a call for help."

Kate's eyes filled; she flew a hand up to cover her face.

Valerie's heart seized, watching torment rack her daughter. Kate wanted to believe her father had longed for her. Valerie never should have said that. But what else? Let her believe the lie? Or was it possible he had tried . . . and things had been lost in the mail? He didn't have enough postage? She pulled Kate in, stroking her back like when she was a child. She didn't know what was true, but she hated that he had barged in and upended their world. It was easier when he was gone.

Kate unhooked her arms and pulled back. She wiped her eyes with her fingertips and thrust her shoulders back. Her chin elevated slightly, and her demeanor abruptly shifted. "You can be angry, but I'm not. We're going to be super close." She nodded like she was trying to convince herself. "He promised."

A rock sank in Valerie's gut. How many times had she been that girl? Buying the used car with the broken window and faulty transmission because the salesman had flashed a smile?

But what if he'd matured? What if jail had humbled him? What if he did want to make up for lost time, and this had nothing to do with him seeking a payout? She'd deprived her daughter of a father with her lies. How could she possibly do it again with no proof he was insincere? She would call that private investigator. Collect all the information before making a decision. "Kate, I'm nervous. Give me a little time before we let him into our lives."

"No, Mom. I've already lost a decade because of your lies. I want a dad!" Her jaw jerked, and she sniffed back tears. "I need *someone* who believes in me."

"Kate," Valerie whimpered, "I believe."

It was like Valerie had said nothing. Kate plowed on. "Now that Colette's no longer my friend and Elise has ditched me . . ."

Valerie's head whipped. "What are you talking about?" Did Elise know Andrew had kissed her? And had axed Kate from their home?

"Well . . ." Kate hesitated. "She . . . She . . ." Her voice quivered.

Valerie instinctively knew she'd misconstrued the comment. This didn't have anything to do with their kiss. "What?"

"The day after the gala roles were posted, Elise and Colette told everyone that Miss Roza gave me the lead out of pity."

"What?" Valerie sat up straighter. "What's that supposed to mean?"

"Apparently, Miss Roza knew Colette had visited the Duncan headquarters, and now she has, like, a billion subscribers on YouTube, and I had a dead father that suddenly showed up. My life is a joke."

Valerie's throat tightened. A big fat knife diced up her heart. "Oh, honey. I'm sorry." She had done this to her daughter.

"Then apparently, Elise said Miss Roza knew Colette would win regionals, so she'd give me the spotlight now since it would be my only chance." Her voice splintered. "I just can't believe Elise would say that. She's been . . ." She stopped.

She's been like a mother to me. Valerie blinked back tears. It took her a moment to collect herself. To shift away from her own hurt to her daughter, who was finally speaking to her again. "You don't believe that, do you? That it was a pity lead?"

She blinked fast. "I don't want to believe it."

"Then don't." Valerie worked to control her anger.

"I'm just so mad at her for saying that!" She balled her hand into a fist. "I can't believe that someone who's always been so nice to me could just . . . change. And Colette thinks it, too." She shook her head. "I'm so stupid," she said with a bite. "I thought we were best friends, but after we both made it to the Duncan, it's like . . ." She shrugged. "Her true feelings are showing."

"What do you mean?" Valerie asked.

"I told Colette about Dad." She swallowed hard. "At first, she was supportive and all, *I'm here for you!* But then the gala routines were posted. And she totally freaked. Now, it's like I don't even exist." Her eyes flashed anger. "Trey doesn't bring me to his house anymore, like he's hiding me from them."

Valerie's heart ached. "I'm sorry. You don't deserve to be treated like this."

Kate's face crumpled, fighting tears, and Valerie's sympathy quickly turned to outrage at Elise. Again. That woman was always creating problems. For a beat, she imagined calling Elise, telling her she'd kissed her husband.

They sat in silence. The room filled with the sound of a TV reporter telling a story of a former rising tennis star. Several years ago, the two-time Wimbledon champion had been attacked by an intruder. A battle had ensued. The perpetrator stabbed the star on her left hand—her dominant hand—and inflicted severe damage to ligaments and tendons. The doctors had warned that her tennis career might be over, but now the reporter was interviewing the star, talking about recovery, rehab, and second chances.

"That's crazy," Kate said.

"What?" Valerie's thoughts had been on Elise.

Kate pointed at the TV. "The man stabbed her in her playing hand. That couldn't have been a coincidence, right? A random attack just as her tennis career was getting ready to take off?"

Valerie looked at Kate, who was intently focusing on the TV and the story of a career-ending attack. A tingle of anxiety coursed through her body. They were both so mad at Elise and Colette. Maybe for slightly different reasons, but nonetheless, the animosity was palpable. Kate's entire body was tilted forward, leaning in as she stared at the TV. And maybe it was because Valerie had just seen Chad, but suddenly she realized how much he and Kate looked alike. She shuddered, thinking about her ex's propensity for violence. Valerie squeezed her eyes shut to clear the memories and clicked the TV off. She prayed Chad had matured, had left his violent tendencies in the past. Her daughter seemed intent on reconnecting with him despite Valerie's warnings.

Kate got up. "I'm going to take a shower."

Once Kate was gone, before Valerie even thought it through, she dialed Andrew. "Do you know what your wife said about my daughter? That Miss Roza pities her because of our sad life? First, she acted like she was Kate's mother, signing her up for that competition after I told

Kate no. Then she stabbed her in the back like an immature teenager. She's hurting my daughter, Andrew. Why?"

"I . . . I don't understand."

"Kate's been through a lot. And your wife is making it worse! Kate is running into the arms of Chad because she feels abandoned by Elise!"

"He came back?" He sounded frantic. "I'm coming over." Before she could protest, he hung up. She dialed back, but he didn't answer.

Twenty-five minutes later, there was a knock on the door. Andrew's hair was ruffled, and he had on a new pair of dark-rimmed glasses that made him look studious. He scanned left and right.

"He's not here. He went to the studio and saw Kate there."

His lips pulled taut. "I don't like this. Him tracking you guys down. Showing up uninvited."

Valerie opened the door and ushered him in. They stood there, looking at each other; she could still feel the heat of his body pressed against hers, and the taste of his lips. She took a step back. "Kate's here," she said, pointing vaguely down the hall.

He nodded and sat. She whispered what Kate had said, how Chad wanted to be involved, and it came at the perfect time because Elise had turned cold to her.

He shook his head in obvious disbelief. "Are you sure? I can't imagine it. Elise loves Kate."

"Not anymore. Not when she poses a threat to Colette's success."

Andrew let out a soft sigh that sounded like defeat. He swiped his hands through his hair.

"It was hard enough when Elise was the perfect mother—everything I could never be. Do you know how tough it was to watch my daughter adore her? More than me?" Tears stung her eyes. "But it's so much worse to watch Kate be crushed and abandoned by her." She wiped her eyes. "I don't know what to do." She threw her hands out, palms up. Which was worse? For her daughter to cling to Elise or Chad?

"You have every right to be upset." He hesitated, then reached out and took her hand.

The gesture, so tender, made tears spring back to her eyes. How could such a good man be married to such an awful woman? She hated Elise! She looked away, embarrassed by her emotions. "I'm tired of being angry, but how can I trust Chad if I have no proof of his intentions? How can I forgive Elise when she's caused me so much pain? And now, she's lashing out at my daughter! I'm sorry. I know she's your wife, but she's being a bitch." She pulled her hand away. His reassuring touch was making her too honest.

He shook his head. "She's always been involved, but lately, it's like something has flipped a switch in her. It worries me. You have every right to be mad. That doesn't make you an angry person."

"No. I am. I'm mad at so many people." She stood up, pacing the living room. "No wonder Kate is searching for a parent—anyone except me. I'm an angry, awful mother."

Andrew walked to her. "Val," he said gently, "you're the only level-headed dance mom I know." He gave her a teasing smile, but she couldn't seem to break loose from the feeling that something was wrong with her. She was hard. That was why Chad had left. That was why Kate had sought refuge at the Carrington house. That was why she and her mother no longer spoke. That was why she hadn't found love.

Andrew reached over and pulled a figurine off the bookshelf. The green porcelain frog was adorned with a pink tutu and ballet slippers. "Would an angry person have something as fun as this?" He danced the frog in the air, landed it on her shoulder. "Only someone easygoing and lighthearted would keep a frog figurine on display."

Valerie couldn't help but smile. "Kate gave me that. For Mother's Day one year," she said softly, glancing in the direction of her daughter's room.

"*What?*" he said with dramatic effect. "The girl who thinks you're angry gave you a fun, thoughtful gift? Like, maybe . . . she loves you?" His face was so animated, his words so reassuring and kind.

She just stood there, looking at him. *I can't stop thinking about you*, he had said. *You make me happy*, he had said. *But no*, she had argued. She wouldn't be the one to break up a marriage. To hurt another woman. Even Elise. Who clearly had no problem hurting her family.

Her emotions were fraught; her head was spinning and exploding with the force of everything she'd learned. It pulsed up through her body with a jolt. Then, like he was reading her mind, he grabbed her and kissed her urgently.

She didn't hesitate, maybe wanting to prove to herself that she was lovable. Maybe just filled with yearning. He wrapped his arms around her, banging the porcelain frog against her spine. "Oh, sorry," he said into her lips, shoving the frog in his coat pocket.

He walked backward, lips never disconnecting, toward the couch. "No," Valerie said. "Kate's here."

His eyes darted around. Then he grabbed her hand, and the next thing she knew, they'd piled into the back seat of his BMW, the butter-leather seats at first frigid, then soon everything hot and sweaty and frantic. They were like teenagers, kissing for the first time. He kissed her neck, sending an electric jolt down her spine. Desire skidded across her skin, but as she rocked herself onto his lap, she caught sight of a water bottle on the floorboard. The name *Colette* emblazoned in pink. Kate had a matching one. The girls. She couldn't do this. "No. Stop. We can't."

He pulled back, his face full of disappointment.

"I'm sorry," she whispered as she eased off him.

"Val," he begged.

"I can't. It's not right." She exited the car before desire changed her mind.

She knew it was the right decision. As she snuck back toward her condo, she thought she'd avoided disaster until, in the light of her neighbor's window, she saw nosy Mrs. Seneca watching.

TWENTY-SIX

At work on Monday, every laboring mother was comforted and soothed by a doting partner. Everyone had a companion except Valerie. She knew she'd made the right decision, but still, she was enveloped by loneliness. Kate had disappeared once again into the depths of dance. Exiting the hospital into the parking deck at the end of her shift, Valerie didn't think her mood could get any worse. Then she saw Andrew standing by her car. He was wearing an expensive-looking overcoat and shiny shoes, straight from work. Putting up a hand, she said, "I thought I made myself clear. I can't do this. You're married."

He gestured to his BMW. "Let's go for a ride. I want to talk."

She couldn't sit in that car again and let every inch of that butter leather remind her of what she had almost done. What, deep down, she still wanted to do. She unlocked her car. "Get in. I'll drive."

He was silent as she clicked her seat belt and started the engine. Silent as she pulled out of the deck and turned onto the highway. "Where to?" she asked. He didn't answer, seeming lost in his own head. She randomly drove, and without realizing it, she wound up in the neighborhood she'd visited so many times, the location of her dream home. She slowed down as she took the winding curves, driving past brick bungalows and well-tended yards. There were rocking chairs on front porches, bicycles propped against garages, young boys tossing a football. It wasn't elaborate or magazine-worthy the way Andrew's community appeared, but it was exactly the kind of place Valerie imagined happy families lived.

"Where are we?" Andrew asked.

"Oh," she said, suddenly embarrassed. "It's . . . um . . . the house I've been thinking about buying is down this road. I don't know why I drove here."

"Show me."

She drove to the end of a cul-de-sac and parked at the curb by the "For Sale" sign.

"It's a nice, quiet street," he said. "The yard is great. The roof looks new."

"Yeah," she said. "I need to set up a time with the Realtor, so I can look inside."

He shifted on his seat, clenched and unclenched his hand. "I can help you. With the paperwork. I know it can be overwhelming."

A slow burn flooded her eyes. He was a good man. Why did he stay with Elise? "Thanks."

They drove back to the hospital in silence. The air was strained, filled with unsaid words. She pulled into the empty space beside his car and stared, giving him a final chance to say what was on his mind. He gave her a sad smile and then darted into his car. She'd started to reverse when suddenly, he honked his horn and rolled down his window. She rolled down hers. "What?"

"Come here," he said. He looked suddenly desperate, his face creased, a glisten of sweat on his brow. Reluctantly, she parked again and climbed into his passenger seat. The smell of leather and his aftershave tugged at her memories. "What?" she said aggressively. She could not torture herself anymore. "Just say whatever it is."

He locked eyes with her, and all at once, the air was electric. "I can't stop thinking about you. All weekend I thought of a million reasons why this could never work. But then I thought if we wait until the kids graduate, then I could ask for a separation. That's what I was going to say in the car, but when I saw that house, all I could think was, I don't want to wait. Two years is too long. I want to be happy now."

Valerie's head buzzed. Her skin tingled. "What?"

"I know you're hesitant, but Val, what you had with that guy . . ." He shook his head. "You deserve so much better. Let it be me." He leaned over and delicately kissed her.

Andrew would leave Elise? For her? He ran his hand along the back of her jacket, up her neck, into the base of her hair. She was on a roller coaster, rising out of the dark dungeon of rejection. But the higher she rose, the clearer the view: If Andrew left Elise, Colette would be devastated. Elise would be furious. And what revenge would they bestow on her? On Kate? With Chad's sudden appearance, Kate's emotions were already fraught. She couldn't bring more drama into their lives. Not now. Her heart thumped in her chest. She had to protect her daughter.

"No," she said. "We have to think of our girls. It's already complicated. We can't make it worse."

He nodded, slowly pulling his hand off her back. He let out a long, disappointed breath. "But I think I'm falling in love with you."

It was like a knife. Exactly what she wanted to hear, but those words would slice their worlds apart.

"I'll wait," he said. "I will."

༄

The next morning, as she got ready for work and looped her lanyard around her neck, she realized her ID badge was not attached. She searched her work bag, her purse, and her car. She recalled Andrew's hands on her back, her neck, and thought how easily it could have slipped and dropped to the bottom of his car. A tingle of anxiety worked its way up her spine. She called him. "I can't find my hospital ID," Valerie said, realizing that she was whispering. Like they were discussing a crime.

He was quiet for a beat. "Do you think it fell off when we were together yesterday?"

"Maybe?"

He let out a muffled curse. "Let me look." She heard the beeps of the car opening, rustling and shuffling. "I don't see it anywhere. Oh no. Colette went out last night and hunted in my car for a lost water bottle."

"You don't think . . ."

But hopeful words of comfort didn't come. He was wondering, Valerie assumed, how they would explain this.

TWENTY-SEVEN

Later, it would all make sense. Why everything happened the way it had. It's not like a war just starts. Everyone gets so wrapped up in their own drama. Toxicity starts sprouting, but no one sees it. Until it's everywhere. Suffocating you.

It started at the studio. It was like everyone wanted to be perfect, to prove some point, that no one could make their bodies work. Muscles cramped. Ankles turned. Miss Roza yelled. They flinched. The moms sat on the bench, their phones in their laps, because suddenly, there was nothing Insta-worthy to post.

Avery was suddenly besties with Emma, and Colette and Kate were flung to the sides on their own. Their friend group had split. And even worse, things with Trey felt effed up. He either glared at Colette or ignored her. Clearly taking Kate's side. And if Kate wasn't with Trey, suddenly, she was off meeting up with her newfound father. He was like her new BFF. Everyone had someone except Colette. Even Mom and Ashton had bonded in the goal of torturing her. Training. Filming videos. Charting food. Counting calories. Watching film. Colette wanted to freak, but anytime she started to scream, she'd remember Mom's tears, her sad voice: *Have I been a good mother?*

In school, Avery cornered Colette. Marcus had DM'd her, asking her to show Colette a message: *You screwed up my sponsor ops. FU! UR psycho! You'll regret it.* Avery stared at her with full-on fear, but what was Colette supposed to do? She'd blocked him and tried to move on. But he kept posting about her. And now he was involving her friends to make sure Colette knew he was still mad.

Two days later, a slate-blue Bronco slow-cruised through Colette's cul-de-sac. She wasn't sure what Marcus drove, but for some reason, she remembered him mentioning a Bronco. Every hair on her scalp prickled. Like she had a head full of lice. She ducked beneath their living room window and watched. The vehicle paused in front of the mailbox, idling. Stupid tinted windows. But still, she knew. What was he going to do? Put a bomb in the mailbox? Toss a match into the shrubs? Graffiti the house? The door angled open. A hand reached out. Her heart pounded. Her breath got shallow. Was she having another panic attack?

Suddenly, a loud thump of bass filled the air. A radio turned up loud, music wafting out an open window. Trey's truck flew into view, speeding toward their driveway. The outstretched hand retracted back inside the Bronco. The door slammed, the engine fired, and the driver hightailed it down the street. As he raced away, Colette saw the license plate. Florida.

Her whole body felt electric. Because what would have happened if Trey hadn't appeared? Was he, like, going to *hurt* her? All because of this stupid social media war? It was just a couple of mean posts! But what if she actually had killed some of his sponsorship opportunities? And he was for real, seeking revenge? Like, maybe she needed a restraining order? She couldn't ask Mom for help because Colette had convinced her the Marcus dilemma was over.

How had everything gotten so screwed up?

Colette needed help. She went to the only sane person she had left: Dad.

She couldn't find him. She checked in the garage and saw his car. Maybe he was on a run. She turned to go back inside but saw through the car window her favorite water bottle on the floorboard. She opened the door and reached for it. Something flickered. A hospital badge: *Valerie Yarnell.* Kate had been in their cars all the time. But not her mom. Holding the ID in her hand fired a feeling Colette couldn't name. Something dark and disturbing. She shoved it in her pocket, then in her sock drawer, keeping her mouth shut. She wasn't even sure why.

The next day after practice, Colette couldn't find Mom. She waited in the lobby. Five minutes later, Mom walked out of Miss Roza's office, saying she'd complained about the air quality in the studio. But her mouth was all twitchy, like she was trying hard not to smile. And Colette just knew: Mom wasn't worried one bit about everyone's breathing. She was up to something.

After that, practice was weird. It was like Miss Roza had put on glasses that only let her see Kate. "Kate! Your turns are very sloppy," she snapped.

"Yes, ma'am." Kate sounded petrified. She tried again.

It was flawless, but Miss Roza got this look like she was ready to unleash holy hell. "Good technique is expected, Kate! Your personality must shine through. That's what will bring this routine to life. Do you understand?"

Kate nodded, but her eyes were buggy and scared.

Colette felt all twingey. Something wasn't right.

The next day, Miss Roza pointed at Kate. "You're bloated! Your body is your instrument. I won't hesitate to make necessary changes if you continue to disappoint me."

Necessary changes? Everyone's eyes darted around. Kate stood speechless, her legs trembling. Avery burst into tears. Practice ended early.

Two days later, Miss Roza pulled Colette up to the front with Kate and asked both to dance the combination. Kate's understudy stiffened, and her face twisted in confusion. Everyone nodded in agreement. It made no sense. Colette had a good role. She wasn't the featured dancer, but she was a front-focused performer. She wasn't Kate's backup. The backup has, like, a 1 percent chance of performing. Kate would have to be dead to give up the solo. And yet, Miss Roza was making Colette practice her moves. It made zero sense. But over on the bench, Mom grinned. Colette's skin crawled.

That's how the rest of the week went: Kate and Colette both rehearsing the featured routine and both perfecting Colette's secondary role, the understudies pushed to the sidelines. No one was brave enough to ask why.

Four days before the gala, Mom came into Colette's room and showed her the Google Analytics for her channel. Subscriptions had exploded. She wanted Colette to "capitalize on the momentum" by filming an extra video each week. "Yeah," Colette said. "Maybe." When would she have time for that? But she didn't want a repeat of the tears.

So, Colette snuck into Dad's office, thinking he could tell Mom it was too much. He wasn't there. Again. She decided to write him a note. Looking for paper, she opened the top drawer of his desk. *With the actual hell?* She gasped. She reached in and pulled out a porcelain frog wearing a pink tutu. For a second, she prayed that it was random. But no. It had to be the frog from the bookshelf in Kate's house. She flipped it over and there, on the bottom, written in Sharpie, was Kate's name. Colette's stomach gripped. What did that mean?

She grabbed the frog, raced into her room, and opened her dresser drawer. She dug through a bundle of socks until she saw the small plastic hospital ID badge: *Valerie Yarnell, RN. Labor and Delivery.* And now this. The frog. From Kate's house. Two things. Two things that belonged to Valerie that had somehow wound up in her dad's possession. What was going on? She blinked back tears. A huge rodent scraped its way through her stomach, its claws piercing her insides, leaving her feeling raw and sour.

Lots of her friends had divorced parents. They were constantly bouncing from house to house. She always focused on the logistics of it—would it be hard to have all the stuff you need at any given moment? Would you have to buy everything in duplicate? But she'd never really thought about what was going on—that the parents were split. The family cracked in two. How did love just die? And if you were a piece of each of them, did that part of you crumble in the destruction, too? Could this be her future?

What she'd never really contemplated was what happened when a parent hooked up with someone else. As she stared at this strange pile of mounting evidence, her heart raced. Mom and Valerie already had a dust storm of conflict. If Dad and Valerie had crossed some line, that friction would cyclone into a tornado. What would happen to her and Kate? Would they get swept up in the storm?

All night, strange dreams played in Colette's mind: Kate's mom, young, pretty, talking to Dad. Laughing. And that day in the pool, when Kate's foot crashed into Colette's stomach and sent her underwater, struggling to breathe. She woke up with strands of blond hair scattered in her sheets, like she'd pulled at them all night. In the mirror, she saw tender pink scalp shining. An actual bald spot the size of a nickel. She rearranged her part and used the blow-dryer to angle her hair to hide it.

Days blended together as Colette worked hard to avoid Mom and Dad, suppressing the idea of their marriage in chaos, his possible cheating. Then, suddenly, it was gala night. Mom, clutching a tube of MAC Ruby Woo lipstick, shoved it in Colette's hand. "Wear it tonight."

She hesitated. How could she wear her signature red lipstick if she wasn't dancing the lead?

Mom squeezed Colette's hand so hard, a knuckle popped. "Wear it," Mom insisted, her lips pulling so tight, her teeth were a white sliver. Like an animal growling. "Promise."

"Okay." Colette's hand shook as she pulled it away from Mom's grip. "I promise."

All day it poured, creating huge mud puddles on the roads and sidewalks. Inside, dancers frantically blotted raindrops off their costumes and shoes. Backstage was chaos. The air smelled like fresh paint and panic. Volunteer moms raced set pieces across the floor and lined them up according to labels on the backs. Other mothers brought in costumes and hung them on racks. Colette walked to the warm-up room, where dancers were stretching.

Emma showed up with raindrops puddled on top of her shellacked hair and dripping down her face. "Look at me!" One set of false eyelashes had skidded onto her temple. "My face is sliding off!"

"Come on. This way. Hurry." Avery grabbed her hand, and they ran.

Outside, there was a low rumble of thunder. Colette thought about the scouts from New York. Would the weather delay flights, cause traffic jams? Was there a possibility they wouldn't be in the audience? Overhead, the florescent lights dimmed and flickered. A twenty-minute warning. She bent down and put the Ziploc bag of bobby pins she was holding into her duffel bag.

"Has anyone seen Kate?" Miss Roza called, walking toward Colette, her cheeks dotted pink. "I want to talk to you both." She swiveled her head left and right. Her voice rose, and she spoke fast. "I thought about this all day. I know it's a last-minute change, but sometimes these things happen. We must do what's best for the show."

Colette stood there, confused, all eyes on them.

"You will dance the staircase solo." Miss Roza's index finger flicked out, aimed at Colette. "You've practiced. You can do it, right?"

The row of dancers stood very still at the barre.

"What?" Colette asked, overcome.

"You will dance the solo. Kate is not ready. At practice, she has been nervous. Stiff. What if she falls going down the stairs? Not only ruin the show, but break a leg? She will do better with less pressure." She said it with her normal, harsh tone, but her face looked different. As if she wasn't sure. Colette's belly was all squirmy. Because no way would Miss Roza ever think Kate could tumble down the stairs. They'd practiced for weeks. And then Colette knew Mom hadn't talked to Miss Roza about "air quality." But this.

Colette shook a little. Because it was wrong. Manipulative. Mean. But Kate had ghosted her for so long, could they ever go back to being friends?

Colette thought of the scouts in the audience. She thought of Kate's mother and the hospital badge, the frog. Was Valerie trying to steal Colette's father? Was it that much different if Colette stole Kate's routine? And as much as Colette hated it, the truth was, Mom's advice was always right.

Colette looked Miss Roza in the eyes. "What about Kate?" she asked.

"She'll be front left. She'll be seen." She sounded like she was trying to convince herself.

The room was silent. No one breathed. Colette understood this conversation would be replayed a thousand times over chats and texts— how exactly it had gone down. She needed to be smart. "Miss Roza, this is your decision."

Her teacher hesitated, then nodded. It was done.

Overhead again, the lights dimmed and flickered. Ten-minute warning. Colette forced herself not to smile. "All right," she said softly. Miss Roza jogged off.

A loud thud made Colette turn. A dropped water bottle rolled across the wooden floor. Standing there was Kate, her face fierce like a tiger's. Kate shook her head slowly. The rhinestones of her headpiece caught the light. The air suddenly went icy cold. Kate's laser stare fired across the open space and stabbed Colette like electricity. A surge zapped the crown of Colette's head, down to the high arch of her foot. She felt both hot and cold, like she was getting the flu.

"Well," Kate said. "Now you'll get what you've wanted every minute of every day since the gala routines were posted." The air was charged, like a current had tripped on a wire. Dangerous. Ready to explode.

Colette's hands shook by her sides. "It wasn't my decision." She made sure everyone heard her say this.

"Oh, really?" Kate stomped over to the rack of costumes and shuffled the wire hangers until she found two identical red dresses. "Two staircase queen costumes. One in my size, and look! One in yours! Now tell me you had nothing to do with this!" She threw the dresses on the ground. Her whole body went completely still, except her nostrils, which flared with every breath. "All along, I've been totally clueless.

I thought we were best friends. I didn't realize you only cared about yourself. That you were secretly plotting to steal this from me. Well, fine." She threw a hand into the air. "Take it! But just wait. I'll get you back. I'll be the one who wins at regionals while you're crushed on the sidelines. Let's see who'll be crying then!"

There were gasps. Someone whispered, "That was toxic."

Avery whimpered. "Guys. Please don't fight."

The overhead lights flashed three times. Outside the warm-up room, people swarmed past, hustling into positions. A high-pitched wail blared in the distance as microphones turned on. "Ladies and gentlemen . . ." Miss Roza's voice boomed from the stage. "Our final sizzling performance . . ."

Colette felt dizzy. She didn't know what to do. The scouts were here. Curtain call was in minutes. She did feel bad. For ten years, Kate had been her best friend. Kate had been traumatized by her mom's lies. Colette didn't want to hurt her, too. But now? The bloodbath Kate had just unleashed? *I'll get you back? You'll be crushed on the sidelines?* Maybe they never were friends. Colette looked at Kate. "It wasn't my decision." Then with shaking hands, she grabbed the red dress and stepped into it.

Dum dum dum . . . The music soared into the air, but the tune was drowned out by the rushing sound roaring inside her head. The odor of fresh paint filled her nose, and for a moment, she thought she was going to be sick. She clutched at her stomach. What had she done?

Colette froze next to the curtain. All she could think about was Kate's resentful eyes, the sound of hate in her voice. A wave of nausea gagged Colette again. She didn't want Kate to hate her. Colette didn't hate Kate. She loved her. Still. Didn't she? Why had she let Mom do this to Kate? To Colette's friend?

"Go!" Emma said with a gentle push from behind. Colette climbed up the back of the giant staircase with wobbling legs. The curtain parted. The spotlight blinded her. For a second, she thought maybe she should mess up. On purpose. For Kate. To make it better.

But then she saw Mom and Ashton in the audience. Front and center. And Colette knew she had to be perfect. She counted the beats of music and began. Emotions welled up from deep in her gut—the guilt, the fear, the excitement charged through her body. Colette pranced down those stairs with swaying hips and a confident stride.

She'd never danced better.

TWENTY-EIGHT

At first it was hard to concentrate on anything happening onstage because Andrew was three rows over from where Valerie sat. His gaze kept wandering her way. The ID badge still had not surfaced. Threads of anxiety lingered between them.

Elise, radiant in a spring green sheath dress with her hair styled down, long and silky, was sitting to his right. She leaned against his shoulder and whispered something in his ear. He nodded. He'd told Valerie that they barely talked anymore; they had become like passing ships in the night. That didn't look like passing ships to Valerie. The intimacy of the gesture was like a knife plunging into her gut. They looked so . . . married. She reminded herself that she was the one who'd said no. He'd been willing to leave.

Elise reached into her purse and pulled out a phone. A red light glowed, and Valerie realized that was what she was supposed to be doing. Of course. All the good mothers recorded their daughters' performances. While she pulled out her own phone, several of the mothers surrounding her jostled in their seats. Whispers circulated. Ling Li spun one hundred and eighty degrees to face Elise. Her eyes were wide, her mouth agape. What was going on?

Valerie looked back toward the stage at the huge staircase and the cluster of dancers dressed in black. For as many of these performances as Valerie had sat through, she still struggled to appreciate what was going on. One time, Kate had told her that you were supposed to experience emotions. So, Valerie tried to interpret the sentiments onstage. Everything seemed tender and romantic—and a bit uneventful, if she was honest—yet an intensity permeated the audience. She didn't understand the commotion, but for some reason, it unnerved her.

Valerie watched Elise clench Ling Li's arm and whisper in her ear. Ever so slightly, she turned and caught Valerie's gaze. Her face looked smug. Valerie looked back toward the stage. Suddenly, a spotlight shone on Colette at the very top of the staircase. Valerie's stomach dropped. Something was wrong. Hadn't Kate said something about being the one to saunter down the stairs? While she'd been contemplating Andrew and Elise's marriage, something sinister had transpired.

Kate was at the front of the stairs, looking stunning yet filled with turmoil. She danced beautifully—even Valerie could appreciate that—but the ferocity and fury that emanated from her limbs was almost scary. Valerie straightened her spine, clenched her fists in her lap.

When the show ended, she quickly exited, then waited in the parking lot, hoping to catch Kate before she went off to celebrate. Out of the corner of her eye, she thought she saw Chad. Unease tingled in her limbs, but then Kate barreled out the back entrance with thick black makeup tears streaming down her face. She flung herself into the passenger seat, slammed the door shut, and cried out, "Drive! Go! I've got to get out of here!"

"Honey, what happened?" She craned her neck in search of Chad, but he was nowhere. Had she imagined him?

"Drive!" her daughter screamed.

"Why are you upset?"

But Kate didn't respond. She sobbed big, heavy breaths and little moans like she was in pain.

"What is it?" Valerie begged as she got into the driver's seat and started the car. "Please tell me. Let me help."

"Colette betrayed me. She ambushed me. She stole my solo."

"What?" Valerie didn't understand.

Through heaving gasps, Kate explained that at the last minute, Miss Roza had decided she wouldn't be the featured dancer. "She said I was not dancing to my full potential. I seemed nervous. With the scouts in the audience, she said it could be a disaster." Kate looked at her mother with utter devastation in her eyes. "Maybe I'm just not good enough."

Valerie shook her head. "No way. I saw you up there tonight." And even though she didn't understand dance, she could tell from the audience's reaction that Kate had done well. "You were amazing." They were both quiet for a moment, only the sound of Kate's sniffles filling the car. Valerie knew they were thinking the same thing. If it wasn't Kate's ability or preparedness that had forced Miss Roza's decision, then what could it have been?

Images flashed across Valerie's mind: Dena witnessing her with Andrew at the Mexican restaurant, her neighbor watching them kiss, the missing ID badge. And now, Kate in tears. Her stomach bottomed out. Was this simply karma? Or had Elise found out and was exacting revenge?

TWENTY-NINE

The streets were dark and wet, but inside the car, the air rippled with sunshine and warm pride. With the rain pounding against the windshield, Elise had to raise her voice to be heard, but it felt natural, like they were simply celebrating. "That was fabulous!"

In the back seat, Ashton was nestled into the deep leather. "I'm not going to say it was *all* my doing . . ." He thrust his chin into the air. "But it probably was." He laughed. Elise joined him; Andrew concentrated on driving.

She'd let him think. Analyze. Because after this performance, there was no way he couldn't realize that all her focus, her *obsession*, had proven effective. Sure, after those flowers had arrived, with the threatening message *Colette is going to crack,* she'd almost stopped. Almost given in to his criticism. But he'd denied it, said he hadn't sent any flowers. And she'd realized the card hadn't been addressed to her. It hadn't been addressed to anyone.

She'd marched over to Miss Roza and told her one of her students was jealous. Cruel. Miss Roza thought none of the girls would send that message. Naturally this infuriated Elise. Anyone involved in a cutthroat industry should understand potential malice could erupt when competition tightened. Even Elise had succumbed back in the day. Of course Kate had sent those flowers to mess with Colette's head! But Elise was gentle in her approach; the teacher barely recognized she was being swayed. And now, here they were. Tonight was perfection.

Andrew had to realize she had paved the way for their daughter to step into her passion and potential.

She would forgive him, she decided, for being absent, for being critical. Because at last, he would understand everything she'd worked so hard for. Now they could move forward in unison, instead of the bizarre alternate worlds they'd been living in. No one had warned Elise that marriage would include strange and unpredictable times when you would ricochet out of love with your spouse, then randomly contract back in. She didn't need a Triple S seduction plan. All they needed was this night. Colette's success.

They walked into the house, where they were greeted by the savory aroma of chicken marsala that Elise had slipped into the oven before they'd left. Ashton retrieved a bottle of champagne and three flutes, then popped the cork with a loud explosion. Elise turned on a playlist, and in seconds, a cheerful song filled the room. "To success," Ashton toasted with a glass raised. He flashed his oversize iPhone in the air. "And to Colette's Instagram and YouTube accounts, which are absolutely blowing up with congratulations!"

A door slammed. A slap of heavy wet shoes against the hard tile echoed over the music. Trey appeared, his face harsh, a trail of muddy footprints stamped across the floor. "What the hell happened?" he barked.

"Trey! You made a mess," Elise scolded.

"I waited after the recital, but Kate never showed up. She never came to Emma's house. We had planned to all meet up and hang out. I called and texted, and she didn't answer. Something is wrong."

Elise hated it when people called it a *recital*. A recital was for amateur dancers performing for their parents. It was a *performance*. How had Andrew and Trey shared a home with two dancers for the last fifteen years and absorbed absolutely nothing?

Trey stepped toward them. Ashton put his drink down; Andrew turned off the music. Elise stood very still.

"What happened? Why is Kate MIA?" Trey demanded.

Elise took a moment and centered herself, working to bring her tone to a casual demeanor. "Kate hasn't been spending much time with Colette lately, so maybe she didn't want to go to Emma's house and hang out."

Trey narrowed his eyes. "No, the plan was that she would be there. All her other friends were going. News flash: The whole world is not about Colette."

"Colette is your sister!" Elise exclaimed. "How about some loyalty?"

"Something happened tonight," Trey said. "Right before the curtain dropped, Kate burst into tears."

"Oh, love." Ashton floated a hand through the air. "At the end of a production, dancers are on a complete adrenaline high! There are often tears!"

"No." Trey shook his head. "Those weren't happy tears."

Tension filled the space. Elise hated the way both her son and husband were looking at her with accusation in their eyes, assuming she was responsible for the controversy. They didn't know her history; they had no right to suspect she could be vindictive.

"Well . . ." Ashton's voice punctured the silence. "It appears there was a last-minute casting change. These things happen. One must learn to go with the flow, as they say. But perhaps your Kate was a bit . . ." He twisted his hand this way and then that. "Taken off guard."

"What?" Trey and Andrew said at the same time.

"What do you mean *casting change*?" Andrew turned to Elise. "What's he talking about?"

"Didn't you notice that Colette was dancing the lead?" Elise asked. Andrew squinted like his vision had affected his hearing. "Huh?"

Elise threw a glance at Ashton. He gave her a pull of his mouth. She swallowed. "Apparently Miss Roza felt Kate had been too cautious at practice, dancing scared. She thought Kate would do better with less pressure. Colette was more equipped to perform the showcased routine." She tried to use a soft, easy voice, like this all made perfect sense.

"Miss Roza decided?" Trey's tone was aggressive. "Tonight? Out of the blue? She let Kate prepare for weeks, then right before the show started, she changed her mind?"

Elise shrugged. "Actually, Miss Roza had been critical of Kate recently. She had Colette practice the staircase solo. It was clear. She was preparing . . . for options."

"The scouts were there tonight. For the Duncan." Trey raised his voice. "And you've gone crazy thinking those scouts wouldn't see your precious Colette dancing the lead."

"Trey!" Elise threw a hand to her chest. "Watch how you speak to me!"

"Maybe shouting is the only way you ever notice me!"

She turned to Andrew for backup, but his face was creased, like he was thinking very hard.

Andrew turned toward Elise. "What did you do?" His voice was low, gravelly. On the verge of hostile. Reminiscent of New York, when all the dancers had ganged up against her.

Elise took a step back. "This was Miss Roza's decision. Not mine!"

The temperature in the room climbed higher. The oven timer beeped. They all jumped.

Ashton squirmed, sweat dotting his forehead. He reached for his glass. "Ah, but this is all good." He guzzled the last drops of champagne. "Because both girls danced exquisitely! In the end, it all worked out!"

"So, the end justifies the means?" Andrew's face was hard and unyielding.

Sometimes it does. But she held her tongue.

Trey jangled his keys in his hand. "It's not right that Colette stole her part."

"She didn't steal anything! The change was made by their instructor!" Elise yelled.

"I don't believe you," Trey said. "And I'm tired of this. You always ignoring me, now ignoring Kate and then backstabbing her. You better make this right, or I'm done." He stormed off.

Elise stood silent, gobsmacked.

Andrew's mouth opened like he was about to say something, but then he looked at Ashton and left the room.

Ashton made a dramatic grimace. "Well, party's over, I suppose." He placed his glass in the sink and hugged Elise goodbye.

Once Ashton was gone, Elise, embarrassed and building a head of steam, grabbed her phone and charged into their bedroom. Andrew was sitting on their bed, taking off his shoes. She stood in front of him, hands on her hips. "Look at this!" She waved the phone in front of him. "Colette's social media is blowing up with congratulations, but her own brother and father aren't happy."

He glared at her. "Your son just told you he feels ignored, and all you care about is Instagram likes? What the hell is wrong with you?"

"I resent that," Elise snapped. "Of course I'm upset about Trey, but he's just a lovesick teen who's hurt because his girlfriend had a setback."

"And why? *Why* did Kate have a setback?"

"I don't know what you're implying. I was in the audience with you, Andrew. I obviously didn't do anything!"

He rolled his lips in tightly. "Is it that far of a stretch? You're obsessed with Colette always being on top. And I hate to think you'd hurt someone—someone who's been like a part of this family—to secure Colette's stardom."

She put a hand to her hip and stuck out her chin, defiant. "After all your criticisms, I wondered: Was I too hard? Was I a horrible mother? But you know what? I asked Colette. And she said no. She said I was helping her, and she was grateful. You don't understand the world of competitive dance, Andrew. But I do! I'm just trying to guide our daughter to achieve her goals! Except you can't see that. You don't see anything I do. You don't see me anymore."

She was wearing a vibrant green dress that hung flawlessly to her knees. She'd gone to the hair salon for a blowout, painted on her berry-plum lipstick. She'd felt like a million bucks, and she'd seen men in the audience take notice. She'd witnessed women's approval. Not her husband's, though. He hadn't batted an eye or said a word. But the night was about Colette. And if he'd finally seen their daughter's potential, recognized all of Elise's contributions, that would have been enough. But now, she realized he hadn't. He still didn't get it. Especially not her role. She was completely invisible to him.

She took a deep breath and steadied her voice. "You've created this image in your mind that I'm a ruthless, obsessed mother. Do I advocate for Colette? Yes. But you know what? Lots of mothers do. In fact, did it ever occur to you that maybe all this was Valerie's doing?"

"What?" His face shifted from anger to disbelief.

"Valerie doesn't want Kate to pursue dance. So, all this time you brand me as fanatic for helping Colette achieve her dreams. But Valerie is fixating, too. She's pushing Kate *against* her dreams. Kate told me that her mother insists she do something practical. So, which is worse, Andrew? To push a child toward their dreams? Or to push a child away from them?"

Andrew fell silent.

The overhead vents suddenly turned on, sending a flow of air down, fluttering the bedroom drapes and rippling goose bumps across Elise's skin. "Is it so far-fetched to wonder if maybe *Valerie* went to Miss Roza and suggested the swap?"

He shook his head. "That's absurd. Even if she doesn't like the idea of a dance career, she wouldn't hurt her child."

"No?" Elise said with dramatic flair. "So, lying about her father's death is not hurting her child?"

His eyes bugged out. "You know nothing about the decisions Valerie had to make to protect Kate!"

"Oh, but you do?" Elise locked eyes with him. Adrenaline pulsed through her veins. Valerie was a liar. Concocting stories to get sympathy. All those hours Elise had spent helping her find a school, get financial help because she felt bad for a young widow. And now she was using some story to garner compassion and attention from her husband! She was a fraud! A deceiver! Just like Kate—the way she'd manipulated Miss Roza to cast her as the lead.

And then, like the devil had ears, her phone lit up with a message. The name on the screen: *Valerie*.

THIRTY

Did you tell Miss Roza to swap roles tonight, so Colette could shine in front of the scouts? Valerie banged out a text to Elise.

She and Kate sat in the car, waiting for a response. For a few minutes, the little word *delivered* appeared under the message, but no dots flashed, indicating no forthcoming reply. They went inside. Kate flopped on the couch, her face smeared in drippy makeup. Valerie looked at her daughter with an overwhelming feeling of ineptitude. She'd brought so much distress on Kate with her lies. And now, this. Another deception. Not caused by her, but still, she felt strangely responsible for all her daughter's agony. She couldn't fix the mistake about Chad, but she was determined to rectify this.

She had just put on the kettle when her phone dinged.

I'm shocked that you would suggest such a thing. I've been nothing but supportive. For years, we've opened our home to Kate for countless meals and sleepovers. I've cheered Kate on at every performance. I even helped her prepare her submission for the Duncan.

Don't you think you should have checked with ME before you entered MY daughter into a competition? Valerie responded, acid swirling in her stomach.

Maybe if you ever came to practice, I would've had a chance to mention it.

Valerie gasped. *What a judgmental bitch!* She pounded out a response:

While you and your overzealous friends are videoing lessons, I'm working an actual job. But even if you think I'm not around, don't think I haven't heard all the Volkov Studio gossip. I know that ever since Kate got a solo, you've disparaged her abilities. And while you bragged about the donations you recently made to the studio, everyone knew it was a bribe to get your daughter back into the lead role.

Elise responded immediately:

We have made monetary contributions to Volkov Studio for years! Our most recent donation was just another contribution in a long line of financial support. You're fabricating these accusations because you want to take the spotlight off your own deceit. Letting the poor girl believe her dad was dead. No wonder she couldn't perform well at practice. And now, more deceit. Laying blame on me when it was YOU who asked Miss Roza for the swap. Because YOU don't want Kate to succeed in dance!

"Oh my God," Valerie said as she slammed her phone down on the counter.

Kate's head popped up. "What?"

"She's trying to say that I convinced Miss Roza to swap your roles because I want you to give up dance. The nerve of her!"

Kate's face sunk back onto the pillow. Her chin and mouth were hidden behind the dark blue microfiber throw. "But you didn't, right?" Her voice was soft and muffled.

"Didn't what?" The kettle boiled. Valerie turned off the burner and poured the water into two teacups. Understanding dawned. Valerie had misled Kate about her father; now she'd question all of Valerie's actions and motives. Disgrace plummeted in her gut. "Of course not."

She set the cups on the coffee table. She sat on the couch next to Kate, a brick of sadness weighing her down. "I don't always understand your passion for dance, and I do worry it would be a hard career, but I'd never do anything to hurt you. Everything with your dad was done out of love to protect you. I know that's hard for you to understand, but I swear, it's the truth."

Kate sat up, her smeary eyes looking earnest. "I know you say that, but he's been so nice. So interested in my life. He texted that he thinks Colette did it, arranged the swap. He's super pissed because he knew the scouts were there. He doesn't want anything to mess up my chance to win the Duncan."

Unease tugged at Valerie's core. So, he was at the performance. And now he's pissed. Because there was a potential roadblock to a cash prize? Or just because he now cared about his daughter? Either way, she knew how something could trigger his vengeance. "Maybe you shouldn't discuss this with him."

"You don't want me to have a relationship with him! You don't want me to dance! What am I supposed to believe?"

"Believe *me*!" Valerie begged. *Not Chad. Not Elise.*

Her phone pinged again. She glanced down, expecting more vitriol from Elise, but it was Andrew. Before she could read his message, there was a knock on the door.

She opened it to find Trey, worry in his eyes. "Kate?" He ran to her.

Andrew on her phone; his son at her door. Elise and Colette across town.

How had they tangled such a web?

THIRTY-ONE

The afterparty was insane, but it was hard to celebrate when Colette kept waiting for Kate to show up and unleash on her. But Kate was nowhere. Way past Colette's curfew, she crept in the back door and stumbled down the hallway when she heard, "Colette, c'mere." Dad sounded kind of slurry. She noticed an empty glass sitting on the end table. "You did great tonight," he said.

"Thanks." She sat across from him.

He pulled his foot up and rested it on the other knee. "I heard about what happened." *Crap.* Sometimes it really sucked having a lawyer for a dad because everything sounded like a cross-examination. "Trey said Kate was pretty upset."

"I guess. But I mean, she had to know it was a *possibility*."

"Really?" He adjusted his glasses. "Why?"

"Well . . ." Colette shifted in her seat. "Because Miss Roza hasn't been happy with her practice. And she started prepping me for the solo, too. So, it seemed obvious, you know?" Heat spread up her neck into her face, sweat beads forming along her hairline.

He nodded slowly. "Did you agree?"

"Agree? What do you mean?"

"Did you agree that Kate's practice was sloppy?"

Her scalp got all tingly. Why was she on trial? "I don't know . . ." She looked away, pretty sure if he looked into her eyes, he'd know the truth: Kate's dancing had been flawless.

"What're you doing?" His voice was sharp. He stood up and pulled her hand out of her hair. "What in God's name?" He leaned closer. "Colette, you have a bald spot. Is this . . . Are you pulling your hair out?"

She felt caught, like she'd been stealing, or doing drugs, or lying on the stand. She looked away, embarrassed. "No. I'm not. I mean, I didn't realize . . ."

He gently released her hand and sat back down. "Are you okay? Are you caught in the middle of this? You weren't pressured into convincing your teacher to make the switch, were you . . . ?" He let the sentence dangle, like it was a question.

Colette shook her head. "No. I had no idea." Her face felt on fire. It was true, she reassured herself. Even if she'd noticed something suspicious, she wasn't involved.

He took off his glasses, cleaned the lenses, then slowly slid them back on his face. "Kate's been your best friend for years. It's been tough for her lately—her dad, now this. She needs a friend. I think you should apologize."

"Why do I have to apologize?" She stood up, protesting. "I didn't do anything wrong."

He had a strange look on his face. "I believe you. I do. It's just . . . complicated. I know you're not at fault, but if someone doesn't make the first move, it might . . . fester."

With an uncomfortable realization creeping up her spine, she knew. He'd figured it out. That Mom had manipulated Miss Roza into giving Colette the solo, but Mom would never admit it. So, he was asking Colette to fix it. Kate had not only been her best friend, she was Trey's girlfriend, and probably felt like a daughter to Dad. But Mom had backstabbed Kate at a time when her life was already in turmoil. And somehow, Colette was supposed to fix it.

THIRTY-TWO

All day Monday, Colette dreaded seeing Kate, knowing she had to apologize like Dad had asked. As if a lame-ass sorry could fix all the drama. But lately, he was the only one on her side, so what choice did she have?

Walking to biology, Colette saw Kate by her locker. "Hey." She threw on a casual tone, like everything was chill. "We missed you at Emma's."

When Kate whipped her head around, her face was straight-up scary. "Are you serious right now?" She slammed her locker shut with a loud crash. Squeaking shoes halted. The clink of lockers stalled. Muffled chatter paused. All heads craned in their direction.

Words caught in Colette's throat; a pulse of fear flooded through her. Why did she feel like she wanted to run? Why did she feel so . . . freaked? "Look, I get why you're upset about Friday." She swallowed. "But it wasn't my idea."

Kate let out one hard laugh. "Ha!" It was creepy. She lowered her chin and looked Colette in the eye. "It was easy to be best friends when you were the star."

Harsh fluorescent light flickered off the freshly buffed linoleum, blinding Colette. She was used to the spotlight, but not like this.

Kate took a step toward her. "But suddenly, I wasn't just the sidekick anymore. Miss Roza noticed how hard I'd worked. Then I got accepted to the Duncan. And I don't think you liked that one bit. I don't think you want a friend who's as good as you, do you?" Her voice was gravelly and menacing. Like an aggressive dog. "Who knew being upstaged would unleash your psycho-bitch tendencies? That you'd royally screw me over?"

The air was thick, hot, and suffocating. Colette glanced at the glass-enclosed fire alarm with a strange urge to pull the lever. An escape. But hundreds of stares froze her in place. "Look . . ." She placed a fist on her heart. "I swear, I had nothing to do with the switch. Can we just forget it and go back to the way it was before?"

Something happened to Kate's face. Her eyes narrowed to tiny black slits—a panther, ready to pounce. "I'll never be your friend again," she said. "I can't believe you're so obsessed with being the best that you'd take something from me. Something that was *mine*." A mottled look of rage flushed her face. "I hate you."

Someone in the crowd gasped.

Colette's vision got blurry. Her heart beat all the way into her ears. She pressed a hand against a cold metal locker to brace herself. She knew she shouldn't say it, but she was so tired of being the one accused. "You think I took something from you, but maybe you should look at what your family is trying to take from mine!"

"What?" Her wrath momentarily morphed into confusion.

"Your dad rises from the dead, and your mom goes running to *my* dad for comfort? Why is your mom's frog statue in my dad's office, huh? Why did I find your mom's hospital badge in my dad's car? *Huh?* Maybe *you* should stop blaming *me* for everything, and take a look at your part in this whole mess!" Sweat dripped down her back. "Because I think *your mom* is scamming on *my dad*! And FYI: He's *married*!"

"Shiiiiiiiit," someone said, dragging it out long and dramatic.

Overhead, the bell rang, loud and clanging. No one moved.

Kate pushed a sweaty strand of hair off her forehead and pulled her mouth into a wicked smile. "Fine. Try to embarrass me. But everyone knows that you stole that role from me. Mark my words: You'll never do that again. I hope you never dance again!"

Kate's words smothered Colette. Her lungs crushed in; she needed air. She pushed through the crowds, elbows and backpacks knocking her. People yelled, but her head was filled with static, like bad reception. The only thing she heard were Kate's words that would play out long and hard into the future:

I hope you never dance again.

THIRTY-THREE

Elise was sitting at the kitchen table, rewatching the video from Friday's performance, when Colette wandered in from school, Ashton following behind. He talked animatedly, waving his phone, but her daughter's face looked pale and drained. "What's wrong?" Elise asked.

Colette put her backpack down. "Kate is, like, really mad at me. About the gala." Emotion crushed her face.

Actually, this was good. A clean break between the girls. Now Kate couldn't use their friendship as a ploy to undermine or steal her daughter's glory. But Elise couldn't say that. Not yet.

Ashton gave Colette a half hug. "I know you feel awkward about the switch, but look how much attention you've received." He flashed his phone again. "Look how many followers you've gained just since Friday night!" Elise walked over and glanced at the screen.

The side door swung open with a creak, and Andrew walked in with his work bag slung over his shoulder. He was home early, and Elise hoped that maybe, like her, he'd been unable to focus with so much strain between them. Perhaps he was finally ready to reconcile.

Ashton continued to scroll, landing on a reel of Colette outdoors, under a blue sky, doing a double pencil turn. "This post was from two weeks ago, but now suddenly, people are reposting."

Andrew walked over. He reached down and took the phone out of Ashton's hand, which Elise thought was obnoxious, but she bit her lip. *God*, she was trying.

He studied the post for what seemed like an extraordinary amount of time before speaking. "This person captioned the photo, *Here's @tinydancercolette killing it at Chastain Park.*" Andrew's eyebrows scrunched. "How did they know it was at Chastain Park?"

Ashton rolled up the sleeves of his paisley print shirt. "Some social media sites have GPS tracking. You can pinpoint location from the IP address of a post."

Colette stood, quietly listening.

"That sounds dangerous." There was a slight uptick in Andrew's tone, concern. "That someone can track you so easily."

Ashton waved a hand through the air dismissively. "No. We *want* people to find Colette! It'll help build her brand. We've got two more weeks to really increase her following." He turned toward Colette. "Today, after practice, let's film another YouTube segment. Capitalize on the momentum from Friday night."

"I think that's a wonderful idea," Elise said. "Don't you, honey?" She looked across the kitchen at her daughter.

"Okay," Colette said, but her thoughts seemed a million miles away.

"No," Andrew said harshly.

Elise, Ashton, and Colette all turned toward him.

He raised his hand in a clear show of authority. "I think we need to stop all this online posting." He sliced his hand through the air like a chop. "Colette is fifteen years old! And people can track her location? That's asking for danger. There are crazy people in this world." His voice thundered across the marble kitchen.

Elise stood, shell-shocked by his sudden assertion. "We can't just stop. Her brand is building. The judges . . ."

"Safety comes first. I need to look into this," he said abruptly with finality. "But for now, no more." He turned and disappeared down the hallway.

Slowly, Colette closed the refrigerator door and walked, as if in a trance. Elise hated thinking how discouraged her daughter must feel.

After all her hard work, to be forced to stop. She was furious at Andrew for taking out his anger about their fight on Colette. Like he suddenly had all the say? That's not how their marriage worked. She didn't like all these changes he was suddenly imposing. The silent treatment. Criticism. And now, dictatorial rule.

"I guess I never thought it could be dangerous. People post stuff all the time, right?" Colette said.

Her daughter looked so contemplative. Elise put an arm around her. She wanted to say, *Your father is angry at me, but he's taking it out on all of us.* Instead, she said, "Dad doesn't understand how all this works—the platform, the opportunities."

Ashton tilted his head, his silver swoop of hair flopping over his forehead. "One can't be discovered if one is hidden away."

"But, like, is it true? That someone could . . . find me . . . from a post?" Colette's expression was unreadable. Intrigue? Or alarm? "Like, even if he lives far away?"

Elise whipped her head toward her daughter. "He who?"

"Oh, uh, you know—I meant, like, maybe that's how Kate's dad found them. Online." Colette shifted uncomfortably. "I'm just asking, like, *anyone* could find me?"

Elise couldn't decipher her daughter's point. Could she be worried about that stupid surfer? But he'd been blocked on Colette's phone, and the last several times Elise had checked, there'd been no new activity between them.

Ashton's gaze drifted from Elise to Colette. "We must decide how to proceed. If you prefer, we will curtail our current social media agenda. If you feel . . . at risk."

"But regionals . . ." Agitation trickled through Elise's limbs, making her hands shake.

Colette averted her gaze, lost in thought. "I . . . I think it would be good to keep posting. Keep building . . . but Dad . . ."

Elise released a breath of relief. Her girl got it. She understood.

Ashton raised a long, delicate hand and lowered his voice. "Well," he said, "we could proceed as planned. With caution. And discretion about what we share with Mr. Carrington."

Colette stood very still; Elise knew this was a defining moment. What would she be teaching her daughter if she advocated lying? But did she want to teach her daughter that just because Andrew was a man, he thought he could overrule them? She was conflicted. Could it be unsafe? Before she could say anything, her phone rang. She answered. "Sus, can I call you right back?"

"No. I think you need to hear this," Susie said.

It was unlike her friend to be forceful, so Elise stepped aside. "What is it?"

"Elise, maybe I was wrong about Andrew, after all." What her friend told her made her stomach drop, her mind crash, her knees go weak. It changed everything.

Elise ended the call, looked at Ashton, then Colette. "Let's proceed as planned. Now."

THIRTY-FOUR

Elise couldn't concentrate. While Ashton worked with Colette in the basement, her mind replayed on a loop what Susie had told her. Avery had come home from school so upset; there'd been a terrible fight between Kate and Colette in front of everyone. Lots of harsh words . . . and accusations . . . about Valerie and Andrew. Elise's mind swirled. Her mouth was dry, and her throat was tight. Exactly what was going on between that wretched woman and her husband?

"Well," Ashton said, "I guess we're done."

Elise glanced over and saw Colette hanging on to the barre like it was a crutch, panting. Why was she so winded? Elise would have to up the cardio workouts. She escorted Ashton out, then zigzagged through their home, hunting her husband, prowling for answers. Silence. He must have gone for a run. Frantically, she scoured for evidence, bolting to his closet, pushing hanging shirts to the side, looking for anything to convict him. She tore through his drawers, his briefcase, his laptop. She didn't even know what she was looking for, but she was desperate to find something—maybe a piece of Valerie's jewelry or her scent on his clothes. But plain, boring Valerie probably never even wore jewelry or perfume. The front door opened; then footsteps clomped across the wooden floor. Quickly, she closed his drawers and grabbed a laundry basket, pretending to collect dirty towels.

He walked into the room sweaty and still breathing heavily.

She cleared her throat. "Can you explain why Valerie Yarnell's hospital ID badge was in your car?" He gave her a blank stare, and in that second, she prayed, *Please*. Maybe Susie had gotten it all wrong. Adrenaline buzzed in her ears as she waited for him to deny everything.

He stood very still and looked thoughtful. "Kate's father had been absent for years, but with his return, Valerie asked for help with parenting logistics. Was he allowed to see Kate at any time? Was he obligated to give child support?"

Elise recoiled. Not a denial. What, then? She crossed her arms.

"Well, that led to a discussion about her buying a house."

"And?" Elise scowled.

"We drove to the neighborhood. I offered advice about mortgages, taxes. She must have dropped her badge inside my car." He walked past her, heading to the shower, but she put a hand up to stop him.

"How does a conversation about child support transition into real estate?" she pressed with a sharp edge to her voice.

He immediately took a defensive stance, shoulders back, chin up, and retaliated. "That's what happens when a conversation is not limited to a single topic, like it is around here."

She flinched. He was the one under fire here, not her. "Don't you think it's convenient that this man who was supposedly *dead* suddenly appears? It sounds like a perfect excuse to go after a handsome rich man to rescue her!" Her heart thumped in her chest. "Are you that stupid? Did you sleep with her?" The words just slithered out of her mouth—tormented and terrified. Had he been conned?

"No!" But his face failed to match his denial.

Tears brimmed. "But you want to?" Her head was woozy, her lungs tight. How could he want Valerie over her? Valerie, who never worked out, who never dressed on trend, who never wore makeup or pruned her eyebrows. "Do you think about *her* when you're with me?"

"What is this, high school?" He shook his head in disgust. He charged through their bedroom into the master bath, his running shoes clomping across the tile.

"It's not an unreasonable question!" She raced after him. "You're the one who's different lately. Not me. You're not interested in our marriage. In us. In this *family*."

At the word *family*, his face softened. He closed his eyes and inhaled through his nose. "I love this family; of course I do."

"Do you love *me*?" Her voice was pitiful, like she was begging her own husband to love her.

Several seconds passed. Elise's stomach plunged, unsure of whether she wanted the truth.

He sighed. "Yes, I love you, but Elise, we have problems. This isn't working. I tried to talk to you about something a few months ago, something really important, but you never listened. If it's not about dance, you tune it out."

Her blood was throbbing in her ears. "So what? You decided to talk with Valerie instead?"

"No. I didn't *decide* anything. We just ran into each other a few times and chatted. She actually listens."

She put her head in her hands and started crying. What if . . . What if he were going to leave her? Her carefully constructed life would crumble. "Please, Andrew. You can't do this to me. I haven't done anything wrong!"

"You're putting so much pressure on Colette that she's pulling her hair out. Did you know that? She has a bald spot!" His hand shot up to the crown of his head.

"What?" Elise gasped.

"I looked it up. It's a sign of anxiety. Listen to me. Stop worrying about yourself and think of our daughter. She's under too much pressure." His voice was harsh but also pleading.

A clamp tightened around her throat. She couldn't talk. Tears filled her eyes. She remembered her days in New York, all the stress, the constant nervousness of losing her contract with the company, the pressure to always be the best, to retain her spot on the stage. Yes, it had pushed her to extremes, to things she wasn't proud of. But Andrew didn't know about that. And it would have been worth it. If she hadn't gotten caught. Was Colette too young for such intensity?

She'd asked Colette if the training was too much, and she'd said she was fine. Andrew didn't understand the commitment of an elite athlete. But she couldn't tell him that. He'd go running into the arms of Valerie, a woman who knew nothing about the harsh reality of competitive dance.

Andrew walked toward the shower, the moment gone. The opportunity lost. All because she was thinking of that horrible woman.

Elise paced the bedroom, seething. How stupid she'd been! She'd almost lost him; how could she have been so blind? After all she'd been through. She'd been robbed of her dreams years ago in New York and had promised herself she'd never let that happen again. But she'd been so focused on protecting Colette from Kate, she'd failed to realize another danger that threatened her: While Kate was trying to hijack Colette's spotlight, Valerie was seducing Andrew. That family was stealing everything that was hers! She balled her hands into fists.

She wasn't about to let that continue.

There was a squeak of the faucet, then the drum of water. Steam escaped from the bathroom in a swirly white cloud, funneling into the bedroom. Could Ling Li have been right all along? She needed to lure him back in? Make him remember all the things he'd loved about her and all the things Valerie could never be. Did this boil down to one more competition? Because Elise knew how to win. She inhaled deeply, then exhaled all her fears and insecurities. Andrew didn't want an angry and obsessed wife. He wanted present and pleasant. She could do that.

She waited until the shower stopped. He emerged with a towel wrapped around his waist, water droplets spilling off his hair. Slowly, she walked toward him and gently laid a hand on his wet shoulder. "I'm sorry, Andrew. I'm sorry I've been overly focused on dance. I had no idea she was pulling her hair. I promise I'll ease up. I'll ask Ashton to cut back training. I'll let Colette have more time to rest, and I'll spend more time with you. And Trey. I'll listen and be present. We can make this work. This family can work." She wrapped her arms around him, and he didn't push her away. She rested her head against his bare chest. She would do whatever it took to keep what belonged to her.

THIRTY-FIVE

Valerie dropped Kate off at school, her daughter exiting the car with only a silent wave. Ever since the gala, Kate had seesawed between sullen and angry, sad and spiteful. It worried Valerie that her daughter had not only pulled away from her but fractured ties with Colette and Elise as well. She barely saw Trey and was spending more time with Chad. Valerie fretted over their growing connection, his potential influence, but what could she do? She couldn't get a restraining order; since his reappearance, he hadn't technically done anything wrong.

Then, amid the worry about her daughter, Andrew had messaged her: Elise is suspicious of us.

What happened? What did she say? But her reply text had gone unanswered for three days. She stopped at her favorite tucked-away breakfast café, deciding to drown her worries in coffee and food. At the entrance, a strange premonition that someone was behind her crawled up her spine. She turned, and there she was: Elise Carrington, as unexpected as a slap across the face.

"Oh." Valerie pulled a hand up to her mouth, startled. Elise was, as ever, effortlessly pristine in the perfect pair of dark-wash jeans, a camel-colored button-down jacket, hair pulled into a low bun, and large leopard-print earrings dangling from her lobes. Who wore such an extravagant accessory on a weekday morning to drop the kids off at school? They stood there, the door still propped open, Valerie halfway inside the small restaurant. Andrew's text flashed through her mind: Elise is suspicious of us.

"Thank you," Elise finally said, taking the door in her own hand. She smiled, her white, even teeth sparkling like those of the former stage star she was.

Valerie attempted to escape into the line at the counter, but the minute her back was turned, she heard Elise's voice, sharp and insistent. "Valerie!"

She took a long, slow inhale through her nose and turned. "Yes?"

Elise took an aggressive step toward her, confrontation splashed across her face. "I was wondering if we could have a little chat?" She tilted her head in the direction of a small circular table in the corner.

"Actually, I'm on my way to work. I don't have time for a sit-down. Sorry." She entered the line to order.

"I thought it would be more discreet at a table, but here's fine. I have a few things I'd like to discuss, and I feel it's a bit more mature to broach a conversation in person rather than via text message." She tilted her chin up with self-righteousness.

The criticism slammed into Valerie like a punch.

Elise inched closer. She had her hands clasped in front of her like she was holding an imaginary axe, ready to attack. "Can you explain why your hospital ID badge was inside my husband's car?" The exhale of her breath rippled through Valerie's loose hair.

Anxiety swirled in Valerie's stomach, churning hot and sour. The look in Elise's eyes was aggressive, territorial, angry. A chilling fear emerged inside Valerie. How had Andrew answered this question? Elise was obviously trying to catch them in a lie. Adrenaline pumped through her body, hard and fast. She touched the café counter to steady herself. She had to get this right. The answer sparked as if he'd whispered it in her ear. "I reached out to Andrew for help with legal questions."

"About your risen-from-the-dead ex?"

Valerie shrank; heat flooded her face. That woman didn't deserve any explanation. She remained silent.

"Andrew's a personal injury lawyer," Elise said with a smirk. "He can't help with your relationship lies."

"He helped me navigate some questions about Kate's father's past." Valerie turned away, but Elise grabbed her shoulder.

"In his car?" Her eyes flashed.

"No." She was trapped in the line, Elise hovering over her, and patrons all around. So, she contemplated, hoping a version of the truth was where he'd gone. "I also asked Andrew for advice about buying a house. It's overwhelming—mortgages, interest rates, and taxes . . ." Her skin felt torn off, exposing her vulnerability. She had no one else to turn to. Her voice cracked. "I think because Kate has always been like a part of your family, he extended that friendship toward me. We drove to look at the house. I guess the ID badge dropped in his car that day." She was horrified to feel tears blur her vision, and she blinked fast, suddenly disturbed by what she and Andrew had been doing while his wife—evil as she may be—sat home, clueless. It was wrong. Like something Valerie would judge if she saw it playing out on TV.

"Yes, he's a good man," Elise said sharply. "But he's my man. My husband." She waved her left hand in the air, flashing an enormous diamond ring.

"Of course he is." The truth of that crashed through Valerie like a blow to the back. He'd said he would leave. But he wouldn't. Because Elise always won.

"I want your little *friendship*," Elise said the word with a bitter smack, "to end. Now. Understood?"

An urge bolted through her to tell Elise: *He wants me. He said he'd leave you.* But she knew that would do no good. The tension was high enough. She stepped away.

The short-order cook cracked two eggs and poured them on the hot griddle with a hiss, a cloud of steam popping into the air. The line edged forward, the strong smell of breakfast foods permeating the air. "The other thing I want to discuss is our daughters," Elise said. "Did you know about their fight yesterday at school?"

"What?" Valerie was staggered by the abrupt change in topic.

"According to all the bystanders, this was not biased testimony only from Colette."

"Testimony?" Valerie interrupted. "What is this, *Law & Order*?"

Elise pursed her lips. "Well, everyone was quite shocked by the sheer malice and aggression that came out of your daughter's mouth." She nodded sanctimoniously. "Kate said that she hated Colette and hoped she would never dance again."

A cold shiver trickled across Valerie's skin. She thought of the hostile look in Kate's eyes all weekend. All those diary entries and how Kate had adored, practically worshipped, Colette. Until she felt rejected. Her recent time spent with Chad—who could be aggressive and hostile. His text that he was pissed about the swap. Had he filled her head with wrath?

"Several people heard," Elise continued. "Not to mention, after Miss Roza swapped roles, Kate told Colette she would win at the Duncan, and Colette would be crushed on the sidelines."

"I'm sure she meant crushed emotionally . . ." Valerie's voice wobbled. "Like how Kate felt after Colette danced her routine at the gala."

"Regardless of what she meant, it sounded like a threat." She ended the word with a harsh *T*.

Valerie was silent, her mind exploding with the realization that Andrew might be the least of her problems. But Elise had no idea about Kate's journals. Or the increasing spite written inside them. The man at the counter looked at Valerie with his pad and pencil and asked for her order. "Egg and cheese on a sesame bagel," she said, sounding shaky. "To go." The cook cracked an egg. Another hiss filled the air.

Elise placed a cold hand on Valerie's arm. Her nails were manicured into sharp daggers. "Andrew and I encouraged Colette to mend fences with Kate."

"That's not what I've heard," Valerie countered. "Kate said you've completely ousted her. Thrown her out like yesterday's garbage."

"She threatened my daughter! I can't go on being Kate's mother—doing your job—when she's bullying my own flesh and blood!"

Valerie recoiled, stricken. Her face flamed with fury.

"She can't sleep, can't focus. Kate is creating so much anxiety that Colette's been pulling her hair out! Kate needs to stay away from Colette. And Trey, too." She pointed a finger like a knife. "And *you* need to leave my husband alone!"

All eyes turned their way.

Valerie grabbed her paper-wrapped bagel, slapped money on the counter, and stormed out. She raced to her car and slammed the door. The engine revved; she skidded away. Her breath was short and choppy, her heart rate ragged. She was furious. How arrogant of Elise to dictate that she and Kate were the toxic ones. When Colette had backstabbed Kate! When Elise had treated her daughter like trash!

But as she drove, Valerie thought about what Elise had accused Kate of saying. Her daughter wasn't vengeful. Was she?

She wasn't hateful. Right?

She could never be violent. Could she?

A dark shiver crawled through her as she thought of Chad's instability: his fluctuating moods, his propensity for high-spirited adoration followed by crashing rejection, then vindictive promises of retaliation. But Kate was not her father. Even if they did share the same DNA.

She drove away, her throat tightening in alarm.

THIRTY-SIX

Since the fight, everyone avoided Colette. Avery was glued to Emma. Trey and Kate were a team. Colette had no one except Ashton, her mother, and forty thousand YouTube followers demanding more and more content. But filming and posting videos had become a secret mission because God forbid if Dad found out. Everything sucked. She was so . . . freaking . . . tired.

She had a minute-by-minute schedule of dance, stretch, strength, cardio, nutrition, hydration, and social media brand building. The other day, her teacher asked where her history essay was, and she almost cried. Today, after Ashton left, she decided to use her twenty-minute scheduled shower time to scratch out that assignment. She zoomed through the kitchen to get her backpack. Mom was at the counter, dicing vegetables.

Trey came in the side door and stared at Colette with a weird look on his face. It was so sad—how they'd become like strangers. Or worse.

"What?" Colette asked. "What have I done now?"

He tossed his keys onto the counter. "I saw you talking to Bates Herndon at school." His words were harmless. His face implied something else. Was everyone watching her?

"What's wrong with talking to Bates Herndon? Why am I being monitored?"

"Everyone knows Bates sells pills, Col. You're jumpy all the time now. You barely sleep. And when you do, it's like you're in a coma. You're acting all jacked up, and I was worried."

"What the hell?" She tried to conceal her complete desperation with outrage. "You know me better than that! I don't put anything processed in my body. You think I'd do drugs?"

Mom's face shot up. She backed into a chair; it toppled and crashed.

"Forget it," Trey said harshly.

Colette's heart cracked. Because Trey did still love her. But she was pushing him away. Before she could apologize, he was out the door.

Mom's face turned white. She turned toward Colette. "Who is this boy? Why are you talking to him?" Her hands trembled; she dropped the knife she was using to slice onions. "Colette," she said, her voice full of questions.

"I'm not doing drugs." Colette tried to escape to her room, her twenty minutes of homework time quickly ticking away, but Mom grabbed her arm.

"If you're lacking energy, evaluate what you're eating. Sugar and carbs are real energy thieves. Also, dehydration—"

"Mom!" Colette yanked her arm free. "I only eat from your highly detailed menu of acceptable items. You'll never meet another fifteen-year-old more dedicated to clean eating. Can't I have a conversation with a guy? Does every aspect of my life have to be examined and criticized?"

Mom stared down at the pile of diced onions, looking flabbergasted. She blinked. "Is Trey right? Are you stressed?"

Colette shifted from foot to foot. So now Mom decided to actually listen to Trey?

Mom had a frightened look in her eyes. "Is it true that you found Valerie's hospital badge in Dad's car?"

Whoa. That was a swerve. "What?"

"Susie called. Avery told her about the fight you and Kate had at school. The things you said. About Valerie . . ." Her voice sounded overly delicate, like a frightened kitten.

It threw Colette. Did Mom not only know about the hospital badge but also the frog statue still hidden under a pile of socks in her drawer?

Mom gave her a thin smile. "Valerie has buried herself in legal trouble because of her lies about Kate's father. Your father was helping her out, okay?" She reached up and ran her fingers through Colette's hair. Her hand grazed right over the bald spot. "Please don't spend another minute worrying about rumors. This family is solid. No need to stress about that. Focus on the Duncan."

Colette nodded, tears spilling. "But Kate . . ."

"Honey." Mom used her thumb to wipe away the tears on Colette's cheeks. Her finger lingered for a moment at the outside edge of Colette's lid, where she'd pulled a few lashes, but if Mom noticed, she didn't mention it. "I know you're upset about Kate. But you can't let her affect your training. You've worked your whole life for this. Don't let someone derail your future."

Colette nodded and wiped the rest of her tears away. "I've gotta do some homework." She waited for Mom to say they needed to stretch or film, but she didn't. Colette fled before she could reconsider.

She sat at her desk, staring at the empty computer screen. This history assignment was so not happening. The more she tried to write the essay, the more she thought about the poster on the wall of Miss Roza's office: *It's time to write our own story.* Yes, Colette needed to rewrite her life.

Now. Before it was too late.

THIRTY-SEVEN

Valerie arrived home from work and checked her phone again. No word from Kate. Elise had stopped driving her home from the studio, and since the big fight, even Avery's and Emma's parents were no longer offering. Kate's training had intensified as the competition neared, so Valerie never knew how long she'd be. She sat on the couch and turned on the TV, waiting for a pickup request.

The door flung open. Kate was flushed in the cheeks, perspiration dampening the crown of her hair. She tossed her backpack and dance bag on the floor without a greeting, still holding her mother at a distance.

"Hi. I was waiting for a text," Valerie said.

"Yeah, sorry. I lost my phone."

"Lost your phone?" Valerie tried to remember if they had gotten insurance. New phones were ridiculously expensive. "Who drove you home?"

"Dad. We'd already planned it. He loves watching me dance. He's so excited for the Duncan." Her words cut through Valerie. Kate had never looked so satisfied.

As Kate began spending more and more time with Chad, Valerie had reached back out to him. He no longer attempted to pull Valerie into his spell; he'd seemed to zone in on their daughter. Worried about letting Kate spend time with someone she felt she no longer knew, Valerie had hired the PI. He'd found where Chad was living—up in their old hometown, renting a small cabin. He was officially working for a rafting and tubing company, but given the season hadn't yet started, he wasn't that busy. He was spending a lot of time in the city. Near Kate.

"Doesn't seem like he's working much," Valerie said, wondering how he was getting gas money for all these visits.

Kate opened a fridge and got a Gatorade. "He's planning to open this awesome business. An adventure park. He's gathering information, investors. It's going to be amazing. He just needs to finalize the start-up costs."

It sounded all too familiar. She sighed. "I'll see if I have insurance on the phone." She took a breath and broached the conversation she'd been dreading. "I heard that you . . . you said some pretty awful things at school. I know you didn't mean it. But . . . it sounded pretty . . . aggressive." *Like something your father would say . . .*

Kate set her mouth into a line of rebuttal. "Well, that wasn't the only thing said at school. Colette made some pretty big accusations about you and her dad."

The air stilled. Valerie's nerve endings fired, hot and alert. "What?"

"I thought she was making stuff up to piss me off. But now I don't know. Maybe that's why Colette backstabbed me. Because she thought you were trying to break up her family."

"That's ridiculous. Andrew and I are just friends." But even Valerie could hear the false note in her voice, the desperate attempt to camouflage her true feelings.

"Uh-huh. Friends." She said it with such a bite, it was like a slap.

∽

Hours later, nestled deep inside a dream, a ringing sound reverberated in Valerie's ears. It was church bells, a fire alarm, the heart monitor at work. Slowly, she rolled over and pulled open her eyes. She blinked and looked at the clock: 2:47 a.m. The phone on her nightstand rang out. Pulling it closer, she saw Andrew's name flashing across the screen. "Andrew," she answered breathlessly. "Are you okay?"

"I'm sorry it's so late. I'm here. Outside. Can you talk?"

"Here? At my house?" She sat up, not certain she wasn't still dreaming.

"I'm sorry. I need to talk to you but couldn't risk leaving while anyone was awake. And Colette never sleeps. Come outside. I'm in my car."

"Okay." Minutes later, after throwing on some sweats, brushing her teeth, and running a brush through her hair, she stepped outside into the cool, moonless night. He was sitting in his black BMW, wearing a lightweight coat and jeans. His hair was rumpled, his eyes heavy with fatigue. When he spotted her approaching, his face softened in a way that made her feel equally thrilled and miserable. The passenger-door locks clicked open, and she sat inside the car, uncertain of what to expect. He shifted his body, gripped and ungripped his hands on the steering wheel.

"Sorry I didn't respond to your text. Elise is checking my phone. I had to delete everything."

She nodded. *Of course.*

He faced her. "Thank you for handling her interrogation so . . . perfectly." He released the steering wheel and touched her arm. "We really are in sync." He smiled sadly. "She believed it. That I was just . . . helping."

"That's good," she said softly.

He paused and pulled in a breath. "All along, I've been worried that Colette was stressed because of Elise—her demands with training." He raked a hand through his hair. "But she said Colette was the one who found your ID. And she found the frog statue from your house in my study. I guess I'd accidentally slipped it in my pocket and then put it in my desk. That's why she's been so anxious. Not sleeping. Pulling out her hair. Because of *me*. Worried I was having an affair." He clenched the front of his coat, his face creased with guilt.

"Andrew, I don't think—"

"I know you said we could be friends," he interrupted. "And I wanted more. I was hoping in time . . . but as much as it kills me . . . I can't be responsible for hurting my kids . . ." He covered his face with his hands.

She stared at the gold wedding band on his finger and knew this was all a product of Elise's manipulation. She had pushed Colette to the absolute brink of insanity with her expectations but pinned their daughter's anxiety on him. Forcing his decision to stay. She reeled with revulsion. That woman would stop at nothing to get what she wanted.

Valerie pulled his hands down off his face and looked into his clear blue eyes. "You didn't do anything to hurt Colette. You're an excellent father. Please don't ever doubt that. What we did was wrong, but your daughter didn't know about any of it, okay?" She kissed him softly on the lips just once and said goodbye. She'd leave him alone. Stop all correspondence. For him, for his sake, for his sanity. Not for Elise. That woman deserved nothing.

THIRTY-EIGHT

Saturday morning, Elise wandered into the kitchen and brewed coffee. Outside, the sky was cloudless and blue, the first signs of spring evident: Bright yellow daffodils sprouted through the ground, and tiny white buds burst from the cherry tree. Her ten-year-old neighbor was already outside jumping on his trampoline. She glanced into the living room, then down the stairs into the basement; no one was home. In the garage, both Andrew's and Trey's cars were gone. Andrew was probably on the golf course, but where were the kids? Why didn't anyone ever leave a note? Anytime Elise left to go somewhere, she left a Post-it pinned to the fridge or sent a text. It was the courteous thing to do.

She added a splash of almond milk to her coffee and sat down with her phone. Opening up Instagram, she saw that Colette had posted to her account twenty-two minutes ago. A selfie, one foot up on the curb stretching her calf. *#earlymorningjog #waytostarttheday #stretchthosemuscles #preventinjury*

Elise smiled, her shoulders easing down. That was even better than a note. After she'd reassured Colette that the rumors about Valerie and Andrew were untrue, her daughter had seemed like herself again. Just last night, Elise had noticed a new sense of resolution in Colette's demeanor, as if she'd made a decision. Indeed, she had. She had committed. A jolt of excitement and hope passed through Elise now. Everything was going to be fine. With Colette, and even with Andrew. Ever since pointing out that his irresponsible behavior had prompted their daughter's distress, a switch had flipped. He was remorseful. Recommitted.

Her phone rang.

She answered it, not even registering that it was an unfamiliar number on the screen. "Hello?" Her tone was bright and chipper, like the chickadees singing at the bird feeder outside the kitchen window.

"Ma'am?" a deep voice said. "This is Officer Jones from the Atlanta Police Department. Do you have a teenage daughter, approximately sixteen years old, blond, petite, wearing black leggings, a purple hoodie, and Hoka running shoes?"

"What?" Her whole body went cold as her chest tightened.

"You are listed as *Mom* under emergency contacts on the phone found next to an unconscious young woman. She was found collapsed on a jogging trail in the park. She has no identification."

"Unconscious? What are you talking about? What are you saying?" Elise's voice edged higher, close to hysteria. She was confused. Her heart throbbed louder and louder. Her fingers and toes went numb. The walls tilted closer.

"I'm sorry to upset you, ma'am. But I think this is your daughter we've found. She's hurt, and we're transporting her to the hospital. Do you have someone that can take you there? Ma'am?"

"Hurt? What do you mean, hurt?" She pulled the phone away, looked at the screen. Was this a joke?

"She may have a head injury," he continued. "We think she might have fallen while jogging. And from the way her leg is splayed out, it appears she may also have sustained injuries to her leg and ankle."

"What?" Elise looked frantically around the kitchen.

She dropped the phone on the floor with a bang. Then she began to scream.

THIRTY-NINE

Scorching pain jolted Colette awake. Sharp, electric bolts of heat shot through her calf, down the side of her ankle, and across the top of her foot. Her bones were on fire. It was unlike anything she could've imagined.

She heard a voice in the distance. Her eyes were heavy; it took actual effort to open them. The bright lights stabbed and blinded her. She turned her head. Pain. Worse than any headache ever.

She waited until the pounding slowed, then forced her eyes back open. It took her a minute to focus. When she did, she tried to figure out where she was. On the wall next to her was a dry-erase board. She squinted through fuzzy vision. Her name was written in red marker followed by *98.6°* and *90/62 at 11:35 a.m.* The bed she was in had metal rails on the sides. There was a tube going into her arm.

That voice sliced through the air again. "You don't understand! She has a major competition in six days!" Colette couldn't see her, but she knew. *Mom.* In total hysterics.

"I'm sorry." A man's voice. "It doesn't look like that's going to happen."

"What?" Mom screeched, making Colette wince.

Colette forced herself into a seated position. The sudden movement made her head throb. "Ow!" She clamped her hand to her face.

Mom raced toward her. The edges of Mom's body were shadowed like there were two of her. She wrapped Colette in a hug. Colette tried not to flinch as her brain slammed into her skull. Mom cried, her tears dribbling down the side of Colette's cheek and neck.

Someone else was there. The man. "You've had an accident," he said. Mom pulled away, stood up straight. Even through Colette's blurry vision, she could see that Mom looked terrible—pale, red-eyed, and frantic.

"How do you feel?" the man asked Colette. He was wearing scrubs and had a stethoscope around his neck.

Colette tried to speak, but her lips were swollen and numb. Her tongue was dry and fuzzy. "My head hurts." She pointed. "And my leg and foot . . ." She looked down toward the pain, but she was covered with a blanket.

The doctor bent over and shone a bright light in her eyes. Colette turned away. He put the little flashlight back in his pocket. "You've sustained a concussion. We're waiting on X-rays to understand the extent of the injuries to your leg and your foot."

Mom buried her face in her hands.

It was crazy, but seeing Mom lose it made Colette feel guilty. Her pain causing Mom so much suffering. "I'm sorry," Colette said, starting to cry.

Mom threw her thin arms around Colette again. "Shh. Shh. It's not your fault. My baby. My poor baby."

It was like something burst open inside Colette. She cried. So hard. Heaving. Sobbing.

"You're going to be okay," Mom said. "You fell while you were running. You're at the hospital now. But the doctors will take care of you."

Colette wasn't sure how long they were like that. She and Mom. Basket cases. But then, it was like both of them suddenly realized the doctor was still there. Mom slowly stood. The doctor waited for her to finish blowing her nose, and for some reason, that made Colette like him.

"Colette," he said, "do you remember anything?"

Her mind felt heavy. The edges of her memory were hazy. Like she was in a dream. "Not really."

He tapped on an iPad. "Do you feel confused?"

"Maybe."

The doctor nodded. "Is there ringing in your ears?"

"Not ringing. But maybe buzzing? Is it the air-conditioning?" Mom looked up toward the vents in the ceiling.

The doctor walked over to a machine by the bed and tapped a button.

The door opened, and her father walked in. His eyes widened when he saw Colette. "When did she wake up? Why didn't you text me?" He raced over and kissed her forehead. "Oh, thank God. How are you? Are you okay?"

"She just woke up." Mom's voice was weak. "Just a minute ago."

"Does she . . ." He didn't finish the question.

"I don't think she remembers anything," Mom said.

Colette hated the way they were talking about her like she wasn't even there. Then she realized her eyelids had fluttered closed. She guessed that whatever the doctor had done to her IV had shot through her like a wave of relief. Her leg felt weightless. The pain was almost gone. The buzzing in her head dimmed. She felt so sleepy.

FORTY

Watching as Colette's eyes softly closed, Elise grabbed Andrew's hand and fought back another round of tears. "Colette? Sweetie?"

"She needs rest," the doctor said.

Elise knew that. It made sense, but she wanted to hear her daughter's voice. She wanted to see her daughter's beautiful blue eyes, to wrap her arms around her, to feel her heartbeat pulse against her own. She felt useless, standing there while her poor daughter was lying in a hospital bed, banged up and bruised. Why couldn't they do the X-rays while she was sleeping? Figure out what the injuries were, so they could make a plan to fix them? She turned toward the doctor. "Can we image her leg now?" He scrunched up his eyebrows like she was crazy, and that irritated her. "I just want to know what we're dealing with!" She hadn't meant to shout.

The doctor paused, hesitating. "It appears she hit her head pretty hard on the concrete." He spoke with a slow, soft tone. "She was unconscious for an indeterminate amount of time." He looked at the iPad. "According to the information we obtained from her watch, the GPS stopped approximately three minutes before the jogger found her and called 911, which means she could have been knocked out for over five minutes. She has a grade-three concussion, Mrs. Carrington. Recovery will take time and significant rest. So, no. We're not doing any tests now."

Elise sighed loudly, frustrated. She pulled a plastic chair over next to the hospital bed and sat. Colette slept for four hours. Elise, Andrew, and Trey sat there in silence, listening to every inhale and exhale. Elise searched on her phone. *Common injuries from a fall. Leg injuries from running. How long until you can participate in activities after a concussion.* Her eyes glazed over. Finally, there was a rustle; then Colette rolled over. Disheveled hair fell out of her ponytail, loose strands dangling around her face.

"Hey, CC," Trey said, resurrecting an old nickname from their childhood. It made Elise's throat clench. The sweetness of his voice, the concern on his face. Why did it take such a tragedy for him to get over their recent estrangement? Maybe now he'd start being nicer to his own mother.

Colette's eyelids rose and fell two times before they remained open. She had the dazed look of someone sleepwalking. Elise went to her bedside. *Don't cry. Be strong.* "How are you, sweetie?" Still, her voice cracked.

Colette attempted to smile. The side of her face where she'd hit the concrete was scraped. As the corners of her lips pulled upward, the damaged skin on her chin and cheek stretched. A pinprick of blood appeared. She pulled a hand to her face.

"Careful." Elise dabbed at the wound with a tissue. She turned to Andrew. "Do you think we should get a nurse to bandage that?"

He nodded. "I'll go find someone."

Elise tucked a strand of Colette's hair behind her ear. "Are you in pain?"

Colette swallowed, tears filling her eyes. She nodded slowly. "A little." Her lips quivered. "A lot." She started to cry.

"Oh no." Elise pulled her into a hug. Her daughter's tears dampened her cheek as her mind raced. Sure, she was in pain now because the injury had just happened. But that didn't mean it was serious. The doctor was wrong; she was certain. She'd probably turned her ankle the way Avery had. Some ice, a day or two of rest, and everything would be fine.

Andrew returned with both a nurse and the doctor. As the nurse applied an ointment to the scrapes, the doctor shone a light in Colette's eyes again. He tapped his iPad. "Colette, I'd like to get some X-rays of your leg."

"Yes!" Elise said a little too aggressively. "I bet it's just a little sprain!"

The doctor gave her that strange look again, but she turned away from him and faced Colette. "Let's find out what happened, so we can get you back in dancing form." She smiled broadly. Andrew placed a hand on her arm, as if telling her to tone it down. She batted him away.

Colette gave a shrug of compliance. She looked so young, lying there against the stark white sheets, her hair almost as pale, her face battered and bruised, her bottom lip still puffy and swollen from the fall. "Okay," she said softly.

The images didn't take long, but now the four of them were waiting for what felt like an eternity to hear the results. Trey went to the vending machines and got Gatorades and snacks, but Elise couldn't eat. Each minute ticked by like individual sand grains slipping down an hourglass.

At last, the door creaked open, and the doctor walked in. He crossed the room to a computer and clicked until images appeared on the screen. Before the doctor even spoke a word, Elise identified the black line slashed across the image of the white bone. Her heart seized; her stomach bottomed out. "It's broken!" She was shocked. Horrified. Tortured. How could this have happened?

There was a gasp. They turned and looked at Colette, pale as a ghost, mouth agape.

Guilt washed over Elise. She shouldn't panic Colette. She went to her. "It's okay. People break bones all the time. We'll heal from this. We'll recover." She felt physically sick. What did this mean for Colette?

The doctor cleared his throat, and they returned their attention to him. "You are correct, Mrs. Carrington. Fractures are quite common, especially among athletes. However," he said, his mouth twitching again, "tibial shaft fractures such as this one are most often caused by a high-energy collision, like a motor vehicle accident, for example. Sports-related injuries that most often lead to this type of break are typically skiing accidents or blunt-force impact from a kick in soccer. To incur this type of a break . . ." He pointed at the X-ray. "With the additional ankle joint involvement . . ." He pointed again toward the screen. "Well, it raises some questions."

"What kind of questions?" Andrew asked.

"Questions about how the injury was sustained." The doctor tapped the computer screen at the location of the break. "I asked Dr. Azar to take a look at this. He's an orthopedist who can often ascertain the nature of the injury based on how and where the fracture sits in the bone. We recently had a motorcycle rider who was struck by a vehicle. From the X-ray analysis, Dr. Azar determined the velocity of impact and that the car was speeding."

"I don't understand," Elise interrupted. "Colette wasn't hit by a car. She was jogging on a trail inside a park."

"Yes, I'm sorry. I'm not trying to confuse you. I'm trying to say that from the assessment of your daughter's injuries, it appears highly improbable that she sustained this oblique fracture and subsequent ankle joint injury simply from a fall."

Beside Elise, Andrew's body went rigid.

Her vision swarmed in front of her. She felt dizzy. Confused. She squinted as if that would help her understand. "What do you mean? What caused it, then?"

The doctor nodded softly. "I'm very sorry to tell you this, but from the information we've obtained and the analysis of Colette's injuries, it appears she was hit with something. Attacked."

"Attacked?" It was Trey who first found the voice to speak. "What are you talking about?"

His words sounded tinny, as if Elise were suddenly standing inside a metal can.

Andrew inhaled sharply. "What are you saying?"

The doctor's voice took on the tone of apology. "It appears someone clubbed your daughter with a blunt heavy object on the leg. Right here." He bent down and mimed a hit to his own outer shin.

Elise wrapped her arms around her chest. "What?" she shrieked.

Trey pulled his hands up to his face and cursed.

Only Colette was silent. The color drained from her face.

The doctor glanced her way. "Colette, we'd like you to speak with the police."

FORTY-ONE

Moments later, a nurse entered the hospital room, followed by a police officer. Andrew's shoulders pulled back, straightening his posture up to his full six-foot-one-inch height. He took a step closer to the bed, angling himself in front of their daughter; something about that protective gesture made Elise want to burst into tears.

The officer shook Andrew's and Elise's hands. "Carl Abbott."

The name flew in and out of Elise's mind like a gust of wind. What was happening? Just a few hours ago, she'd been brewing coffee in her kitchen. Now she was staring at a shiny badge. Her daughter had a splint on her leg and cuts on her face.

Abbott pulled a chair from the corner of the room and dragged it up to the very edge of the bed. "Miss Colette Carrington?" His voice was soft and encouraging.

"Yes." The undamaged side of her face climbed up into a half smile, piercing Elise's heart.

"I'm going to ask you a few questions about this morning, okay?"

She nodded, looking timid. It took every ounce of restraint for Elise not to tell this man to leave her daughter alone.

He pulled out a small pad and a pen, like they did on TV shows. Elise waited for a director and an audio tech with a microphone because this had to be acting. This had to be a movie. This couldn't be real. "What time did you leave your house this morning?" he asked.

Colette glanced at her wrist, but her watch had been removed earlier, taken as evidence to be dusted for fingerprints with the rest of her clothes, shoes, phone, and earbuds. "I think it was . . ." Her voice was gravelly. She took a sip of Gatorade. "It was around eight thirty?"

"She posted on Instagram at 8:37 a.m. She was standing in our driveway at that time," Elise said. Andrew stiffened by her side. Now he knew. They'd continued the online campaign.

The officer nodded and wrote. "And according to the watch's GPS," he continued, "you had run three and a half miles at a seven-minute pace—wow, that's impressive—when the incident occurred. That's very good data for us to be able to ascertain the exact time the attack happened."

At the word *attack*, Elise flinched.

"What do you remember, Colette? Do you recall jogging in the park?"

"Yeah." She sounded far away and groggy. "I remember running." She looked up at the ceiling, then gripped the side of her head again.

"This is too much!" Elise shouted. "She's still in pain."

But Colette swallowed and shook her head slightly. "It's okay, Mom. It's coming back a little. I remember a song came on that I wanted to skip. I looked at my phone." She mimed dipping her chin. "I guess I tripped. A pain sliced up my leg, and my head crashed onto something hard." She touched her hairline. "Then everything went black."

Abbott's pen was poised above his notepad. "Colette, do you remember seeing anyone suspicious on the trail?"

"Suspicious?" She squinted. "What do you mean?"

"Did you ever feel like anyone was watching you? Following you?"

"Watching me?" She knitted her eyebrows. "I mean, I passed some people on the trails walking dogs or jogging. But when I fell, I was in the shaded area, which is quieter. Fewer people. I remember that because I had on my sunglasses, and suddenly everything seemed darker."

He cut his eyes down and nodded slightly.

"What?" Andrew asked.

"The shaded part of the trail," the cop repeated. "Trees, bushes, where someone could hide and wait."

"Oh my God!" Elise closed her eyes, trying to block out the visual of someone cowering in the shrubs, waiting to hurt her daughter. Every muscle in her body tensed.

Colette's face scrunched up. She looked at her foot, then back up at the officer.

Elise's insides ripped in half. Her poor, innocent daughter.

"That damn YouTube channel!" Andrew yelled, his jaw set hard. "And her Instagram posts! Is that how they knew where to find her?"

Elise whimpered. Was this her fault? She hadn't listened to Andrew's concerns. She'd let her daughter post her locations to everyone.

"There are sick people in this world," Andrew said through gritted teeth.

Abbott was scribbling notes. "I need more information on this. You have a YouTube channel, miss?"

Colette nodded, avoiding her dad's penetrating gaze.

"How many views does a typical post get?"

Colette massaged her scalp. "My last video had about seventy thousand."

"Oh." The cop's eyebrows shot up. "We're not talking amateur stuff here. Tell me your channel name."

Colette told him while Elise pulled up a link on her phone and held it out for him to see. Her hand trembled. She felt the weight of Andrew's stare as he examined the recent additions.

Colette's eyes darted from one person to the other; Trey reached out and took her hand. She sat very still, the blood draining from her face. They were all quiet for a beat, letting the unthinkable settle in.

"Do you think that's what happened?" Andrew asked. "A crazy stalker from the internet?"

Abbott drew in a long, deep breath. "It could be. This is typically a very safe part of town. The incident occurred at an atypical time—early morning, broad daylight—as if the person knew Colette's schedule. Knew when to expect her. That could fit the profile of an online stalker."

Colette averted her eyes, gripped her hands in her lap.

"Son of a bitch!" Andrew shouted, clenching his hands into fists.

Elise shivered. This was all her fault. She should have listened to her husband. Acknowledged that he had a valid concern. She wrapped her arms around herself, trying to stamp out the cold that iced its way through her veins.

The officer bit his lower lip.

"What?" Andrew demanded. "Is there something else?"

A small flush dotted the man's cheeks. He looked from Colette back to Andrew, then swallowed. He appeared uncomfortable, which dropped a stone of worry into Elise's stomach.

"The circumstances here, well, they're a little unusual." He pointed toward Colette's arms. "There's no bruising or scratching on your arms or hands, indicating there was no fight. There were no eyewitnesses screaming and frightening the perpetrator away. Rather, we have what appears to be most likely a planned violent attack with the desire *only* to injure. Not to kill, abduct, or sexually assault." His face made an expression of bizarre curiosity, lips pursed, forehead creased. "We don't have all the information yet, but what this all strongly suggests is . . ." He paused.

Elise's eye twitched.

Andrew's face tightened.

Trey turned and looked at the cop.

Colette blinked. Her mouth dropped slightly open.

The air stilled. Everyone looked intently at the officer. The room went cold.

"Well, we can't rule out the possibility that this assault was planned with the sole intention to hurt Colette." He leaned toward her. "Can you think of any reason why someone might want your leg broken?"

FORTY-TWO

Saturday morning, Valerie woke to an empty house. Kate's replacement phone still hadn't arrived, so she had no way to contact her. If she went in early to clean before dance, who had driven? Chad? She hoped it was Trey.

Later that afternoon, Valerie's phone rang. It was the studio number. "Hey," Kate said with an edge. "Trey never showed. Can you pick me up?"

"Of course." She was relieved there was no mention of her father. She quickly headed out. In the parent lounge, Miss Roza and Kate were waiting.

"Valerie," Miss Roza said in her brusque manner, "I want to let you know Kate's training is progressing wonderfully. She is ready for regionals. She will be good." She tapped a beefy hand on Kate's shoulder, and they all stood there awkwardly. Valerie hadn't spoken to Miss Roza since the gala, and she knew this unusual display of praise was her way of apologizing for the switch. Kate reached into Valerie's purse while her instructor spoke and dug out her mother's phone. She frantically texted. She was like an addict, Valerie thought. Getting a hit of endorphins now that she held a precious phone after going an entire morning without.

Miss Roza removed her hand from Kate's shoulder, and with that, they turned to leave.

"Kate, that was very rude," Valerie said once they were in the car.

"Sorry. I was trying to find Trey. It's not like him to no-show. He's not answering, and Colette wasn't at dance. It's weird. Something's up."

They drove the rest of the way in silence. Inside the condo, Kate went straight to her bedroom, still clutching Valerie's phone. Valerie sighed, too tired to demand it back. As she sat down, a familiar ringtone echoed from down the hall. A moment later, Kate walked out, a look of disgust on her face.

"Well, look," she said, dripping with judgment. "It's your *friend*." She held the screen toward her, the name *Andrew* flashing.

Valerie's heart immediately went into overdrive. She snatched the phone. "Don't talk to me like that," she retorted. She turned her back and clicked the green "Answer" button. "Hello?"

"Hey." His voice was clipped. "Have you heard what happened?"

Instantly, her mind flashed to Elise. Had she found out about their kissing? "What?"

He let out an audible breath. Then with a shaky voice, he said, "Colette was attacked."

"What?" She sucked in a breath. "What are you talking about?"

He was quiet for a moment. Muffled sounds of him crying filled the air. Valerie's heart squeezed. "Someone . . . someone . . . hit her while she was running in the park. The police haven't found the weapon."

Weapon. The word slammed into her. "Oh my God," she said, dumbfounded. "I . . . I can't even imagine. I don't know what to say." Her voice quivered. "Is she okay? Did they catch the guy?"

The line went silent. Eventually, he said, "No, they haven't found who did this. She has a concussion and several fractures in her ankle and shin. It's going to be a long road to recovery. The doctor said even if they can avoid surgery, it will be at least six months of physical therapy. Probably more."

Valerie's legs weakened. She put her hand against the wall to steady herself. "How is she? I can't even imagine . . ."

"I think she's still in shock. She doesn't remember being hit—which is a blessing. Honestly, Elise is in worse shape." He paused. "The police insinuated it was someone who knew Colette, knew her schedule, and wanted to hurt her . . ." His voice hitched.

"Wait, what? They think someone hurt her on purpose?" Her head swam; her pulse accelerated. A prickle of anxiety crept up her legs as she thought of the fight at school. The terrible things everyone had heard Kate say. The text from Chad saying he was pissed about the gala.

"The cop said Colette was all over the internet. People can be jealous or obsessed. I don't know what to think. Val?" He sounded strange. Cautious. "Tell me Kate was with you this morning, so I can tell Elise to stop making crazy accusations."

A cold chill blew over her. Goose bumps sprouted across her skin. "What?" She was frozen, paralyzed. "She was at the studio. She's been home since two." It came out offended. "How can you ask that?" But hadn't she just allowed herself to contemplate the same thing?

"I'm sorry," he blurted. "But you have to understand with all this fighting and the things said . . ."

"I have to understand? Kate is not violent! She's a fifteen-year-old girl. This is my daughter you're talking about!" Valerie's thoughts raced, her heartbeat throbbing in her ears. She'd told Andrew about Chad's unpredictable moods and violence. Could he wonder about genetics? No. He hadn't read Kate's journals. There was no merit to this accusation. "Tell me you never believed it was a possibility. Please."

"I'm not saying I think Kate did anything wrong . . ."

"It sounds like you are."

"No, it's just . . . Elise can be . . . persuasive. And I guess for a moment, I wondered if Kate found out about us, and it was the final straw." He paused. "But no, I don't think . . . I'm fried, Val. My family is in crisis. Everything is a mess." He sounded pitiful, but Valerie couldn't comfort him. Her entire body was on edge, her mind reeling.

My family is in crisis. And there it was. He had never belonged to her. He never would. His family had suffered a tragedy, and he'd do anything to soothe them, vindicate them. But would he . . . could he possibly turn on Valerie? Side with Elise and point the finger at Kate? And if he did, what would he find?

"I hope Colette recovers quickly," she said. "I've got to go." Feeling sick, she walked down the hallway to talk to her daughter, her thoughts blowing her world apart like a grenade.

FORTY-THREE

"Of course she has an alibi!" Elise shrieked. "She's a fifteen-year-old girl. She doesn't have the brute strength to club a leg and impose long-standing injuries." She gave Andrew a patronizing look like he was an idiot. "She paid someone to do it for her!" She paced around the kitchen island, her head buzzing, her mouth dry. They had been home from the hospital for three hours, and she'd been unable to do anything other than rack her brain for ways to prove her theory. She knew from experience the depths to which dancers would sink to secure their future. She was not proud of the atrocities that had taken place in New York, but she'd never broken a bone . . . at least not on purpose. This was outrageous! Criminal!

Andrew walked in front of her and put out a hand. "Elise, stop. I understand that you're upset, but these things you're saying . . . they're insane."

She narrowed her eyes.

"Think about it," he said. "Colette is all over the internet. Pictures, videos, social media, and YouTube. Her electronic footprint is far-reaching. She has people all over the country watching her." He shook his head with a disgusted grimace. "I tried to warn you. There are sick people out there that prey on young women." His jaw tensed. "That makes more sense."

"Blah, blah, blah," she said with a snarky expression. "Do you really think our daughter was brutalized by a complete stranger when, just days ago, Kate threatened her? In front of everyone? She said, 'I hope you never dance again!' She's angry about the gala, and now she wants her out of the Duncan. So, explain to me how your theory makes more sense?" She gave him a death glare.

He rolled his eyes in disapproval. "Kate's practically family. Colette is like her sister. They're fighting, but she's not going to hurt her. She's not vicious."

"Not vicious?" Her voice edged higher. "Colette's ankle and shin are crushed in seven spots." She held up seven trembling fingers. "It's no coincidence this happened right before regionals. How can you not see that? This is not the act of some sick predator, Andrew! This was the premeditated revenge of a jealous rival! Several girls overheard Kate say, 'I'm going to be the one who wins at regionals, and you'll be crushed on the sidelines.' *Crushed!*"

"Teenagers say stuff they don't mean." He waved a hand like a dismissal, and that infuriated her.

"You think that was random? To me, it sounds like motive."

The side door slammed, making the plantation shutters rattle against the windows. Trey walked in, anger splashed across his face. "I could hear you all the way outside, Mom. Do you actually believe Kate, the girl you used to love, the girl who practically grew up in our house, my girlfriend, has somehow plotted to attack Colette? Seriously?"

Energy pulsed through Elise's body like she'd downed a double espresso. Why did everyone refuse to accept this as a possibility? How could they be so shortsighted? "Rivals can be malicious. There are hundreds of stories like this. It's not as crazy as you think!"

"What's going on?"

They turned. On the far end of the kitchen, Colette stood, leaning on crutches, her face tilted in curiosity.

Trey moved into the room. "Mom thinks Kate planned all of this." He pointed at Colette's leg in a cast. "The attack."

Darkness spread across Colette's face like a storm cloud. "You think Kate would hurt me?" Her voice hitched with horror. "On purpose?"

Elise looked at her daughter. She was washed out, a pale photocopy of herself.

There was a distant ding. Colette reached around to retrieve her phone from her back pocket. A crutch fell to the ground; she lost her balance, wobbling on one leg, her arm flailing for something to hold on to. Andrew raced over and caught her before she fell to the floor. It was too much for Elise to see—her perfect daughter, once so coordinated that she could hold an arabesque in a windstorm—on crutches. Elise's resolve hardened. She'd find a way to prove her theory. Get revenge!

Trey and Andrew helped Colette over to a chair at the kitchen table. She read the text. "It's Avery and Emma. They want to come over."

"You just got home from the hospital," Andrew said. "I think you need to rest."

"Maybe she needs support from her friends," Elise said, suddenly grasping for an opportunity to needle the girls' opinions, to see if they agreed with her.

"Yeah," Colette said. "I do kind of want to see them."

Andrew sighed. "Okay. But not for too long." He propped Colette's leg on a chair, got her a glass of water, then disappeared.

A few minutes later, Ling Li, Emma, Susie, and Avery arrived. "Oh my God!" the girls screeched, racing over to hug Colette. "So," Emma said, "how bad is it?"

"It looks way worse than when I sprained my ankle," Avery said.

Colette's eyes brimmed with tears, but she sat up straighter and blinked them away. "I'll be okay. It's just going to take . . . time." Her voice broke.

Elise's lip quivered. Susie put a hand to Elise's shoulder. "I'm so sorry," she whispered.

"Are you scared?" Avery asked cautiously.

"Like, to think whoever did this is still out there?" Emma asked. "Like, what if they're obsessed with you or something?"

Ling Li made a scolding gesture, pursed her lips, and whispered, "Stop."

"Or . . ." Elise said, before she could stop herself. "Maybe it wasn't a stranger."

"Marcus?" Avery whispered.

"What?" Elise snapped. "No." *For the love!* Elise was so tired of everyone's stupidity. "That's been over for weeks."

Colette flushed. "Mom thinks Kate somehow orchestrated this whole thing." She rolled her eyes and shook her head like, *Insane.* Emma and Avery exchanged glances, neither saying a word. Colette startled. "Come on. You guys can't possibly think . . ." Her voice dropped off.

A pulse of adrenaline spiked through Elise. Maybe they weren't so dumb after all. The kitchen was eerily quiet for a moment.

"Well." Emma let out a long sigh. "Avery and I made a pact to stay out of it. The fight." She cast a look toward Avery. "Because it's been weird since the gala, you know?"

Avery nodded. Her eyes were wide, frightened.

"Yeah, but . . ." Colette's voice was laced with incredulity. "But Kate? I mean, I know we've been in a throw down, but guys, she's been my friend since we were, like, five." She sounded desperate, looking from one to the other. "You don't actually think Kate *hates* me, do you? She's been a bitch, but I don't *hate* her."

Everyone was stone still, the only noise the sound of birds chirping outside the window.

Emma looked toward Colette. "When we first heard about the accident, obviously, we didn't automatically think, *Oh, Kate did this.* But Mom said the cops think it was intentional?" She grimaced dramatically. "It's your landing leg, and it's a week before regionals—"

"And everything's been so . . . *savage* between you two," Avery interrupted. Susie gave her daughter a death glare. She clamped her mouth. "Sorry."

Elise sat very still, every nerve ending firing.

"At the gala," Emma started, "I was backstage and saw Kate. She was watching you climbing to the top of the staircase. The lighting was shining from behind, so you were in silhouette. You looked . . ." Emma looked down, blushing. "Beautiful." She stood and raised her hand, miming Kate. "She made a fist and had this mean look on her face." Emma scowled. "And she whispered something."

"What?" Colette was breathless.

Elise hinged forward. "What did she say?"

Emma hesitated. "I shouldn't say. I mean, I'm not sure . . ."

"She told me," Avery blurted out. "She thought Kate whispered, *I hope she falls. I hope she breaks her leg.*"

Elise gasped.

Colette's mouth dropped open.

Ling Li rested a hand on her daughter's arm. "But you're not sure, Emma."

"No," Emma admitted. "But then at school . . . the fight . . . The things Kate said—"

Avery interrupted: "They were, like, *a warning.*"

Elise's insides buzzed. She was not crazy. Other people had doubts about Kate, too.

Across the table, Colette looked sucker punched. "Kate was mad. I get that. But, guys . . ." Her voice cracked. "I know she didn't do this. She wouldn't hurt me." Tears brimmed her bottom lids.

Suzie's gaze pierced her daughter with reprimand. Avery looked panicked. "I shouldn't have said anything."

"That's not true!" Elise said too abruptly. She softened her tone. "It's okay for you to voice your opinion." She took Colette's hand. "I'm sorry. It's awful to think a friend could betray you."

"But . . ." Colette stammered. "I can understand if she's secretly happy I can't compete against her. But this is ridiculous." She pointed at her leg. "I can't believe you think she hates me enough to hurt me. Kate didn't do this!" she yelled. "We've been best friends for ten years!"

Avery and Emma looked down at the table.

Elise whispered, "But not anymore."

FORTY-FOUR

Valerie knocked on Kate's door. No answer. Opening it, she found her daughter sitting on her bed, headphones on, laptop on her thighs.

Kate glanced up, then pulled her headphones off. "I heard."

"About Colette?"

"Yeah. That sucks." She leaned back against her headboard.

That sucks. Valerie shuddered, recalling Chad telling the police years ago: *Yeah, it sucks that he tripped and broke his ankle. But it's not my fault. I can't help if I have a loud voice and it startled him.* But this was Kate. Not Chad. Valerie sat down on the bed. "Who told you?"

"It's all over Instagram." Kate pointed to her laptop screen. There was a photo of her friend with *Prayers for Colette!* written beneath.

Valerie looked at Kate. Her best friend had just been violently attacked, and yet she sat there with no emotion on her face, no fear in her voice. When Valerie pulled her legs up onto the bed, her daughter stared at her in a way that suggested she didn't want to have a conversation. Valerie chose to ignore it. She held out her phone. "I'm sorry your new phone isn't in yet. I'm sure you feel out of the loop. Do you want to call her or Trey?"

Kate shrugged. "Yeah. Maybe later." Her eyes drifted back to the computer.

Valerie had to restrain herself from grabbing the device and flinging it into the trash. How could she be so blasé? "Kate," Valerie pressed, "how do *you* feel about it?"

Kate hesitated, yanking her hair out of the elastic and refixing her ponytail. Stalling. "I mean . . . It's rough."

Valerie bristled. It's *rough*? "I think you should call her." She waved her phone in the air.

Kate gave an exasperated head shake. "I, like, *just* found out, Mom. Let me process, okay?"

It was true. Still, Valerie's throat was suddenly dried out and raw. "But you will?"

She hesitated, looking down.

"Look, I know things have been strained, but it's time to put that aside and be supportive. She's been through something terrible."

"I've been through a lot, and she hasn't exactly been supportive to me!" She flung a hand to her chest.

Valerie swallowed, her mind filled with turbulence. "Kate, please. Be the better friend."

Kate stared at her long and hard, then finally said, "Yeah, okay."

But it didn't sound convincing.

Monday at work, Valerie and Jazmin assisted in an intense delivery that required vacuum extraction and extensive reassurance that the infant's head would, in fact, morph back into a round shape. Afterward, they sat in the break room. The cleaning staff had just left, and the pungent smell of Lysol permeated the air. Valerie had immediately texted Jazmin after talking to Kate about the attack. Jazmin had reminded her that Kate was a good girl; of course she was capable of sympathy for Colette. Her initial reaction had probably been a product of shock. But now, feet up on the coffee table, hot tea in their hands, Valerie told Jazmin that Kate had stayed holed up in her room for the rest of the weekend. "Did she ever reach out to Colette?" Jazmin asked.

Valerie threw her hands out, palms up. "Not from my phone."

Jazmin tilted her head and made a face like, *Don't worry.* "Think about it from Kate's point of view. Colette had just royally screwed her over. She still has a lot of anger. I'm not saying Kate is happy about what happened, but I can understand the conflict."

Valerie leaned back against the couch and felt her face twitch.

"What?" Jazmin asked.

Valerie closed her eyes for a long moment and inhaled deeply. "Apparently, Elise thinks Kate is responsible."

"Responsible?" Jazmin asked. "For the attack?" Her voice tinged with disbelief.

"Yup."

"That's ridiculous," Jazmin said. "There's some underlying hostility between those two, sure, but come on! She's fifteen!"

From inside the pocket of her scrubs, Valerie's phone rang. The line was instantly flooded with heavy sobbing, gasps of air, a faint whisper of her daughter's voice lost somewhere in between. "Kate?" She plugged her other ear with a finger, her heart starting to pound. "What's wrong?" She listened as Kate's words spouted out, taking a hard hold on her lungs.

"What's going on?" Jazmin asked.

"Okay, calm down," Valerie said into the phone. "I'll be right there." She ended the call and stood frozen, her body like a statue. "At school. The kids are saying terrible things. Repeating Elise's crazy idea that Kate's responsible. Someone wrote *jealous evil bitch* on her locker with a Sharpie."

"What?" Jazmin's voice rose in anger. "Go get her!"

Valerie stared blindly at her friend. The antiseptic smell became overpowering, making her feel sick.

Jazmin pointed to Valerie's locker. "Get your stuff and go to her."

Valerie nodded, unable to find words. Her head was swimming.

"I'll tell everyone that you had a family emergency. Are you okay? Do you want me to drive you?"

She realized she was crying. She wiped her eyes with the sleeve of her shirt.

Jazmin pulled her into a hug. "Everyone knows this is crazy."

Valerie rested her cheek against the scratchy fabric of her friend's scrubs. "This is all Elise's fault." She squeezed Jazmin one last time, got her purse from her locker, and raced away to the parking deck.

Once in her car, she dialed Andrew, who answered on the first ring. "Valerie?" He sounded surprised. "Are you okay?"

"No!" she shouted. The tears jammed up in the back of her throat, making her voice shake. Her hands trembled on the steering wheel. "I'm not okay. Kate said people at school are making accusations that she's responsible for Colette's injuries. That's insane, Andrew!" She slammed on the brakes, almost rear-ending a black SUV in front of her. Her chest tightened.

Across the phone line, she heard the sound of shuffling papers, a distant voice, then the door closing. "Jesus," he said under his breath.

"Did Elise start this?" She didn't know why she even asked that, because she was absolutely behind this horrendous rumor.

He was quiet for a beat. "She's been sneaking around making phone calls and abruptly hangs up when I walk in. She slammed her laptop shut when I came too close. Last night, when she was in the shower, I snuck down and looked at her browsing history. She's pulled up all these websites—dozens of them—about sports rivalries that turned violent. There were unfathomable stories about people sabotaging their competition."

"Kate didn't do this!" She gripped the steering wheel so tight, the skin around her knuckles stretched thin.

"I know. I know," he said. "But she found all these stories that validated her ideas. So now she's convinced."

"Convinced? What? That Kate was involved?" Silence. "Do *you* think Kate was involved?" Dead air. "Andrew?" Her voice escalated.

There was rustling on the other end, then a faint, "Um . . ."

"She's just a girl!" She pulled the car into the school parking lot and turned off the ignition. "Tell your wife to stop this harassment. Leave Kate alone." With that, she clicked the phone off and went inside to rescue her daughter.

FORTY-FIVE

Elise was sautéing shrimp in lemon and oil when she turned around to see Andrew standing right behind her. "Oh!" She startled and put a hand to her throat. "When did you get home?" She saw the keys in his hand, his spring jacket still buttoned.

"Just now." His eyes locked on her in a way that felt like a restraint.

Self-consciously, she smoothed the front of her apron and tucked a loose wisp of hair behind her ear. She lowered the gas burner to simmer and placed the spatula on a spoon rest. A breeze blew in through the open window, smelling of fresh-cut grass, a scent she normally relished; now, she only felt the chill. She closed the window.

Andrew, watching her with an unfamiliar intensity, set his keys down. "I heard things got heated at school today. Accusations were made about the accident."

Tension gripped her spine. His voice took on an edge; his jaw clenched, so he was almost baring his teeth. He was ready for a fight. Well, fine. But she shouldn't be the one under fire. "And who exactly did you discuss this with?" She put her hands on her hips. She would call Valerie right this instant if . . .

"Trey told me."

"Oh." She pulled her hands down.

"Elise, look, I understand the inclination to think after the fight they had that Kate might be . . . looking for revenge. But there's no proof! You can't blame someone without evidence."

Elise's breath caught. He was looking at her with pure disgust.

Elise inhaled long and deep, forcing her fury aside and making the decision to save her family. She plastered on an apologetic expression: eyebrows pulled in, mouth slightly downturned. She reached for his hand. "I'm sorry. You're right. Emotions are running very high. But you weren't there." She pointed toward the kitchen table. "It wasn't *me* who brought up the idea of Kate's involvement." She clutched at her chest. "Emma talked about Kate's jealousy and outrage about the gala. Then Avery chimed in. She used the word *savage* to describe Kate's recent behavior. That was her word, Andrew, not mine."

He stood very still, his expression not relaxing but also not resisting.

She continued. "I know," she said dramatically. "I shouldn't have allowed that discussion in front of Colette. I was . . . selfish. They were validating my fears. Because I've lived it, Andrew. A life where people were jealous of me, tried to undermine me." Andrew raised an eyebrow, so she plowed on while she had him under her spell. "It's awful. What envy can do. But I've had years to recover. Everything is so fresh and raw for Colette. I didn't even know they were talking about it at school, but still, I made some phone calls and arranged for someone to come talk to her about how upsetting this all is."

"Oh." The muscles around his jaw relaxed. "Really?"

She shrugged softly. "I only want what's best for our daughter."

He cocked his head in that lawyerly way he used when speaking to a client. "I'm glad you realized your mistake and took actions to correct it. It'll be good for her to talk to a professional."

Elise pulled him into an embrace. She reached up and ran her fingers through his thick hair and placed a gentle kiss on his neck. Of course, he thought she'd meant a counselor. She did not correct him.

⌒⑨

The next day, the temperature rose into the seventies. The sky was a perfect watercolor blue with wispy clouds on the horizon. The dogwoods lining the curb had budded overnight, creating a stretch of white blooms as far as the eye could see. People jogged, pushed strollers, walked dogs. Elise felt the energy in the air and was eager to see how the afternoon meeting would go. She had purposely not told Colette about it, hoping to stave off questions.

Colette was in the living room, her leg propped on the ottoman. Elise approached her. "I've asked a woman to come over today and talk to you about the accident."

Colette reared back. "About what? A plan to get my leg healed and me back onstage? I'm so tired. Can we do it another day? Please? Just walking with crutches and dealing with the pain is exhausting me."

"No." Elise waved a hand through the air. "That's not what this is about." She sat on the chair opposite her daughter.

Colette looked equally relieved and confused. She rested back against the couch cushions. "What, then?"

Elise thought of Andrew's quick acceptance of the idea of a counselor, and she decided to play on that. "I've been worried about you, honey. Not only have you experienced a physical tragedy, but you've endured emotional trauma, too. The lost opportunity to dance at regionals and the underlying fear that your best friend may have betrayed you."

Her mouth pulled down. "Mom, come on. Kate didn't do this."

Elise looked at her, her head tipped a fraction to the side, like her brain couldn't handle the weight of possible deception. She was so trusting. For a moment, Elise wondered if she should let it all go—all the speculation—to maintain her child's pure heart. But no. Her long-ago buried hostility bubbled up inside. People who deceived others under the guise of friendship should be punished.

She touched Colette's hand tenderly. "You heard Avery and Emma. They had more than a little doubt about Kate's intentions." She noticed Colette's resistance, the way she tensed up and turned slightly away. She softened her voice. "I thought it might be easier to talk this through with an outsider." She thrust a hand to her heart. "A completely unbiased opinion."

As if on cue, the doorbell rang. It was Lori McMillan, dressed in black slacks and a lightweight leopard-print blouse, her hair cut into a shiny shoulder-length bob. She pulled her shades up into her hair and extended a hand. "So nice to meet you. When I heard about your situation, I have to say, I was intrigued."

Elise had phoned an old friend who worked at the newspaper. "Yes. But I'm sure you can understand, right now, Colette's emotions are . . ." She glanced into the living room and lowered her voice. "Conflicted. She's still in denial. It might be better for you . . . in terms of gathering information . . . if she doesn't understand the outcome."

Lori's eyes squinted in confusion.

"I don't think Colette will be as forthcoming if she knows this is for the media."

Lori was silent.

"Maybe it's best if you don't say where you work?"

Lori hesitated. "That's not exactly good practice."

Elise bristled. "Oh. Of course." She placed a hand on the woman's shoulder. "You do what you're comfortable with. I'm just saying my daughter might not give you as much detail if she thinks her words will be broadcast for public consumption."

Lori inhaled slowly through her nose, then nodded and walked into the living room. "Got it."

Elise signaled for her to sit in the overstuffed armchair, facing the fireplace. That afternoon, she had arranged several picture frames in a semicircle across from that chair. It was a collection of photos of Colette and Kate, in costumes and dance poses, varying ages spanning their decade-long friendship. She'd made sure to select shots where Colette stood center stage while Kate was off to the side, a clear depiction of the dynamic between the girls.

Lori held out a hand toward Colette. "My name is Lori. I'm going to talk to you about what happened this weekend, okay?"

Elise smiled, happy about Lori's choice to keep silent about exactly why she was there.

Colette shook her hand. "Sure."

Lori pulled out a phone. "Is it okay if I record this?" Colette shrugged. Lori placed the phone on the coffee table and asked Colette to tell her about the accident.

With a shaky voice, she recalled the details.

"I'm so sorry," Lori said, sounding sincere. She paused, shifted on her seat. "I heard you'd been accepted to dance at the Duncan Dance Prix next week."

"Yeah," Colette said.

"Congratulations. That's very prestigious." Lori threw a glance toward Elise, then looked back at Colette. "I've also heard there's another dancer from your studio who's been invited to audition."

"Yes. Kate."

"Can you tell me about Kate? Is she a good dancer?"

"Yes." Her mouth tightened in a tempered look of panic.

Elise pointed at the display of photos. "Colette and Kate have been friends for years."

Lori glanced at the pictures.

"Yes. She's been . . ." Colette hesitated. "Well, she's been like my sister." Her voice wobbled.

Lori nodded. "But in the last few months, your mother told me that tension has been brewing. There was an incident at the studio's spring gala, wasn't there?" She let the sentence dangle like a question, but Colette remained quiet.

Elise broke the silence. "Yes. And now these two *friends*"—she used finger quotes—"were set to compete against each other for one of the few coveted spots to advance to the final competition in New York City this summer."

"It's hard to be friends when you both want the same thing." Lori looked at Colette. "Do you think Kate is maybe . . . happy that you're no longer a threat to her success?"

Colette shrugged noncommittally. "Maybe she feels like there's less competition now, but she's not responsible for this." She pointed down at her cast. "It was just . . . a freak accident."

Elise was frustrated by her daughter's inability to even consider Kate's culpability. "It was no accident. It was an attack."

Colette averted her eyes toward her leg.

Lori rolled her pen between her hands, making a clicking sound each time it moved across her ring. "There are tons of stories about rivalries turned violent. Have you heard of Tonya Harding and Nancy Kerrigan?"

Colette's eyebrows squished together. She pulled out her phone and tapped. She read from an online search. "The 1994 Winter Olympics turned into a tabloid frenzy after Harding's ex-husband orchestrated an attack on rival figure skater Kerrigan by clubbing her in the leg." Colette put her phone in her lap and stared vacantly at the wall, the skin bunching around her eyes as if pained. Then she blinked and sat up straighter. "But they weren't friends."

Lori nodded, as if accepting this rebuttal. "There's the story of US skater Mariah Bell, who was accused of intentionally slashing her rival with the blade of her skate during warm-ups at the 2019 World Figure Skating Championship. And then there's Wanda Holloway—the Pom-Pom Mom. Have you heard that story?"

Elise scooted to the edge of her seat. "Who?"

"Wanda Holloway, the mother of a high-ranking high school cheerleader. There was an upcoming tryout for a competitive cheer squad; Wanda worried that her daughter might lose a spot on the team to another top-tier athlete. So, she hired a hit man to kill the rival's mother."

"Kill the mother?" Elise's voice rose an octave. "Why kill the mother?"

"Because Wanda thought if the girl was distraught over her mother's death, she wouldn't perform well at the tryouts, and that would clear the path for her own daughter's success."

"That's horrible," Colette said sharply.

Elise's mouth dropped open, her mind spinning. "The *mother* orchestrated the attack?"

"You'd be surprised how often parents get involved. Did you hear about the Pennsylvania mother who created deepfake videos of her daughter's cheerleading rivals to get them kicked off the team?"

"Yes . . ." Elise said slowly. "I did."

"Don't go there, Mom," Colette snapped. "Valerie doesn't even want Kate to dance. She doesn't consider me a threat."

No. But Elise was a threat to Valerie's ultimate mission: to get Andrew. All her conniving for legal help had backfired. She needed a new plan. Valerie knew if Elise was upset about Colette's injury and focused on her daughter's recovery, that would clear the path for Valerie to swoop in and seduce Andrew. Good God! It made so much sense! This attack wasn't only about opening a window of opportunity for Kate; it was also a way to drive Andrew away from Elise. Her palms began to sweat. She reached for her water and took a long gulp. Both Kate and Valerie benefited from Colette's injury.

Lori pulled out a notebook from her purse. "So, tension bubbled between you and Kate as you prepared for the competition. Did she do or say anything that could make you suspect she might be involved in this attack?"

"Kate didn't do this!" Colette barked.

Elise, ignoring Colette's outburst, turned to Lori. "Just the other day, Kate said Colette would never dance again."

"No, Mom. She said she *hoped* I'd never dance again. That's different."

Lori scribbled in her notebook. "Still, those are very strong words."

Colette looked down at her leg, her shoulders sagging as if a huge boulder of acceptance had crashed onto her.

"Half of the school overheard this *threat*."

"I see." Lori wrote furiously. "And the police haven't closed the case?"

Elise shook her head, a smile creeping across her face. Wouldn't it be satisfying when they did? The whirling sound of the garage door opened. "Well," Elise said nervously, "my son's home. We should wrap this up. It was so nice to talk to you. Thank you so much for your time."

Lori stood and walked over to Colette. "Wishing you a speedy recovery, my dear. Get back out there and show them nothing can hold you down." She smiled and walked toward the front door, Elise following.

Once out of earshot, Elise whispered, "Thanks so much, Lori. Do you think you have enough?"

"Oh yeah," Lori said animatedly. "I do have to reach out to Kate for her side of the story."

Elise prickled. "Is that absolutely necessary?"

"Well, actually, it is. For responsible journalism, I must at least make an attempt to contact them for a rebuttal. I'll reach out today or tomorrow; I'm hoping to get this article into Friday's edition. I'm going to push for front page of the community section. I think it will spark a lot of buzz."

FORTY-SIX

As Mom walked the woman to the front door, Trey came into the living room. "Who's that?" he asked.

Colette was sitting there, blown apart. It had been hard enough listening to Avery and Emma talk about how toxic she and Kate had become. All night, Colette had imagined people making crazy memes about them. *Frenemies.* But then she had to listen to this random woman spout stories about revenge and violence. The woman and Mom nodded like this made perfect sense—that Kate attacked Colette. As if! She wanted to tell them that one time Kate actually scooped up a spider and shoved it outside, so Colette wouldn't kill it. But she didn't. Because she was still thinking about the Kate from before. And now, according to everyone, Kate was different. She was jealous. And violent. Maybe she'd hated Colette all along. Colette felt so stupid.

She wanted to turn it around, tell Mom this was all *her* fault. She was the one who'd said training would break Colette's body. Mom was the one who demanded those early-morning miles.

"Is it true?" Colette asked Trey. "That Kate hates me? That she's, like, *happy* I'm out of the Duncan?"

His face hardened. He glared at Mom, whispering with that woman. "You're letting her get to you. She's insane." He pulled his ball cap down low and looked back at Colette.

The back of her throat went dry and scratchy. "I don't want to believe it. But . . ."

"But what?" He cut her off, his eyes turning cold.

"But . . ." Colette's voice hitched. She hated how weird things had been between them. It was like he picked Kate over her. And that hurt. Tears formed.

He softened. "What?" He tilted his head, curiously. "You can't honestly think Kate has anything to do with this."

"No. Of course not." She looked away, afraid to show her emotions. "But Emma and Avery told me some things Kate said that were really bitchy. Like maybe . . ." She stopped, not knowing how to say what she feared. "Look, I know Mom's going crazy, okay? I know Kate didn't hurt me. But what if it's true that she cares more about her own success then being my friend?" All those hours of them together in the basement . . . She'd thought they were bonding, but what if Kate was just using Colette? For the space? The equipment? For Mom's help? Had Colette totally been played? Her nose started to run. She wiped it with her sleeve.

Trey sat on the coffee table in front of her. "Have things been weird lately? Yes. I'm not gonna lie; she was really mad about the gala. She felt stabbed in the back."

Colette had felt that knife, too. It had hurt her to make that choice. But how could she explain that no matter what she did, someone would be mad at her? Mom or Kate. She thought Kate would take it better. Maybe she was wrong. And she'd never realized how it would toss Trey into the fire. She just wanted her brother back. Her friend back. Their trio.

"Come on. Kate loves you. She always has. I was with her last night, and she was worried that you'd actually believe the crap these jackoffs are saying."

"Really?"

"But I'm telling you, if Mom doesn't cut this shit out, it's gonna destroy any chance of you guys ever being friends again."

Colette looked over at Mom, standing in the sunlit foyer. She had this huge ear-to-ear smile and was tapping that woman on the shoulder.

They shook hands, and then, just before leaving, the woman winked. Colette's stomach clenched. Mom was up to something; she could feel it. Colette needed to act fast before Mom blew her world even further apart. She had to prove to Mom that Kate wasn't responsible for the attack. And maybe there was still a small part of Colette, despite Trey's reassurance, that needed proof that Kate's feelings for her were genuine.

A spark of impulse shot through Colette's body to the tips of her fingers. There was a sacred place where Kate let all her feelings out. Her notebooks. Colette needed to get her hands on them.

The answer to Kate's truth, the evidence of her true intentions, was buried somewhere in those written pages.

FORTY-SEVEN

Valerie woke to a whisper in her ear and breath against her cheek. She rolled over, pulling a pillow against her head, assuming she was nestled inside a crazy dream. But then came a tug on her arm. The voice grew louder. "It's all my fault."

Blinking her eyes open, she saw a shadowed face looming above her. She almost screamed, but her vision adjusted; it was Kate. She lifted herself up and tried to calm her banging heart. "What?"

Kate, face filled with terror, pressed a hand onto Valerie's arm. "It's all my fault."

Panicked, Valerie rubbed her eyes and turned on the lamp. What had she just said? Surely she'd heard wrong. Her heart began to thump. "What?" she repeated.

Her daughter's face was illuminated in the soft glow of light. Dark shadows hollowed out the undersides of her eyes. Her chin came down. She looked at Valerie through her tear-streaked lashes. "When she stole the staircase solo from me, I was so mad. I hated her. I wanted something bad to happen to her. I wanted her to hurt as much as I was hurting." She screwed her eyes shut, her chest heaving with each jagged breath.

Valerie tried desperately to clear her mind, to mentally bulldoze away the grogginess, to understand what her daughter was trying to confess. She heaved herself up, sitting against the headboard. "What are you saying?" There was a clamp around her throat, a brick pressing her heart. "Did you . . . Did you do something?" The words came out as a choke.

"I was so mad at her." She sobbed, her whole body shaking.

Please, God. Please, no. "Kate, what did you do?" Every muscle tensed.

"I wanted her to hurt. I wanted her to . . ." She wailed. "To suffer."

Valerie blinked, trying to process her daughter's words. "Kate, calm down. Take a breath."

"Our friendship is so complicated." She clenched her fists.

"Yes, that's true." Valerie leaned in to see her daughter more clearly. "Still, just because you were mad at someone, that doesn't make you responsible for an attack."

Kate covered her eyes with a hand to shield the light. "But, like, deep down, maybe there was part of me that *did* want her out of the competition."

"You can't wish an injury on someone. You didn't do anything, right? Kate! Look at me."

Kate put her hand down. Her eyes were bloodshot and swollen. She remained silent.

"Kate?" Valerie begged. Terror had risen into her throat, strangling her.

Slowly, Kate shook her head.

Valerie stared at her, trying to believe, but the dread in her daughter's eyes sent a chill across her skin. "Nothing?" Desperation echoed across the room. "You knew nothing about this?"

She inhaled slowly, rolled her lips in, and then finally, "No."

A flood of tears pushed into Valerie's eyes. "Okay," she said. She patted the space on the bed next to her; Kate laid her head down on the pillow. She reached for her mother's hand like she used to when she was young. Before dance. Before Chad. Before Valerie had screwed everything up. Valerie held her daughter until she drifted off to sleep.

This was like all those nightmares that had plagued her when Kate was a baby. But then she would bolt out of bed, covered in a cold sweat, and blessedly realize it was just her imagination gone dark. This, now, was real. Valerie eased out of the bed, guilt running through her veins. God have mercy on her for doubting what she should be sure of. But Kate's eyes. Her clenched fists. The way she looked so much like her angry, unstable father.

She tiptoed into Kate's room. Sitting on her desk in plain view was her most recent notebook. Valerie picked it up and flipped back a few pages to the night of the gala. Sitting down on the carpet, she crossed her legs and read, her heart ticking.

I hate her! It was premeditated. Strategized. She stole the staircase from me!

I thought she was my friend! My best friend.

All this time, I've been such an idiot.

I believed her when she told me I could do it. That I could be a professional dancer. That one day we'd live together in a big city and be in a company together. I thought those were honest, kind words—but it was all BULLSHIT! And I felt bad when Marcus hit on me. I would never steal anything from her!

But I had to watch her steal MY SOLO, perform MY MOVES with such perfection, there was no doubt she KNEW she'd be dancing that routine. She is a thief. A double-crosser. An enemy.

As my spotlight lit up her face, I wished she would miscount, misstep, land a jump wrong, twist an ankle, pull a muscle, crack a bone, break her back, so she would never dance again.

She was amazing. Of course she was!! Because she knew the freaking SCOUTS for the Duncan were there!!!!!

I HATE HER!

I will get her back someday.

I will. I will. I will.

Valerie's hands shook as the shock swept over her. A new fear spiraled down into her gut, and she flipped back in the notebook with dread.

Tonight, Mom and I watched tennis on TV. A reporter talked about a player named Petra Kvitová. Back in 2016 she was ranked number two in the world. One day a man attacked her. He slashed her hand with a knife. It was bad. The doctor said she might never compete again because it was her playing hand. Like an attack to a dancer's dominant leg— the landing leg.

A random attack—but the end of a career.

I wanted to know more about it. But when I googled "tennis star attacked with a knife," a different story popped up. Back in 1993, a man rushed out of the stands and stabbed Monica Seles in the middle of a match. She didn't play for two years. And when she returned to tennis, she was never as good. But here's the kicker: The guy who stabbed her? It wasn't that he hated her—he just was a huge fan of Steffi Graf—one of Monica's biggest rivals. He wanted to take Monica out of the competition so Steffi could win.

Valerie shut the notebook, her heart pounding, her throat parched with despair.

She wanted to believe Kate would never do anything like this. Kate was a sweet, loving, kind girl. She had never been vengeful.

But those words. Those stories. That determination.

If someone else ever got their hands on those notebooks and read about Kate's anger toward Colette, her fascination with violence to athletes . . . Well, she might as well lock her own prison cell.

FORTY-EIGHT

Elise lowered the temperature on the thermostat. It was too early in the season for air-conditioning. Outside, it was a pleasant seventy degrees with a gentle spring breeze, but Elise was sweating. She absolutely refused to believe this was menopause or perimenopause or any of the other preposterous ideas Ling Li had just spouted. But her face was flushed, her armpits damp, and her skin felt sunburned and scorched. She took her glass of ice water and pressed the sweating side against her cheek.

Sitting at the kitchen table, Ling Li pulled her cardigan tight around her torso and made a dramatic shiver. Elise rolled her eyes, then waved her hand like a fan in front of her face. Ever since the reporter had left, Elise's internal thermostat had been on overdrive. She was a windup toy ready to vibrate. She'd phoned Ling Li and Susie and told them to come over immediately. The minute they'd arrived, she'd recounted the visit with Lori and all the stories of violence between rivals. Then, rubbing her hands in satisfaction, she told them about the Pom-Pom Mom and her mission to sabotage her daughter's top competitor.

"Are you suggesting that Valerie is involved?" Susie's face pinched. "I've always heard she doesn't even want Kate to dance."

Elise let out a loud, frustrated breath. Why did she have to explain everything to everyone? "You're right; she couldn't care less about a dance career for her daughter. She didn't hurt Colette to propel Kate's success. Think about it. You were the one who called and told me about Valerie's ID badge in Andrew's car . . ."

Susie squinted. "But I thought they both said it was a real estate thing?"

"Which I called bullshit on, by the way," Ling Li said. Elise jerked with the harshness of those words and what they implied. Ling Li softened. "Not that I'm saying they're having an affair . . . just that *she* wants one."

Elise swallowed. "Yes. Exactly."

"Sorry, Elise. I'm not following." Susie shook her head. "Valerie was trying to . . . needle her way into Andrew's life, and he helped her because that's the kind of man he is—not realizing she was plotting to seduce him. But what does that have to do with . . ." She lowered her voice and pointed in the vague direction of the living room, where Colette sat, legs propped up, watching TV.

Elise got up and tiptoed, sly like a fox, then peered around the wall to check on Colette. Inching her way back to the table, she spoke softly. "When Valerie realized her scheme to bait Andrew wasn't working, she concocted a new plan. If Colette was injured, I'd be frantic and give all my attention to my hurt daughter. She hoped Andrew would feel neglected . . ."

"And she could swoop in and steal your husband!" Ling Li stood up with her hands theatrically outstretched. "All the while, repairing her relationship with her estranged daughter because Kate obviously wouldn't be hanging out here anymore!"

"Yes!" Elise shouted. It all made perfect sense.

"You think *Valerie* attacked Colette?" Susie's face blanched. "I don't think . . ."

"She could have hired someone," Ling Li suggested, her ponytail swaying side to side as she nodded.

"Oh." Susie went wide-eyed. "A hit man? Like in the mob?"

Ling Li sat back down, panting slightly. "Why not?"

Elise's mind raced. The pieces of the puzzle were all fitting together.

Susie's teeth chattered. "Elise, do you think maybe we can make it just a smidge warmer in here? The windows are frosting over."

Self-conscious, Elise got up and adjusted the thermostat. She ran a paper towel under cold water and held it to her neck.

Ling Li watched her. "Dena told me about a nurse practitioner who does a cocktail of hormones that could get you back on track."

"I'm not in menopause! I'm only forty-three! Geez." She fanned her face. "I'm just . . . processing. But it all makes sense! Right? I'm going to call the police and tell them to investigate Valerie."

Susie looked skeptical. "Sweetie, you know I love you. And this all has been quite tragic. But . . ."

"But what?" Elise snapped.

Susie took a breath. "Things are sounding a little . . . unrealistic." She grimaced. "Valerie doesn't have a lot of money, right? I can't imagine her paying for a hit man. Plus, she doesn't seem the type, you know? I'm just not sure . . . Didn't Andrew think it might be an internet stalker? That kind of makes more sense. Or what about that surfer boy who was obsessed with Colette? Avery said he posted a lot of scary things online. Teen boys don't like rejection. And Colette told Avery that she saw him drive by her house not too long ago. Have you checked your security cameras? Maybe he wanted . . . revenge?"

"Hmm." Ling Li tilted her head, curious.

"Seriously?" Elise gestured toward the window. "We know our neighbors. Don't you think someone would say something if a car was just lingering? It wasn't that boy! It was the premeditated plan of Valerie Yarnell!"

Susie rolled her lips in. "Maybe you should talk to someone. Like a therapist? You know Molly from Pilates? She sees a counselor over on Lenox."

"I don't need a therapist! That's why I called you guys! If you think I'm nuts, then I won't say anything. But if you think there's even a shred of possibility that Valerie could be linked to this, then I'm going to call the detectives and point them in her direction. Let *them* find the evidence." She looked frantically from Susie to Ling Li, her heart positively on fire.

Susie looked down at her cuticles.

Ling Li shrugged. "Why don't you sit on it for a day? Let the idea marinate, and we'll reconvene in the morning."

Elise sighed heavily, deflated.

"Check the security tapes," Susie said. "Just to make sure."

Elise nodded and walked her friends to the door. Surely silly Surfer Boy wasn't involved in this, right? She'd monitored Colette's phone. The boy had been silent. Unless Colette had somehow erased recent threats? Was that possible? Reluctantly, she opened her laptop and found their security camera footage from the last several weeks. She would peruse the tapes and report back what she already knew: Nothing. Nothing. Nothing. Then . . . wait. *What was that?*

She rewound the film, squinting at the dark image. *What the hell?* She checked the date and the time, her pulse quickening. Her neck went clammy. She pulled up the calendar on her phone to double-check. *My God.* Dread mixed with confirmation. Of course! Of freaking course!

That bastard!

It was the night she and Andrew had discussed their marriage. She'd agreed to ease off Colette's training, and even though he'd insisted it was all innocent, he'd promised to stop talking to Valerie. According to their security camera footage, later that night, Andrew had driven off at approximately 2:00 a.m. To break off things with Valerie, no doubt. Obviously, they were a little more involved than he'd admitted to. That liar. That cheat!

And what had happened next? After Valerie's heart was broken? Their affair ended?

Days later, their daughter had been viciously attacked.

If that wasn't revenge . . .

She exhaled deeply, wiped the sweat from her brow, picked up her cell phone, and dialed the police.

FORTY-NINE

Kate was at the studio with Miss Roza, doing last-minute preparations for the upcoming competition, so Valerie decided to take advantage of the mild temperature and go for a walk. She and Jazmin changed out of their scrubs into workout gear and laced up their running shoes. Her phone rang.

Valerie stood, frozen, listening to the voice on the line. In a daze, she sat down on the hard wooden bench. "Okay. I understand. I can come right now. Yes. Thank you." She ended the call and turned to Jazmin. "That was the police." Her words came out slowly, like she was speaking in a foreign language. "They want me to come in for questioning."

Jazmin stiffened. "Questioning? About what?" Defensiveness seeped into her voice. "About the attack?"

Valerie nodded.

"Are you kidding me? That's ludicrous. And illogical. How could they possibly think you had anything to do with that?"

Valerie felt like she had suddenly been coated in a heavy, viscous jelly. Her vision was oily, her tongue thick. Her feet moved as if through marshmallows, sinking and sticking. "I don't know." She grabbed her purse. "I guess I'm going to find out."

"Absolutely not!" Jazmin held her hand out in a stopping gesture. "You can't go to a police station without a lawyer." She jutted her chin like a mother forbidding a teenager.

"I have nothing to hide." Valerie massaged her temples where a viselike pressure squeezed around her head.

"You might say something that's misunderstood or misconstrued. They're going to grill you about Kate. You get that, right?"

"She was at the studio and then with me the rest of the day. It's an airtight alibi."

"You're her mother. There's nothing airtight about that." Jazmin pulled out her phone. "I'm calling that lawyer who helped Peter's son with his DUI."

"Jaz, we're not going to be able to get a lawyer to meet us at the police station in fifteen minutes." She walked toward the exit. "I can handle it. There's no merit to the accusation. They're probably just trying to appease a hysterical mother."

They walked through the cool cement parking deck toward their cars.

"I know, but still," Jazmin said. "I'm worried. You've never set foot inside a police station. Trust me; it's scary. Even if you've done nothing wrong, by the time they're through with you, you'll be confessing about the day Kate played hooky in middle school."

"Kate never skipped school."

Jazmin let out a dramatic breath. "I don't think you understand."

She did. She'd do whatever it took to protect her daughter.

Valerie clicked open the doors to her car, and they both climbed inside. She started the engine, and Jazmin fell silent. They were at the station in five minutes. Jazmin stayed in the waiting area as Valerie followed a woman down a long cold corridor into a small room. The slate-gray walls had a thick foamy texture to them that she assumed was a form of soundproofing. There was a square wooden table and four black plastic chairs. The air was stale with a faint smell of mold and bleach. She sat.

A moment later, two men dressed in blue uniforms entered. Her eyes were immediately drawn to the pistols nestled inside their holsters at their waistbands. A slick of sweat trailed down her back. The older officer had a head of white hair and a thick midsection. He introduced himself as Officer Abbott, then gestured with an extended hand to his partner, Officer Jones, a tall, dark-skinned man with an angular face and light hazel eyes. He was about Valerie's age and movie-star handsome. They both sat in chairs across from her. She couldn't stop staring at their uniforms, the shiny metal nameplates on their chests.

The younger cop pointed to a camera in the corner of the room. "We'll be recording our conversation."

The word *conversation* should have eased her nerves. After all, they hadn't said *interrogation* or *investigation*, but still, now she wished she'd listened to Jazmin and called an attorney.

"I'll get right down to it," Officer Abbott said.

The handsome cop gave her a quick smile and a small bite of his lower lip, which almost seemed . . . flirtatious? A tingle of both desire and relief washed through her. Because damn, he was good-looking, and also, he wouldn't flirt unless this was simply routine. Right?

She gave him a tiny grin back and tried to relax.

"We want to ask you some questions about a young lady named Colette Carrington," Abbott said. "Are you familiar with her?"

"Yes."

"Are you aware that she was attacked while jogging in the park this past Saturday?"

"I am."

He tapped a pen against the wooden table, making a *thud-thud* sound that echoed loudly in the small, sparse room. He sat back in the plastic chair and waited. His expression was probing, unnerving her. Like maybe it wasn't just routine. *They'll just sit there, and let you dig your own grave,* Jazmin had warned her. *Don't feel like you need to fill the silence.*

Valerie worked hard to remain quiet. She wouldn't rush to defend Kate. This was just unreasonable ideas spouted from a crazy mother who was frantic because she could no longer live vicariously through her daughter. She glanced toward the hot cop, her possible ally, but his head was down.

After a long silence, Abbott cleared his throat. "Did you know that according to the Bureau of Justice Statistics, only thirty-eight percent of nonfatal violent crimes are committed by strangers?"

A thud of dread dropped on her. "No. I don't know much about . . . crime."

He pulled out a small black notepad and flipped it open. "You have a daughter named Kate Yarnell. Is that correct?"

"Yes."

"She's fifteen years old?"

"Yes."

"Kate has been a student at Volkov Studio for the last five years, where Colette also is enrolled?"

"Yes."

"Both Kate and Colette have been selected to compete at the upcoming Duncan Dance Prix national dance competition in the regional division this upcoming weekend at the Ferst Center?"

"Yes."

"Would you agree that Colette has always been the better dancer?"

Valerie startled. "I think that statement is a matter of opinion. Not fact."

Officer Jones gave a slight nod of conciliation.

"Fair enough," Abbott said. "But would you concede that your daughter might feel that Colette was her biggest competition at this upcoming event?"

"No." Valerie's tone was insistent. "There will be close to five hundred dancers this weekend, from all over the Southeast. I think it's impossible to know who will be Kate's biggest competition."

He tapped his pen against his notepad with a loud thud. His jaw twitched like he hadn't been expecting a rebuttal. "Okay. But wouldn't it be fair to say that the girls, who were once friends, have now shifted to rivals?"

"Do the two have to be mutually exclusive? Can't you be friends with someone who is also competing for the same thing?"

"Are they?" he asked quickly. "Are they still friends?"

Valerie swallowed. She thought of Jazmin's warning: *Don't get trapped into saying something that can be misconstrued.* "I think that's a question only Kate and Colette can answer."

The two men exchanged a glance that Valerie couldn't interpret. A few moments of silence went by. "Are you aware that a week ago, your daughter and Colette had an argument at school where several students heard Kate say, *You'll never dance again?*"

Valerie bunched her hands in her lap, trying to squeeze away her panic. "Teenagers often say things they don't mean."

"But it's noteworthy," Abbott said, "given that, just five days later, she was assaulted."

"Kate was at the studio during the time of the attack." She couldn't believe this was actually happening. She was defending her daughter to a cop, providing an alibi, as if Kate were an actual suspect.

"Class didn't start until ten, but she was there earlier to clean, correct?"

"Yes."

"Alone?"

"Uh . . ." Valerie didn't know.

"That particular morning, the instructor told us she didn't arrive until fifteen minutes before the lesson. Since there are no security cameras at the studio to confirm whether your daughter was there or not, that leaves Kate with no alibi for several hours."

A cold blast of panic shot through Valerie's insides.

He consulted his notes and changed gears. "A few weeks ago, you were seen by your neighbor. She claimed you were outside your condominium arguing with a man about money. She described the man as tall and muscular, with shoulder-length blond hair. She had never seen him before."

The words sent something straight through her, like a train rushing past, the loud wind growling through the air.

"Can you tell me who that was?"

"It was Kate's father—"

"Chad Jensen?" he interrupted. "Birth date June 6, 1989? The name listed on Kate's birth certificate? The person you had claimed was deceased?"

A feeling of doom descended. This was straight from Elise's mouth. She'd gotten the police to believe her! Valerie straightened. "Last I heard, telling a lie was not a crime."

He stared at her for a long time. Goose bumps popped along her skin. "And you were arguing about money?"

"Yes. He was mad I hadn't sent him money . . . several years ago . . . when he needed it."

"Does he still need money?"

"I don't know his personal finances."

"Could he potentially benefit if his daughter won a very substantial cash prize at the upcoming competition?"

Tiny little needles scratched the back of Valerie's throat. "Well, that money would belong to Kate . . . if she won it." Her voice wobbled.

"But Kate and her father have gotten close lately, correct?"

She was silent.

"If Chad thought Kate would share that windfall, it would make sense that he might want to reduce the competition?"

Valerie bit the inside of her cheek and tried to not show the panic that was pouring through her. Why did he have to show up? At the absolute worst time?

Abbott pointed to his partner, who read from his notes. "Chad Jensen has quite a record. Let's see. He was arrested and charged with assault for breaking someone's nose."

"A man criticized how he was loading his lawn mower onto his trailer. Chad was embarrassed . . . and flew off the handle. But he paid the fine, and that was it. No further charges. And it was a long time ago." Valerie felt kicked in the shins. That cop had looked so nice. He'd smiled at her! If she wasn't sitting, she would buckle to the floor.

He flipped pages. "There was a restraining order and a drunk and disorderly in Georgia. Then we hit the list from Costa Rica: another assault, trespassing on private property. Then, of course, the manslaughter conviction."

Her mind raced. "I understand Chad has had some issues in the past. But he's matured. He's received help for his anger." She had no proof of this, but she could only hope. "Since his release, he's been an upstanding citizen." Had he? She didn't know. Her insides burned. How many times had she sworn she was done defending him?

Abbott made a dramatic expression: eyebrows raised, mouth drawn, and a head tilt that seemed to say, *Does it even matter?* He continued. "Colette was assaulted while running in Chastain Park. Chad's vehicle was captured on police-monitored security cameras parked at the entrance to the same park on Thursday afternoon, two days before the attack."

"What?" It was a gasp.

"What was Kate's father doing there when he lives two hours away?"

Foreboding dropped into her bones. "I . . . don't . . . wait! He picked Kate up from the studio that day."

"Could it be they were scouting the location? Setting up plans?"

"Absolutely not!"

Officer Jones gave her a sad look that pierced her gut. "I'm going to have to ask for your phone. And Kate's phone. To examine calls and messages."

Valerie slid her phone across the table "Kate . . ." Anxiety spread through her like a slow poison. "Kate lost her phone." On Thursday. The day Chad was in town. Her heart catapulted into her throat. The men stared at her. "She's a teenager! They lose things all the time."

Abbott scribbled notes. "We'll need to get our hands on those phone records. And of course, we'll be speaking to your daughter." He pulled his mouth into a phony smile. "Is there any reason *you* might want to see Colette injured?"

Valerie's spine straightened. "Why would I . . . ?"

"Were you having an affair with Colette's father, Andrew Carrington?"

"No. We're friends." Heat scorched her face.

"Your neighbor, who clearly has all eyes and ears on your community, claims she saw you and a gentleman in the back seat of a black BMW. She didn't get the license plate number, but she said there was a UGA plate on the front bumper. Guess who drives a black BMW with a UGA license plate?"

Her heart seized in embarrassment, shame, and fear.

"There are no divorce proceedings in the process for the Carringtons. One could speculate the rage a woman might feel if she believed a man would leave his wife and then didn't. Passion and scorn can provoke revenge."

"Why would I go after Colette?" Valerie's voice wobbled.

"Because a great way to torture a woman is to hurt her child." A vortex of insinuation filled the room.

"This is unbelievable." Valerie put her head in her hands. Somehow, they suspected not only Kate but Chad and now her? Panic poured through her body.

The cops were silent. Abbott scribbled one final note, then tucked the notepad back into his pocket. "Thank you, Ms. Yarnell." They both stood and stuck meaty hands out toward her.

She shook, realizing her palm was damp with sweat. Then they were gone.

And she was left with nothing but fear.

FIFTY

Colette sat on the couch, scrolling through Netflix trailers. She thought that being out of the competition would let Mom back the hell off her. She was dead wrong. Now, instead of hovering over her training, Mom practically levitated above the couch, commenting on Colette's every move. *Is that what you're going to watch? It's just garbage for your mind. Is that what you're going to eat? It's just garbage for your body.*

Now Mom wandered in with kale chips and water. She took the remote from Colette's hand. "Oh, look! There's a new season of *Cheer*!" Because *that's* not garbage.

The side door creaked open. They heard aggressive stomping through the kitchen, then Trey bounded in, face red with rage. "This shit has to stop!"

"Language, Trey," Mom scolded.

"First, all the gossip. Then, the locker graffiti. Yesterday Kate found a Barbie shoved in her backpack. It was missing a leg. Today, she didn't come to school and she's not answering my messages. Someone said they heard her mom was at the police station. Being questioned! What if they do that to Kate, too? What the hell, Mom?"

Mom shrugged, all innocent. "Why are you mad at me? I didn't put a Barbie in her backpack."

"But you're the one who started these crazy rumors. I told you to fix it, but you haven't."

Colette closed her eyes, feeling strangely responsible. Of course Kate hadn't hired a hit man. Come on! But because Colette was injured, Kate was suffering, too.

Mom let out a dramatic sigh like, *Oh, you stupid fools* and sat beside Colette on the couch. "Both of you have had uncontested lives. Do you know what I mean by that?" she asked. Trey and Colette were silent. "You're both attractive, talented, and have financial resources. You've never looked at someone and thought, *If only I had that.* Or worse, *I wish she didn't have it so easy.*"

"Kate isn't like that," Trey said.

"You're very gracious in your defense of her. But trust me, people you think you know can harbor deep-seated feelings of jealousy and revenge." Mom fiddled with her wedding ring, hesitating, then nodded as if giving herself permission. "Sit. I'm going to tell you a story I've never told anyone."

Trey relaxed his shoulders and tilted his head, looking curious. He sat.

"Right before I met your father, I was living in New York with my best friend, Gina. We were both soloists at a company. You have to understand," she said, looking at Trey, who was unfamiliar with the structure of dance companies, "contracts are renewed annually. So, you can be friends with the other dancers, but you're also always competitors for a job." She paused, tapping her chin, almost like she was crafting a story instead of retelling it. "As I got more stage time, strange things began to surface—torn shoes, glass shards, all the cliché sabotage. I assumed it was random jealous dancers. Never Gina. We were friends.

"I refused to let those antics get to me," Mom said. "I continued to earn the attention of the director and choreographers. Then, quite out of the blue, I became fatigued. Not run-of-the-mill tired. I was walking through mud, seeing stars when I stood too fast, forgetting basic routines."

"Were you not eating enough?" Colette asked. She knew dancers were notorious for cutting calories and exercising on little fuel. She wondered if that was why her mother had such a detailed nutrition plan for her. Colette had always been annoyed by the inflexible menus, but maybe Mom had learned from experience.

But Mom shook her head. "No, that wasn't it. They made me see a dietitian, but I was eating well. I went to the doctor. They did blood work and tests. No one could figure out why I could barely do a kick, let alone perform an intense routine. But contract renewals were coming up, so I kept trying, until one practice, I was so dizzy, I felt like I had taken a hallucinogenic drug. The colors of everyone's clothing smeared together. My legs wouldn't cooperate. I felt like I was walking on a rocking ship. Voices rose in my ears above the music, calling my name, and everything went black."

"What happened?" Trey asked.

"I'd fallen off the stage. I had a grade-four ankle sprain. I couldn't dance for eight weeks. I lost my contract. Gina was promoted to prima."

"What was wrong?" Colette asked. "Why were you sick?"

Mom smiled a strange smile, like she was transfixed by her own story. "Our apartment was very small, and Gina and I shared a bathroom. I had a bottle of Valium in the medicine cabinet. That's antianxiety medication. I was really nervous about moving to the city, and my doctor had prescribed it in the event I had a panic attack."

Colette straightened her spine. She'd never known her mother struggled with anxiety. Her mother seemed so confident. Colette wondered if she should talk to her mom about the time in the closet, or when her heart raced at night. Was there a medicine that could help her?

"I never took any of those pills," her mother said. "Not one. But after my fall, I rummaged for an ibuprofen and came across that bottle. It was half empty!" Her eyes narrowed, and her face pulled tight. "A sinking feeling told me to look up the side effects of Valium. Drowsiness. Dizziness. Low blood pressure." She ticked off the words on her fingers, her voice ringing in a strange triumph. "Gina had drugged me! She had started fixing my coffee in the mornings. She crushed those pills and gave them to me so I wouldn't be able to perform well. But when I pushed through, because I was so determined, she increased the doses so I could barely function! So she could steal prima from me!" She stood up, her eyes glazed over and her hands clenched into fists.

"Did you tell the director?" Colette asked.

Mom scrunched her nose and parted her lips, looking like an angry Chihuahua. "All she had to do was say the pills were mine. My name was on the bottle. She called me an addict! No one believed me. I lost everything because of her!"

Trey and Colette were silent. They'd never understood why Mom had given up her ballet career. "You could have gone somewhere else," Colette said.

"Yes." Mom cast her eyes to the ceiling. "But I was devastated, shocked that someone could be so vengeful." She swallowed. "I learned that when people fear their future is at risk, they can do desperate things."

It suddenly became clear why Mom was laser-focused on Kate. Her own betrayal had influenced her opinion.

Trey's face was hard. He stood. "I'm really sorry about what happened to you, but just because someone backstabbed you doesn't mean everyone is evil. Kate would never hurt Colette."

Mom stood. "Trey, you're blinded by your infatuation with Kate. You don't see her danger!"

"Kate was at the studio when it happened," Colette reminded her. She had an alibi.

"Her mother helped her plan it, so it could go down while she was accounted for."

"Valerie?" Colette threw her hands out. "Are you serious?"

"She wants to steal your father from me! Both Valerie and Kate want to hurt us!"

"You're crazy." Trey walked away.

"Why is it so far-fetched?" Mom called after him. "That woman lied about Kate's father! She's deceitful!"

The side door opened. Dad walked in, his eyes blazing, waving a newspaper in the air. "What the hell is this?" he barked. "Are you out of your mind?" He slapped the Community section down on the coffee table. There, splashed across the front page was a picture of Colette and Kate and a headline that screamed: A Twist of Fate, or a Turn of Hate?

Colette's body went cold. She picked up the paper, scanning the text. The reporter wrote of a dance competition turned dark. Friends turned rivals. Her words . . . Twisted and filled with accusation.

Her parents argued, but their shouting was muted and distant, like Colette was underwater. At first, it seemed like Mom was spiraling recklessly, but her story proved competition could bring out the worst in people. Avery and Emma admitted to doubt. And this reporter cooked up a very convincing story.

Did Kate really hate Colette? Did Valerie really love Dad?

How had everything gotten so out of control?

FIFTY-ONE

When Valerie's phone rang, she grabbed it and escaped into her bedroom. She'd left several frantic messages for Chad to call her. "Chad," she answered. "Please tell me you had nothing to do with the attack on Colette Carrington!"

"What?" He sounded annoyed. "I hear nothing from you for weeks, even after I tried to reconnect, to coparent, and then you finally call with accusations?"

She closed her eyes. She wouldn't let him paint her as the angry woman. "The cops think you might have assaulted Colette to help Kate win the Duncan so you could get your hands on the prize money."

"That's ridiculous! I've got nothing to hide. Let them question me."

"Well, the first thing they're going to ask is why were you at Chastain Park last Thursday?"

"What?" He was confused. Or faking. She truly didn't know. "I got into the city before Kate's lesson, so I went for a walk."

"Well, they think you and Kate went to scout the location of Colette's attack."

"Why would I hurt some girl I've never even met?" His tone was all too familiar. Defensive, yes, but also with a hint of, *Are you kidding me?* She could imagine him flashing that football hero smile; nothing is ever *his* fault. But soon the swagger would spiral into rage if she wasn't careful.

"That prize is a huge amount of money. Something that could help you set up this new business you've told Kate about."

"I know how to get a business loan."

"Oh yeah? Then why haven't you done it? Is it because your history and credit aren't exactly stellar?"

"Don't get all pissy with me! I didn't bludgeon some girl!" he spat.

She'd gone too far. But this was the direction the cops would pursue. "You better have a clear-cut alibi for last Saturday, the day of the attack."

He made a frustrated grunt, then finally, "I went for a trail ride Saturday. What are you, the freaking police?" Classic Chad: overconfidence, defensiveness, anger, then condemning the accuser.

"I'm just trying to remove suspicion from my daughter. And since you've shown up, Kate's been more aggressive, more hostile, and now there's this attack. You've created a lot of problems!" She tried to control her tone, but anxiety crept forward.

"That's not what Kate says. She said you created problems with all your lies. That's why she's more hostile. Because she's upset with you!"

"Look," Valerie tried to temper her resentment, "I've let you spend time with Kate, believed your intentions, but what am I supposed to think when the police build a convincing case against you? Kate will be devastated if you did this! Tell me you didn't!"

He was silent for a moment. "I didn't, Val. Come on." His tone softened; she could almost imagine the tilt of his head, the pleading look in his eyes, the half rise of his lips into that crooked smile. "You know me better than that. I was trail riding on Saturday. In the mountains. Hours away from Atlanta."

"Can anyone verify that?" Her voice clogged with tears.

She heard him let out a long breath. "I was alone."

Her palms sweat, and her heart raced. She thought of Kate's late-night confessions of hate, her diaries filled with vengeance. Chad's anger that flared like a lit match. Could they be a team? Securing what Kate wanted—a win—and what Chad needed: money.

Just then, there was a knock at her bedroom door. Kate came in, not waiting for a reply. She held her MacBook. "Have you've seen it?"

"I've got to go." Valerie ended the call with Chad.

Kate placed the laptop in front of Valerie. The screen showed an article from the local Atlanta newspaper. She scanned the text, quickly at first, then slowed down as the content sank in. Her neck cramped with strain. "I can't believe this," she said. But actually, she could. Because had she really expected anything less from Elise? If she was brazen enough to contact the police, why not the media as well? Hatred sliced through her. The only saving grace was Elise didn't know Chad's history and what the police had implied. But how long until she found out?

"We should tell our side of the story," Kate said.

Valerie took a deep breath. "That woman tried to contact me. I didn't realize she was a reporter. I thought it was someone being nosy. I deleted the message. But I did tell our version. The cops brought me in for questioning."

"What?" Her eyes went wide. "When? Why didn't you tell me?"

"Yesterday. I didn't want to upset you. But they'll want to talk to you, too."

Kate tossed her laptop down and threw her arms around her. Valerie took her in, the clean, Ivory soap smell of her, the feel of her taut, muscular arms. It had been years since they'd embraced this way— but now, she was scared. She wanted her mother.

Valerie rubbed her daughter's back. "There's nothing to link us to this crime." She dug deep to really believe that. "It's obvious Elise is trying to create drama right before the competition to rattle you. Don't let it. You've worked so hard." She blinked back tears. She wouldn't let her know the police were suspicious of Chad. She'd protect her daughter. She'd do whatever was necessary.

Kate leaned against her shoulder. "What do we do, Mom? How do we make this stop?"

Valerie thought how she'd wished for her daughter to return to her, to talk to her, to need her the way she once had. And now those wishes had been granted. Her daughter needed her. Wanted her help. She had been divided from Elise.

She had never dreamed that reality would have such a price.

FIFTY-TWO

"Are you out of your mind?" Andrew's voice boomed across the kitchen as he waved the newspaper in the air.

"A Twist of Fate, or a Turn of Hate?" What a brilliant title for the article. When Lori, the reporter, emailed her a copy of the column she was thrilled with the results. She wouldn't let Andrew's fury diminish her satisfaction. Things were really working in her favor. The story she'd concocted about her time in New York had been well received by Colette and Trey. They didn't know she had flipped it on its head. That it was Gina's pills that Elise had found. It started small—Elise breaking the pill in half and crumbling it into Gina's coffee. Then the whole pill, and on the day of Gina's fall, two doses. But what was Elise to do? Gina had been trying to push Elise out. To take her spot on center stage! Elise had to eliminate the competition and secure her future. But Elise had never resorted to brutal violence. It wasn't her fault that Gina fell off the stage and sprained her ankle. And Elise hadn't realized Gina was sleeping with their director, so when she pointed the finger at Elise, the stupid man believed her. Elise countered accusations by saying the medicine belonged to Gina, that she was an addict, but Gina spread her legs, kept the director on her side. Elise was kicked out, made an example. Like other dancers weren't sabotaging one another all the time.

Worst of all, the director called several administrators at other companies in the area. Ballet was a small world. No one wanted a dancer who drugged her competition. When Andrew came along, it was her ticket to a new location. A fresh start.

She'd never told anyone the true story, but the edited version had not only placed Elise in a sympathetic light, it allowed Colette and Trey to recognize how athletes could undermine competitors in the name of success. It had been a wonderful moment. But now, Andrew was baring his teeth like a damn tiger, waving the newspaper in the air.

"You're destroying Kate's reputation! With absolutely no proof." The tips of his ears burned red, driving home to Elise just how furious he was. This was serious. The safety of their marriage—of their family—hung by a thin, delicate thread.

Elise glanced over at Colette, gave a small gesture for her to leave. She grabbed her crutches and disappeared. Elise turned back toward her husband. "Andrew, listen." She was calm, trying to soften his fury. "Remember those flowers? That nasty message? I'm sorry I assumed they were from you, but it made sense at the time. You'd harped on the fact that I was pushing Colette too hard. But afterward, I realized the card wasn't addressed to me . . . It was meant for Colette. From a jealous rival! I called the florist. They didn't have a credit card receipt or a Venmo transaction. The person paid *in cash*. To cover their tracks. And guess what? I asked if it was a teenager who'd ordered those flowers, and they weren't sure but said that sounded right!" She extended her hand. *There you go.* "It was *Kate* who sent them as a threat. *Colette is going to crack*. My God! How were we so blind?"

Andrew's jaw clicked. "That's not proof. That stalker from Florida is a teenager. And why did I have to hear about him from an outsider?"

"Who?" Elise demanded. "Valerie? Of course she throws Surfer Boy into the mix to overshadow her daughter's guilt."

"Elise!"

She rolled her eyes. "I took care of that online problem. I blocked him. Monitored Colette's phone. He's no longer an issue."

He shook his head in disgust. "We don't know who attacked her! But you're destroying a girl who's been part of this family. What's happened to you? You've never been vindictive."

Rage boiled under her skin. "What about you?" She flung a finger out toward the window. "Why does our security tape show you driving off in the middle of the night? Right after you told me Valerie was *just a friend*, and you would prioritize us!" She pounded her hand on her chest. "Where did you go at two a.m.? *Huh?* Did you race off to have one final screw?"

His face blanched. "I didn't sleep with Valerie!"

"Don't you think it's a little more than coincidental that after you supposedly quit your *friendship* with Valerie, two days later our daughter was attacked?" She waited for an excuse, a rebuttal, a look of distress, remorse, something . . . but his face remained hard.

She knew she was in trouble. She'd expected him to beg her for forgiveness. To admit something—anything—but no. He was silent. This chasm was far deeper than just a fleeting attraction to another woman. Accusing him wasn't the way to rectify this situation. She had to find a new approach. She'd never used tears as a weapon, like all those women on TV dramas. But suddenly, her eyes filled. She made a choking sound, her emotions seeping out. "You love her. That's why you think these things about me. Because you're trying to find a reason to leave me." She sat down on the kitchen chair and threw her hands over her eyes. And then she was crying actual tears. Because it all seemed too real. The possibility of what she was saying.

The air was still. He looked positively shocked by her unusual tenderness.

"I don't know what to believe," he finally said, running a hand through his thick, wavy hair. "You're telling me you're not responsible for this?" He pointed at the paper on the counter. "For real?" He looked conflicted.

Lying was tricky. She'd learned that the hard way in New York after being trapped in a spiderweb of deceit. But a crisis was upon them. Drastic measures needed to be taken. "Andrew, I had no way of knowing what that reporter was going to write. She asked if she could meet with Colette to ask some questions. I thought it was going to be commentary on rising crime in safe neighborhoods." She shrugged dramatically.

He sat down and sighed deeply. "This is all such a mess."

"I know. Our poor girl." She took his hand. As long as she still had him, she'd won half the battle.

FIFTY-THREE

Valerie and Kate left early Saturday morning to head toward the Ferst Center for the first day of the Duncan Dance Prix. The curbs and nearby parking lots were clogged; they had to drive a few blocks away to find an available deck. Valerie wondered if all the cars could possibly be here for the competition, and for the first time, she realized maybe she'd never truly understood the magnitude of this event.

They walked quickly, the spring air damp and cool, until they arrived at the red brick building. People gathered around in clumps outside the entrance: young dancers, adorable in tiny tutus and tights; preteens and teenagers dolled up in heavy makeup and glitter. As they walked toward the glass double doors, a swarm emerged from behind a large figure-eight statue and raced toward them, pointing cameras and microphones in their direction. "Kate! Can you tell us your version of the story? Is there really that much animosity between you and Colette? How do you feel about your rival's attack and injury? Did you have anything to do with it?"

"Valerie Yarnell? What is your comment on the allegations against you and your daughter?" Voices shouted over each other as Valerie stood frozen, completely shell-shocked as the accusations fell like a sledgehammer.

It was Kate who recovered first, grabbing her mother's hand and pulling the door handle. It opened halfway, then stopped hard against the large leather loafer of a reporter. He stood, eyes squinting, mouth parted like a predatory animal. "How do you respond to the mounting evidence against your daughter?"

Valerie glared at him. "How dare you!" she barked. "We have done nothing wrong. There is *no* evidence!"

But the man spouted the indisputable facts: the gala controversy, the fight at school, the threats Kate had shouted.

Valerie saw Kate visibly crumble under the allegations. She had to defend her daughter. But how? Her thoughts scrambled; she needed to redirect their interest. And suddenly, it was there—the words Andrew had said about his wife when he and Valerie were at the Mexican restaurant: *Elise is secretive about her time in New York. I often wonder what transpired, how far she would go to get what she wanted.*

What did Elise want more than anything now? For Colette to be number one. "Have you considered this?" Valerie announced to the swarm of reporters. "Is it possible that Elise Carrington would rather have an injured child than one who isn't the champion?"

The crowd fell to a hush. Valerie yanked the door, and she and Kate disappeared inside.

Once inside the foyer, they darted down a random hallway, away from any camera flashes. Kate leaned against the wall, her chest heaving. "You don't really think Elise . . ."

Did she? Days ago, she would have said, *Of course not.* But now, her rage for that woman was boiling. "I just needed them to stop hassling you."

Kate nodded, wiping tears. "I can't dance. Not with those people out there."

Valerie was ashamed. Months ago, she'd hoped her daughter would abandon this competition. But not like this. She took in a breath and cupped Kate's chin with her hands. "Don't let them win. After what you've gone through, most girls would have buckled. I'm proud of you." The words cracked with emotion. "You've been strong. Keep being strong."

"Okay." It was a whisper.

They walked back toward the lobby, following signs that directed the dancers toward their proper locations based on their age group. Kate gave Valerie a hard hug and headed down a long, crowded corridor.

She stood there motionless, watching her daughter shrink smaller and smaller as she walked away. She backtracked toward the lobby, entered the theater, and found a seat. Scanning the audience filling in all around her, she didn't see any reporters. Just groups of families clustered together, cameras and phones resting in their laps, paper programs rustling in their hands.

The lights dimmed. An elegant woman introduced fifteen judges seated below the stage. "This weekend, four hundred dancers will compete at our Southeast regional competition for one of the twelve spots to advance to the finals at Lincoln Center in New York City. At that prestigious competition this summer, one hundred scholarships will be awarded, and for the few top-tier students, the ultimate prizes: Cash! Agent contracts! Dance company admissions!"

The audience erupted into thundering applause.

The woman onstage smiled and waited for the clapping to die down. "Winners will be announced Sunday afternoon, when the award ceremony begins at four p.m. Good luck to all!" The lights dimmed, the curtains parted, and the first dancer appeared.

Valerie tried to pay attention, but one performance slid into the next, all blurring together. If she'd paid more attention through the years, maybe she would understand why the crowd oohed and aahed at certain moments, why the woman next to her gasped and flailed her arms dramatically for one jump but the previous jump garnered no reaction.

The woman leaned closer and whispered, "That was amazing, wasn't it?"

"Uh-hmm," Valerie answered evasively.

"When does your child perform?"

She looked at the program. "Not for another hour."

"Waiting is so hard, isn't it? My name is Janel." Her face was full of energy, her hands fluttering holding her program. "My Mia doesn't dance until two p.m. It's torture for me; I can't imagine how hard it is for the dancers!"

"At least you seem to understand what's going on." Valerie gave a tentative smile. "I'm Valerie, and I'm a little lost." It hit her like a sucker punch that she'd gotten everything wrong. She'd thought if she worked more so she could buy the nicer house in the better neighborhood, Kate would want to spend time with her. But really, all Kate wanted was someone who took an interest in what was important to her. That's what had drawn her to Elise as a mother figure. Elise cared about dance, and Valerie hadn't. "I'm a working mom, so I missed a lot. I never became well versed in dance." She gestured toward the girl onstage, springing up and down with intense vigor. "I should have taken the time to ask questions and comprehend it, because my daughter loves it." The weight of the words, the reality of her decisions to disengage from her daughter's passion, sank down onto her heart. Her insides were scooped out and hollow. "I'm a terrible mother."

Valerie was horrified. Why was she admitting her life's failures to a stranger?

Before she could career down a road of embarrassment, Janel did the most unexpected thing. She extended her hand and rested it on top of Valerie's. "Oh, sweetie," she said. "There's no way you're a bad mother. Just the fact that your daughter is here means you've done something right. You've provided her with instruction, and a working mother models discipline and diligence. No one makes it this far without a solid foundation of work ethic and grit."

The words covered Valerie in a soft pillow of kindness. "Thank you," she said, "for saying those things."

Janel pulled her hand back and waved it through the air, dismissing the enormity of her graciousness. Then she ever so slightly leaned toward Valerie and began explaining. "That jump—that's a difficult move because it requires both power and flexibility. Not everyone can do both . . . Multiple double tours are hard because of timing and coordination . . . Oh! That's a mistake. She didn't land cleanly."

The minutes ticked by, and then, without even realizing the time, Valerie tapped her new friend's arm. "That's her. My Kate."

They both fell silent. The music thrummed. Kate began to dance. "Oh! Her choice . . ." Janel said breathlessly. "Such a classic standard variation, but with your daughter's build and physique, it's clear she knew, or her coach knew, that there's an increased prominence of athletic proficiency over stylistic purity."

"What does that mean?" Valerie looked at Kate onstage, fluttering and prancing like she was being guided and pulled by an invisible wire.

Janel smiled. "It means your daughter is not only an excellent dancer; she's a tremendous athlete." Onstage, Kate threw her body into the air, did a three-hundred-sixty-degree spin, then landed on one arm. Janel put a hand to her mouth and gasped.

"What? Did she make a mistake?" Valerie's heart banged.

"No." It was a whisper. "She just completed a one-handed chair flare." She burst into a huge, proud smile. "Mark my words. Your girl is going to New York."

FIFTY-FOUR

The phone shook inside Elise's hands as she scrolled through her social media feed. *New controversy amid the "Twist of Hate" case in Atlanta where a promising dancer was mauled just days before an international competition. Could the injuries have come from . . . her mother?* What in God's name? Her disgust was so palpable, her whole body buzzed.

At that very moment, Kate was dressed in costume, hair shellacked into a bun, eyes lined black, lips painted red. Probably MAC Ruby Woo red, stolen from Colette's signature look, just like she'd stolen this opportunity. And they had the gall to voice her as the culprit? Her hand clenched into a fist.

She walked into the living room where Colette was watching some inane baking show—immersed in the spirit of a TV competition to replace the one she should be attending. A surge of righteous indignation boiled. *I'm going to get even.* But how? She texted Ling Li: Available to chat?

Three white dots appeared, then disappeared. Elise waited. Ling Li was never without her phone. After three minutes, Elise texted: ???

Those three dots appeared and disappeared again. Another minute passed. Finally, her reply: Actually, I'm not available right now.

Elise sensed mischief: Where are you?

The dots played their games again, taunting her. The girls wanted to see the competition. So, Susie and I took them.

Waves of betrayal, rage, and resentment crashed over Elise.

"What's wrong?" Colette asked, and Elise realized she must have cursed out loud.

"Oh, nothing." Her tone was fake cheerful, camouflaging her fury. "Going to get a drink. Need anything?"

"Maybe a hot chocolate?"

Elise's vision blurred. What was this crazy time warp she was living in where her friends were cheering on Colette's rival while her daughter was watching baking shows and indulging in endless thousand-calorie drinks?

Everything was crashing down. All her dreams. Her plans for her daughter's future were imploding and crumbling like that faulty soufflé on TV.

Another text from Ling Li: Maybe you should come watch.

Why would I do that? Her palms sweated. She almost dropped the phone.

Because we just saw Kate's first performance, and I think it's important for you to know—and I don't mean this to upset you or anything—but she was really good.

Elise's face flamed. Sweat collected at her hairline. She held her phone, staring at the words that kept coming.

I think you'd agree that Kate didn't really need to "take Colette out of the competition," like maybe we all thought. She's pretty solid on her own.

"Hey, Mom," Colette called from the living room. "Can I have whipped cream? The kind from the can? Not the Cool Whip."

Elise's eyes burned with tears. What was happening? Nothing made any sense. Her daughter was a star, not someone who requested whipped freaking cream! She had to do something! She scrolled through her contacts as she got the hot chocolate out from the cabinet. She dialed.

"Detective Abbott." He answered on the first ring.

"Hello! It's Elise Carrington. I'm following up on the investigation into Colette's attack. Are there any impending arrests?" Her breath beat against the phone as she grabbed a mug.

He was silent for a beat. "I understand your family has endured a great trauma, and you're angry and seeking . . . justice. We're working very hard to uncover the nature of the crime against your daughter, and once we have definitive information, we'll certainly let you know."

Her heart banged. He was giving her the runaround, some BS script to appease her. How the hell had they not arrested Valerie or Kate? Had the world gone absolutely bonkers? "But you're looking into the friend? And her mother?" She didn't want to be pushy, but come on!

"Actually, I'm not allowed to discuss an ongoing investigation, but . . ." he said, lowering his voice, "we did uncover something." *Oh!* Her heart jammed. "There's been an online war of sorts between your daughter and a boy." There was rustling of papers. "He posted several threats against Colette online."

Not another person who thought Marcus was responsible for this. "He's just a boy she briefly dated. He doesn't even live here . . ."

"Recently, he posted, *Shit is coming your way. It's only time until we're even.*"

Elise shook her head. "No. Nothing has been posted in a month. You're moving in the wrong direction. That was a teenage . . . lover's quarrel. This"—she pointed toward the living room where her daughter sat—"is the act of someone who wanted her out of the competition!" She hadn't meant to yell.

He was silent on the other end until finally, he cleared his throat. "We'll keep you abreast of any new developments."

She reined in her rage and sugarcoated her tone. "Thank you, Detective. I very much appreciate your efforts."

Well, it was up to her. She couldn't even count on the police to do their job. She wouldn't let Kate steal her daughter's future. She had to put an end to this. But how?

Her mind zigzagged across ideas, hitting roadblocks. When she brought the drink into the living room, one of the judges on TV was speaking to a contestant. "I heard your mother has a rare form of leukemia," the judge said as the contestant teared up. "And if you win this competition, you plan to use the prize money to pay for her medical bills." The woman nodded, and the audience cried, "Aw."

And all at once, the answer shone on Elise like a ray of sunshine. Forget the police. The way to stop Kate's theft was through the judges. Many of them were from other parts of the country and hadn't heard of Colette's attack and Kate's obvious involvement. As evident on Colette's baking show, when the judges knew a contestant's backstory, their opinions were swayed. For better. Or for worse.

She set the mug of hot chocolate down and kissed Colette on the forehead, then raced back to her desk. She pulled up the article online and copied the link. Then with shaking hands, she emailed: In case you're unaware of the controversy . . .

FIFTY-FIVE

Valerie and Kate had spent Saturday evening with Janel and her daughter, Mia, who were from Alabama and staying in a hotel. They'd invited Valerie and Kate to use the pool with them. Kate and Mia hit it off immediately, trading stories of demanding instructors, painful joints, blackened toenails, and dreams of professional dancing. Valerie confessed to Janel the scandal that had rocked her and Kate's world. On Sunday morning, Janel stood protectively by Valerie's side as they passed the crowd of reporters.

In the auditorium, they sat side by side, awaiting the awards ceremony. When the announcer walked onstage, Janel gripped Valerie's hand. They had only just met, but their kinship was instant. It was the kind of relationship with another dance mom Valerie had thought was impossible: one without judgment, without a hierarchy. Onstage, as the announcer took the microphone, blood rushed through Valerie's veins in frantic anticipation. She turned twice, looking for the source of the thumping in the air, only to realize it was her heartbeat, pulsating inside her head.

"This is the fruition of a lifetime of effort, discipline, and perseverance," the announcer said. "While I'm impressed with each and every one of you, only the top twelve scores qualify to advance to the finals this summer in New York." She took a dramatic pause and consulted an oversize index card in her hand. "The following students have made the list. When I call your name, please come up onstage."

The names smeared together into a long string of syllables, Valerie's grip on Janel's hand tightening with each passing winner. Then, finally: Katherine Yarnell.

Valerie beamed as Kate stood from the rows of contestants and tentatively walked up the stairs and into the limelight. She wore a simple black dress and two-inch platform sandals that made her tower above the other winners. She was so beautiful, Valerie's heart swelled with pride. She deserved this. Not as retribution for the hell Elise had put her through; not even as compensation for all the discouragement and ill advice Valerie had given. Kate deserved to win because she was the best. Pure and simple. How had Valerie failed to recognize her child's pure God-given talent mixed with her fierce determination? How had she managed to muddle her view only to see fear rather than possibility?

Her daughter could make it as a professional dancer. Valerie hoped the world would understand. Kate didn't need to sweep Colette out of the competition. She was good enough on her own.

When Kate returned to the lobby after the ceremony was over, she gave Valerie a huge hug. Just as Valerie was about to gush with pride, Kate pulled back. "Dad!" Valerie followed her gaze and saw Chad's truck parked by the curb just outside the glass door. Kate bolted toward him. Valerie reluctantly followed.

Chad got out and embraced his daughter. "You were amazing, Tiny. I knew you'd win!"

Valerie was hooked in the gut hearing his nickname for Kate, knowing she was falling more and more under his spell.

She looked away, unable to stomach their growing bond, when something caught her eye. Chad's truck door was open, and on the cloth driver's seat, there was a faint stain. It was copper colored, in the shape of two small clovers, small but undeniable: a splatter of blood. She was a nurse and understood that blood could never be fully washed away, no matter how hard someone tried to make it vanish. Remnants of hemoglobin lingered in fibers.

Chad saw her looking. "I had an accident on my bike. Scraped my knee up pretty bad."

It could be true. Or not. She looked around but didn't see any more reporters. "Did you ever speak to the police?" she asked.

"Yeah. I showed them that I used my Starbucks app to get a coffee at eight a.m. that Saturday, then used a credit card at one p.m. for lunch. Both locations were in the mountains. Even though it was a five-hour gap in time, I think he recognized there wasn't enough time to drive to the city and back." He playfully nudged Kate's shoulder with his own. Just a fun-loving dad. Not a former criminal. Not someone in need of cash. Not someone who could convince anyone of anything with a flash of charisma.

"So that was it?"

"Look, don't worry about it," Chad said with his easy grin. "We have nothing to hide. Right, kiddo?" He wrapped his arm around Kate. She smiled up at him.

Valerie prayed that was the truth.

FIFTY-SIX

It was all over Snapchat. So many pictures of Kate, dancing onstage, at the awards ceremony, smiling and crying. Tears of joy.

Colette should have stopped scrolling. Not because she was jealous or pissed; strangely, she wasn't. Instead, she was empty. She snuck cookies and milk, hoping the forbidden snacks would fill her. But instead, she just felt sick.

Avery and Emma were blowing up her phone, but she turned it to Do Not Disturb and went to bed at 7:00 p.m. She took a pain pill because she hurt. Not only in her leg. Everywhere.

She pushed her face into her pillow and cried.

∞

Mom said Colette didn't have to go to school. But she *had* to go. There was something she needed to do. She walked down the hallway, slowly, still on crutches. Everyone had strange looks in their eyes. She knew they had all seen the awards ceremony on TikTok. People eyed Colette like she was a great white circling for a kill. She *was* looking for Kate; they were right about that. Just not for reasons they thought.

Kate was nowhere. Colette thought she saw Kate's long curly hair, but it was Maddie Mathew's new extensions. Colette thought she heard Kate laugh, but it was Chloe Smith's voice, raspy from allergies.

Colette was on her way to biology, listening to Avery talk about her new crush. They rounded the corner, and there Kate was. Standing by Trey's locker, alone, her thumbs racing over her phone. Her hair was a little frizzy. She seemed taller, older, prettier. Like she'd just returned from a vacation, a newer, better version of herself.

Avery looked up. Her eyes widened. She gestured with a jerk of her head that they could quickly escape into the classroom.

Maybe Colette should have, but she didn't. She needed to see Kate's face, her eyes, her expression after her win. It was the only way for Colette to know what was really going on between them. Because too many people thought Kate hated her. She had to know if it was true.

Colette waited. Beside her, Avery tensed. Everyone in the hallway slowed, looking from Kate to Colette. Their faces distorted into a smeary blur in the side of Colette's vision. She stared only ahead.

Kate looked up, and their eyes locked. Someone opened the door, and a gust of wind blew Kate's hair across her face. Suddenly, they were seven, on top of SkyView downtown.

Kate! Look at how small the people are. They look like little bugs. Ants marching!

I can't see! My hair is blowing in my eyes.

They kept staring at each other as the hallway fell to a hush. Slowly, hands raised; phones turned on and pointed in their direction.

Another memory: Miss Roza had pulled them from the crowd of students.

Most aren't ready for solos this young, but the two of you are special. The two of you are ready.

Did you hear that, Kate? We're special. Just the two of us.

Kate blinked her eyes. Her lips opened like she wanted to say something, but no words came out. The crowd was restless. Someone took a step closer. Still, neither of them spoke.

Did you know Atlanta is hosting the Southeast regional competition of the Duncan? We should totally try out for it!

You, for sure. But me? You think I'm ready?

Kate! Of course you're ready! You're a great dancer!

But not as great as you.

You are. Trust me.

Across the hallway, Kate closed her mouth, and her eyes turned glassy. Like she could also hear all the memories, too. That emotion flashing across her face—was it sadness for the friendship they'd lost? Or was it guilt?

FIFTY-SEVEN

Valerie opened the door and dropped her keys on the console. "Kate? Guess what? Peter and Jaz sent you the cutest congratulations cupcakes." She walked toward the kitchen, where Kate sat at the table, her face a splotchy red, her eyes swollen and tear-streaked. "What's wrong?" Nervous, Valerie tossed her bag down and went to her daughter.

Kate's chest heaved in and out as she struggled to wrangle the words. "I saw Colette today at school." She sucked in a breath. "I just thought everything was going to be okay. She didn't seem mad. That I won." She covered her face with her hands. "I'm so stupid!" she wailed.

"What happened?" Valerie asked, panic rising as a flutter in her chest.

She pointed to her new replacement phone.

Valerie saw fourteen voicemails. She pressed "Play."

"Good morning, this is Beverly Clark calling from *The Atlanta Journal-Constitution* in regard to an article that ran last week about rivalry gone wrong. I was wondering if I could do a follow-up interview—"

Delete.

"Hello, this is Roger Redington from *USA Today* calling for Miss Kate Yarnell for comments regarding recent allegations that injuries Colette Carrington sustained from an attack while jogging might be—"

Delete.

"I'm trying to reach a Kate Yarnell. This is Sarah Kane; I'm a reporter from the *TODAY* show. I'd like her take on allegations that she was responsible for removing her biggest rival from this weekend's competition. In light of her win, people want to hear her side of the story."

Delete.

The messages tumbled like snowballs, growing in size and speed. Valerie hit "Delete" several more times until a high-pitched voice sliced through the air and made her hold her breath.

"Hello. This is Tamara Suches calling from the Duncan Dance Prix headquarters. It has been brought to my attention that Kate Yarnell's regional win has undergone reconsideration due to suspicious circumstances surrounding an accident involving another dance student. Here at the Duncan Dance Prix organization, it is our mission to promote positivity through the spirit of competition, and we fear this scandal may smear our presence within the dance community. I'd like to discuss this decision with Kate as soon as possible." She left a phone number, then only a dial tone filled the air.

"They can't do this," Valerie said. "They can't take this away from you!"

Kate looked up at her mother, her cheeks wet with tears. "They just did."

FIFTY-EIGHT

Elise pulled the pan out of the oven and called everyone to dinner. One by one, they found their ways to the table. She studied Andrew's face, even though every expression he'd made over the last few days had been branded into her brain. He'd been less angry, but he had slid toward quiet detachment.

She removed the aluminum foil from the casserole dish. Mediterranean scents of cinnamon and allspice filled the air. Silverware clanked as plates were filled, and everyone ate in silence. Tree limbs rustled in the wind, tapping against the window. Bluish-gray storm clouds had rolled in and bruised the sky, an ominous foreboding that matched the general disposition of her family. She felt heavy with the task of fixing them.

When the doorbell rang, they all glanced at each other across the table. Trey went to answer it. A familiar voice filled the air. Elise's shoulders tensed; a look crossed Andrew's face, at first one of confusion, followed by alarm. Trey returned with Valerie standing next to him. She wore her usual scrubs—navy blue and wrinkled. Her hair was disheveled, her eyes red.

"I'm sorry to interrupt," she said. Her gaze slid from Elise, past Colette, and landed on Andrew. There was a sudden, microscopic tremble in her lips as she looked at him. Which made Elise's spine straighten.

Valerie cut her eyes back to Colette. "I know you've suffered a terrible tragedy, and my heart breaks for you. I understand your disappointment, and maybe the instinct to . . ." Her voice broke. She swallowed, shut her eyes briefly, then continued. "To want to blame someone. But I had nothing to do with this attack. I would never want to hurt you, or anyone. More importantly, my daughter had nothing—absolutely nothing—to do with this." She blinked quickly, then mashed an index finger to the corner of her eye. "Kate has had to tolerate rumors, taunting, and bullying at school. We've been questioned by the police. Our phone records have been seized and analyzed. Detectives have interrogated Kate's father and my neighbors. It's horrible and embarrassing. But I've endured it because . . ." She paused, threw her hands out. "There's nothing to link us to this crime."

"I—" Elise began, but Andrew put a hand on her arm. She looked at him—the way he stared at Valerie with intense concern, the way his eyes looked almost watery with empathy. Her stomach bottomed out; he was looking at Valerie the way he used to look at her. She felt sick. Was it possible his fascination with this woman was not just a midlife crisis? Not simply a result of boredom after years of marriage? Could he actually have fallen in love with her? Dread needled its way through her body.

"I've said nothing," Valerie continued. "Even amid all the social media slander and the newspaper articles and the rumor mill throughout the community. I've tried to teach Kate how to have grace under fire, to reassure her that the truth would prevail. But now—to strip my daughter of her win . . ." Her face contorted as she tried not to cry.

"What?" Andrew, Trey, and Colette all said in unison.

"What are you talking about?" It was Colette's voice that rose above the rest.

Valerie sniffed back fresh tears. "A woman called today from the Duncan headquarters and officially retracted Kate's win because of this scandal."

"That's ridiculous!" Andrew stood.

At first, Elise had a pulse of pure adrenaline and satisfaction. The article had worked its magic. But looking at her husband's distraught face, red spreading all the way to his ears, made her refocus.

"We'll make this right," Andrew said, his words sounding like a promise. A vow. He walked toward Valerie; it was not lost on Elise how Valerie looked at her husband with blatant adoration. Elise burned with indignation. He was married to *her*! This was their home. Their family. He was still tethered to them.

"We?" Elise walked over and angled herself in front of her husband like a shield. "Why are *we* responsible for her daughter, Andrew?" Her tone was enraged and possessive.

He ignored her, and that stoked her fury. Heat burned her eyes. She looked at Colette and Trey, like two stone statues, mouths agape, faces seized with shock.

"I don't know who else to turn to." Valerie's voice dropped to despair, almost tender.

Elise thought she might explode. This woman would stop at nothing to take everything from her! She grabbed her husband by the shirtsleeve. "Andrew." She tugged territorially.

Staring at Elise's hand on Andrew's forearm, Valerie took a step backward. "I . . . I'm going to go."

Elise held tight to her husband's clothing, her mind like a tornado, whirling with an absolutely disastrous thought: What if he followed her? Had she come so close to mending her marriage only to lose it all?

Valerie walked out, the heavy front door shutting behind her with a whoosh.

Andrew yanked his arm away. "What did you do?" Disgust distorted his face.

"Me?" Elise yelled. "What did *you* do?" She pointed toward the front door. "Why did she come here, Andrew? To talk to *you*? I thought you put a stop to your *friendship*!" She spit the word out. "Or is it more than that? I deserve the truth!"

"Guys!" Colette screamed. "Stop!"

FIFTY-NINE

Dad stormed off. Mom stood there for a second, not moving, like she was the one with the broken bones. Then, something flashed across her face, and she chased after him. Trey and Colette looked at each other. "I can't believe they took away her win." Trey reached for his phone. His thumbs flew over the screen. "Kate is innocent. There is no *scandal*."

"I know." This was a freaking nightmare.

He stared down at his phone. No response. "Kate must be going insane. She worked so effing hard for this! And they took it away?" He looked up. "Do you think . . ." He didn't finish. Maybe he was afraid to say it out loud because it was too awful. But who else? Why else?

"Yes." Colette nodded. "Of course it was Mom. But how?"

He had a scowl on his face. She realized it wasn't just her who was losing something. If Mom kept up all her vengeance, not only would Kate and Colette never be friends again, Trey would no longer have a girlfriend.

"She's out of control. We have to get her to stop this shit," he said. "But what can we do? The police still don't have any answers. How can we convince her it wasn't Kate?"

Colette had been thinking about it a lot. Kate's diaries. Selfishly, Colette wanted an unedited look at what Kate thought about her. Could Avery and Emma be right that Kate was happy Colette was hurt? Out of the competition? She desperately needed to know. But maybe the diaries wouldn't be just for her own benefit. She felt guilty that Kate's life had turned to complete crap because of Colette's injuries. "What if . . ." She stopped. It would never work.

"What?"

"You know how Kate writes in her journals all the time?"

Understanding fell across his face. "If Mom saw that Kate never wrote anything bad about you, never had any intention to hurt you . . ."

"Maybe she'd be willing to drop this."

He nodded and got her crutches. She hobbled down the hallway beside him toward their parents' bedroom, where voices boomed through the wooden door.

"I didn't make that decision! The organization did!" Mom yelled.

"Only because you've done everything in your power to promote this crazy rumor!"

"Why is it so crazy? We still don't have any answers!" Mom sounded completely unhinged, like a bad soap opera actress. "Give me another option! Show me the person who hurt my daughter! Give me a reason they mangled her beautiful body. Until then, what else am I to believe?"

Trey pushed the door open, and there they were, standing a few feet apart, looking like their normal parents, which was weird because they weren't acting normal.

"Mom," Colette said, and they turned, looking surprised.

Dad took a step back. Mom smoothed her hair. They both stared at them.

"Even if we don't ever know who attacked me," Colette said, "if we can prove that it wasn't Kate, can we call the Duncan headquarters and tell them to give her back her win?"

"Colette," Mom said with a heavy sigh, like she was disappointed.

"It doesn't feel good." Colette's words wobbled with guilt. "It feels . . . like we're trying to destroy her life."

"She destroyed *your* life!"

"Elise!" Dad shouted so loud that the bedroom windows shook. The drapes rippled in the aftermath.

"Fine." Mom put a hand on her hip. "How do you propose we get this *proof?*"

Colette looked up at the elaborate molded ceiling, searching for a way to propose this idea. She inhaled deeply. "Remember when Avery and Emma told us the terrible things Kate said? I'll admit, it made me wonder what she really thinks of me. Would she really be happy if I was hurt?"

"Of course she isn't happy you're hurt," Trey interjected.

"You're so gullible." Mom sneered in disgust.

"*No*, I'm not!" he shouted.

Mom shook her head like a dismissal.

"*Stop!*" Dad fired at Mom. "Stop ignoring your son."

Mom's eyes bulged. "I don't."

"You do," Trey said, sounding small, like a child. He stared down at the shiny wooden floor.

They were frozen. Fractured. Like ice splitting.

Colette reached out and put a hand on his wrist. Because her brother, her friend, had endured his own tragedy with Mom. Colette was just so wound up in her own storm, she hadn't noticed.

"It's just—" Mom started.

"No. It's nothing," Dad interrupted. "Stop acting like Trey is a roadblock to your theories. Listen to him."

Mom's mouth jerked. "Fine. Tell me."

Trey hesitated, looking at Colette, then back at Mom. "Everyone knows Kate writes everything in her journals. If I ask her if we can see them, then we'll know her true feelings. It'll be obvious. How wrong it was to ever doubt her. I'll bet she's never written anything mean. I'll bet she was horrified when Colette got hurt."

"And then we can all agree to stop pointing the finger at Kate. We can accept that it was just . . ." Colette choked on the words. "A random attack. We can call the Duncan and tell them it's all been a mistake. Insist they give Kate back her win."

Mom breathed in long and deep through her nose. She ran a finger over her eyebrows, smoothing the hair. The room was quiet, tense. Finally, she spoke. "I can't imagine a teenager would let anyone read her diaries." She looked relieved as if she'd succeeded in dismissing the idea.

"If it means an end to this," Colette said, "I'll bet she will."

SIXTY

The next day, while Valerie and Kate were together in the kitchen cleaning up after dinner, there was a knock at the door. It was Trey. Kate ran to him, fell into his arms, and cried softly.

Valerie stayed in the kitchen, giving them a morsel of privacy, but also watching with a strange mix of wonder and incomprehension about how Kate could be so loving with Trey when it was his mother who'd imploded her whole world.

He pulled out of the embrace. "I have the perfect way to fix everything. To get you back into nationals this summer."

Kate stared up at him, hope blossoming across her face.

"Your diaries," he said matter-of-factly. "You write everything down, right?" He didn't wait for confirmation. "If we show them to my mom, it'll be obvious that you love Colette and that you're innocent."

Kate's face paled. "You want to read my journals?" Her voice wavered. Valerie peered around the wall and saw panic written on her daughter's face.

"Well, not all of them. Maybe. I don't know. The last two years."

She swallowed and didn't move.

Valerie stood very still, watching.

"No. That's . . . No." Kate shook her head. "I'm sorry, but those are private."

"Kate." Trey's voice rose in clear frustration. "I know it might seem embarrassing or whatever. But it's the only way to fix this. You don't get it. Mom's, like, going crazy. She's one hundred percent convinced that you and your mom plotted to hurt Colette. All so you could win the Duncan. And now that you did win?" He widened his eyes. "She's never gonna let this go. Unless we can show her."

"Show her what?" Kate sounded on the verge of hysteria.

"That you had nothing but nice things to say about your best friend."

Dread flashed in Kate's eyes. She took a step back. Valerie understood why her face was frozen, why her shoulders shuddered like an earthquake was rocking beneath her feet. She thought back to all the entries she'd read. Pages filled with venom and thoughts of revenge. Filled with facts about athletes who'd suffered career-ending injuries. And brutality.

Kate's face hardened. "Why do I have to prove anything to your mother? It's none of her business what I write. Or how I feel." Kate's voice banged across the condo. "You have no right to even ask!"

"Kate." Trey's tone quieted, pleading. "I know she doesn't deserve anything right now. She's been a total psycho. Trying to sabotage your future—"

"Wait." She raised a hand. "You're admitting that *she's* the reason they took away my win? That headquarters didn't just randomly hear about this, but *she* told them?" Her face hardened; her jaw clenched.

Trey shrugged. "I don't know, but come on—this is Mom. She gets what she wants. And she wants you to suffer . . . like Colette. That's why we have to prove to her . . ."

Kate's hands gripped into fists. "She wants me to *suffer*?" She inhaled sharply, her face taking on an expression Valerie remembered from childhood tantrums: eyes bulging, teeth grinding, the vein in her neck throbbing.

Valerie darted into the living room. "Kate, it's okay." She looked at Trey. "I don't think your mother has any right to demand anything from us. We don't have to prove anything. The police are investigating. Not your mother."

"She's not asking to see them. It's me." He pointed at his chest, insistent. "I'm trying to find a way to fix everything. I thought the diaries could help her see that Kate is a good person; then she'd call the Duncan and ask them to change their decision." He sounded so sincere, it softened Valerie.

"Well, I think after a decade, she should know Kate's true nature. So, no. She doesn't get to lay eyes on her personal property."

He deflated.

Valerie squeezed Kate's arm in solidarity and walked into the kitchen. As she washed dishes, she heard muffles of her daughter and Trey arguing, then a softened, whispered conversation. A little while later, Valerie wandered back into the living room and said that she was going to bed. Trey took the hint and got up to leave. Valerie left, letting them have their goodbyes. She was removing her contact lenses and washing her face when a bloodcurdling scream filled the air. Her heart racing, she ran toward it.

In her bedroom, Kate stood, arms outstretched, face white. "He took them."

"What?"

"Trey stole my journals!" Her face was white, her voice high-pitched and panicked.

Valerie ran to the bookcase and saw an empty space. She glanced over at the empty desk. "How?"

Kate shook her head, her eyes unfocused, shackled in fear. "I . . . I don't know." A crease formed between her eyebrows; then her mouth dropped open. "I went to the bathroom while you were washing dishes. He must've snuck in here and shoved them under his hoodie. I can't believe this!" She threw her hands out into the air and just held them there.

As if expecting a cop to appear and wrestle her into handcuffs.

SIXTY-ONE

Valerie wrapped her arms around her daughter.

Kate's face crumbled in what Valerie could only describe as panic. "Some of the things I wrote . . . I mean, there were times when I was mad, or hurt, or really jealous, and . . ." Her lips trembled with horror. "I never would have written those things if I knew someone would read them!" She pitched slightly forward and screwed her eyes shut, like she was going to collapse right there on her bedroom floor.

She eased Kate down onto the duvet and sat on the edge of the bed. "Look at me." She tilted her chin up and met her gaze. "Those are your personal journals. You have the right to say anything you want inside those pages. They can't say you're guilty of anything other than being mad unless you actually wrote: *I'm going to hurt Colette. I'm going to get someone to break her leg. I'm going to take her out of the competition.* You didn't write that, did you?"

She expected a quick, robust, "No," so when Kate sat there, her mouth slightly twisted like she was chewing the inside of her cheek, Valerie felt as if a sharp set of canines had bitten into her, too. Could it have been possible that somewhere nestled inside one of those journals was an entry she'd missed? Words that not only held vitriol but possibly some misguided intention? Something that could be wholly misunderstood? She thought she'd seen anything that could be misconstrued. But she had to know she hadn't missed something. "Kate?"

Kate's face was sunken, her eyes vacant, her shoulders hunched. She looked scraped from the inside out. She turned away and buried her head in the pillow with a muffled, "No. Of course not."

"Okay, okay." Valerie exhaled long and deep. "As long as you didn't write that, you'll be fine." She hoped that was true.

SIXTY-TWO

Elise sat on one of the stools at the kitchen bar, looking at the menagerie of porcelain bunny rabbits and delicate painted Easter eggs. Earlier that day, she'd unpacked the boxes of holiday items and spread them all over the marble counter. Usually, she loved decorating for spring—filling the house with fresh flowers and cheerful Easter ornamentation. But today she couldn't find the joy. All day, they'd just sat there. Now, after cleaning the kitchen, she looked at the Lenox porcelain miniature bunnies gazing adoringly at their mother. When was the last time her children had looked at her with admiration? Or even gratitude? Somehow instead, they confronted her like she might require a straitjacket. They were all on a mission to prove she'd cracked. Like a damn Easter egg dropped to the floor. She was furious! After she'd carefully crafted that story to place her as a victim, just like her daughter. They still didn't get it. She banged her fist against the counter.

She picked up a peach-colored alabaster egg from the embossed glass basket, reared her arm back, and with all her might, hurled it across the room. It smashed against the tile backsplash with a satisfying crack and shattered into pieces. She reached for another. Then another.

She was on her fourth egg when Andrew raced into the room and shouted, "Elise! Stop!" She turned and saw him, wide-eyed as he took in the destruction. "What the hell?" He went to the closet and got a broom and dustpan.

The side door swung open. In walked Trey, breathless, a stack of books in his arms. "I got Kate's diaries." He walked toward the hallway and yelled up the stairs. "Colette! Come here!"

There was a slow thumping down the stairs.

Then, the four of them crowded around the bar.

SIXTY-THREE

Valerie opened the fridge and scanned the contents, wondering what she could scrounge up for dinner. Kate wandered out of her bedroom, still wearing her pajamas even though it was 6:00 p.m. She plopped down on the couch and flipped on the TV. Valerie had let her skip school again. They should have felt some relief. Chad called and said the police had officially released him from the investigation. They'd found two witnesses who'd corroborated his location the morning of the attack. Valerie conceded to the fact that he was truly innocent. The blood in his car must have actually been from his skinned knee.

But fear still immobilized her. Why had the police not called and cleared her and Kate from suspicion? After Kate had discovered her journals missing, she'd texted and called Trey but hadn't heard a word back. Almost twenty-four hours had passed, and Valerie's stomach clenched every time she thought of what she might have missed in those pages. Could there be an entry lurking that framed her daughter?

She sent up a small prayer that she'd missed nothing and grabbed a box of spaghetti from the pantry. In her heart, she believed her daughter was innocent. She did. But anxiety lingered. As she turned on the stove, there was a thud in the distance. Realizing it was the door, a cold stab plunged through her. She glanced over at Kate, whose face was filled with equal dread. With weak legs, Valerie walked across the room.

Andrew, Trey, and Colette. Better than the police.

"May we come in?" Andrew sounded formal. That sent another swell of panic surging through her.

She swung the door wider, and they entered.

Kate sat up, looking at Trey with both anger and fear in her eyes. He placed the stack of diaries on the coffee table. No one said anything for a moment. Trey's and Kate's eyes stayed locked on each other.

"I can't believe you stole those," she said, her mouth twisting in resentment. "You went behind my back." She took the books into her shaking hands and pressed them to her chest. "I'll never forgive you."

"I did it for you," he said softly. "To help you." He sat down next to her on the couch.

She turned her head away. "You didn't answer my texts! Or my calls! If you were trying to help me, why did you ghost me?!"

"I didn't ghost you. I was defending you! Trying to prove that you had nothing to do with Colette's attack."

For an awful moment, everyone was quiet. The air was thick, stagnant, and suffocating.

"We read your journals," Colette said.

Kate took a shaky breath. Her face lost all color and went completely still.

"It's okay," Trey said, putting a hand on her arm.

She batted it away. "No, it's not okay. Those were my private thoughts. That was a place for me to . . . to get out my feelings and not worry that anyone would see them." She stood, looking ready to race away, but Colette hobbled in front of her.

Tight pressure rose in Valerie's lungs; she took in a long gulp of air. Her poor daughter. She should have told her what she'd done. Scrubbed the diaries clean. But she'd been embarrassed to admit her snooping.

"Stop," Colette whispered. "Don't leave. Don't be embarrassed. I . . . I was . . . grateful."

Kate's mouth gaped in shock. "What?"

"For all the things you said. About us. Our friendship. About me." She sat across from Kate and laughed a little. "It kind of made me feel famous. Like I was really slaying it with my hair and makeup and outfits."

Valerie took a deep breath, and her whole body relaxed, realizing she'd gotten every passage filled with Kate's rage. If she'd missed something, this conversation would be entirely different. A lightness filled her chest. As awful as those entries were, her daughter was guilty only of anger. And wrath. Not execution. She'd been a horrible mother. Not only had she failed to realize how talented Kate was, she'd doubted her innocence. She'd tossed and turned at night and wondered . . . what if? Guilt gripped her at the core. She'd let Chad's history influence how she viewed her own child. She looked at her precious girl, sitting on the couch with complete confusion on her face.

Andrew laid a hand on Valerie's arm. "I'm so sorry," he said, "for what this has done to your family." He spoke to her with such tenderness, it made her ache. "For everything you've been through."

Across the living room, puzzlement still plowed across Kate's face. "I . . . I don't understand."

Valerie closed her eyes. How did she always screw things up? Even when she tried to protect her daughter, she failed to inform her, leaving her unprepared.

Andrew reached into the pockets of his dark jeans and pulled something out. "I called the Duncan headquarters today," he said to Kate. "I spoke to a woman named Tamara Suches." He placed a small square Post-it Note onto the table. In thick black marker were a name and number. "I've explained that there was a misunderstanding, and you shouldn't be punished. They said if you and Colette agree to do a promotional video on mental health in athletes, addressing rivalry, jealousy, stress, and bullying, your regional win will be reinstated. You'll be back on the roster for New York this summer. You can call her to discuss everything."

Kate slowly spun her head to look at him, skepticism on her face. She started to speak, but it was like her words were caught. "So . . . Elise finally believes that I didn't do anything?"

Trey, Colette, and Andrew all darted their eyes frantically. Valerie knew Elise would never accept their innocence. Trey stood. "Well, it's over," he said. "We can celebrate your win. Finally. If you can forgive me."

Kate still looked shell-shocked and pale, her breathing shallow. "I don't know . . ."

Andrew walked toward Valerie. A million silent words passed between them with just their eyes. He gestured for them to step aside. He whispered, "The police questioned me. They know about . . ." He glanced toward the door, his car outside.

"I know," Valerie said. "They brought it up with me, too."

"I told them you had nothing to do with this."

"They have my phone records, my bank statements, my GPS locations. I don't know what more they need to finally clear me." Her voice edged up.

He laid a hand on her arm. "They have nothing. Because you're a good person. You'd never do anything like that." He gently squeezed. "I'm sorry." And she knew that he meant for everything. For getting too close. For complicating their lives. For ensnarling the two families. For letting accusations mount. For giving them each a glimpse of what might have been, in a different world.

"Me, too," she whispered.

"I always knew you couldn't raise a daughter who'd hurt someone."

Valerie took a shaky breath. And finally, she believed it. She was a good mother. When the stakes were truly raised, she'd come through. She'd protected her daughter. And wasn't that all she had ever wanted? All those nightmares that had woken her, gripping her with fear that she'd lost her grip on the stroller, left the baby in a hot car, slid a bundled infant into the oven . . . maybe that was all preparation for when it truly mattered. Right now.

"And Chad?" he asked.

She shook her head. "I don't know. He seems . . . genuinely interested in Kate. He hasn't asked for money . . . says he's working on putting together a business plan." The private investigator had nothing scandalous to report. She shrugged, like, *I guess I'll believe him.*

"You know, if you ever feel uncomfortable, I'll be here. In a heartbeat."

They stood for too long, just looking at each other. She knew that he was also feeling the judgment of their kids, and that's when Valerie knew, really knew, there could never be anything more between them. She took a step away.

"I should go," Andrew said.

Colette levered herself up from the chair, grabbing her crutches and propping them under her arms. She looked toward the door and hesitated. Then her face twitched as if she was making a decision. She pulled something out of the back pocket of her jeans. Valerie squinted and saw it was an old photograph of Kate and Colette around the age of six. The girls were decked out in petal pink costumes, hair pulled into high buns, huge grins splashed across their faces. Colette slid the picture across the coffee table.

Kate looked from the picture to Colette, still utterly baffled.

"It's my fault. All of this," Colette said, sitting on the coffee table in front of Kate, pulling at her hair.

Kate scrunched her eyebrows up. "Huh?"

"I'm the one who made everything change between us." There was a quiver of emotion in her voice. "When Mom saw how good you'd gotten . . . she freaked. Like, she suddenly realized that I had competition. She has this whole big life plan for me." Colette used air quotes, and her voice hitched on the words *life plan.* "And it only works if I'm the best." She tugged at strands of hair.

"You *are* the best," Kate said softly. She reached up and touched Colette's hand. "Stop doing that."

Colette put her arm down. "Mom's spent so much time and money trying to help me. Like, her whole life is about me becoming a professional dancer, you know?"

"Yeah," Kate agreed.

"When Miss Roza gave you the staircase solo, Mom went crazy, and I . . . I panicked." She bit her lip. "I was worried that you . . ."

"What?" Kate's voice pitched up.

"That you'd be better than me. I don't know what Mom did or why Miss Roza made the change, but when she did, I took it. I'm sorry. I get why you were pissed. But instead of just telling you that I was trapped between you and Mom, I buried it. I focused on my practice. Let us get . . . toxic." She swallowed. "The more I tried to ignore what was happening between us, the worse it got. Then everything went crazy. I'm sorry. I knew all along you didn't have anything to do with this." She pointed at her leg. "Of course you didn't. I wish I'd found a way to shut it down sooner."

Kate was quiet, glancing between her journals and the photograph.

Colette tapped the books. "You need a lipstick color, too. Your own signature look. You can absolutely pull it off." Kate flushed and gave a tentative smile. "Go to New York," Colette said. "Win. Dance for them both." She pointed down at the picture. "For everything they always wanted." She left the picture on the coffee table, turned, and hobbled out the door.

Trey leaned down and gave Kate a soft kiss before following his sister.

"But . . ." A soft whisper of confusion escaped Kate's lips.

The door shut as they left.

Valerie walked toward her daughter to explain.

SIXTY-FOUR

Hearing the garage door open, Elise quickly shut down the website she was scrolling through. If Andrew thought a few juvenile diary entries were enough to convince her of Kate and Valerie's innocence, he was wrong. Couldn't he tell Kate was obsessed with Colette? The way dancers had always envied Elise. Sure, she'd allowed him to make the phone call to the Duncan, but that was because his outrage was almost frightening. She had, for an awful minute, thought he was ready to walk away. Because of Kate? And her gangly mother? Oh, hell no. So, fine. She'd let Kate have her regional win, but she'd be damned if she'd let Valerie have her husband. And just because she'd acquiesced to the Duncan call did not mean she would back down. She would uncover a way to incriminate those Yarnell girls if it were the last thing she did. She just needed to be strategic.

The door opened. "How was your visit?" she asked, walking away from the computer.

"Fine." He eyed her with suspicion. "Assuming your *headache* is all gone?" There was clear implication in his tone. But she wasn't about to go over to that woman's house and apologize.

She massaged her temples. "Some ibuprofen dulled the pain. What did they say?" She thought she saw him roll his eyes as he walked away, which stuck in her side like a thorny barb. "Andrew! I'm not going to be ignored!" She cringed as soon as the words came out, thinking she sounded like a deranged woman from the movies. But this was her husband!

He stopped, spun around, and looked at her.

"These last few months you've blown right by me like I'm invisible," she said. "Like my only purpose is to put meals on the table and pick up your dry cleaning. At first, I thought I was being insecure because I'm getting older, and this world is not kind to women after a certain age."

He sighed. "I think everyone would agree that you're still beautiful, Elise. Is that what you need? To hear how gorgeous you are?" He spit out the words like there was venom in his mouth.

"No," she snapped, "but don't act like I'm exaggerating. You're the one who went off and found a younger woman!"

He crossed his arms. "I didn't *go off and find a younger woman*. You pushed me out. Six months ago, I tried to tell you that I made some bad investments, and I was worried about our financial security. But every time I tried, you cut me off to talk about spending another thousand dollars on damn dance!" He balled his hands into fists.

"What?" Elise backed against the counter, feeling punched in the gut. "You lost all of our money?"

His jaw was set hard, like his back molars were grinding. "Oh, don't worry. Your gravy train is back on track. I'm building our accounts up." He turned to leave, but Elise grabbed his arm.

"That's not fair. I've never been a gold digger. We were both broke when we met. We built this together." She extended her arms toward their elaborate, upscale home. "I like nice things, yes. But so do you. I'm not obsessed with money."

"No. But you're obsessed with Colette's future. Using that money not for what *she* wants, but for what *you* never had. Molding her into the person you could never be."

It was a smack across the face. Worse—a knife through her heart. Tears came. Real ones. "I can't believe you just said that." She let go of his arm. Didn't he know that once words slipped out, you could never reel them back in? "Do you even love me anymore?" She felt her face crumble.

He was obviously unfazed by her blatant distress. He looked like he was having a business discussion, not a heartfelt marital dispute. "Are you sure you want to have this conversation right now?"

"What?" She gasped. He was supposed to say, *Of course I love you. For better or for worse. Until death do us part.* He'd taken a vow!

"Because I'm not sure, actually." He continued to blow her world to pieces. "I thought I did. I thought I could forgive all your fanatic desires. But now, I'm not sure I can love someone who could be so ruthless. Who could seek to destroy a teenage girl's life." He turned to leave again.

Her head squeezed tight, thoughts scrambling across her bruised brain. "Andrew, you don't understand!" She chased after him. "Just listen. Please."

"I'm done hearing your excuses."

"This isn't an excuse. I promise. It's a story. A reason. You have to listen." She'd never felt so anguished. So absolutely wretched. "It might help you to see my side." He turned and looked at her with utter distaste. She felt on the verge of complete collapse. "Please," she begged.

"Fine." He threw his hands out in exasperation. "Tell me your *story*." The word sounded like an insult.

They stood there, in the space where the kitchen met the foyer—bridged between the heart of the home and the exit—and she repeated the inverted story she'd told the kids. Not only would it open his eyes to the brutality between rivals, it could earn her some compassion. She explained how at the time she'd been able to bury the betrayal of her best friend because Andrew had swooped in and taken her on a new adventure. But now, she couldn't help but think Kate was doing the same thing to Colette. "The police called while you were gone. They cleared that boy from Florida. They have absolutely no other leads. This makes sense." When she finished, she stood before him, her heart throbbing with vulnerability. He had to understand now.

"Why didn't you tell me?" he asked.

"I was afraid you'd think I was concocting a story to support my theory."

"No, why didn't you tell me back then, in New York?"

She was silent.

"Was I just an escape route? A second-best option?"

"No!"

"It kind of sounds like it."

"Andrew . . ."

"No, Elise. I'm sorry that happened to you; truly, I am. But it makes me feel like you betrayed me. By not being honest back then and even now. Maybe I could have understood your overreaction a little more. But it doesn't justify your behavior. It doesn't make it okay for you to push our daughter to the brink of insanity to live out your unfulfilled dreams. It doesn't forgive your actions against Kate and Valerie." He pulled his shoulders back, towering above her, his whole face rigid with indignation and determination, boring holes into her heart. The air was still and shocking.

She realized with utter devastation that they were standing on a precipice, and the sheer drop-off was frightening. She would never convince him to accept her theories of Kate's and Valerie's culpability. If she pressed, it would be her that plummeted, not the Yarnell girls.

She had a choice to make, and it wasn't hard to figure out. "I'll go to therapy," she said abruptly. "I'll work through all these . . . issues." She fumbled on the word but quickly recovered. "I'll ease off Colette and support whatever future she chooses. I'll rebuild my relationship with Trey." The adrenaline pumped so hard through her veins, and her heart throbbed so loud in her ears, she thought she might have a stroke. "I'll do it, Andrew. Once a week. Twice a week, if you want. But you have to stay away from Valerie. That's the only way."

He was silent.

"I don't understand how this all happened. Me keeping secrets from you. You keeping secrets from me. But we can start over. Build our trust. Build our money. Build back our family."

"I can't promise that'll fix it, Elise. These last several months—"

"But you'd be willing to try?" she interrupted. "Try to forgive me? To work on our marriage?" She walked toward him, pressing her nose into his button-down shirt, taking in the smell of him.

"I don't think you can let this go. And I'm not going to sit around and watch you—"

"I can!" She inhaled and breathed in the scent of his cologne. "I will," she lied.

SIXTY-FIVE

Kate looked up toward Valerie. "I don't get it. I said I hated her. I said I'd get revenge. I imagined her with broken bones." Her eyes were watery with guilt and bewilderment.

Valerie took one of the journals from Kate's lap. She flipped through the pages, then rested it on the coffee table. "Not even a trace."

"Trace of what?" Kate picked up the book and looked at the ink splashed across the page.

"A trace that some entries were even there."

Kate's eyebrows squeezed together, and she began reading, turning pages, scanning the text faster. "Wait." She flipped back and forth. "They're gone."

Valerie nodded.

She looked back down, her cheeks flushing pink.

Valerie took a deep breath. "There's an ambiguous line between love and hate. Between friendship and rivalry. Sometimes things we say, or things we write, especially in the heat of the moment, cross those lines. It didn't seem fair to let someone read those tender feelings and maybe misunderstand the intention."

"You read my journals?"

Valerie dreaded admitting that she'd violated the basic code of parenting: Respect privacy. She had prepared a defense for that, but staring at her daughter's honey-colored eyes, it evaporated from her brain. "I'm sorry," she said simply. "I was at a loss. You were never around. You never talked to me. I worried that you hated me—that I was failing you as a mother."

Kate sank down on the carpet cross-legged and leaned against the love seat.

"I hoped your entries would tell me what you really wanted from a family—from a mother. I wanted to understand what you were finding at the Carringtons' that I didn't know how to provide."

Kate's face took on the perplexed look she often made when doing a complicated math problem. "Wait. Are you saying you read my journals before Dad showed up? Before the accident? Before Elise started accusing me?"

Oh, crap. She grimaced. "I was truly only looking for ways that I could connect with you better. But instead, you mostly wrote about Colette."

"Do you think I'm terrible?" she asked softly.

"No." Valerie sat beside her daughter on the floor. "Friendships are complex. Especially one where two people want the same thing."

"But some of the stuff I wrote—it could've been really bad. Taken the wrong way."

"Yes. I do think we need to address some of that—your anger and aggression."

"But you know I'd never . . ."

"I know." She honestly did. At last. But still. "You need to know a little more about your father." She told her about the violent mood swings, the obsessions and crashes, the arrests in Costa Rica. "I know it's not an excuse for me to lie, but I was trying to protect you from the hurt I experienced living with him, loving him."

Kate wiped at her eyes. "Okay. He seems . . . not like that at all." Her eyes looked desperate, wanting her father to stay this way: interested, present, kind.

"I know." Maybe he was medicated? Maybe he was in therapy? Or maybe it would all crash down again. She didn't know. But if Kate wanted to try and build a relationship with her father, how could

Valerie deny her that? She would insist they all sit down and have a conversation about how they would move forward. There would have to be rules, boundaries, and a lot of therapy. For all of them. Valerie swallowed the scratchy ball of fear in her throat. "I hope he's different, Kate. I really do. I want nothing more than for you to have a loving, stable relationship with him. And I'll let you spend time with him. But there will be rules. You have to promise that if he ever starts to act differently, you'll tell me. Immediately."

Kate nodded as a tear fell down her cheek. "I don't think he'll be like that, Mom. I really don't."

"I hope you're right." But still, Valerie knew she'd be saying prayers every day.

After a few moments, Kate looked back at her books. "How did you figure out they'd ask for the journals?"

"I didn't. But I worried someone would."

Kate flipped through the pages. "It looks so clean. How'd you do it?"

"Hair-dryer. If you heat the spine, it loosens the glue, and you can tear the page out with no evidence."

"Wow," Kate said. "Google?"

Valerie chuckled. "Guilty."

They stared out the window at the late Friday evening traffic. People were leading their normal, ordinary lives. Going to dinner. The movies. To friends' houses. Valerie would never take for granted another mundane Friday evening. "Are you mad? That I snooped?"

"Have you looked through my phone, too?"

"How? You always have it in your hands."

Kate let a small smile creep across her face. "I'm sorry you felt desperate. I know I've been a little absent."

"A little?" Valerie said with a raised eyebrow, and they both laughed. She stood up and walked toward her bedroom, Kate following. Lifting the edge of her mattress, Valerie pulled out a stack of papers, Kate's loopy cursive filling them. "Not the most inventive hiding place. It's a good thing the cops didn't show up with a search warrant."

Kate took the pages. "I never want to see these again."

Valerie nodded. She rummaged through her drawers until she found a box of matches. They walked onto the patio. She stuffed the pages deep down into the bottom of a metal garbage can and handed Kate the matchbox. A flame lit, hot, red, and satisfying. Kate tipped the match to the edges of the pages, and instantly, the smell of singed paper filled the air. Together they watched all the words turn brown, then black, then curl up, burn, and disintegrate into ashes.

SIXTY-SIX

Valerie and Kate had settled back into their routines. The school year was nearing its end, and when Kate wasn't at the studio practicing, at physical therapy sessions with Colette, or at counseling, she was spending time with Chad. So far, he'd been available, calm, and friendly. Even to Valerie. He'd agreed to therapy himself, and it seemed to be working. She hoped it would continue. Things hadn't rebounded so easily with Trey. Even though he hadn't been privy to her embarrassing and scandalous journal entries, Kate still felt hurt by his betrayal. Valerie had overheard his ongoing pleas of forgiveness, and eventually, her daughter had acquiesced. And then, everything seemed almost normal, except Kate told Valerie she still felt a strangeness around Elise—who smiled and acted like the drama was behind them but emanated an air of constant suspicion, even after the police had officially cleared Valerie and Kate. They declared the attack was random, and the case was closed.

On a warm Saturday morning, Kate wandered into the kitchen dressed in sweats, ready to go to the studio. She and Miss Roza had worked on a new routine for the upcoming nationals, and the training schedule had picked back up. "What are you doing?" Kate asked, looking at Valerie's open laptop. "Searching real estate?"

"Nah," she said. "I told the Realtor I wasn't in the market for a new house anymore. I think we're fine right here." She pointed toward the screen. "I'm booking tickets to New York."

Kate leaned toward the screen.

"Help me pick a hotel. Do you want to be close to where the competition is? Or maybe in Times Square?"

༄

Afterward, Valerie dropped Kate off at the studio and then drove to the sandwich shop to meet Jazmin for breakfast. Standing in line, she heard a voice call, "Valerie Yarnell?"

It was the younger police officer—the one with hazel eyes, a strong jaw, and gorgeous dark-brown skin. He walked over, and they shook hands. "James Jones," he reminded her. "How are you? How's your daughter?"

"We're good. Thanks." She released his grip, but their fingers entangled for just a moment longer. She took in all the things she hadn't noticed while too distracted in the interrogation. He was tall and solid, wore his dark hair cut short; his eyes had a golden ring around light-brown irises.

"Crazy," he said with a little head shake. "The whole thing."

"Yeah. And they never found who did it?"

He clicked his tongue. "Sure didn't. Strange case." He tilted his head in a joking way. "Hope that doesn't make you think any less of our expertise."

She smiled and felt a tingle across her skin. Was he flirting? Yes, he was. "Not at all."

"Well, I'm glad to hear that." He lingered, leaning against the counter.

Across the shop, Jazmin appeared at the glass door. She spotted Valerie. Her gaze traveled to the cop, and her jaw hinged open.

Valerie gave her a wide-eyed expression and shrugged.

Go! Go! Jazmin mimed with a hand wave, then ducked back into her car.

James glanced over his shoulder, then back at her. "Are you meeting someone?"

She quickly looked back toward him. "Oh, um, no." Valerie shook her head. "Just thought I saw a friend, but, uh, I didn't."

Something teased on his lips that was more than just a smile. It felt like an invitation.

And maybe, just maybe, she was finally ready to bust through that wall around her heart. "Would you like to join me?" she asked.

A small dimple appeared deep in the side of his cheek. "I think I'd like that very much."

SIXTY-SEVEN

Colette exited the physical therapy office with a pamphlet in her hand. "Dr. Buchanan gave me some exercises to try."

"Oh?" Elise took the papers and helped her daughter into the car. She would have preferred to be at the appointment, to ask specific questions about initiating at-home rehabilitation, but her damn psychologist was available only at the same time as Colette's PT. Andrew thought this was *a perfect way to ease Elise out of every aspect of Colette's life*, as he'd so lovingly put it. Whatever.

Janet Mumsford, PhD, was a clinical psychologist who specialized in parenting therapy, which Andrew thought was the best place for her to start. Dr. Mumsford—*Call me Janet*—a redheaded woman with a penchant for button-up cardigans, incessantly talked about parenting styles and their effects on the mother-child relationship. Blah, blah, blah. She liked to nod and swing her eyeglasses between her fingers while making deep, audible sighs, as if processing massive amounts of information. It drove Elise absolutely bonkers. But she nodded along, sharing about her uninvolved mother, agreeing with great dramatic gusto that yes, that could be why she took such an opposite approach in her parenting style.

Now, she parked the car and glanced at the paperwork again. "Wouldn't it make sense to do both stretch and strength?"

Colette shrugged. "He said start with this."

Elise groaned. She'd send him an email with additional questions later. Once inside, she found a yoga mat and unraveled it on the living room carpet.

Colette looked at her with raised eyebrows. "You want me to do the exercises now?"

Elise glanced at her watch. "I'll need to start dinner soon, so yes."

"Okay." Colette got down on the floor and spread her legs out in front of her. After a moment of holding a static pose, she said, "I was thinking, maybe we should incorporate something like this into my channel. At-home therapy after an injury?"

"Your channel?" Elise squatted down next to her on the floor.

"Yeah, I mean, I know all the YouTube stuff was for creating a brand before the Duncan, but, well, I did develop a following. I kind of feel bad just abandoning them."

"Hmm. Good thought." Ideas sparked in Elise's mind. Yes. They could use this off time to create compassion and empathy, so that when Colette returned to the stage, her following would be doubly invested. She opened up the notes on her phone and saw the last few things she had jotted down while waiting on buttoned-up Janet. *Could you hire a hit man on the internet? How can I access Kate's and Valerie's computer search history?* She hit "Save" and opened a new note. *New topics for YouTube channel,* she typed. "Tell me more."

But before Colette could elaborate, Elise's phone dinged with a text. Then another. And another. She opened the message from Ling: E?? WTH??

Her heart jumped. What? she responded.

She clicked on Susie's message: Hon, have you been on Insta? You probably should . . . explain.

A zing of panic cascaded across her brain as she opened her socials. *Oh, crap.* Her heart accelerated. Dena, gossipmonger, absolute rumor-rager. How? How did she find out? Her palms were sweating as she enlarged the image. It was a picture of Miss Roza's computer, open to an email from Elise: Yes, you are right. I'll make the check out to you, not the studio. And I think we should wait to announce the switch on Friday. Minutes before curtain. So there's no time for a rebuttal.

The comments on Dena's post were snowballing.

Did she pay her off?

I don't know who's worse—the mother or the teacher.

They're both bitches!

Elise's heart hammered. Her limbs went liquid. The side door slammed.

"Elise!" Andrew's voice. Loud. Aggressive. Did he know?

She darted to the mudroom, attempting to concoct a story to explain to everyone, but before she could escape, there was Andrew, standing in front of her. She saw a flash of something on his face she'd never seen before. Not just anger. Contempt. Elise's heart went cold.

"I was thinking about your story and something kept bothering me, but I couldn't figure it out," he said with his head cocked, cross-examination mode. "Then it hit me. I saw your last performance, remember? After, you said you were taking a break. To have time for me. And the thing is . . ." His voice dropped low, eerily calm. "You didn't have a sprained ankle."

"What?" Elise's heart jammed up. Why was he looking at her like that? Sweat trickled down her spine. "You're forgetting. I had a limp. I never complained. I'm strong . . ."

He grinned that smug, closed smile he used when he knew he'd won a case. "It took me a minute, but I remembered because it was an unusual name. Your director. Bernie Byrd. When I googled, it came right up. Funny how his version of events was quite different."

Panic skittered across every nerve ending in her body. "I can explain."

"We're done. I've already contacted a divorce lawyer."

"No!" She ran toward him, but he turned away.

Over his shoulder he called, "Face it, Elise, it's over. It's all over."

SIXTY-EIGHT

Tell me more. That's what Mom had just said, then proceeded to dive into her phone. Then leave. It had been like that for months. Anytime Colette wanted to talk, she never got the chance. It was always time to practice, time to video, time to plan Colette's life. If only Mom had listened, Colette would have said: *I'm feeling overwhelmed. I'm feeling pressure. I never feel good enough. It's hard to always be perfect. I'm suffocating. Stop making me choose between you and Kate. Stop making me hate my best friend. I'm drowning. I'm desperate.*

But Mom hadn't asked, and Colette hadn't said anything. Instead, Colette decided to go all cryptic and send Mom flowers. *Colette is going to crack.* That was what Dad had screamed. She hoped if Mom thought Dad was super pissed, she'd ease off. But no; that's not how it went down. *Mom* cracked. Tears. *Am I pushing you too hard?* Oh my God! The guilt! What a backfire. Then Colette had to work harder and complain less because every time she wanted to crumble, she saw Mom's crushed face, swollen eyes, and Colette knew she had caused that.

Mom started going to a shrink. A lot of mothers do. Emma told Colette that her mom said it's the only reason she doesn't die of boredom. When Colette asked if Mom was going because of the rumors about Dad and Valerie, she said no. She needed to talk to someone because seeing Colette hurt had been terrible.

And that made Colette feel even more like a piece of crap. She could never get anything right.

She must have let it show on her face because Mom said, *It's not your fault.*

Colette just nodded and said, *Okay.* Because that's how she'd play it. None of it had been her fault. The case was closed. And no one would ever know. On her MacBook Air, there were eighty-four deleted Google searches about foot and leg injuries. It had started as possible content for her channel—prevention of injuries. But as the competition drew closer, and pressure mounted, and panic attacks plagued her in the middle of the night, the searches took on a new meaning. A possible way out. Because if Colette were injured, she couldn't dance, right? And if she couldn't dance, Mom would lay off. Leave her and Kate alone.

But that seemed a little extra, so Colette strategized. Most of Mom's issues were with Kate. About how good she'd gotten. How maybe she could beat Colette. If somehow Kate dropped out, that would be the perfect solution. They could still be friends, and Mom would relax. So, Colette hid her science project, hoping that the failing grade would piss off Valerie, and Kate would get yanked from the Duncan. But that didn't happen. If anything, it just made Kate a little suspicious of Colette.

Colette was stuck. She could have the Duncan and Mom's approval or her friendship with Kate. She couldn't have both. Or maybe . . . as she went back to her Google search, she thought there was another option.

It was a fine line. Finding a break that would take her out of the competition but not leave permanent damage. How, though? A fall at the studio? A stumble down the staircase? But somehow those things would be her fault, and Mom would be forever disappointed in her.

Then Dad freaked about the location tracker on social media, and Colette had the perfect solution. A random attack. Someone who knew where she was because of her posts.

Everyone would be so thankful she was alive that the whole idea of winning a stupid competition would be forgotten. Later, she could dance again. Mom wouldn't be as high-strung because, hey, she'd still be healing. It'd be a freaking celebration to get back onstage. And then she could actually enjoy the thing she loved.

But if the injury were too severe, she'd risk never being able to dance again, or worse, she could wind up with a permanent limp.

So, she researched obsessively. She read forums. She contacted people who'd had foot and leg injuries, asked very detailed questions. All in the name of research for her injury prevention channel, of course.

When Colette first approached Bates Herndon, the guy at school, he'd assumed she was after pain meds. "No," she said all cryptic. "But what if I want something you don't sell? Like, how would I get my hands on something that's illegal. Like *big-time* illegal."

He laughed at her. She was wearing a pink baby doll dress. She understood the disconnect. But she kind of teared up and told him she was *desperate*. And she was. At that moment, an injury felt like her only way out.

"What do you need?" he'd whispered, but she shook her head and wiped her eyes. She was out of her league, but she was smart enough to know that no one, *no one*, could have any hint about what she was planning. That was crucial. She bit her lip and looked pathetic. Everyone knew how much stress she'd been under. He probably assumed she was after some superpotent drugs.

He sighed. "Okay, listen to me. Leave your phone at your house or the dance studio. Anywhere. But do not have it with you. Then go here." He wrote down an address. "Don't put this location in your phone, okay? It's a diner on the other side of town that has public-use laptops and Wi-Fi. Get on the dark web, and search for what you need. Don't use your name, credit card, Venmo, or anything that links to you."

"The dark web?"

He put a hand to his head like, *You're such an innocent little baby.* "Forget it. You're going to get yourself in trouble."

"No! Please. Help me." She took a step closer. Tears came, and truthfully, she wasn't trying to get her way. She was just so damn desperate.

He stared at her for a long time. Then he let out a long exhale and told her how to find it. "Be careful," he said. "There's a lot of scams. And a lot of scary shit. Don't screw yourself." He reached over, touched her arm, and asked one more time if he could help. He might have been crushing on her a little. She smiled, thanked him, and told him she was good.

She waited. She didn't want the assault to happen too quickly after their chat. Bates got a bad rap, but the kid wasn't stupid.

The diner was a crap hole in a bad part of town, but what did she expect? She followed his instructions to find the dark web, and holy crap, she almost left the place in tears. There were some truly effed-up people in this world. She learned that for $50,000, she could hire someone to commit "death by torture." But a beating ran about $2,000, unless she wanted a facial scar, which jacked up the price. *For real?* That was the moment she almost bailed. But something inside her knew that if she wanted to keep Kate as a friend, and if she wanted the never-ending pressure to stop, this was her only option.

She searched until she found what she thought was the best match. Two days later, she met a guy with a very scary-looking tattoo that wrapped around his neck and up his face. She paid in cash and gave him a picture, printed off the internet, of the anatomy of legs and feet. She used a red marker and drew arrows on the picture to show the exact spot where he needed to hit her. He told her he wasn't doing the job. "The purchaser never meets the contract," he said, sounding too formal for his appearance.

"But, but . . ." She stammered and tried to explain the absolute importance that he couldn't hit at the knee. That would be a death sentence. In her research, she was shocked that it took a ton of force to crack a shinbone. The internet said it took approximately two hundred pounds of pressure to produce a tibial fracture using blunt force with a small hammer. If the hit were dead-on, it'd be a smooth break, making for an easier recovery. But if he hit at an angle, it could cause cracks with heavy distortion, ragged gaps, and a much harder road to repair. She told him all of this, but Tattoo Guy didn't look like an anatomy wizard; he didn't exactly seem to grasp the greater physics behind velocity and force. For a moment, she reconsidered. But she knew she was going to break one way or the other: mind or leg.

She chose leg.

What she didn't realize was that because she was running when the impact hit, her ankle joint would buckle and cause a spiral fracture down into her foot. She definitely didn't consider that she might hit her head so hard, she'd get a concussion. When she woke up in the hospital, she was totally confused, barely remembered that she had planned the whole thing. The pain was far worse than anything she could have ever imagined. And for a hot minute or two, she thought she had ruined her life.

Stupidly, when she'd dreamed this up, she never even considered the police and an investigation. Luckily, Tattoo Guy and the contract man were both far more familiar with the world of crime. They had worked out all the details to make everything untraceable.

It was planned out flawlessly.

Even Bates had been duped. After the assault, he'd come to her looking totally tortured. "I feel so bad," he'd said. "I never should have let you go to that place. That was a sketchy part of town. Some dude could have seen you there and become, like, *obsessed* with you or some shit. What if that was your stalker? Some guy using the Wi-Fi? I'm so freaking sorry."

What perfection.

"Not your fault, Bates. No worries."

She'd thought it was a wrap. Except one thing that she never could've predicted: Kate.

When Mom had first pinned the attack on her, it was almost comical. The girl danced, wrote in her journals, and sometimes watched HGTV. How could anyone think she was capable of masterminding an attack on her best friend? Colette figured the rumors would die down when they found no proof.

Right.

Instead, Avery and Emma sat at their table and talked about how much Kate hated Colette. Then the idea that Dad and Valerie were involved in some crazy affair had complicated things even more. Suddenly, everyone was convinced that Kate and her mother were somehow responsible.

It was insane. Sure, there had been tension between them. Rivalry. Competition. Betrayal. But deep down, Kate was still Colette's best friend. Was she hers? A part of Colette wondered if what Avery and Emma thought was true.

Colette needed to know if Kate felt the same, or if all along she had been duped. She knew the journals were the answer.

There was nothing that showed the hatred Avery and Emma had insinuated. If anything, Kate liked Colette almost too much. But it was nice. To be adored like that. Colette couldn't let Kate lose everything for something she didn't do.

Of course, Mom's eyes still twitched anytime Colette said Kate's name, but she'd let Dad call the Duncan and fix everything, so that's how Colette knew it was all going to be okay. In the end, it would all be worth it. She had her friend back. Her recovery was going to take longer than she thought, but she'd be fine. She would walk again. Maybe she would dance again.

But mostly, she'd finally be free of all the pressure to win, win, win. And she could just be happy.

ACKNOWLEDGMENTS

It truly takes a village to get a story out of your head, onto the page, through the long and difficult submission and editorial processes, and bound into a book. Without the help of many people along the way, I would not be here.

I am deeply indebted to Liz Winick Rubinstein for plucking my manuscript from the pile and giving me a chance. Your vision for this book along with Emily Cottingham's suggestions helped elevate this story to a new level.

From our very first conversation, I knew Chantelle Aimée Osman not only connected with my story but with my writing style, passion, and ambition. Working with you has been easy and enjoyable, an absolute dream. My appreciation is endless. Thank you to Faith Black Ross for a seamless, simple editorial process. And to the rest of the team at Lake Union—assistants, copyeditors, designers, marketing, and salespeople—your expertise and diligence are invaluable.

Benee Knauer, I could fill an entire page with gratitude for all the things you've given me. You entered my life as an exceptional developmental editor but over time became a mentor, life coach, and friend. Thank you for pushing me to make hard choices, then holding my hand as I did. I'm forever indebted.

The road from young adult to adult author has been incredibly long and curvy, and without the endless support of my writing community, friends, and family, I never would have persisted. Thank you to all my

WFWA friends for their constant support and enthusiasm, particularly Elizabeth Gillman, Sarah Berke, and Spencer Byce. Thank you to my Lake Union author friends who've been so generous with advice and encouragement, particularly Hadley Leggett, Christine Gunderson, Rosa Kwon Easton, Sharon Ritchey, Sofia Robleda, and C. I. Jerez. Our Zoom calls and Slack messages have been a lifeline.

Thank you to early readers of this manuscript: Cass Briggs, Kim Derting, and Lidija Hilje. Your early feedback was instrumental in advancing this from awful first draft to something manageable. Shelli Johannes Wells—you are the ultimate plot whisperer. Thanks for always asking the right questions, finding loopholes, and offering incredible suggestions. Thank you to Camille Pagán and Sarah Pekkanen for your generous offers to blurb. You are true literary citizens.

Thank you to everyone who schooled me on dance, particularly Sarah Shane, who fervently told me there would be no "recitals" at this level. I tried hard to watch videos and interrogate dance moms and instructors, but I'm sure I've made mistakes in portraying a true preprofessional dance program. I apologize for any inaccuracies.

To my close circle of writer people—Katie Anderson, Sarah Frances Harding, and Shelli Johannes Wells—can you believe we met over a decade ago at a conference? A million thanks for all the Marcos, the years of writers' retreats, and events. We started out as writing colleagues and ended up as friends. I love you guys.

To my other Marco girls—Shannon York and Paula Harper—thank you for your endless support and love. Thanks for teaching me to celebrate every step of the journey. We've been through a lot together, and there's so much more to come.

I'm so blessed to be encouraged, supported, and loved by so many friends far and near. Thanks to my high school girls: Cass, Kristen, and Amy. My Blue Ridge clan: Shannon, Cami, Susan, Crista, and Carrie. My tennis ladies: Piper, Allyson, Wendy, Deborah, and Renee. A million hugs to my optometry best buds, Jenny and Colleen; life is better with you. You all keep me happy and sane. One of the greatest gifts in life is friendship, and I'm so blessed to have received it many times over.

Love and thanks to my sister, Jackie, for everything.

Thanks to my family, far and near. I've always said my family's antics would make a great book or TV show. Consider yourself warned.

To Sam and Izzie, thank you for being nothing like the teenagers in this book. You were crazy insomniac infants, but the teen years have been a joy. I love you.

Finally, thank you, Chris, for listening to me talk about my characters like they're real people. We all know you're not actually listening, but thanks for pretending and nodding at appropriate times. I know you'll probably show up to my book launch wearing a shirt that says, *It was my idea* or *I'm the ghostwriter*, but I'll let you get away with it because you make me laugh.

Finally, to the reader, thank you for picking this book and giving me a chance. As an author, my biggest hope is that you were entertained.

ABOUT THE AUTHOR

Photo © 2021 Vania Stoyanova

Jennifer Jabaley is the award-winning author of *Lipstick Apology* and *Crush Control*. She won Georgia Author of the Year in the young adult category and was nominated for the Pennsylvania Young Reader's Choice Award. Jen is a practicing optometrist. She brings sharp focus to eye care by day and to storytelling by night. She lives in the north Georgia mountains with her sports-obsessed family and two rescue dogs. For more information, visit www.jenniferjabaley.com.